THE
RED
WHITE
AND BLUE

a novel by
JOHN GREGORY DUNNE

SIMON AND SCHUSTER
NEW YORK

Published by Simon and Schuster
A Division of Simon & Schuster, Inc.
Simon & Schuster Building
Rockefeller Center
1230 Avenue of the Americas
New York, New York 10020
Simon and Schuster and colophon are registered trademarks of Simon &
Schuster, Inc.
Designed by Anne Scatto/Levavi & Levavi
A signed first edition of this book has been privately printed by The Franklin
Library
Manufactured in the United States of America

10   9   8   7   6   5   4   3   2   1

Library of Congress Cataloging in Publication Data

Dunne, John Gregory
    The red white and blue.

    I. Title.
PS3554.U493R4   1987   813'.54   86-26025
ISBN: 0-671-46380-2

"Smile," words by John Turner and Geoffrey Parsons, music by Charles
Chaplin.   Copyright 1954 by Bourne, Inc., now Bourne Co.   All rights reserved.   Used by permission.

"Me and Bobby McGee" by Kris Kristofferson. Copyright © 1969 Combine
Music Corporation. Used by permission.

This book is for Diana Phipps
It is for my brother Dick and my sister Ginny
It is for Jim Didion
And finally, reluctantly, it is for Earl McGrath

History is an account, mostly false, of events, mostly unimportant, which are brought about by rulers, mostly knaves, and soldiers, mostly fools.

—Ambrose Bierce

BOOK ONE
GENEALOGY

I
_____

WHEN THE TRIAL BEGAN, we left the country.

All things considered, not a bad first line. Showy. Perhaps even a little vulgar. An attention-getter. That was something I had learned from Marty Magnin. You got to grab them by their nuts right away, Marty Magnin always said. That's what making pictures is all about. You fade in on the sky. Then you cut to a plane. The third shot you blow up the goddamn plane. Somebody gives me an opening like that, I could write the goddamn picture. . . .

When the trial began, we left the country. . . .

The trial is a touch Marty Magnin would appreciate. Whose trial? What's the charge? Who do we root for? And this "we." Who's this "we"? You and a broad? Me and a broad, Marty. She puts out, right? Really, Marty. Already I like it, Marty Magnin would say. You ever seen a crappy trial scene? You get stuck, always throw in a trial scene. A Jew lawyer, a mick judge, maybe the D.A.'s shtupping the blonde. What blonde, Marty? You're the writer, for Christ's sake, why am I paying you fifteen grand a week for, I got to do everything for you?

Twenty grand a week, Marty.

Then for twenty lousy grand a week, you ought to be able to come up with a blonde. You're a Mel, you know that?

11

No, Marty, I didn't know that.

All writers are Mels. Mel Tolkin, Mel Frank, Mel Shavelson, Mel Pincus . . .

I'm Jack.

A mick translation of Mel. Producers are named Marty. Just remember one thing . . .

What's that, Marty?

In this town, the Martys hire the Mels.

The gospel according to Marty Magnin. The Martys hire the Mels. Once, on the way from Asolo to Cortina, for a tryst with (God help me) Lottie French, I stopped for gas in the foothills of the Dolomites, in a town called Mel. In the local trattoria, I bought a postcard with a view of the town—CITTA DI MEL (BELLUNO)—and sent it to Marty Magnin with the inscription, "This is where screenwriters go to die." Some time later, when I asked if he ever got the card, he answered, "Martys die in Cortina."

Here is another piece of wisdom offered by Marty Magnin: Nuns and midgets, that's the ticket. Your story's got a nun or a midget in it, you can't go wrong. Just so long as they're below the title.

There is a nun in this story. Below the title. She was buried in a shallow grave in Chalatenango Province, Cristo Rey, C.A. The man who shot her was, by all the unofficial accounts, wearing a Mickey Mouse sweatshirt. The gun he used to shoot her was an Ingram Mac-10 with a flash suppressor. The nun was a Sister of Mercy and her name was Sister Phyllis and the seven shots from the Ingram Mac-10 with flash suppressor fired by the man in the Mickey Mouse sweatshirt had obliterated Sister Phyllis's face.

To a cradle Catholic like myself, Sister Phyllis seemed an odd name for a nun. The nuns I remember from parochial school had names like Sister John Bosco and Sister Annunciata and Sister Mary Magdalene. There was a photograph of Sister Phyllis Emmett in the newspapers when she died, a picture taken when she was a postulant and her face was still intact. It was a sweet round moon face, its baby fat encased in coif and veil. She wore rimless glasses and the right temple of her glasses was stuck to the frame with a wad of adhesive tape—a trademark of sorts. I cannot recall her ever wearing glasses in full repair. Sister Phyllis had been sexually assaulted before her face was shot away and she was buried in that shallow red clay grave in Chalatenango Province, Cristo Rey, C.A. She was wearing Lily of France cotton bikini panties and when her body was uncovered the bikini panties were wrapped around her ankles wrong side front, as if someone had put them back on in haste. Try as I can, I am unable to imagine Sister John Bosco or Sister Annunciata or Sister Mary Magdalene in Lily of France cotton bikini bottoms.

It was Leah who identified Sister Phyllis's body. Leah Kaye. Leah was my first ex-wife. It was coincidental that she was in Cristo Rey, C.A., when Phyllis Emmett was killed, but not accidental. Leah was attracted to places and situations in which words like injustice and revolution figured. Social activism was a narcotic to which she remained addicted most of her adult life. Sometimes I accompanied her on these crusades, more often not. It was not that I was resistant to the winds of change. It is that I am more comfortable as a spectator than as a player. I am a profligate lender of moral support. I commit to a policy of heroic caution after an intensive study of the instant replay and the freeze-frame, the stop action and the reverse angle. We were an odd couple, Leah and I.

Leah had no difficulty identifying Sister Phyllis, even though the body in the shallow red clay grave had no face left. A pair of broken rimless glasses stuck together with adhesive tape marked the gravesite. And a PHYLLIS EMMETT name tag was sewn into the Lily of France cotton bikini bottoms. That old parochial school convent training. Know your own things. Avoid the temptation of taking items belonging to the other girls. The nuns who had instilled in Phyllis Emmett the idea that name tags were a safeguard against Satan's overtures would have been gratified by how useful they were when she was dispatched to her eternal reward.

There is also a midget in this story. Again below the line. Ramona Leon. Sister of Onyx Leon. And Leah's devoted secretary during the good years, and the not so good. The first time I slept

with Leah she was a young lawyer working for Onyx that summer when he began organizing the farm workers. I suppose it is
not strictly accurate to say that Leah "worked" for Onyx. Leah
was incapable of "working for" anyone. She bullied Onyx, as she
tried to bully everyone, offering advice as if it were the Sermon
on the Mount. Leah the implacable, Leah who wore her moral superiority as if it were a knight's armor, Leah whom I loved, and
still love.

When Leah left Onyx and returned to her law practice in Oakland, she took Ramona Leon with her to answer the telephone
and to make coffee and to be yelled at. I think it would help explain Leah if I told you that she called her law firm The Justice
Department. There are those who thought the name reflected her
sense of humor, but of course she had none; the name did, however, attract the attention she always claimed she never tried to
seek. Among the psychic cripples of radical politics who composed the bulk of Leah's practice, Ramona Leon, with the hump
on her back, was not an oddity. In that ratty storefront filled with
sagging couches and overflowing secondhand file cabinets and
broken chairs and posters that screamed NO or pledged POWER to
some constituency or other of the dispossessed, Ramona Leon's
good cheer was an unfailing constant in an atmosphere of otherwise suffocating rage and anger and suppressed violence. Less
than four feet tall, Ramona fit perfectly between Mercury Baker's
legs when he forced her to fellate him, holding her captive with
his thighs, as if she were in a vise, Ramona in her Peter Pan collar,
her dress cut so as to minimize the hump disfiguring her back,
and Mercury in the prison denims he always wore, even after his
release from Folsom, the white P stenciled on both pant legs and
also on the back of his faded soft blue work shirt. The bitch go up
on me, Mercury Baker told Leah by way of explanation, and I
think for the first time in her life Leah knew what it was to be
afraid.

Nuns and midgets, that's the ticket. A Martin Magnin Production.

Good Christ, what a cast.

II

_____

I AM, as you have probably gathered by now, a screenwriter. This, however, is not a Hollywood story, although a fair amount of it takes place in the gilded venues where celebrity and political action make common cause. Screenwriting is not an ignoble profession. It is just one that does not require a great deal of ego investment, and that suited me perfectly. The most to which a screenwriter can aspire is to be a co-pilot, and again I was a good fit.

"This is Jack Broderick," Marty Magnin said to the Duchess of Simsbury at the Royal Command Performance at the Odeon in Leicester Square. "He's my writer." As if I were a possession, like a poodle, bought and paid for. "One of my writers anyway. You can always get a writer."

The Duchess of Simsbury held out her hand. "How lovely." She was wearing a tiara, and the tiara was paste, but I did not tell Marty Magnin that. I had rewritten the picture being shown at the Royal Command Performance, but Marty Magnin had asked me as a personal favor not to petition the guild for a credit arbitration. The writer he wished to be credited with the screenplay was the son of a man from whom Marty wanted a favor, some-

thing about the transfer of funds from an account in a bank in
Berne to an account in a bank on Grand Cayman, the object, I
was sure, being to defraud the United States government. "You
don't ask for a credit, kid"—Marty had the irritating habit of always calling writers "kid," which was particularly grating to me
as he was four years younger than I—"and I'll tell you what I'll
do. I'll give you a plane ticket, first class, I'll put you up at the
Connaught, you can ball anyone you want, I'll bill the picture." It
did not matter to Marty that I could afford my own plane tickets,
being rich, or to be more precise, having been born rich. Writers
were Mels and Mels could not possibly be rich or know about the
intricacies of the banking regulations on Grand Cayman. I saw no
point in reminding him that my father had investigated Grand
Cayman when Marty was still in the mailroom at the William
Morris Agency and that he had found it wanting in the kind of
security that he demanded, in other words bank officials who
could not be bribed, bought or rented. And so in my room at
the Connaught—Marty of course had the Oliver Messel suite at the
Dorchester—I slept with Diana Simsbury on the afternoon of the
evening Marty hoped to sleep with her following the Royal Command Performance.

"How is Bro?"

Bro was my older brother. He was a Benedictine priest. The
only times I had ever heard Diana mention him were on those
odd occasions in various hotel rooms around the world where we
happened to spend, because we could find no good reason not to,
the afternoon (never the evening) in bed. "Fine," I said.

"I read about him all the time."

"Yes." Bro was the kind of priest people who otherwise had no
interest in the Catholic Church read about. His entry in *Who's
Who* numbered forty-three lines. There were fourteen honorary
degrees, only two of which, I should point out, came from Catholic universities, the more primitive academic stalags of the Irish
and the Catholic announcing their implicit disapproval of him by
the withholding of their LL.D.'s. Trustee. Chairman. Fellow.
Member. Director. Recipient. Medalist. Foundation. Institute.
Fellowship. Commission. Committee. Council. Delegation. Congress. Society. It was a hymn of public service in the interest of
both church and state.

Diana Simsbury calibrated the sag of her breasts in the mirror on the bathroom door. "And that wife of yours . . ."

"Leah?"

"I saw her on the telly. Some kind of Vietnam retrospective. There was a clip of her in Hanoi. With that actress. Carlotta . . ."

"Lottie French."

"Anabel says she's a lesbian." Anabel Rutland is my second ex-wife. And my last. Her grandfather owned 129,000 acres in Riverside and San Bernardino counties. "Are she and, uh . . ."

"Are she and Leah what, Diana?"

Diana got back into bed. "She was wearing a helmet."

"Leah?"

"Her friend Carlotta."

"What kind of helmet?"

"The kind American pilots wear. Like a spaceman's. It belonged to this American who had been shot down. It was white. And his name was stenciled on it. A Jewish name. Fiebleman. Fischl."

"Was he there?"

"Oh, no. Just your wife."

"Ex-wife."

"And her friend. And some North Vietnamese. Everyone was smiling. The footage came from some French TV crew. Robin Day did the commentary."

I was suddenly very tired of Diana Simsbury.

"She had this ring. Your wife, I mean. Ex-wife. It was made from the metal of the plane that had been shot down. It looked just like a wedding ring. She held it right up to the camera."

I knew all about that ring. It was the kind visiting American radicals were given in Hanoi. Signifying the solidarity of the revolutionary struggle against the capitalist oppressor. With this ring I do thee wed. Leah lost hers after she got home. First it was confiscated when she went through customs at JFK. She sued to get it back, not because she particularly wanted the ring but as a matter of principle. Then when the ring was returned she never wore it because she thought it was ugly. It made her finger green. She gave it to me as a Christmas present—we never exchanged presents until we were divorced—and I gave it back to her on her birthday. That made her laugh. She kept the ring loose in her purse until finally one day—by accident, she insisted—she threw it into the exact change bucket at a toll booth on the Golden Gate Bridge. Lottie French auctioned off the ring she received in Hanoi at a benefit for Mercury Baker. Marty Magnin bought it for three thousand dollars, which perhaps coincidentally was the same amount he had contributed to The Committee to Re-Elect the President. A long time later, on the Concorde home from the Cannes Festival that spring before Bro and Leah died, Marty told me that he had given the ring to Fidel when he was in Havana trying to arrange a remake of *Casablanca*, his version set against the background of the Cuban revolution, with Warren and Meryl and Sydney to direct. There was a metaphor to be found in those two rings, but then and now I did not care to investigate it.

Diana Simsbury rearranged the pillows on the bed, putting one under her buttocks.

"I didn't know she was a communist."

"Who?"

"Your wife."

"Ex-wife."

"Whatever."

The idea that Leah was a communist was another contribution of Anabel's. I was quite sure. First Leah was a lesbian, now she was a communist. Anabel was a constant source of mischief.

"She's worse than a communist, Diana. She's a Jew communist."

"Really, Jack."

The intended irony was wasted on Diana Simsbury. In any event, it was what passed among the Brodericks as a family joke. "Jew" was the adjective my father always used to define Leah. My son married a Jew lawyer. Jack's Jew wife. Jack's getting a divorce from that Jew lawyer. The Jew lawyer my son used to be married to. My father used "Jew" the way other people might use tall or short or fat or skinny. The word had the kind of unequivocal precision he always demanded from his employees and his children, one of whom—me—he regarded as less productive than an employee.

My father was the sort of rich man whose wealth was of such a dimension that it had to be diagrammed with a cartoon when

The New York Times Magazine tried to estimate his net worth. Hugh Broderick, the puppeteer, manipulating the marionettes of his empire. There were arrows that connected TRUSTS to ENTERPRISES to PORTFOLIOS to LAND (not real estate, but LAND; I remember being impressed by that) to FOUNDATIONS & MEMORIALS. Of course my father did not talk to the *Times* and said he had not read the story, although he also said the figures were wrong, leaving the distinct impression that the estimate was too low. There is no contradiction here. My father never read anything longer than a single page prepared by a subordinate. I once asked him how rich we were. He did not reply, not because we had been rich for so long he thought the question in poor taste, but because the money was so new he thought the room might be wired.

That was when I was still a child and my mother was still alive and I attended parochial school and clapped the erasers after school for Sister John Bosco and Sister Annunciata and Sister Mary Magdalene. I was an altar boy who even today, some thirty years after I lost my faith, can still recite the Latin responses I learned by rote: *"Quia tu es, Deus, fortitudo mea: quare me repulisti, et quare tristis incedo, dum affligit me inimicus?"* I never bothered to learn what this meant, and can translate now only with the help of the New Marian Missal I found in my pew at Old St. Mary's the morning of my brother Bro's funeral: "For Thou, O God, art my strength. Why hast Thou cast me off and why do I go sorrowful whilst the enemy afflicteth me?" Considering all that has happened, a not inappropriate response.

III

My mother's death, when I was still in school, put an end to what my father called "that parochial school nun stuff." A Catholic education, at least in the formative years, was the one concession on what she considered her children's behalf that Gertrude Mary Mahoney Broderick was able to wrest from her husband. And so I memorized the Baltimore Catechism and mimed faith as if I already knew it was something I would one day drop as I would a bad habit.

My mother belonged to that generation of pious Catholic women who knew the feast days assigned to each saint. January 21, Saint Agnes. January 21, the feast of Saint Agnes, she would say brightly at breakfast. That's who Saint Agnes's Home is named after. They do such good work for the unwed mothers, the nuns at Saint Agnes's. January 22, Saint Anastasius. Ed Kiley's the new pastor at Saint Anastasius, Hugh, did you hear that? January 23, my father's birthday, Saint Raymond of Pennafort. I don't understand why your parents didn't name you Raymond, Hugh. An observation she made every January 23. Raymond Broderick, she would say, trying the name out. Ray. Ray Broderick. Mrs. Raymond Broderick, my husband's named after Saint Raymond of Pennafort.

Every summer my mother went to Lourdes the way other women went to Southampton or Malibu or Cap d'Antibes. As if she were a ship's chandler, she would purchase hundreds of vials of the healing holy water which she would then duly distribute the following Christmas to an ever-increasing network of priests and nuns and to the fallen young women incarcerated in the Houses of the Good Shepherd who were the special beneficiaries of her novenas and her charity. She was never less than vigilant on the behalf of the less fortunate. BRODERICK TURKEYS BRIGHTEN HOLIDAY FARE OF POOR. An annual headline I remember from my youth. My mother gave away a thousand turkeys at Thanksgiving and another thousand at Christmas, earning ecumenical blessings before ecumenism was in flower.

With chauffeur and limousine and fur lap robes, she visited the sites of the better known miracles, never missing a pilgrimage or a Holy Year, charting her life by the nine First Fridays, gathering plenary indulgences, this holy innocent who did not need them, as if they were campaign ribbons. In a sense they were. My mother's constant peripatetic reconnoitering of God's battlefields enabled her to remain publicly ignorant of my father's flagrant infidelities. I am sure that she offered them up, as the devout women of her age and station were taught to do with a husband's indiscretions, every humiliation a marker against her time in purgatory. Their marriage was celebrated as a happy one, and the convenience suited them both, and so on their terms perhaps it was. She died, appropriately enough, at Fatima. It was her favorite shrine, the rigors of central Portugal compensated by the fact that it was only a day's easy travel from the Ritz in Madrid, her considered opinion being that Lisbon was no place to spend even a night. *Gertrude Mary Mahoney Broderick was a lay guardian angel,* the archbishop of San Francisco said in his eulogy at her funeral. *Hers was a life dedicated to the humble who will inherit the kingdom of heaven.*

With my mother's cerebral hemorrhage and fortune now so vast that even he had difficulty tracking it through the tax havens and loopholes in the Internal Revenue Code where most of it was sheltered, my father at last felt free to jettison the baggage of Irish Catholic guilt and ethnicity that was Gertrude Mary Mahoney's dowry when she came to him in marriage. (That she was an only child, and her father dispenser of those easements and zoning variances and rights of way controlled by the San Francisco County Planning Commission, was part of the dowry that went unmentioned by my father.) As a family, we moved to a larger stage. The Brodericks became citizens of the world of celebrity, touching down in Palm Beach and the Hamptons, in the south of France and on private islands in the Aegean, logging in safari time on the zebra stripes of El Morocco. Mass was where we went to be photographed with the cardinal. My sister Priscilla made what *Vogue* called "a brilliant match" and *Time* "the merger of the year" with Dickie Finn, the president's younger brother, with twenty-four ushers and the cover of *Life*, but then, as with our mother, a vein burst in her skull and she was dead at twenty-nine. My father grieved for Priscilla more than he had for his wife. Our mother, my father, his wife. In those phrases, perhaps, you can discern the chill among the Brodericks.

The summer that Priscilla died was also the summer I married Leah. My sister's death in fact was the catalyst that transformed what had been a cool and somewhat distant and disapproving acquaintanceship into a connection. Perhaps if the president had not stayed at my father's house in San Francisco after Priscilla died the connection would never have been joined, and this story never played out.

There are those who claim, even today, that Priscilla was in bed with President Finn when she died, but in fact her affair with Fritz Finn had been over for more than a year. It was Tuck Bradley who was her gentleman caller that summer, and Tuck was at Bohemian Grove with Dickie and me when we got the news. The first person Dickie called was Fritz, who was in Los Angeles at a fundraiser, and because the Grove was fogged in and the Sonoma County Airport closed down, the three of us had to drive down to the Bay Area with the Secret Service man assigned to Dickie, with the result that Air Force One beat us to San Francisco. I suppose that is where the story got started about Priscilla being in bed with Fritz. Years later, in fact, Marty Magnin even wanted me to do a screenplay based on the rumor. "Nobody's got to know it's about your sister, kid," Marty said. Typical Marty. He had a mind activated by a thousand story conferences. Let's pitch a few ideas around, Marty would say. It was a command, not a request. Marty pitched, the writer caught. In Marty's eyes, the writing of the screenplay was an incidental afterthought. Pitching was the important part.

In this instance, Marty's pitch had Secret Service men getting Priscilla dressed and it had a helicopter and a Lear jet and an un-marked ambulance and servants who were paid well to keep their mouths shut, and who knew what would happen if they didn't. I pointed out to Marty that as Priscilla had died in her own house the Secret Service would not have had to get her dressed and onto a Lear so that she might be discovered in her own bedroom. "I didn't say I was married to the idea," Marty said. "I just said broad strokes, we fill in the cracks later." I also pointed out that Marty had seen Fritz at the very moment he was supposed to be in bed with Priscilla. He had not only bought an entire table for Fritz's dinner in L.A.—ten plates at $1,500 a plate—but had even told him a dirty joke at the $2,500-per-person cocktail party in Fritz's suite at the Beverly Hilton before the dinner.

This I learned from Fritz himself the morning after Priscilla died when we were having coffee in the living room of my father's house on Washington Street. The Secret Service and the police and the television cameras were camped outside—as in-deed, later that same day, was Leah, who came to get arrested, and was successful—and inside the house the president of the United States was imitating a movie producer whom neither Dickie, Tuck nor I had ever heard of. Fritz Finn's main virtue perhaps is that he is an inspired mimic and he had been capti-vated by the way Marty, through sheer force of will, could shout a whole room full of $2,500 Top People into silence so that he could tell an off-color story. " 'Mr. President, Mr. President, what's a Jewish-American princess's favorite position? I mean, when she's balling, Mr. President?' " Marty's voice could cut through metal, as I was to learn when we finally met, and Fritz had it down cold. " 'Facing Rodeo Drive, Mr. Presi-dent.' "

Fritz often acted as if the world existed only to make him laugh, and laugh we did that morning after Priscilla died, myself and Dickie and Fritz and Tuck, brother and husband and lovers of the recently deceased, good soldiers all, tacitly acknowledging that blood and bed tied us, through Priscilla, one to the other, any joke at the expense of this unknown Marty Magnin character covering whatever private embarrassment we might otherwise have displayed about personal connections known to us all. Only Bro was missing. He was in Quito for a meeting of the Eucharistic Congress and was unable to make plane connections that would bring him back to San Francisco in time for the funeral. The cable he sent was among his papers at the Widener Library at Harvard, the papers I went through after he died to see if I could find some clue as to why what happened had happened. I quote it in full because it so suggests Bro:

BEREFT STOP MY PRAYERS ARE WITH YOU STOP SAID MASS FOR PRISCILLA THIS MORNING IN ARCHBISHOP'S PRIVATE CHAPEL STOP SO DID CARDINAL ANDOLINI THE DELEGATE FROM THE VATICAN STOP HE ALSO ATTENDING CONFERENCE AS POPE'S PERSONAL EMISSARY STOP ANDOLINI TELEPHONED HOLY FATHER AT CASTEL GONDOLFO TO PASS HIM THE NEWS STOP HIS HOLINESS ASKED TO SPEAK TO ME STOP POPE EXPRESSED HIS PERSONAL REGRETS AND PROMISED TO OFFER A MASS FOR PRISCILLA HIMSELF STOP HOLY FATHER ALSO ASKED ME TO EXTEND PAPAL SYMPATHIES TO DICKIE AND ALL THE BRODERICKS STOP AND OF COURSE TO FRITZ AS WELL STOP VAYA CON DIOS STOP BRO END MESSAGE.

The cable was vintage Bro. Even Fritz Finn was impressed. " 'And of course to Fritz as well,' " he repeated, his face split with that famous crooked smile that camouflaged his basic unpleasantness. "I suspect Bro is trying to tell me that His Holiness really does have more divisions than I do."

In any event, Marty Magnin preferred his scenario to the actual version of events, and when I complained to him that Priscilla was after all my sister, he said, "Listen, kid, who's better qualified to write it, then? Mel Pincus?" That Leah was outside the house

on Washington Street and was subsequently arrested was another
subplot that Marty thought I might explore. The Brodericks were
the source of an infinite number of screenplay ideas for Marty,
and I guess that is why he kept me around.

IV

OF COURSE IT WAS THIS VERY ATTITUDE that made me such a disappointment to my father. In his scheme of things, no Broderick was meant to be "kept around" by the likes of a Marty Magnin. "My father." It is like saying "my dentist" or "my analyst," but I do not know how else to refer to him. I stopped calling him "Daddy" when I went to Hotchkiss. The word seemed to breach the reserve of two people, father and son, who found it difficult to comprehend each other, and over the next twenty-five years, until his stroke, when the matter became moot, I never addressed him directly. I made eye contact or cleared my throat to get his attention when we were together, and when I called on the telephone and he rather than a servant or a secretary answered, I would always say quickly, "This is Jack," an announcement that precluded the necessity of further familiarity. What my father wanted, or to be more accurate, what he thought his wealth and his always unpaid services to the nation entitled him to have, was a son in the White House, president of the United States, but one son became a priest and the other, even worse, a writer, and the closest he came to the aspiration he so devoutly desired was a daughter who was the sister-in-law and for a season the dalliance

26

of a president, although I suspect, if truth be told, that Priscilla dallied more with Fritz than he with Priscilla.

With Bro, there was at least the compensation of fame. It was Priscilla who first called him "Bro," short for "brother," because she could not, when she was a child, pronounce Augustine, his given name, and the nickname stuck, the name by which he was known to presidents and papal envoys and to the Holy Father and to abbots and cabinet ministers and advance men and pundits and newscasters and talk show hosts and the selected mighty on all those commissions and committees on national goals and national purpose and national aims and national solutions on which he served. He had entered the seminary after Harvard, an event recorded by both *Time* and *Newsweek*, who treated it less as a vocation than as a career decision. On this subject, I give Bro the benefit of the doubt.

We moved around a lot after my mother died, city to city, country to country, and wherever we stopped there was always an elegant monsignor or a disputatious prelate hovering in the vicinity of my father, seeking his favor and of course his money. We were never exposed to the Catholicism of novenas and mite boxes and cake sales in the parish hall and diocesan tours of the Emerald Isle and the funny thing that happened to Onions Galliher, him with the walleye in the Department of Parks, when he goes out to the ball game at Candlestick there with Father Edso Kiley and the Mercy nuns from over to Holy Sepulchre. This brand of parish Catholicism suggested an Irish experience that my father despised, one whose roots deep in the Mission District of San Francisco he had taken pains to expunge with money and position. It was in the Mission that my immigrant great-grandfather, fresh from the boat, had settled industriously poor, and it was from the Mission that my grandfather had fled incipiently rich, owner of Broderick Towing, the small tugboat company plying San Francisco Bay that my father was to parlay into the Broderick fortune. My father had no romantic illusions about either Ireland or his grandfather's steerage ticket from the bogs of Sligo. As if he were pursued, he tried to put distance between himself and what he perceived as the sour envy, the servant mentality of those Irish less driven than he. Harps and micks, he

called them, kissing the ass of Fainting Phil Devine, the Domini-
can, and calling it a four-leaf clover. This diction was the only
legacy he kept from his parochial school past. It was a diction he
in fact savored, brandishing it as a caveman would a club, finding
it especially useful as a preemptive regulator in the circles he now
traveled. I think now that it was the reality behind the language
that he saw in me, the caution and contented mediocrity that he
always associated with the immigrant Irish.

On the run, as it were, ours became a world of tutors and private chaplains with a taste for port and Jansenism. As my father
was more or less honest in his business dealings, and as his liaisons were always discreet (and usually with the wives and
daughters of friends, which kept them so), the priest who was a
man of the world was a regular visitor at the Broderick table. In
his teens, Bro became a dinner table theologian, debating the her-
esy of his fancy with whatever Jesuit provincial who happened to
be into the Stilton at that moment. My father encouraged him out
of a basic dislike of all priests—he regarded what he derisively
called Holy Mother the Church as just another supplicant
pressure group, on the same order as the AFL-CIO or the National Association of Manufacturers—and this turned out to be a
tactical mistake, because in so doing he lost Bro to the Church, a
contribution of infinitely greater value than any check he might
have written or bequest he might have made. Bro had a zest for
intrigue that the Church with its Byzantine cabals more than satisfied and a talent for doing exactly what he wanted, or perhaps
the exact opposite of what my father—our father—wanted.
"There was no epiphany, Daddy," was the way he explained his
vocation, and the juxtaposition of "epiphany" and "Daddy" cap-
tures the drollery with which Bro was always able to deflect the
full weight of the power and wisdom that my father thought his
many hundreds of millions of dollars gave him.

Thus Bro became a man of God, never missing a meal or a
presidential commission, Augustine Broderick, O.S.B., seconded
by the Benedictines to wherever he was posted by higher secular
or ecclesiastical authority. There was speculation that he was
homosexual, as there always is when a man of affairs chooses celibacy, but I am assured by no less an authority than Diana Sims-

bury, who knew him when he was at Harvard and she the randy and unhappy wife of a particle physicist (Ivor Simsbury was still two husbands away), that such was most definitely not the case. I think that Bro was simply not prepared to accept the ambushes of family life and that he accepted celibacy in its place as a game he was very good at, a game that did not interfere with the position he had staked out for himself, a Richelieu of the atomic age.

His obituary was accompanied by a whole page of newspaper photographs. There was Bro with the pope and Bro with the nuncio. Bro in Prague and Bro in Cracow and Bro in Jakarta and Bro in Saigon and Bro in Cristo Rey. Bro with prime ministers and Bro with Warsaw Pact premiers and Bro with Latin dictators who wore tinted glasses, this the Bro who advised Fritz Finn that it was the better part of wisdom never to get too tight with any country whose leaders wore sunglasses at night. Bro with Fritz and Bro with Jack and Bobby and Bro with Mercury Baker and of course Bro with Leah, Leah whose face, as it usually was in newspaper pictures, was partially hidden behind a bank of microphones, Leah who in those same newspaper photos had the startled look of someone who had never become entirely used to flashbulbs.

The same was certainly not true for Bro. It was Leah who first said that flashbulbs kept Bro's tan even, and after appropriate consideration, Bro requisitioned the remark as his own, dropping it into interviews in that self-mocking manner that so beguiled profile writers, and when he died, the crack was repeated in both the AP and the UPI obits, sent out over the wires as evidence of the wit and style of the late Father Augustine Broderick, O.S.B. I would like to think that Leah might have laughed, but probably she would have forgotten that she ever said it, or if she had remembered she would have denied saying it, because Leah liked to maintain that she never engaged in small talk, most specifically in the tart code of malice and gossip, which she considered time-consuming, and for her the wasting of time was the ultimate sin. Of course she did gossip, but I will grant her that small pretense. In any event, Leah died with Bro, rendering my conjecture about whether or not she would have laughed academic, just another failed stratagem to repel grief.

V
_____

I HAVE NO MAP except for that grief. It is a chart that offers no true narrative course. Notice "true." In the telling of this story I think I have lost my trust in truth as a fixed point with determinable coordinates. Nor am I sure that truth as an absolute has any relevance here. Leah's truth is not the world's truth, nor is it Bro's, nor even mine. In any event, I meant "true" in the sense of "straight," as narratives are meant to be plotted—beginning, middle and end. But I have begun at the end, and I drop anchor where the tides take me.

And so I return to my father.

I think that what he minded about Bro's decision to become a priest was only partly the loss of a son to whom he had assigned an ambition more his than the son's. I think what he minded even more was the possibility that he would no longer be able, inveterate meddler that he was, to pull strings on Bro's behalf. He had, however, been a global insider for more than forty years, keeping houses and apartments and hotel suites in many of the more interesting cities and capitals in the world, and he could no more keep his hands off Bro's vocation than he could stop himself from telling a president or a prime minister that his economic recovery

program was a chucklehead's wet dream. Hugh Broderick—I find
it emancipating to think of him that way—was sui generis. He
knew everyone who mattered and he had something negotiable
on those he did not know—a small vice, a minor vanity, a recher-
ché taste, a tiny lapse—and what he knew he would not hesitate
to use, if ever it became necessary, would use if only to confirm
his own crabbed view of the world. He was not so much a businessman as a predator of other men's businesses. Traveling fast,
traveling light, he struck and moved on and struck again, the corporate raider as commando, always leaving the running of his
companies to flunkies who were as disposable as Kleenex. His
cable address was "Mongoose," and I suppose that said it all, ex-
pressing as it did both his technique and, implicitly, his contempt
for the victims who made it so easy for him. Whenever we met,
he would never mention his endeavors, in part, I am sure, because
he thought me incapable of understanding them, in larger measure, I am equally sure, because he was bored by the demonstra-
ble fact that the making of money came so naturally to him.
Instead he would talk exclusively about Bro, about whom he had
warned Bro to watch out for, about whom he had seen and whom
he had set straight in the furtherance of Bro's career in the
Church. He talked, I listened, offering only the occasional punctuation of irony.

I remember the business about the archbishop of San Francisco.

"He said he wanted Bro to do a little parish work, it would be
good for him, he started to say it would give him a little humility,
but he thought better of it. I set him straight quick enough."

"I'd bet on that."

" 'What's he going to do?' I said. 'Wear a whistle and referee
some CYO game between Our Lady of Lourdes and that bunch
of dago kids at Mother Cabrini that smokes pot in the dressing
room and masturbates to beat the band, I know their type and
don't you think I don't.' "

"His Excellency must have enjoyed hearing that." And I had
not the slightest doubt that my father had put it to the archbishop
in exactly those terms. Hugh Broderick was, after all, the man
who called Leah "my son's Jew wife" and he had once referred to

Martin Luther King as a "jigaboo" at a White House dinner. It was the way he talked, a way that demanded attention without any unnecessary waste of time getting it, and if some people thought him a loose cannon, then so much the better for him.

"He caved in."

"I'm not surprised."

"Soft as spaghetti, that one. And twice as slippery."

"You must have made a very persuasive argument."

"I asked him how he was enjoying his house in Balboa. And the boat."

"I didn't know His Excellency was a sailor."

"I bet you didn't know he has a hundred twenty-five feet of beachfront either. Where he parks the boat. Five grand a front foot."

"I didn't know the archbishop business was that good."

"He's got his paws into something called discretionary funds."

"Which gives him the discretion to pick up a nice little place in Balboa, I suppose."

"That's the idea," my father said. I have never known anyone with his capacity for being so invigorated by any hint of human frailty, and the higher the station where it manifested itself the happier he was.

"Balboa's a nice place to make a retreat, I'm told." I always played along with him. "You mentioned a boat."

"You can hide the Jesuits on it, it's so big, and nobody would ever find them. Good riddance if you ask me. Never could stand that Jesuit la-di-da. Nancy boys with airs, that crowd, that's all they are." The Jesuits were an old hobbyhorse. "Worker-priests with the styled hair and the manicures. Blessing machine guns and bringing the word to dwarfs and darkies." So much for the Jesuits. He returned to the boat. "He renamed it. *The Pink Lady* is what he calls it now."

"After anyone we know?" I knew the rhythm of these conversations, knew automatically what questions to ask.

"Marie Funicello. Widow of the late Finbar Funicello. The society bandleader from San Jose." My father permitted himself a small harsh laugh. "He played at all the best communion breakfasts and Knights of Columbus banquets. 'The Irish-Italian

Hummingbird' is what he called himself. He looked like a chicken croquette. The harmonica was his specialty."

"And the widow Funicello is close to the archbishop?"

"The house in Balboa's in her name."

"I thought it might be."

It was a variation of the litany I had heard at the Carlyle and the Connaught, the Plaza-Athénée and the bungalow he maintained year round at the Bel-Air. The fact was, however, that Bro really did not need my father's intervention and, as difficult as it was for him to acknowledge it, my father knew it. He had the manners of a tire iron, but he was never stupid. As for Bro, he was if not smart a quick study, with an ability to assimilate and refine what was useful in the ideas of those who were smarter than he, while at the same time discarding what was not useful or what was off the point. With that uncanny political barometer he always had, he sniffed the winds of change before they began buffeting the Church, picked up the prevailing breeze of ecumenism and tacked before it. He knew the top-seeded atheists and the latest Eskimo mystic; the president sent him to Selma unofficially and the governor, equally unofficially, to Attica. Bro was a pragmatist when pragmatism was much in fashion, the moral underpinning of what we used to call Camelot; he defended Teilhard in the corridors of the Vatican, "not successfully," he once told me, "but well, which is perhaps more to the point." Jean-Luc Godard polished Bro's French and the Holy Father's secretary of state, Rocco Cardinal Lampedusa, instructed him in the nuances of Italian profanity. "He's got the brains of a codfish cake," Bro said of his Vatican mentor, "but balls like brass knuckles." It could have been my father speaking, quantifying worth by the ballsiness of the balls. Bro was Hugh Broderick's son, and never more so than when he felt free to ignore him with impunity.

Never once did my father complain. When circumstances brought us together, he would still talk only of Bro, repeating to me the latest admonitions he had given him. The stories I heard over those years collide now in my mind and fuse into one: "I told him about that one and don't you think I didn't. He's one of triplets, I bet you didn't know that. It's not something he likes to talk about. There's no money in it, like being one of the Dionnes, and a sweet racket that was. Triplets. It's not the sort of thing you like to hear about a future vice president. Ha. The third one never quite hatched. A little fellow, he looks like a dachshund, but not quite so tall. The other brother eats Velveeta with a spoon and drinks prune juice. He was appointed to this board to come up with famous people from Illinois to put on postage stamps. He backed George Washington . . ."

I would pick at my shrimp salad and wait for him to call for the check, never quite sure which triplet looked like a house pet and which was into the prune juice. We both knew he talked about Bro because it spared him the necessity of talking to me. I was the other son and to my father I must just as well have been eating Velveeta with a spoon. I was what I am, a successful failure. I am aware of the paradox in that line, the glib irony, which is perhaps why I am a failure and equally possible why I am a success. Being as rich as my father had made me allowed me to nourish a small talent for irony, irony being the vehicle by which the essentially second rate arrive at some kind of superiority. Screenwriting is the profession for someone of this temperament. The pay is good, the responsibility is small, the emotional stake minimal.

That I appeared satisfied was the worst of my sins in my father's eyes. Not marrying Leah, not my "Jew wife." He liked Leah, and she liked him, at least well enough to sleep with him. Leah had been called a lesbian and a communist and a traitor and a nigger lover and so was not fazed at being called a Jew, which at least had the virtue of being true. Anabel was another story. My father detested Marshall Rutland, Anabel's grandfather, the one who had amassed those 129,000 acres that he subsequently alchemized into Rutland Enterprises and left to his granddaughter. There had been a deal years back that had ended badly, I suspect to my father's disadvantage, because he never mentioned it, and his dislike was still broad enough to include Anabel. "She marries jockeys," he said, and that was his last word on the subject, but one that, deliberately or not, quite firmly categorized me in his eyes. In fact, Anabel had only married one jockey—Kenny Carpenter—but she had also married a ski bum—Billy Killian—and a tennis bum—Johnny Baxter—and is currently married, until the divorce becomes final, to a tramp flier, Teddy Shaffer. Notice that I am the only one of Anabel's five husbands whose Christian diminutive does not end in the sporty letter *y*. And of course I am the only one who after the divorce did not get a Rutland pension. Kenny runs the Rutland stables, Billy the ski resort in Colorado, Johnny the tennis ranches across the country, and Teddy is the chief pilot of Rutland Enterprises and of its small air force of seven planes. It was a unique kind of alimony to which I was not entitled because I was rich. Not that Anabel did not try.

"I hear that Paramount is available," she said one night in bed. "If the price is right . . ."

"I'm not interested."

"What makes you think the deal depends on you?"

"Because you have a history of pensioning off your ex-husbands."

"And what makes you think you're about to become an ex-husband?"

"Teddy Shaffer."

"Oh."

"Just 'oh.' "

"I didn't think you'd heard about that."

"You've never been very discreet."

"No." She slid down and positioned herself for fellatio. It was the way Anabel would try to avoid what could become an unpleasant scene. "Are you hurt?"

"Of course not."

"I think I'll pass on Paramount, then."

"Yes. I wasn't cut out for the executive life."

"I gave some money to your ex-wife."

"She prefers to be called Leah. Even by you."

"She just barged in and asked for it. Demanded. Flat out. She wouldn't leave until I wrote a check. It was for some Negro defense fund." Busy fellating, Anabel could make "Negro" an obscene word. "That colored man was with her. The murderer . . ."

"Mercury Baker."

"That's the last time I want to see her, Jack. No more money . . ."

"It's cheaper than buying Paramount."

"Fuck you, Jack."

"Jesus, Anabel."

And so my second marriage came to an end. Not long after, my
father suffered the stroke that makes him today an elderly vegetable, a boiled potato who at least was spared the pain and tumult of
Bro's death, and Leah's. He is cared for at the house on Washington Street by a round-the-clock team of doctors and nurses and
paramedics, the best that money can buy, I am assured by Dickie
Finn, who took over the running of the Broderick empire after the
stroke with that flair for logistics and management that has made
him so effective an executor of other people's money. Dickie
never remarried after Priscilla died, I suspect because he thought
another wife might have compromised his chance to manage the
Broderick domain, he being as much a student of Hugh Broderick's volatility as Bro, or myself. On Dickie's orders, my father's medical reports were sent to me every week, complete to
the looseness or irregularity of his bowels and the color of his
stools. It was a humiliation in which I took not even the tiniest illicit pleasure. The doctors said his cognitive functions remained
relatively and surprisingly stable after the initial massive infarction and so, at Dickie's explicit instructions, the newspaper was
read to him every day, column after endless column, and he
stared at the television set that Dickie insisted remain turned to
the Dow-Jones ticker channel on the cable network, even though
there was never the slightest indication that my father saw or
heard or understood or cared. Every morning he was dressed, always in a suit and tie, and he sat on the terrace in his wheelchair,
his legs covered by an afghan, looking down at the Bay below,
where the Broderick tugs had made the first of the Broderick millions.

It was on the terrace, not long before Bro and Leah were killed,
that I first met Lizzie. I was in the habit, after my father's stroke,
of flying up from Los Angeles to see him every other week, something I had of course never done when he was in full possession of
his faculties. As always, I had taken an early plane and arrived
unannounced. It was the best way to avoid seeing Dickie, who
lived around the corner on Broadway and usually did not look in
until late in the afternoon, by which time I was, if lucky, already
gone. I was let into the house by Peter, the butler, who since my

father's incapacitation had taken on a slightly unctuous *droit de seigneur*, as if he were already anticipating the codicil in the will in which he expected to be mentioned. With exaggerated self-importance, he was always prepared to tell me which of the staff he had been forced to dismiss and of the household misdemeanors that had precipitated the severance. Mr. Broderick was already on the terrace with the latest nurse, Peter said, she seems to be working out better than the previous ones, especially that Guatemalan who . . .

"Thank you, Peter."

I stood in the French doors leading to the terrace. The nurse's back was turned. She did not see me. She was leaning close to my father, and for one startled moment I thought she was whispering obscenities into his ear.

" 'Bad enough he was offed taking a shit,' " I heard her say. " 'But he was pounding his hound there in the crapper. Whacking away at that thing, it looked like a fucking clarinet. He had the shits. The way you stop the shits, you eat the peanut butter in the C rations, forget the grape juice, it's the grape juice that makes you crap . . .' "

It was a moment before I remembered the cadences. Richie Kane. Specialist fourth class, USAR. Door gunner. 322d Aviation Company. 55th Aviation Battalion. Bien Hoa. South Vietnam. 1969.

Richie Kane.

She was reading from my one published book, a collection of interviews I had taped when I was in Vietnam. I was officially a correspondent, a free lance accredited to a number of magazines whose editors assumed that, because I was a Broderick, I might have doors opened to me that were closed to other reporters. Near the end of my second year in Vietnam, by then anesthetized by the war, I began to teach a night remedial English composition course to GIs and marines at Bien Hoa as a University of Maryland extension course lecturer. To the troops, I was just a rear-echelon pogue, but because I was a civilian and had spent time in the field I was more or less accepted. Every evening when the slicks and the medevacs and the gunships returned from whatever mission they had been on that day, I would discourse about vo-

cabulary and punctuation and paragraphing to grunts who had
spent most of the hours since predawn lift-off roaming the
boonies in their flak jackets, praying that a VC bouncing betty
would not jump out of the ground and blow off their genitals. I
never knew why they came to my course instead of getting drunk
or stoned or a blowjob through the barbed wire from the whores
who nested outside the base perimeter, but I did not think it was
because of the way I taught the fundamentals of sentence structure: "Every complete sentence must have two elements, a subject and a predicate. The subject is called a noun or a pronoun
and the predicate is called a verb . . ."

Richie Kane.

Of all my students, the one in whom I took the most interest.

I made no move to indicate my presence. I wanted to listen. In
her sureness that she was alone, and her only listener uncompre-
hending, the young woman read so unselfconsciously that Richie
Kane's terrible story became in some unexpected way erotic.

" 'He gets it all wrong, this colored guy,' " she read. " 'He
throws away the peanut butter and drinks the grape juice every
time. It's really not like taking a shit, it's like pissing out your asshole. So he's in the crapper there beating his meat and letting go
and this incoming round lands right outside the latrine, he never
knew what fucking hit him . . .' "

Richie Kane.

The book was called *Grunts*. All I really did was cut into a
narrative my interviews with both my students in Rem. Eng.
Comp. II and anyone else who would talk into my tape recorder.
(One of the peculiarities of the college credit extension curriculum at Bien Hoa was that there was no Rem. Eng. Comp. I, an
omission that seemed to sum up the entire Vietnam adventure.)
To my surprise, *Grunts* was a considerable success. It was a full
book club selection, made *The New York Times Book Review*
best-seller list for eleven weeks, was widely and well-reviewed,
had a respectable reprint sale and is still in print. I think the reason for the book's success was that the interviews were anonymous, making it impossible for any reader to identify that son or
husband or brother who claimed to have torched a village or
fragged a platoon leader or strangled the infant the Saigon whore

said he had fathered. I never knew how much of what I taped was true and how much that particular form of braggadocio that is the by-product of fear. Never knew and of course never asked.

Richie Kane.

She was reading Richie Kane's contribution.

I try not to dwell on the obscenity of coincidence.

Suddenly she was aware that I was there. She turned around, but continued to read. " 'He's got his pants down around his ankles and his joint in his hand, both hands, it happened so fast he never even let go of his cock . . .' "

She closed the book. There was not a sign of embarrassment. I looked at my father. He seemed to have shrunk still further into his suit since I had last seen him and there appeared to be more brown liver spots on his hands and his forehead.

"I'm Jack Broderick."

She looked at my book jacket photograph. "You had a beard then." For a moment she examined my clean-shaven face, as if trying to decide which she preferred. "I'm Elizabeth Innocent."

She was tall and slender with a small bosom and dark hair and dark eyes and a wide cinemascopic mouth. She was wearing jeans and a deep lavender blouse, unlike all the other white-uniformed medical police who had trooped through the house. I saw my father move imperceptibly in his wheelchair, as if he were trying to look up at her, and for an instant, with that habit of promiscuity that is the only personality trait I inherited from him, I wondered if anything had happened between them.

"He never read the book." He had told me that writing it was as much a waste of time as the war that had inspired it. It was artfully put, as I realize now were most of his blunter pronouncements if they were carefully parsed.

"Then he made a mistake," she said.

I was not prepared to argue the point. "Innocent," I said. "I've only seen that name once before. In a churchyard cemetery in the Cotswolds. A village called Lechlade. The churchwarden's name was Bentley Innocent."

"We're not related. Unless he's Italian." A quick smile. "The name is really Ynocenzo. I changed it to Innocent."

"Are you?"

"I hope you don't think you're the first man to ask me that question."

Lizzie, sweet Lizzie. Shelley wrote a poem about that churchyard in Lechlade: ". . . here could I hope that death did not hide from human sight sweet secrets . . ." Lizzie is the sweet secret of my middle age, and a stranger to most of the events I am about to describe. With me, she made up the "we" of "When the trial began, we left the country." On a trip around the world. The expression made Lizzie giggle. Lizzie with her uncomplicated view of sex.

It was Lizzie to whom I confided in those long months we were away, Lizzie who while trimming her toenails at the Peninsula in Hong Kong or plucking a hair from the aureole of her breast at the Raffles in Singapore would tote up the body count of the story, the KIAs, the DOWs, the wounded. I will try not to burden you with motive. Motivation, Marty Magnin is always telling me, is a very poor explanation of character. I will only say that this is the story of many people in many places, but essentially it belongs to Leah and to Bro and, because without him there is no ending, to Richie Kane. I had thought I played a supporting role, but I have come to see that it is my story as well, perhaps mine more than anyone else's. I remember the day it began, that day in Beverly Hills at Jimmy Dana's funeral, the first of the three funerals I attended that week.

VI

"JIMMY'S SCRIPT was a piece of shit."

Marty Magnin, reeking of Pinaud Lime Sec cologne, his sense of the appropriate still intact, edged into the pew next to me. His shirt was open four buttons down and the smell of the cologne seemed to be emanating from the underbrush of salt-and-pepper hair on his chest.

"Last week you told me it was not your run-of-the-mill piece of shit," I whispered back, irked that I had been pushed off the aisle. I at least had been a friend of Jimmy Dana's, close enough to know that he wanted Cole Porter music played at his funeral and the theme songs from the seventeen movies he had written. The minister had not been perplexed by the request. Frank Sinatra had sung at funerals in the chapel at All Saints, and the Supremes.

"Last week Lottie French was interested," Marty Magnin said, looking around the chapel for people he knew. Marty was always acutely uncomfortable around people he did not know, people at whom he could not wink or cock a finger or pucker his lips in a parody kiss. The imitation walnut casket, topped as per Jimmy Dana's funeral instructions with a single white musk rose scotch-taped to its cover, seemed to make him uneasy. Across the aisle, on the other side of the casket, Callie Dana, Jimmy's first wife, sat stiffly in her Adolfo suit next to Frankie Pierson, his second, and beside Frankie sat Wally Pierson, the business affairs vice president at Fox who was her current husband. Marty Magnin coughed until he got Frankie Pierson's attention and then blew her a kiss punctuated with a thumbs-up. Out of the side of his mouth he said, "That's a sweet piece of ass. I guess I don't have to tell you that, though, kid."

Marty Magnin's elbow nudged me in the ribs. Jimmy had evidently talked. I suppose Jimmy Dana had been my closest friend. Jimmy Dana, the screenwriter, as he was always called, or sometimes, in the interest of simplicity, Jimmy Dana, the writer. Jimmy was one of those people who needed a modifier to screw his identification into place, to distinguish him from any other Jimmy Dana who might be lurking on the landscape, Jimmy Dana, the accountant, say, or Jimmy Dana, the realtor. He and I had shared a lot of things over the years, including our wives. Not Leah, but Anabel during that brief period we were married, and Frankie. Mainly, however, we shared credit. Jimmy had never once received a solo screenplay credit. It was as if his name were ". . . and James Dana." Or occasionally "James Dana and . . ." Ampersand Dana, he often called himself. With the proper irony of the good dinner guest. Marriage did not really suit Jimmy. He was a professional extra man, veteran of a thousand dinner parties, never too proud to accept when called to fill a last-minute cancellation. The crowd filling up All Saints reflected his status. Wives mostly, the hostesses who printed his name on their place cards. Not their husbands. The husbands could not find the time to attend the funeral of an extra man. It was a touch Jimmy would not have failed to appreciate.

"Why did Lottie back out?" I did not normally approve of the accepted practice of talking shop at Hollywood funerals, but as I had written the original script Marty had hired Jimmy to rewrite, I had a certain interest in how it turned out. The screenplay was rather loosely based on the charge of the Light Brigade.

"She said she didn't want to play any more commies," Marty Magnin said.

"Florence Nightingale wasn't a commie, Marty."

"Well, she wasn't a barrel of laughs either," Marty Magnin said. "I never should've fired you, kid."

I didn't answer. The organist segued from "Night and Day" into "Begin the Beguine." I looked around to see if Anabel had come. I was interested in her latest husband candidate. Timmy Tatum. A surfer. There seemed to be a commotion at the rear of the chapel.

"You see the TV cameras outside when you came in?" Marty Magnin whispered. There were beads of sweat around the plugs of his hair transplant. The transplant had not taken and now the plugs rose out of his scalp like hirsute fire hydrants.

I had arrived before the television crews, but was not surprised by their presence. The local news the night before had covered the opening of a new Mercedes dealership in Sherman Oaks. Jimmy's funeral had at least the news value of that.

"A guy like him." Marty Magnin motioned toward the casket. "A lot of fun. But lousy credits. You see the last one? *Soft Focus.* Opened the Reykjavik Film Festival. The Cannes of the north. In the crapper. So why the TV boys, then? Network. Heidi Hayes. CBS." Marty snapped his fingers suddenly. "She wasn't one of his, was she?"

"Marty. A little respect for the dead."

"I could never understand all those girls of his," Marty continued, as if I had not spoken. "Fucking him was like fucking your way to the middle."

Blessedly the service began, cutting off Marty Magnin's meditation on the sexual attraction of Jimmy Dana. I had orchestrated the funeral. Jimmy and I had often talked about death, the inordinate fear of which we both shared. He was always, in the years we were friends, making notes for his funeral, switching the hymns and the psalms, typing up each new version of his leave-taking and inserting it into the old Episcopal prayer book which was the only thing he took with him when he left Lake Forest after his father shot himself. Callie Dana was clutching this battered old prayer book when I arrived at Jimmy's house in Trancas after his heart attack. He had been in his kitchen making a cassoulet—Jimmy was a determined although not a very good cook; as with his work he needed to share the credit—and when he was stricken he fell against the stove and the pot tipped over and the cassoulet had horribly burned his face. There in his Book of Common Prayer were the latest instructions, neatly typed and dated just two weeks before. *This is what I would like for my funeral . . .*

It was a simple document, calling for a short Episcopal service, "beginning with 'I am the resurrection and the life' etc., through 'The Lord gave and the Lord hath taken away, blessed be the name of the Lord.'" The Twenty-third and the Thirty-ninth psalms. "From my own prayer book," Jimmy had written. "I want 'green pastures.' None of that 'verdant meadows' shit. No lessons. No speakers, especially not Mel Pincus." Mel Pincus was the president of the Writers Guild and had once been described by Jimmy as "the best friend of the recently deceased," a regular at every Hollywood funeral, always ready with a spurious anecdote for the trade papers emphasizing what he invariably called his "close personal friendship" with whoever it was who had died. "Then: 'Man, that is born of woman, hath but a short time,' etc. The commendation I like is for the burial of the dead at sea (p. 337, my prayer book, and you better point it out to Reverend Morehead, he read from Kahlil Gibran's *The Prophet* the last funeral I went to at All Saints) even if burial is not at sea. Figuratively it's always at sea. A hymn I like is 'Holy, Holy, Holy,' up-tempo and triumphant. At the end of the funeral, 'America the Beautiful,' but you could skip that, I just happen to like it." In pen he had written, "Give my prayer book to Callie," and then he had signed the document, "Jimmy."

It is odd how well you think you know someone, someone who has cuckolded you and who you in turn have cuckolded, friends through it all, and yet how little you actually do know that person. "Holy, Holy, Holy" and "America the Beautiful"—I would have figured Jimmy for William Blake, "Jerusalem," say, and "The Battle Hymn of the Republic," lugubrious and down-tempo. But what Jimmy wanted, Jimmy got, except for Mel Pincus, who during the time I was talking to Marty before the service began had slipped into the sacristy and convinced Reverend Morehead, as pink and as bland as a bottle of Pepto-Bismol, and half as smart, that he was Jimmy's best friend and had even given him the recipe for the cassoulet he was cooking when he died, salt-free, low-sodium, he'd be alive today he watched his salt, I told him that a hundred times, Reverend, he had this lousy ticker he didn't tell anybody about but me, these studios, you see, they hear a heart murmur you can't pick up without a U.S. Air Force listening device, they don't give you insurance, and that's one of the things we're going to take up in the next negotiation with the producers, and you can bet your sweet buns on that, if you know what I mean, Reverend, we owe it to Jimmy . . .

And so after "Holy, Holy, Holy," up-tempo and triumphant as ordered, Mel Pincus suddenly materialized on the altar, wearing a double-breasted blazer that was mysteriously color-coordinated with his henna toupee, and perched on top of his toupee, even though this was the most assiduous of Anglican services, was a wine red yarmulke. "Jimmy, and friends of Jimmy," Mel Pincus began, "and everybody was a friend of Jimmy's . . ." It was as if he were the MC at a Friars Club roast. Jimmy and Mel, Mel and Jimmy, every reminiscence beginning with, "Jeez, I remember one time . . ." There were first the good old days at the Writers Guild, Jimmy and Mel, a team to reckon with, fighting against the indignities done to screenwriters by studios and actors and directors, "and there was one thing I told Jimmy," Mel Pincus said, "and he never forgot it, that's the kind of guy he was, 'Jimmy, in this business,' I said to him, 'in the beginning is the word,' and he says to me, 'Mel, I never thought of it that way,' I swear to God, that's what he said . . ." My mind began to wander at this point, the question of whether Mel Pincus had ever heard of Genesis not fully engaging my imagination. Beside me, Marty Magnin was fighting against sleep, kept awake not by Mel Pincus's anecdotal assault but by a steady banging in the vestibule of the chapel, and when I looked around I could see a television cameraman in a blue down jacket and a mesh baseball cap that said SUPER BOWL XIX setting up his camera and lighting equipment. Television, I thought, would at last give Jimmy the solo credit he had so often been denied, but even in this benign wish Jimmy would once again come up short.

I dozed, then snapped awake when Mel Pincus began his peroration about Jimmy Dana, the man. A kind man, a gentle man, a truthful man. Although not, Mel Pincus added with a chuckle, patting his claret-colored yarmulke, a boy scout. But if truth be known, a lonely man. "Yes," Mel Pincus said, "Jimmy was a lonely man, and I know just how lonely he was." I doubted if outside the men's room at a Writers Guild meeting Mel Pincus and Jimmy Dana had ever been alone with each other. "If I hadn't seen him in a long time," Mel Pincus said, "the phone would ring and a voice would say, 'M.P., J.D. here . . .' That was a code we had. I was M.P., he was J.D. . . ."

Marty Magnin stirred at my side. "Let's get the cows to Abilene."

I tried to hush him. "I want to hear how this story comes out."

"You didn't put this guy on the bill, did you?"

I shook my head. "It's Reverend Morehead's idea, I think."

"He must not have all his face cards, that minister." Marty Magnin was suddenly transfixed by Mel Pincus's yarmulke. "He's wearing his beanie, Jack. I didn't know they allowed you to wear one in this kind of church . . ."

"Marty, please . . ." I was totally involved in Mel Pincus's fancy. The net on his toupee glistened with perspiration.

Mel Pincus continued. " 'What's up?' J.D. would say. 'Is your sauna unoccupied?' And he would drive into town and we would go into the sauna and afterward we would schmooze for an hour or so. Only after he left would I stop and think, 'He drove all the way in from Malibu to use my sauna in West Hollywood.' Now I know there are a lot of saunas he could have used in Malibu that are a lot closer than mine in West Hollywood. And I said to myself, 'M.P., it's a very lonely man that makes that trip . . .' "

And a crazy one who would think that Jimmy Dana had ever made it, I thought. But at last Mel Pincus was finishing, his eyes raised toward the chapel ceiling, focusing on where he thought heaven might be. "So long, J.D.," he said to the rafters. "I'll see you in a little while, and when I get up there, I'll give you a call. 'J.D., M.P. here,' I'll say. 'What's up? Is your sauna unoccupied? . . .' "

He left the altar like Jimmy Durante saying good night to Mrs. Calabash, as the organist, with an exquisitely unconscious sense

of timing, launched into "Just One of Those Things." Across the
aisle I could see the muscle in Callie Dana's jaw twitching like a
metronome. I think she was trying desperately not to laugh at
Mel Pincus and his demented reminiscences. Laughter might
have compromised that icy self-control Callie had cultivated for
as long as I had known her, making her in whatever the situation
a forbidding presence occupying the moral high ground. Her implicit disapproval of even the most benign scene was like a constant and impenetrable fog, which was why I found her struggle
not to laugh at her ex-husband's funeral so affecting.

It was now Reverend Morehead's turn. After Mel Pincus, the
minister's reading of "Man, that is born of woman, hath but a
short time . . ." seemed oddly comforting. Next to me, however, I
could almost feel Marty Magnin becoming bored. An Anglican
funeral service was more time than he had planned to give Jimmy
Dana. The role of friend was not one in which Marty felt entirely
secure, at least for a long-term engagement, which for him was
perhaps an hour. Time was far too important a commodity to
waste on friendship, so in recompense he indulged in extravagant
gestures that passed for friendship. There was no occasion too insignificant for a gift or a memento. Flowers, candy, telegrams,
Tiffany lighters, Cartier watches and obscene cakes, a Marty
Magnin specialty, from a place he had discovered on Santa Monica Boulevard, cakes with peppermint candles shaped like phal-
luses rising from marshmallow testicles and on the frosting little
chocolate vaginas, cakes topped by spun sugar figures copulating
or buggering or fellating, with marzipan lettering that said, A
SWELL FIRST DRAFT—IT REALLY CAME OFF—MARTY.

Now his head was swiveling around like a gun turret on a bat-
tleship. There were people to see and deals to make, perhaps even
in the Episcopalian enclave of All Saints. Then under his breath I
heard him mutter, "That fuck."

I knew he did not mean Jimmy. Not even his worst enemies
could have summoned up the energy to call Jimmy "that fuck."
Jimmy was never dismissed with more than a shake of the head, a
raised eyebrow, a tightening of the lips. "That fuck" did not
apply. In Marty Magnin's litany of saints, "that fuck" could only
be Bobby Gabel. I looked around. There he was, across the aisle,

five rows back. Even in church, Bobby Gabel looked as if he were smoking a joint. He was wearing straight-legged jeans and tan boots and a black silk shirt and a beige cashmere sweater vest. No chains. Bobby Gabel had once told me that anyone who wore chains was "not into revolution." He could say things like that without emphasis or irony, I think because he was the most un-selfconscious man I have ever known. Marty Magnin despised him. Of course Marty always wore two or three strands of gold chains that disappeared into the hedgerow on his chest. Marty Magnin was not into revolution. Except as an "area." To Marty, "area" had a very special meaning. An area was a subject he could have developed into a screenplay. Revolution as it was defined in the sixties thus became a marketable area. As in, "You think that cunt that's the lawyer for that schwartze, what's his name . . ."

"Mercury Baker."

"He's a revolutionary, right?"

"Maybe."

"He wants to blow up the Golden Gate Bridge. That's a revo-lutionary the way I look at it. Or a nut case."

"Maybe."

"Don't be a pain in the ass, Jack. A straight answer is what I pay you for, right?"

"Right, Marty."

"So this cunt that's the lawyer for this schwartze, she's a good area, right?"

The lawyer to whom Marty was referring was of course Leah. At that point in our association, it had not registered on Marty that Leah was my ex-wife. It would not really have mattered if it had. He would have called her "that cunt, no offense, kid." As he will, until the day he dies, call Bobby Gabel "that fuck."

Actually Bobby Gabel was a perfect area, although perhaps too sophisticated an area for Marty Magnin. At home in Havana and Hanoi, Managua and Tripoli, conversant with Fidel and Yasser, Leah and "the Merc," which is what he always called Mercury Baker. He had raised his fist in a solidarity salute in most of the gloomier capitals of Eastern Europe and cut cane and threshed wheat and milled rice in the more publicized tropical revolu-tionary paradises, all the while clipping coupons on the 122,000

shares of Federal United Pictures stock left to him by his grandfather, an early motion picture buccaneer who had left the ye-
shiva for Hollywood where he had founded Federal and changed
the spelling of his name to Gable, as in Clark. Bobby has reverted
to what he called "the Jew spelling," because he was "into truth,
although not into Israel." Occasionally he produced a picture,
usually in the Third World, and in season, and he would return
to Hollywood with what he always described as "dynamite
dope," which he was into with as much if not more fervor than he
was into revolution. Bobby Gabel was quite a piece of work and I
rather liked him in the way you can sometimes like people for
whom you have total contempt, which is equally reciprocated.
Jimmy Dana had liked him, too, but for reasons that had more to
do with Bobby's dynamite stash.

I don't think Jimmy would have liked the keening of the girl.
She was sitting next to Bobby Gabel and sobbing in great gulps,
the mascara running down her cheeks like two polluted rivers.
She was also chewing bubble gum. Jimmy would have liked that.
Chomp, chomp, then a spasm of sobs, and then more vigorous
chewing until a large lavender bubble was produced that exploded over her face. She could not have been more than sixteen.
Jimmy always had liked them young. And the gum chewer was
his last great love. Her name was Bitty. Bitty Crane. Bobby
Gabel had introduced Bitty to Jimmy. There was never a short-
age of nubiles around Bobby, most of whom looked like Ruma-
nian gymnasts, small of bosom and underdeveloped in the pelvis,
eager students of his dissertations on the people, cannabis sativa
and cunnilingus. Bitty had a mother. Bev. Bev was Jimmy's penultimate great love. Bev was also crying. More discreetly as befit
her greater age. Bev was thirty-four and she was not chewing
gum. Mother and daughter. The perfect three-decker sandwich
Jimmy had always been searching for. "You know, Jack," he said
the last time we talked, "my pubic hair is turning gray."

I considered a number of possible replies. "What does Bitty
think?"

"She thinks it's cute."

"And Bev?"

"She thinks it's distinguished."

Cute and distinguished. The difference between youth and age.

Marty Magnin poked me in the ribs again. "The day I told him his script was a piece of shit, you know what he said? He said his pubes were turning gray."

Dear Jimmy. Sharer of credits and also sharer of the fancied humiliations of his advancing age. I linger on these memories of his funeral, recall and am comforted by them because just a few short moments later I was to be plunged into the maelstrom where clarity was shattered. The organist played one last Cole Porter song—"What a Swell Party This Is," Jimmy at his ironic best—and then Reverend Morehead read from the burial of the dead at sea. "Unto Almighty God," he intoned, "we commend the soul of James, our brother departed, and we commit his body to the deep . . ."

Another nudge from Marty Magnin. "Where's he going to be planted? In his pool?"

I pretended not to hear and leaned forward to catch the end of the commendation. ". . . through our Lord Jesus Christ, at whose coming in glorious majesty to judge the world, the sea shall give up the dead . . ."

As it would soon give up mine.

Reverend Morehead, arms outstretched, palms fluttering, motioned the congregation to rise. Slowly I got to my feet as the organist slipped into a fanfare for "America the Beautiful." With ministerial gusto, Reverend Morehead began the singing, joined at first by a few voices, and then a few more:

> "O beautiful for spacious skies,
> For amber waves of grain, . . ."

Now the congregation was getting into the swing of it. Except for Bobby Gabel, who remained ostentatiously seated, as he always did during the singing of "The Star-Spangled Banner" in his hundred-dollar courtside seats at the Laker games, in his eyes a protest. I wondered if he would have stood had I told him to consider "America" as spelled with a "k." Beside him, Bitty Crane snapped her fingers and hummed along loudly, as she did not appear to know the lyrics:

". . . purple mountain majesties
Above the fruited plain! . . ."

At the end of the first chorus, the congregation began to file out
of the chapel. As Callie Dana passed my pew, she stopped and I
kissed her on both cheeks, at the same time handing her back
Jimmy's prayer book, thus completing my obligation to the deceased. Behind Callie, Frankie Pierson winked, a wink that I suppose was intended to summon the memory of an undulating pink
hairline-thin caesarean scar. It was the last rational memory I was
to have that day.

I remember images, sounds, "America the Beautiful" still blar-
ing from the organ, myself noodling under my breath, ". . . And
crown thy good with brotherhood," adding as if I were a finger-
snapping, microphone-cord-whipping Vegas headliner, ". . . a
great big gang of brotherhood," playing to the television cameras
that pressed forward, to Heidi Hayes who was so close that I
could see the zit on her chin that the No. 10 pancake makeup did
not quite conceal and smell the Ma Griffe on her wrist when she
shoved her microphone into my face.

I still was not assimilating that the cameras were for me, not for
Jimmy, nor for the cadre of minor film nobility who I assumed
would highlight the soft news segments of the local newscasts
that evening, "Movieland turns out to attend last rites . . . coming
up right after this . . . stay tuned . . ." Many of the mourners did
indeed think the cameras were for them and I can remember how
they acted. Bitty Crane cried on cue for each camera in turn and I
saw Bobby Gabel put his hand over the lens of a TV Minicam as
if the cameraman were an FBI agent filming an illegal demonstration and then he pulled a hat over his face, a soft Borsalino that he
had worn for that express purpose on marches and sit-ins all over
the country. But of course none of the television crews was interested in Bobby Gabel. All I heard was a jumble of words. Augustine. Leah. Glide Memorial. Had I heard? Had I been in touch
with my brother recently? Was I still in contact with my ex-wife?
When were we divorced? When had I last seen her? Him? How
close were they? Were they lovers?

I confess here that "lovers" is one of those words that has always made me laugh helplessly—there is a Victorian prissiness
about it that makes me want to make a circle of the thumb and
forefinger of one hand and ram the forefinger of the other in and
out like a piston—and I am afraid that on all three networks there
was a shot of me trying to suppress a giggle. I looked around trying to make sense of all these questions I did not yet understand
and I can remember wondering why so many mourners at Hollywood funerals wore jeans and suede. Over the heads of the surrounding press, I could see Bobby Gabel put a line of coke on his
fist. He snorted it deliberately, first one nostril, then the other, all
the while never taking his eyes off me.

It was Marty Magnin who saw that I was simply not compre-
hending what the melee was all about. He elbowed his way to my
shoulder and shouted into my ear, "Somebody knocked off your
brother."

"What?"

"Killed. Bang-bang. Rat-a-tat-a-tat-tat ..." In moments of
stress, Marty would often revert to pertinent dialogue from pictures he had produced, and the one that seemed most appropriate
to this occasion was a thriller called *Sing Sing*.

"Bro?"

"Blew him away."

"Leah?"

"Her, too."

"Where?"

"San Francisco. On the steps of Glide Memorial."

"Perfect." I'm afraid I did say "Perfect," and I'm afraid that
made the networks, too.

All through this exchange Marty was trying to lead me away,
shoving reporters and cameramen aside. His Mercedes 450SL
was standing in front of All Saints in a No Parking zone, top
down. He opened the door and shoved me inside the car. I was
now beginning to function, able to piece the fragments together.
Bro had been shot. Leah had also been shot. Apparently together.
In San Francisco. Outside Glide Memorial.

It was then that I saw Jimmy Dana's casket, unattended, sitting
on its trolley on the sidewalk next to the hearse. The funeral

director and his pallbearers had simply abandoned it there, like a stolen supermarket cart, and joined the other mourners crowding around Marty's Mercedes, jumping up and down behind the press and the camera crews, trying to see what was happening. Parked directly in front of the Mercedes was the funeral limousine in which Callie Dana sat. I could see her staring out the rear window at me, clutching Jimmy's Book of Common Prayer in her hand. At the same moment, I saw Bitty Crane steal the white musk rose from the top of the casket and put it in her hair.

"They were assassinated," Marty Magnin shouted over the din as he climbed into the driver's seat.

"By whom?" I remember now that Bitty Cranc took the bubble gum from her mouth and stuck it under the casket. Such was my dissociation I also remember wondering how I would get back to All Saints to pick up my car if I left with Marty.

"Some guy called Kane."

"Richie?"

Marty revved the engine. "You know him?"

"Oh, shit."

That also made the networks. As did Marty's vanity license plate, caught by the cameras as his 450SL gunned away from the curb.

4NIC8.

My sentiments exactly.

BOOK TWO

SFO

I

_____

FRITZ FINN WAS IN THE WHITE HOUSE when I first met Leah. It was the year before my sister Priscilla died. Of course I had been aware of Leah for some time before that. She was a woman attorney at a time when women attorneys were relatively rare and she attracted the sort of cases, even as a young lawyer fresh out of Boalt Hall, that were irresistible to a city editor. There was first of all Harriet Hecht. Harriet Hecht was a graduate student in Liberation Studies who had taken over the student radio station at San Francisco State and live, on the air, she had called the college chancellor "gism face." The newspaper I worked for, the newspaper my father owned, got particularly worked up over Harriet Hecht. STUDENT CALLS CHANCELLOR "———— FACE," the headline screamed. The range of possibilities for ———— FACE was endless, and a source of lively speculation in the city room when the story first broke on the wire. The FCC immediately yanked the station's license. Leah's response was prompt: LAW-YER CITES FIRST AMENDMENT. The headline neatly stated Leah's entire case, a defense that caused my newspaper's editorial page to froth and foam about the "perversion" of the Constitution by "youthful ideologues with no allegiance to the majesty of the

Anglo-Saxon legal system." It was an opportunity that Leah could not let pass without comment. She read the editorial at a press conference covered by all the local radio stations and television channels and then smiled sweetly at the cameras and said, "That means I'm a kike, right?" It was a nice move, putting my newspaper on the defensive and shifting the focus from Harriet Hecht to Leah Kaye, a lonely lawyer battling establishment prejudice. In retrospect I am sure it had more than a little to do with Leah's being able to wangle Harriet Hecht a suspended sentence. Not that Leah was satisfied with the verdict. She called it a miscarriage of justice. A limitation on freedom of speech. A violation of the First Amendment. That combination of phrases I was to hear so often in the years of our marriage and divorce.

I was a columnist for the newspaper my father owned, much to his disgust. His contempt for the press was balanced only by the profit the newspaper returned, and when the profits began to diminish he rid himself of the paper with all the emotion he expended on the firing of a chauffeur. I had graduated from Princeton without distinction, and because I could not think of what else to do, I went to OCS and spent the next two years in the Marine Corps as a second and ultimately a first lieutenant. The Korean War was long since over and it was peacetime duty. I went from Lejeune to Twenty-nine Palms to Pendleton, a platoon leader with a swagger stick under my arm, content with the orderliness of a line company and the freedom until my tour was completed of not having to make a decision about what I intended to do with the rest of my life. My father had settled five million dollars on me when I was twenty-one—I was to receive another five million when I was twenty-five—and because I had an ingrained suspicion of whatever he did, I came to regard the ten million as a pension given to a son from whom he expected little, a bribe to remain a well-paid remittance man, following the sun.

Instead I went to work for his newspaper, which to him was much the same thing. As an undergraduate, I had been an indifferent reporter for the *Daily Princetonian*—I was after all a Broderick, my father owned a newspaper, there was never any question that I would not be welcome at the *Prince*—and when I left the Marine Corps, with no particular vocation toward going systematically through that first five million, I told him I would like to work for his newspaper for no other reason than it was the only skill other than commanding a rifle platoon I seemed to have. I think he was surprised that I asked him for a job. Not that I would have won points had I not asked him. He would have regarded that an idle gesture of independence, especially from a son with five million of his dollars. Nor did he hesitate to act on my behalf on the grounds that I was his son. That after all was what money and the power that went with it were for. He ordered a functionary to order the editor to hire me, and that was that.

Needless to say, I was regarded with some suspicion in the city room. The more charitable of my new colleagues thought I was unqualified, the less charitable that I was an unqualified management spy. I kept my mouth shut, moved into a small apartment on Green Street, at the edge of Chinatown, lived more or less on my salary and not on the income of my father's settlement—a worthless boast I am more than aware. In time, I learned that I not only liked my job but was also very good at it. I was the perfect sidebar reporter, the kind who wrote about the deaf old woman and her fourteen cats who lived in the Haight across the street from the family of nine killed in the fire set by their son-in-law, recently released from the state mental facility in Napa. I gave the names of all fourteen cats and described the smell of the kitty litter as the deaf old woman rambled on about the son-in-law from across the street, such a nice boy, really, quiet, don't you know, we used to talk about what to feed the cats, he was partial to the 9 Lives, I like the Tender Vittles myself, the tuna chunks, that's my favorite, and the liver, that's a nice treat, too, he liked the finicky eater's menu, I guess it takes all kinds . . .

When I was given the column, I called it "All Kinds . . ." There was a line drawing of me next to the logo and as the column became more entrenched the drawing began appearing on the advertising posters the paper placed on the exterior of the city's buses and cable cars, a sure sign that I was becoming a local personality. I confess with some embarrassment now that "All Kinds . . ." was a celebration of the "little people," an attitude I was too callow then to realize was insufferably patronizing. Not that it escaped my father's attention on his occasional stopovers in San Francisco. "The butcher, the baker, the candlestick maker— you're very tight with that whole bunch of deadbeats now, aren't you?" His only comment ever on my column, but at least an implied admission that he read it.

I was more or less living that year with a woman named Wendy Chan, the same Wendy Chan who sits in now as the relief and weekend anchorperson on the "CBS Evening News," but who was then a young reporter on a non-network channel in San Francisco. I watch Wendy now, Wendy of the Chanel suit and the TelePrompter expertise, and what I remember most about her was the voice of the police dispatcher in the background. Wendy Chan insisted on keeping the radio in the bedroom of her apartment on Russian Hill tuned to the police band, even when she was making love. There was always the chance that a story might develop. The dispatcher's voice was as dispassionate and uninflected as the captain's voice on the cockpit recorder of a jetliner just before it crashes, the voice that is always heard on the nightly news with the captain's last words superimposed on the screen, "Hello, Houston tower, this is Eastern 455, it looks like we're not going to make it . . ."

I learned the California Penal Code that year, saddled to Wendy Chan. "All units, code two, 211 in progress, niner-two, repeat niner-two Turk, that's the corner of Taylor, the establishment is called Morrie's Liquor Barn, code two . . ." Passion mixed with the static. "Available units, possible 261, eleven forty-seven Mariposa, repeat eleven forty-seven Mariposa, top-floor apartment, alleged victim female Caucasian . . ." Wendy Chan did not really have breasts. There was a slight swelling on either side of her chest and in the center of each swelling a dark symmetrical aureole the size of a fifty-cent piece and in the middle of each half-dollar a nipple like the cap of a toothpaste tube. "All units, proceed with caution . . ." I played with the toothpaste caps. "All units possible 187 . . ." Wendy Chan once abandoned me in mid-coupling for a 502 at the corner of Jones and Geary, a Carey limousine, and to Wendy a rented limo meant money, rock and roll, visiting film stars, possession, controlled substances, top of the news, Wendy Chan reporting live . . .

I was happy.
More or less.

It occurs to me now, all these years later, that Wendy Chan
never really talked about anything but her own work, and only
insofar as it related to her professional progress: how she performed in comparison to her colleagues and her competitors (an
evaluation seldom burdened either with charity or self-
effacement), how her performance was appreciated by her superiors, and finally what her chances were of promotion or, even
better, being hired by a network outlet, preferably in Los Angeles
or Chicago or, the ultimate prize, New York. At any rate by an
O-and-O, a channel owned and operated by the network, where
she would have the chance of catching the eye of some news department vice president to whose wagon she could hitch her rising star. In those days of my youth, I found the nakedness of her
ambition engaging, as was her ability to grade any story only by
its capacity to advance the career of Wendy Chan.

By her standards, Leah Kaye was a good story.

"He was a snitch," Wendy Chan said. We were in the bedroom
of the apartment on Russian Hill. Wendy Chan pulled on a joint
and absently scratched the wispy beard that disappeared between
her legs.

I took the joint and concentrated on the toothpaste caps on her
chest. Her bush reminded me of Ho Chi Minh's goatee. "Her client?"

"No," Wendy Chan said with some irritation. "Her client
killed the snitch."

"Oh." I was really not paying attention. I had a column due the
next day. The choices seemed limited. There was the menu at the
Friendly Sons of Saint Patrick Dinner the night before, where
every course was named after a local political worthy. Tomato
McKiernan au Spinach. Judge McKiernan of the Bankruptcy
Court. Boyle Beef with Sauce Henningan. Boyle & Henningan,
the contractors, whose Chapter 11 petition would be heard in
Judge McKiernan's court. Fettucine Clougherty. Miles Clougherty, the public works commissioner, once indicted for taking
kickbacks from Footsie Boyle and J. Michael Henningan, Esq.

Case dismissed. By Judge McKiernan, when he was on the Superior Court bench. A possible column, but hard to explain in seven hundred words. With the column appearing five times a week, I only seemed to think in increments of seven hundred words.

"In Folsom," Wendy Chan said. On the bedside table, the police band crackled. A 643 in Bay View. In a garbage can. 643. Disposal of fetal remains. Jesus. No column in Section 643, California penal code. I took a substantial hit.

"This snitch . . ." I lost my train of thought. It must have been the Panama Red. Great stuff, Wendy Chan had said. Wendy always had great stuff. Top of the line. Primo. A column. I still needed a column. Perhaps the fake monsignor in Oakland. The Very Reverend J. Gregory Pottinger, O.F.M. First initial, middle name. Always good for a laugh, that combination. J. Gregory was a confidence man. According to his rap sheet. With a history of appearing at disaster scenes and offering aid and comfort both to survivors and the relatives of the victims. "Subject gains confidence of relatives," the rap sheet read, "and later burglarizes their houses." A smooth MO. Not bad at all. The Roman Collar Bandit. Last known appearance in San Jose when the PSA 727 went down. Oh, oh. Uh, uh. No laughs there. Scratch the monsignor. Maybe the snitch. "This snitch," I repeated. "How did he get knocked off?"

"He was drowned."

"In Folsom?" It had to be the grass. "I didn't know our slammers had swimming pools these days." I laughed. Uproariously. As if what I had said was funny. Dope always made me think I had the gift of wit. "How do you drown someone in the slammer?"

"First, you tie him down," Wendy Chan said, holding up one finger. Wendy Chan's major gift as a reporter was an ability to make even the aberrant seem somehow explicable. The explanation needed only to be broken down into its proper components. One, two, three, four, QED. "To his bunk." Up went a second finger. "Spread-eagled." A third finger. "Arms and legs."

I concentrated on the four fingers. The answer seemed no clearer. "And then what?"

She hesitated. "And then you tinkle in his mouth."

"Tinkle?" I seemed to have missed a beat. A whole movement. The primo Panama, no doubt.

"Pee." Wendy Chan blushed. She had the morals of a mink, but she could never bring herself to say the Anglo-Saxon words for the bodily functions. Pee. Tinkle. Potty. Number two. This restraint was the most delicately Chinese thing about her.

"Someone pissed in his mouth?" I was suddenly not sure I wanted to hear the end of this story. On the police radio a unit was dispatched to a 647 in Franklin Square.

"Not someone," Wendy Chan said. "A lot of people. Seventeen in all."

"And he drowned?"

She nodded. The joint glowed in her mouth. She began to run her hand over Ho Chi Minh.

"In an ocean of piss," I said. "A Mediterranean of urine." An Adriatic, an Aegean, a Caspian. Murder is rarely so original. And yet. A question nagged. I framed it slowly. "How did they keep his mouth open?"

"With a pencil."

The fact had such an appalling simplicity that I found it almost impossible to assimilate. "A pencil."

"A number three soft Dixon Ticonderoga." I wondered who but Wendy Chan with her passion for specificity would note not only the name of the pencil manufacturer but also the quality of the graphite. She held a thumb and forefinger two or three inches apart. "It was only a stub."

"Of course," I said. "Obviously." I was trying hard to be cool. "A whole pencil wouldn't fit." Not what I would call a penetrating observation. I tried to imagine the victim with a number three soft Dixon Ticonderoga stub propping his mouth open. I wondered if he had been told how he was going to die. Of course. This was Folsom. Telling him would have been part of the fun. A rule of the game. "And he drowned, this snitch," I repeated, as if seeking verification.

"According to the autopsy report," Wendy Chan said. A finger went up. "He choked on the urine." A second finger. "Asphyxia." And a third finger. "The foam extruding from his nostrils indicated . . ."

"For Christ's sake, Wendy, spare me the details."

"Weird," Wendy Chan said. "Really weird."

It was perhaps not the way I would have chosen to describe the incident. "You're going to cover it, then?"

"The station won't let me say pee-pee on the air," Wendy Chan said. She blew a marijuana smoke ring and ran her hand down the inside of my leg. On the police band, the 647 in Franklin Square had turned into a 240 and more units were dispatched. "And it's the pee-pee that makes it a good story."

"I suppose."

"It makes me mad."

"I can see why." Her hand kept traveling my thigh. Perhaps I could be more helpful. "Can't you say 'liquid waste'?"

"What's that?"

"Pee-pee." With a start I realized I was falling into her vernacular.

"Out of sight," Wendy Chan said. "Hey, thanks." She removed her hand from my leg, pinched the ember from her joint and crimped the end. Then she put the roach in a Band-Aid can filled with other butts. As always methodical. By the numbers. One, two, three, four. Periodically she would strip the roaches in the can and with the remains make new joints. "Liquid waste," she said now. Like an actress, she gave the phrase different readings, texturing her delivery, then put it into a larger context: "Informed sources say that 'liquid waste' was forced down the victim's trachea . . ." As she practiced, she rolled another joint and placed it on an open matchbook on the bedside table. The postcoital smoke in readiness. Then she adjusted the volume on the police band and turned the digital clock so that it was facing the bed. "Liquid waste," she repeated, this time with slightly ironic italics, and then, "You want to fool around again?"

We fooled around. It did not eradicate the image of the number three soft Dixon Ticonderoga keeping the windpipe open to receive liquid waste.

"She can really pick them," I said later. Wendy Chan was getting dressed, the postcoital joint hanging from her lips. She was meant to cover a rock-and-roll press party scheduled to begin at three A.M. in an abandoned warehouse south of Market.

"Who?"

"That lawyer . . ." I had forgotten her name.

"Leah what's her face," Wendy Chan said. "Kaye." She put a flower behind her ear and pirouetted in front of me. "Flower or no flower?"

"Flower," I said. "Who is this guy anyway?"

"Jimi Hendrix. You sure you don't want to come?"

"No." I was not in the mood for a light show at three o'clock in the morning. "And I don't mean Jimi Hendrix. I mean her client. The one who dreamed up the pencil."

"Baker." Wendy Chan adjusted the white camellia in her hair and surveyed the effect in the mirror. "Mercury Baker. It's a cute name, don't you think?"

It was the first time I ever heard Mercury Baker's name. Jimi Hendrix, the white camellia, the police band and the number three soft Dixon Ticonderoga engraved the moment indelibly on my memory. In retrospect I think it was the terrifying ingenuity of the pencil as much as any other factor that helped fix the legend of Mercury Baker so firmly in the public consciousness. Had it not been for Wendy Chan's mention of the number three soft Dixon Ticonderoga that night between fooling around and Jimi Hendrix's press party, I suspect that I would not have ventured several days later to the county courthouse to attend a preliminary hearing in the Mercury Baker murder case.

Of course Leah Kaye was also an attraction. Especially after The Justice Department was firebombed the day before the hearing.

II

"IT WAS THE ABRUZZOS THAT DID IT," Joe Kenna said. "Or so I hear from someone. You know the Abruzzos?"

"Oakland," I said. "Hoods. I don't know them. Personally, I mean."

"I didn't think you knew them personally," Joe Kenna said. "I mean, I don't see the Abruzzos being all that tight with your old man. I try to work that out in my mind, it don't really play. 'Hi, Carmine.' I can't picture him saying that, your old man. 'Guido, you ginney fuck, how you hitting them?' That's one I got trouble with, too. You know who they are, though. You just never had them over to chow there, the house on Washington Street."

"That's about the size of it," I said. With the small smile I favored to deflect the slight edge present whenever any colleague on the newspaper made reference to my father. We were sitting in the spectators' seats in Department 34 of Superior Court. Joe Kenna covered the courthouse for my paper. My father's paper. I think he was the last reporter in San Francisco who still wore a hat, a crumpled old gray fedora with a feather in its sweat-stained hatband. His jacket was as always covered with a fine layer of cigarette ashes. He was dying of cancer and it did not seem to disturb him unduly.

"You ever met them, you wouldn't forget them," Joe Kenna said. "There's Carmine and there's Guido, you already know that. Carmine's the brains, Guido's the muscle. Unless it's the other way around, I don't know. You talk brains here, you're talking less brains than a jar of Skippy peanut butter. The muscle, that's something else. They look like a pair of cement mixers. About that size, I mean. You see them, they're always dressed in white, you can't miss them, with all the white they wear. They look like they just got off the bus from Cleveland. Always the white shoes, patent leather, what else? White pants. With a big red windowpane check. White belt, patent leather, like the shoes. They wear a tie, it's a white tie. White on white shirt, except the shirt's always unbuttoned, gives the hair on the chest a chance to breathe. It looks like a Brillo factory down there. The only place they got more hair than on their chest is in their ears. The army, they could give jungle training in those ears of theirs. For the Green Berets and them . . ."

Joe Kenna suddenly began to cough into his handkerchief. The strain of the racking eruption turned his face nearly purple with the effort. When the coughing finally subsided, he heaved his breath in and out, testing his labored respiration. "Son of a bitch," he said finally.

"You all right?"

"It's a real pain in the ass, that cough. Lets me know the meter's running. In case it slips my mind." He smiled. "Fuck it. Maroon jacket. Double knit. With white buttons, naturally . . ."

I had lost the thread. "Who?"

"Guido," Joe Kenna said. "Abruzzo." He picked up his description of the Abruzzo brothers as if there had been no interruption. "Carmine likes the royal blue. With the white stitching on the lapels, it makes a nice contrast. That's how you tell them apart. Guido's the one in the maroon, Carmine's the royal blue. About a size fifty-eight short for each of them. I figure, I figure they had to whack out about six hundred and forty-four polyesters easy, get enough skins to slap just one of those babies together . . ."

"I get the picture," I said. I looked around as Joe Kenna caught his breath. Department 34 was beginning to fill up with the flotsam and jetsam of the morning's calendar. The overflow settled in

the jury box, lawyers with imitation leather attaché cases perched
on their knees whispering to their clients. I was struck as I always
was in the courthouse by the furtiveness of the criminal justice
system, by the casually accepted reduction of the human experience to the lowest common denominator. In the row behind me, I
heard someone say, "The only thing I know about physics is that
shit floats." The metaphor of the courtroom, in which nothing
was said and everything implied. I had spent my earliest days on
the paper in the courthouse with Joe Kenna. My editor's idea. He
was convinced on the basis of no evidence whatsoever (except
that I was a rich man's son) that I had a few illusions I should
lose. This was a mistake in judgment of a dimension that inspired
little confidence in his ability to evaluate either character or the
news. Like all that Thomas Jefferson shit, he said, equal and exact
justice to all men of whatever state and persuasion, shit like that, a
couple of weeks in the courthouse with Joey and you'll be a new
man. I did not become a new man. I was too much Hugh Broderick's son for that. No one had to point out to me that most of the
faces in detention were black and brown. Crime was the cottage
industry of the underprivileged; whites made bail. Self-
evident truths. The courthouse was the ultimate game show, the
game being life itself. An idea that had the tautological banality
and reverence for cliché that so often turned up in my column—
and were perhaps the reasons I was so successful a columnist.

An attorney in a forest green blazer tapped Joe Kenna on the
shoulder. "Joey," he said expansively. "How are you, Joey?"

"Dying," Joe Kenna said pleasantly.

"I hear that," the lawyer said. He evinced neither surprise nor
sympathy, but kept looking at me, as if waiting to be introduced
and wondering if Joe would get around to it before going to meet
his maker. "Mim Gagliano tells me. You're on chemotherapy,
Mim says."

"Mim's on the money."

"I thought Mim was shitting me. He's a big kidder, Mim." The
lawyer turned to me. "Vincent Carpi."

"Jack Broderick." I was immediately engulfed in a two-handed
handshake, the left hand traveling up my elbow and back.

"Is that a fact?" Vincent Carpi said. "I thought I recognized you. From your picture on all the cable cars there." He waved a finger in my face. "It doesn't do you justice, that picture."

"I bet you're glad to hear that, Jack," Joe Kenna said. "From Vincent here. Taking the time to check out the artwork on the public transit system. Seeing if the likeness favors you. Looking out for your interest, as it were. That's Vincent. Friend of the fourth estate. Vincent wants to be a judge. Vincent thinks his name gets in the paper often enough, the governor might see it. 'That Vincent Carpi,' the governor might say, he's feeling soft in the head that day, 'that Vincent Carpi's got the makings of an eminent jurist.' In case you're wondering why Vincent came over to say hello, check my pulse, tell me today's the first day of the rest of my life, maybe get me to mention his client, the one he's going to plead into Vacaville an hour from now. He doesn't want to take up the court's time, Vincent. He's always thinking up ways not to waste the court's time, it's a nice angle, I want to put that in my story. He's got so many people in Vacaville, Vincent here, they ought to name a cell block after him, he should've been a prosecutor, he's got so many clients there. I hear this one only sticks up things beginning with the letter A." Joe Kenna paused for effect. "A gas station. A liquor store. A delicatessen . . ."

"What can I say?" Vincent Carpi beamed. For reasons I had always found mysterious, the lesser lights in the county courthouse had always sought out the elaborate scorn of Joe Kenna as if it were some form of benediction. "This guy . . ." Vincent Carpi jerked a thumb at Joe Kenna and looked at me. "Is this guy going to be missed or is this guy going to be missed?"

"My eulogy from Vincent Carpi," Joe Kenna said. It was equally strange to me how he seemed to enjoy all the attention being paid to his imminent demise. "Who, if truth be told, actually came over here to meet you, Jack, I bet, right, Vincent? 'Oh, it's that Jack Broderick.' Like he never heard of your old man before. He thinks your old man might drop a word in the governor's ear, you tell him to, Jack, tell the governor he likes the cut of Vincent Carpi's jib . . ."

"Joey," Vincent Carpi said. "Such a big kidder." He reached into his pocket and then pressed a card into my hand. "My card. Call me. I'll buy you lunch."

"There'll be white blackbirds, that happens," Joe Kenna said.

"Joey," Vincent Carpi said. He checked his watch. "I got to be going."

"And not a moment too soon," Joe Kenna said. He watched Vincent Carpi move across the courtroom and attach himself to another group. "He handled this hooker once, Vincent. Jonelle Something. Washington. Roosevelt. One of those presidential names the colored hookers all seem to have. Like she was born in the White House and was only peddling her ass to save up enough to put Daddy's face up there on Mount Rushmore . . ." He seemed to be talking not to me but to some unseen biographer, as if he were trying to get it all down, to prevent death from erasing the record of his memory. "Cleveland. Jonelle Cleveland. That's it. Anyway. She clips out a trick, Jonelle. Two shots right in the pump, she could've made the Olympic pistol team, she puts them so close together. So he puts her on the stand, Vincent, and he says to her, 'Now, Jonelle, you tell His Honor exactly what happened.' And Jonelle, she says, 'Your Honor, he wanted me to satisfy his dog.' I swear to God. And with that, Vincent, he brings the dog into the courtroom, Department Seventeen downstairs. A German shepherd, name of Bruno, I've seen elephants in the circus smaller than Bruno. Of course he gets it thrown out, Vincent, case dismissed." Joe Kenna looked at me and smiled sadly. "There's a million stories in the naked city. In case you're still wondering why I come down here, I got so little time left."

"That's what I figured."

"You know what chemo's like, Jack? It's like putting on a rubber after you fuck. You're on chemo, you can count the laughs you got left, and Vincent Carpi's one of them." He paused. "Who were we talking about anyway?"

"The Abruzzos."

"Speaking of laughs," Joe Kenna said. "They're a barrel of them all by themselves. Guido, he was busted once nine, ten years back, assault with a deadly weapon, the deadly weapon was a blowtorch. A real sweetheart, our Guido. It was Carmine he was trying to heat up with that blowtorch, by the way. A little family argument, Carmine says, he don't press charges . . ."

I knew Joe Kenna well enough not to interrupt. Ask him the

time and he would tell you how to make a watch. And throw in a history of Switzerland. The information was usually useful.

"They're small potatoes, Jack," Joe Kenna said. "But there's a good living in small potatoes. Numbers, girls, protection. Some smack, a little loan-sharking. Nothing spectacular, nobody gives them a whole lot of trouble, they're only selling to niggers, so what the hell. They're keeping the peace, you want to look at it that way, and that's the way the cops look at it. Carmine and Guido put a little in the kitty, the cops leave them alone. Then along comes this crazy Jew lawyer. A broad. She's going to organize the ghetto, she says. 'What ghetto?' Carmine and Guido say. 'They like to live this way, the niggers. Reminds them of Africa or something.' She's very big with the slogans, this broad. She puts up posters. 'Power to the People,' her posters say. 'The Revolution Starts Here.'

"Now that wasn't exactly what they had in mind, Carmine and Guido, the revolution starts here, when they set up shop over in Oakland there. She wasn't part of the package, they don't know how to handle her. Some coon gets out of line, tries to muscle in on the action, they ice him, it's as simple as that. They whack him out, they go to confession, tell Father Lombardo or some other ginney priest, 'Things got a little out of hand,' like that takes care of the mortal sin. You think he asks them to spell it out, Father Lombardo? He gets the picture. 'Say a good act of contrition, my son, see you next week.' Nobody gives a shit, you get what I mean?"

"You have the gift of clarity, Joe." However long-winded, I thought. I could tell by the sudden flurry of activity that court would soon be in session. The clerk appeared from the door leading to the judge's chambers and the court reporter was setting up her recording machine. One of the two bailiffs adjusted the fit of his holster to his hip while the other took up a position next to the door through which the defendants who were in custody in the holding tank downstairs would enter the courtroom.

"It's different with some white broad," Joe Kenna continued. "You ice someone like her, someone's in the newspaper every other day, someone's got clients that call the chancellor of San Francisco State gism face and nice things like that, someone else might start to get curious, and that's the last thing they want, Carmine and Guido. You know what she calls that law firm of hers?"

"The Justice Department."

"He doesn't understand that, Carmine," Joe Kenna said. "He's a businessman. Why doesn't she open up a bail bond business, he wonders. A neighborhood like that, the niggers always in trouble, there's a lot of money in bail bonds. Uh, uh. That's not what she has in mind. You know what she wants to teach the niggers over there? I mean, so they can protect themselves? Against the pigs?"

I shook my head.

"Jujitsu," Joe Kenna said in disbelief. "I swear to Christ. Jujitsu. Every jungle bunny over there's carrying a piece, and she's talking jujitsu. I mean, they're jiving and shucking and pissing in their pants, they hear that, the jungle bunnies. 'Teach the bitch how to shoot,' they say. Talk about things are getting out of hand. The cops are getting interested, naturally, and a bunch of cops running around, well, that's bad for business. So they decide to pay her a social call, Carmine and Guido, welcome her to the neighborhood, like a ginney welcome wagon. They're prepared to be reasonable, they'll give a little, she wants to open up a bail bond business, they'll back her. That's Carmine's idea . . ."

I tried to conjure up the scene of Leah Kaye dealing with Guido and Carmine Abruzzo.

"They talk, she listens," Joe Kenna said. "They think they're getting somewhere, Carmine and Guido. And then she says, what's her name . . ."

"Leah Kaye . . ."

"Yeah, Leah Kaye. And then this Leah Kaye broad says, 'This mother is going down.' 'Whose mother is going down on who?' Guido says. 'I don't like to hear no dirty talk from a woman.' 'I mean, the whole capitalist system,' she says. 'You said somebody's mother,' Guido says. He's a slow study, Guido, you take his blowtorch away. Then this Harriet Hecht shows up, puts in her two cents worth, you know the one I mean?"

I nodded. "The one from San Francisco State."

"The one with the toilet mouth, that's the one," Joe Kenna

said. "She's working over there with this Leah Kaye at The, uh, Justice Department, she calls it."

"Leah Kaye was her lawyer."

"Better she'd have lost the case, you want my opinion. Better for her this Harriet Hecht spent some time in Chino, getting her pussy finger-waved."

"What happened?"

"She's a real big mouth, this Harriet Hecht. She says to Carmine, 'Our American blacks are the cutting edge of the Third World's war against imperialism.' 'Fuck that,' Carmine says. He doesn't know what she's talking about, but he knows he don't like it. 'Long live the people's war,' she says. That's a war Carmine's never heard about. He'd like to slap her around, Carmine, but he needs to keep cool, just to keep Guido in line. She's wearing this T-shirt . . ."

"Which one?"

"Harriet Hecht. She's wearing one of those T-shirts with the words printed on it, people wear nowadays. 'What's it say on your T-shirt there?' Carmine says. Trying to be friendly, cool things down. She sticks her tits right in his face so he can get a good look at what it says. 'Fellatio Is Freedom,' she says. 'What's fellatio?' Carmine says. He thinks it's some new kind of pasta he's never heard about. 'Cocksucking,' Harriet Hecht says.

" 'That tears it,' Guido says. 'They're worse than the jigaboos, these people.' Carmine has a helluva time getting him out of there before he starts to tear the place apart . . ."

"That was when?"

"End of last week," Joe Kenna said. "Thursday, I think. Maybe Friday."

"And the fire was Sunday night, early Monday morning."

"Two days after they pay their little visit, Carmine and Guido," Joe Kenna said. "It could've been a coincidence. Burned the joint out pretty good, I hear."

"She said it was the cops that did it." I took that Tuesday morning's newspaper from my jacket pocket. A headline on the front page read, KAYE ACCUSES POLICE IN FIREBOMBING OF OAK-LAND OFFICE. There was a photograph of the scorched and still smoldering interior of The Justice Department and an inset photo of Leah Kaye. I read aloud from the story. "Miss Kaye said that the arson attack on her office constituted an example of 'pig terrorism.' Her allegations were vigorously denied by Oakland police chief William H. et cetera . . ."

"I was in her shoes, I'd say the pigs did it, too," Joe Kenna said equably. "There's not a hell of a lot of mileage pointing the finger at Carmine and Guido. The Abruzzos aren't going to put you on the front page."

I noticed Wendy Chan entering the courtroom. "Liquid waste" had apparently passed the muster of her superiors. And of course the fire in Leah Kaye's Oakland office had changed the focus of the story.

"So it was the Abruzzos."

"Jack, you'll never pin it on them," Joe Kenna said reproachfully.

"Never crossed my mind, Joe. Just something to file away. The passing parade. Vanity fair, Oakland division."

"That's what I hear then." Joe Kenna smiled sadly. "I'm on chemo, Jack. People tell me things."

III

LET ME DIGRESS.

The hearing that morning in Department 34 of the San Francisco County Superior Court was of no more moment than any of the hundreds of others over thousands of hours that Leah argued in dozens of courtrooms across the country in the course of her twenty-odd years as an accredited member of the bar. It is perhaps only important to me in that this particular hearing was the first time I had ever laid eyes on Leah Kaye in person. I have the transcript of that morning's hearing. I retrieved it after Leah died for the simplest of reasons: I wanted to trigger my memory. Of course the memories so triggered bear almost no relation to the arguments heard and the testimony recorded in Department 34 on that third Tuesday in March so many years ago.

Consider, for example, the title page of the hearing transcript:

THE PEOPLE OF THE STATE OF CALIFORNIA
Plaintiff

−vs−

EUGENE BAKER
aka MERCURY BAKER

Defendant

APPEARANCES
  For the Plaintiff   EVERETT FELDMAN
                                Deputy District Attorney

  For the Defendant   LEAH KAYE, ESQ.
                                Attorney-at-Law

                                ALEXANDER FAHR, ESQ.
                                Attorney-at-Law

On the look of it, an unremarkable document. But to me a page rich with nuance and the secrets of personal history. Take EUGENE BAKER aka MERCURY BAKER. In court or out, I never once heard Leah refer to him as "Mercury." It was always "Eugene," a name so unthreatening, and one she pronounced so soothingly, that she might have been talking about Eugene Ormandy. It was as if she were trying to distance herself and her client from the homicidal violence the authorities attributed to the man called "Mercury." By such devices the criminal attorney was able to maintain her objectivity.

And then there was ALEXANDER FAHR, ESQ. Attorney-at-Law. Alex Fahr, as I later learned, was Leah's lover. His word, one that lent him a status he did not in fact enjoy. Leah's fuck. Or perhaps, in the interest of precision, a fuck of Leah's. Off and on. Over the years. When he was available. Availability was always Alex Fahr's long suit. He was a lawyer on the fringes of the radical movement, often present at the defense table at the more celebrated political (as they were invariably called by the faithful) trials, but never actually allowed to question a witness or argue a motion. Alex was tolerated because he had a victim's credentials and through these credentials access to the show business money that funded so many of these courtroom spectaculars. His father was Pluto Fahr, a vaudeville second banana who emigrated to Hollywood and fame and fortune, first in two-reelers and then in a series of cheap features he had the wit to buy back after the war from the fly-by-night operators who had gone broke financing them. These he sold to television, becoming in the process the first major prime-time comedian, a man with a bitter wit made palatable by a walleye and no chin. He had his own top-rated live

weekly show, jumped from CBS to a lifetime deal at NBC and
then one afternoon in 1951 his career collapsed when the writer of
one of his early short features named him a communist before the
House Committee on Un-American Activities. Pluto Fahr never
appeared on live television again. His series—"Pluto's Lives"—
was canceled, the network deal abrogated, his boat sold, his house
auctioned. He was finally resurrected in the early sixties when his
shorts began showing again on daytime television, but by this
time Pluto Fahr was hopelessly senile. He would appear at fund-
raisers and benefits, usually with an opulently breasted young
woman into whose cleavage he would invariably bury his chin-
less face. It was a gag always good for a laugh and then Alex
would appear, the victim's son, and ask for pledges for the Pittsburgh 6 or the Cleveland 10. It was at such a gathering that I actually asked Leah to marry me.

So you see what I mean.

Eugene and Alex.

Triggering the memory.

I found the transcript in the Bekins warehouse in Oakland
where Leah stored all her court documents, each filed alphabetic-
ally and cross-referenced by date. Her orderliness was the aspect
of Leah that most surprised me when I came to know her. Mess
was the given of her professional life, mess in the form of murder
and rape and the most appalling violations of the human contract,
mess in the face of which she often seemed indifferent if not actually callous. Perhaps in compensation, she was in her private
life almost pathologically intolerant of mess, was in fact neat and
well-organized to the point of compulsion. Her pencils were always sharpened (she never used a pen because pens leaked), her
desk free of clutter, her clothes arranged by color and season. She
scheduled dental and gynecological appointments weeks in advance, noting in her daybook both the time of the appointment
and its purpose—"plaque scaling" or "Pap smear"—as well as the
doctor's telephone number in case she had to cancel. Her handwriting was precise and with its curlicues and perfect circles so
feminine it could almost be called dainty. A further contradiction
as a radical role model was the inordinate amount of attention she
lavished on her appearance, an affectation that made the less toler-

ant of the radical revolutionary community regard her with a certain suspicion.

It was in fact Leah's outfit which first caught my attention in the jammed courtroom that morning, I think because I had programmed myself to expect the camouflage fatigues of the *compañera* in the hills. She was wearing a white silk blouse and an Italian suede skirt and stockings and high-heeled Charles Jourdan shoes. As a part-time observer of the women who populated my father's world, I had a passing knowledge of fashion and designers, many of whom had run up clothes for his various mistresses, and I found myself, as the courtroom proceedings wore interminably on, calculating the cost of the outfit worn by the counsel for the defense.

I said that this digression was about memory and not really, or at least entirely, about the Mercury Baker hearing, and in memory there is more to learn about Leah, more to complicate the picture, than in all the neutral and densely typed pages of the hearing transcript. What I remember now is that in all the years I loved her, and that is all the years I knew her, Leah never wore trousers, even when the wearing of a skirt would cause the more militant of the sisterhood to accuse her of being antifeminist. The reason was prosaic. She had a recurring vaginal yeast infection that was exacerbated by the wearing of pants, so much so that she could not even wear underpants or panty hose. I did not know it then, but she was naked under that Italian suede skirt, not as a political statement but as a gynecological necessity. Nor did I know then, as I knew later, that in her purse there was a bottle of the Flagyl capsules she used to treat the infection, and that she was never without. This is information that does nothing to illuminate the hearing, but it does perhaps indicate that a woman from whom the phrase "pig terrorist" could spring so effortlessly, thereby identifying her in some quarters as dedicated to the forceful overthrow of the United States government, could also be afflicted with the commonplace hygienic malfunctions of the politically uninvolved. These were just things I knew, details I could not pass on, that day when Bro and Leah were killed, to the network reporters clamoring for comment, as proofs of love, indicators of love.

. . .

The purpose of the hearing in Department 34 was to rule on where Mercury Baker would be incarcerated when he was tried for murder under Section 187 of the California Penal Code. Leah had already won a change of venue to San Francisco on the grounds that Sacramento County, where Folsom Prison was located, could not provide a venire that would not be biased against a maximum-security Folsom inmate. Now she had petitioned the court to have Mercury Baker remanded to San Quentin rather than to the San Francisco city jail. The reason, she told the bench, was that her client had an older half brother, one Elrod Baker, aka Germany Baker, who was currently a member of the inmate population at San Quentin. By remanding Eugene Baker to San Quentin for the duration of his own trial, Leah argued, the court would thus allow him to reestablish contact with a sibling he scarcely knew. This, she said, would be a humanitarian gesture by a criminal justice system (and I use her own words from the transcript) "some would call racist." I was struck, reading the record, by the delicacy of the construction, the use of the subjunctive and her avoidance of the pronoun "I." In the courtroom and for the record, Leah was fastidious in her use of the language. Hers was a style fluent in the more evasive verb tenses, a style based on parenthetical innuendo and cleverly buried qualifiers. She lived on the perimeters of a contempt citation, but at this juncture of her life she rarely stepped across the line.

Of course Leah did not feel impelled to tell the court that Germany Baker was presently on Death Row in San Quentin, having been tried and convicted for shooting and killing a policeman in South Sacramento. This murder occurred eleven days after his release from Soledad Prison, where he had served seven years for sticking up a gas station, during which stickup his partner had shot and killed the station attendant. Germany Baker had turned state's evidence against his former cohort, providing the testimony that helped send him to the gas chamber. During his eleven days at liberty following his release from Soledad, Germany Baker was positively identified by eyewitnesses as having committed two armed robberies, one attempted rape, one assault with a deadly weapon (a lug wrench) and one count of grand theft auto (the car was stolen from a used-car lot in Stockton after Germany Baker had beaten the salesman with the lug wrench in the presence of the newlyweds who had already put down the cash to buy the car). This spree preceded the murder of the policeman in South Sacramento.

Leah mentioned none of this nor did she mention that Germany Baker had exhausted his appeals and that a date had been scheduled for his execution to be carried out in the San Quentin gas chamber. Needless to say, this information was passed onto the court by Everett Feldman, the prosecutor. He also argued that it was not for the prisoner or his counsel to select the site of his incarceration, such incarceration (and again I quote from the record) "not being intended as a form of family therapy, as counsel for the defense would have the court believe." In any event, the prosecutor advised the bench, San Quentin was in Marin County, and thus out of the jurisdiction of a San Francisco court.

I do not think Leah seriously expected her motion to carry. It did, however, give her an opportunity to work on a defense, to see how it would play for the record but before a jury was chosen and sworn. The transcript does not indicate how effective her performance was. I can see now the point of the simple and expensive clothes. The white silk blouse and the Italian suede skirt drew attention to her, as did her diminutive size. She became a well-groomed, non-threatening presence, and when she bent and whispered into the ear of Mercury Baker, sinister in his prison denims with the white letter P stenciled on the back, her arm draped casually on his massive shoulder for support, she was somehow able to make him appear less threatening also.

Leah was always a believer in the value of effect. In later years, after we were divorced, she took to wearing a large square-cut diamond solitaire in court. She bought the ring herself, I suspect as an aggressive act, a reaction against the expectations of her radical sympathizers. She liked it and she wanted it, and no one could ever tell her what she could and could not do. She claimed that women on a jury always noticed the ring. I do not know how true this was—I have never put much faith in the totemic rituals of courtroom psychology—but I do know she would always play with that ring when she talked directly to a jury, twisting it con-

stantly around her finger as she laid out her scenario of the events
in question. One more note about sartorial effect. If her client
were a woman, Leah would arrange at least once during the trial
for the defendant and herself to wear identical pairs of shoes,
which Leah of course bought and provided. Again she said it was
for the women on the jury, who in some subliminal way might
perhaps wonder how the defendant could be as guilty as the state
claimed if she and her attorney went shopping for matching
I. Miller black pumps. I mention these things only to indicate that
however often Leah was portrayed on radio and television and in
the newspapers, most especially my father's, as simply a courtroom harridan mouthing slogans and cant, she was also not immune to the usual vanities and superstitions that instilled
confidence into her fragile psyche, and might even have helped
her clients.

Although harridan she could be.

And slogans and cant she did mouth.

"Who is the real criminal?" Leah said that morning in Department 34. "The man imprisoned? Or the society that imprisons
him?"

Eugene Baker was a "political prisoner."

"A black activist."

"Put behind bars for his opinions, opinions which challenge
the moral authority of racism and its true believers who command every level of society's hierarchy."

Eugene Baker was an "uppity nigger. In the eyes of his cap-
tors."

So said Leah Kaye.

She had a gift for this kind of rhetorical flourish. When she
called Mercury Baker an "uppity nigger," it was as if an electrical
current went through the courtroom. The number three soft
Dixon Ticonderoga and the urine that caused the victim's asphyxiation she brushed off as allegations the state could not
prove, allegations which in any case were not pertinent to the
motion under consideration. Leah had the ability to make murder
seem a form of affirmative action, a balancing of the scales, a viable option available to those who saw themselves as victims of a
white totalitarian oppressor class determined to destroy them. It

was the dexterity with which Leah was able to tie this rhetoric to the concept of reasonable doubt that made her so formidable a trial attorney. That and a willingness to get down and dirty with the prosecution if the situation demanded.

And sometimes if it did not.

I refer to the record.

To trigger the memory.

I see Alex Fahr at the defense table. He was wearing a dark tan poplin suit and a blue button-down shirt and a black knit tie. The top button of the shirt was open and the tie slightly askew. He was losing his hair and there was a furtive look about him. He kept whispering into Leah's ear, as if his advice were an indispensable addition to her defense strategy.

I see the flash of irritation and impatience that passes across Leah's face whenever Alex Fahr bends toward her.

I see Mercury Baker, a huge and menacing grin plastered to his face as it was throughout the proceeding.

I see the judge. He appears to be dozing on the bench. His name is Langhorne Crotta.

I see Everett Feldman. He takes note of Mercury Baker's omnipresent grin and begins referring to him as "Smiling Jack."

Leah objects. "Your Honor, I would ask the court to have the people refer to my client by his given name, which is not, as Mr. Feldman seems to think, 'Smiling Jack.' "

I quote from the record:

MR. FELDMAN: Your Honor, as Miss Kaye's client seems to regard this entire hearing as some kind of private joke for his benefit, with that silly grin all over his face, I think it is entirely appropriate to call him Smiling Jack. I think when this case goes to a jury we will see if Smiling Jack here still thinks murder is a laughing matter.

JUDGE CROTTA: It is not necessary to lecture the court, Mr. Feldman. Miss Kaye, your objection is overruled. I see no harm in Mr. Feldman's reference. You may proceed, Mr. Feldman.

MR. FELDMAN: Your Honor, the issue before the court is whether Smiling Jack here ...

MISS KAYE: Your Honor ...

JUDGE CROTTA: Miss Kaye.

MISS KAYE: Your Honor, as long as we're in the area of court-room etiquette, I should point out with some reluctance that the district attorney has been flatulent all morning. Perhaps it was something he had for breakfast. But if Mr. Feldman insists on referring to my client as 'Smiling Jack,' then I think it's only fair that I be allowed to refer to Mr. Feldman as 'Windbreaker.'

JUDGE CROTTA: Miss Kaye, you're out of order.

I see Leah rising, shielding her face with her hand from the prosecution's table, turning her head away from Everett Feldman, her look indicating that she is smelling something bad.

MISS KAYE: Your Honor, I would like to request a recess.

MR. FELDMAN: Your Honor, I object.

MISS KAYE: Your Honor, this courtroom should be cleared and fumigated.

JUDGE CROTTA: Miss Kaye, I said you were out of order. If you bring this up again, I will hold you in contempt.

I see Mercury Baker laughing. I see Judge Crotta asking Leah and Everett Feldman to meet with him in chambers. I remember that Everett Feldman did not refer to Mercury Baker as Smiling Jack again. I remember that when he ran for district attorney several years later his opponents in the primary taunted him with the name Windbreaker and that he finished a distant third.

Judge Crotta denied the motion to have Mercury Baker remanded to San Quentin. In the corridor outside Department 34, Leah Kaye did not seem particularly concerned. She stood in the glare of the television lights, Alex Fahr at her side, and answered the shouted questions of the reporters who crowded around her. I lingered at the edges of the throng and watched as Wendy Chan thrust a microphone in Leah's face.

"Miss Kaye, do you think that the firebombing of your office had anything to do with your activities in this case?"

Alex Fahr nodded vigorously, cocking his finger at Wendy, as if registering for the cameras his approval of the aptness and astuteness of her question. Leaning toward the microphone, Leah managed at the same time to step in front of him, relegating him to the background, a balding head bobbing behind her shoulder. A smooth maneuver, all the more so in that it seemed unintentional.

"Insofar as I think there is a concerted effort to oppress black and other minorities in this country, then of course I do," Leah Kaye said.

A very cool customer, I thought. Her answer had artfully not excluded the Abruzzos in case there was anyone aware of that version.

"But you're white," Wendy Chan said.

"And all the more dangerous to the pig terrorists because of it," Leah Kaye said softly. "Because I am a witness."

"Witness to what?" Wendy Chan had the virtue of persistence.

"Witness to the campaign of racist oppression against all minority peoples, Miss Chan."

Not bad at all. "Miss Chan" was a good touch. Automatically designating Wendy Chan as a member of that minority population. It was a designation I knew would not please her.

Wendy Chan tried to frame another question. A male television reporter with styled hair that glistened under the bright camera lights elbowed her out of the way. I could hear Wendy Chan protest: "Hey, wait a minute, buster . . ."

"Fuck you, you had your chance. Leah . . ." The reporter was aggressively familiar. "Leah . . ." A piercing whistle from between his teeth to get Leah Kaye's attention. "Leah, you never mentioned Lionelle Partridge in court today. Any reason?" Lionelle Partridge was the name of the drowned victim.

Leah Kaye stared at the questioner. "Lionelle Partridge was the agent of a racist political system."

The reporters pressed closer, waving their microphones as if they were dueling swords. I could barely see the top of Leah's head. "Leah . . . hey, Leah . . . give us a break . . . what do you mean by that . . . hey, Leah . . ."

And then the answer, in that equable voice her opponents found so maddening: "I mean that Lionelle Partridge was an informer."

That was the quote that made the news that night. I watched

the film at five, six and eleven with Wendy Chan. Wendy Chan who did not like the safari jacket she had been wearing on camera when she watched herself at five. Wendy Chan who thought she was wearing too much eye makeup when she watched herself at six. Wendy Chan who said, "Let's fool around," when she finished watching herself at eleven. Wendy Chan who always found her flickering image on the television screen a powerful aphrodisiac.

I thought of Leah Kaye as I coupled with Wendy Chan to the urgent litanies of the police dispatcher. Leah in her white silk blouse and her Italian suede skirt, her left hand shielding her eyes from the television lights, repeating at five, six and eleven, "I mean that Lionelle Partridge was an informer." Her words measured, her verdict clear. There is a penalty for informing in a state penitentiary, and this penalty was meted out to Lionelle Partridge. At five, six and eleven, I tried to focus on the system of priorities under which Leah Kaye seemed to operate. In her world, the victim was irrelevant except as the catalyst of his own fate.

A construct I worked out while I rocked beneath Wendy Chan.

"Good piece," was Wendy Chan's verdict on the film at five, six and eleven.

IV

THERE WAS, HOWEVER, ANOTHER PART OF THE STORY that I neglected to tell Wendy Chan, only partly because she tended to
discount as unimportant any information she could not cut into
her filmed reports. It happened after the television lights were
turned off in the corridor outside Department 34 and the TV reporters had dispersed to film their stand-ups on the courthouse
steps. The stand-up is a ritual of broadcast journalism that has always amused me, each reporter staking out a particular step like a
streetwalker establishing territorial rights in a doorway or under a
lamppost. I watched Wendy Chan fluff her intro three or four
times until finally, with some irritation, she complained that I was
causing her to blow her lines because I was in her eyeline. I
shrugged and gave her the finger with more asperity than I either
intended or felt and rather than wait for her to finish I went back
inside the courthouse. I thought I might talk to the clerk upstairs
in Department 34—I had the newspaperman's weakness for
clerks and bailiffs and marshals and court reporters both as story
sources and repositories of ultimate courthouse wisdom—and so
it was in that almost deserted courtroom I finally came face-to-
face with Leah Kaye.

She was standing at the defense table, stuffing the manila folders Alex Fahr was handing her into the big old-fashioned leather briefcase she carried for as long as I knew her, one with straps and thick brass buckles and leather so soft it was already creased and cracking. Alex was discoursing on the events of the morning and how they might be played in the press, but Leah Kaye did not appear to pay him much attention.

Until he saw me.

"We're in conference," Alex Fahr said when I popped my head into Department 34.

"Sorry," I said, at the same time easing myself through the door. I pretended to be looking for something I had lost.

"No questions," Alex Fahr said. "We've already given our statement to the media."

At least he knew I was a representative of what I was sure he would call "the straight press," as if he were inflicting a mortal wound.

"Actually, Miss Kaye did the talking," I said pleasantly. He brought out in me a rudeness I try, not always successfully, to keep in check. "You were the cheerleader."

Alex Fahr flushed. "Just who are you anyway?"

"His name is Broderick," Leah Kaye said quietly. "Jack Broderick." She looked me up and down, measuring me as she would an unfriendly witness. "On the bus posters." A description made more patronizing by the way she drew it out ever so slightly. "His father's a fascist."

"Hugh Broderick," Alex Fahr said. "Of course. Hugh Broderick." He was always explicating the obvious as if he were the first to perceive it.

I said nothing. My father would not have appreciated my coming to his defense. Especially in this company. He never bothered to defend himself and in any event he would have thought me unequal to the task.

"Why are you snooping around here for anyway?" Alex Fahr said. I knew he was trying to impress Leah.

I permitted myself a small languid smile. It would have spoiled the effect to say I was in Department 34 only because I had been in Wendy Chan's eyeline.

"I'll see you later, Alex," Leah Kaye said. In that surprisingly quiet voice with the note of finality in it. She was not uneasy.

"We have a meeting, Leah." Alex Fahr knew he was being dismissed, like a subaltern from a staff conference.

"Later, Alex."

"With the People's Coalition."

"Later."

"It took a long time to set this up."

"Later."

"Leah, we should talk." He paused, ostentatiously not looking at me. "In private."

"You know the agenda, don't you?"

"Of course."

"Then you can start the meeting without me."

Alex Fahr started to speak, thought better of it, touched Leah on the arm, nodded curtly to me and then disappeared down the aisle, through the door and into the corridor.

She strapped her briefcase shut, then sat down in her chair, arms crossed. "Are you still fucking that Chinese girl?"

I should emphasize here that her tone was perfectly pleasant. Leah always believed in securing the initial advantage, and shock more often than not was the tactic she used. It was one of the ways in which she resembled my father. In retrospect, I see the inevitability of the sparks that flashed between them.

"That's none of your business, is it?" I could see Alex Fahr peeking at us through the window in the courtroom door. He ducked out of sight as soon as I spotted him. I gestured toward the door. "What do you need him around for?"

She did not bother to look around to see who I was talking about. "He has his uses." It was not the most enthusiastic reference I had ever heard.

"Other than raising money?"

"Raising money is reason enough," she said. "This kind of trial is expensive. The pigs have unlimited resources. We don't."

"And that's it?" I realize now the innuendo was unmistakable.

"We screw occasionally, if that's what you're getting at."

A lesson learned. She would always call a bluff. "I think we've exhausted that subject," I said. An attempt at sarcasm that succeeded only in making me sound like a prig.

"If it makes you uncomfortable."

I can smile now. Until the day she died, Leah had the ability to keep me off balance. To cover my disarray, I took a notebook and a ball-point pen from my jacket pocket.

She shook her head. "No notes. Off the record. I'm talking to you for one reason."

I returned the pen and notebook to my pocket. "Which is?"

"I don't often get a chance to meet the pig establishment up close. I seem to scare them."

"I don't think you'd scare my old man." I could not remember ever before referring to him as such. "Old man" implied a familiarity that did not exist.

"Then that's the first good thing I've ever heard about him. Do I scare you?"

"Not especially." Certainly not as an associate non-voting member of the pig establishment, a club to which I belonged by birth but not by instinct. In other ways, however, I was not quite so sure. "How do you know I'll honor off the record?"

"Because I read your silly column." She had a way of concealing the hostility that was so much a part of her makeup by using a tone of voice as matter of fact as the one she would use repeating a telephone number she had just looked up. "You write about stray dogs and lost cats and giving the little guy in the corner candy store a pat on the back for a job well done." A remark that not only proved she did read me but also displayed an affinity for the jugular in even the most commonplace of matters. In fact I had written a column about a corner candy store owner in the Haight who had kept a SWAT team supplied with M&M's and Almond Joys during an all-day shootout and then had refused a citation from the mayor, he was only doing his duty, the candy store owner had said. I saw no reason to tell her he turned out to be a bookie. "You know what I think?"

I was not sure I wanted to know, but I was sure she was going to tell me.

"He's tougher than you, your father." She paused to smooth a crease from the white silk blouse, the kind of maddening gesture I came to appreciate over the next twenty years, demanding as it did that the object of her attention wait upon her private passion for neatness. When everything was in place, she looked up, as if surprised I was still there, and said, "I bet he hates that column of yours."

She was like a dentist, always probing, looking for the inflamed nerve, the pockets of decay. I changed the subject. I had no intention of allowing her to perform oral surgery on my relationship with my father. "The word is that it was the Abruzzos who torched your place."

"So?" A second lesson learned. She had the ability never to act surprised, no matter what surprises the unexpected brought.

"You said the cops did it."

"I said the pigs did it. You think the Abruzzos don't qualify as pigs?"

I did not answer.

"The pig police leave them alone so long as they keep things quiet in the neighborhoods. And we know how they keep things quiet. That's as good a definition of pig terrorism as any I know."

A circumstantial argument, but I admired the way she put it together. Innuendo without accusation. And needless to say, without accountability. I looked at the courtroom clock over the bench. I was sure that Wendy Chan must have finished her stand-up by now. And gone off without me. I did not worry that she would come upstairs looking for me. Wendy's calendar was too full. The fast track beckoned. For which I felt a sense of relief.

"Lionelle Partridge," I said.

"What about him?"

"You said he was an informer."

"He was."

"The agent of a racist political system."

"He was."

"You also mentioned that Mercury Baker . . ."

"Eugene Baker," she corrected.

". . . had a brother."

"Elrod Baker."

"Also known as Germany Baker. How'd he get that name?"

"His father's name was Elrod."

"I mean Germany."

"He was in the army there."

"Stockade?"

She nodded.

"Now you also said that Germany Baker . . ."

"Elrod Baker . . ."

". . . had done time in Soledad."

"The district attorney said that. I didn't."

"But he did do time in Soledad?"

Again she nodded.

"He stuck up a gas station."

"That was the charge."

"And he was convicted of that charge, right?"

Another nod.

"And during that stickup, the gas station attendant was shot."

"I was not involved in that case."

"But you raised no objection when the district attorney put this into the record."

"My objection would not have been sustained."

A roundabout way of agreeing with me, I thought. "And when he went to trial, Germany Baker . . ."

"Elrod Baker . . ."

". . . said his partner killed the attendant, not him." I felt like a prosecutor laying out the evidence. It was an attitude that Leah often forced me to strike through the years. "In fact, he copped a deal, testified against his pal and his pal went to the gas chamber based on his testimony."

She stared at me coolly. I was sure she already knew where I was heading. The secret of being a good trial lawyer, she would often tell me later, was learning to anticipate.

"So if Lionelle Partridge was an informer . . ."

"He was."

". . . and the agent of a racist political system by being an informer . . ."

"That's right."

". . . then what does that make Germany Baker?"

"Elrod Baker."

"I don't give a fuck what you call him. What does that make him?"

She leaned back in her chair and folded her hands on her chest, her forefingers creating a steeple on which she rested her chin. I

noticed for the first time that her nails were painted a deep pur-
plish red. "It makes him my client's brother."

No apologies, no excuses. Not that I had expected any. "And
that makes a difference?"

She stood up and checked the lock on her briefcase. "It does to
me."

"That's hardly consistent."

"And you find a virtue in consistency."

Actually I believe in the ad hoc as a kind of faith, the lay temple in which I worship, but to keep the conversation going, I said
yes, I did believe in the virtue of consistency.

"Of course you do," she said. "In other people and when it
suits your purposes."

"Like you."

She did not even shrug. I watched as she began to check her
makeup in the mirror of a tortoise-shell compact. Even her sun-
dries were stylish and I supposed expensive. Here was another of
those discrepancies I found so intriguing. She dropped the compact into a leather purse and then wound a dangling thread
around a loose button on her Burberry raincoat. I wondered if the
woman in the Burberry would ever wear a FELLATIO IS FREEDOM
T-shirt. Probably. If she thought the situation demanded. For a
moment I speculated on what her thoughts on the freedom of fellatio might be. A mental videotape I erased only with difficulty.
She began gathering her things. I wanted to prolong the conversation. I grabbed a name. The right one, as it turned out. "I'm still
interested in Lionelle Partridge," I said.

"Why do you keep bringing him up?" For the first time there
was a definite edge in her voice. "He was a snitch. They called
him Canary. It was even on his jacket. 'aka Canary.' This wasn't
the first time. He had a history. That's why the Department of
Corrections moved him from San Quentin to Folsom. He
snitched on someone at Q. There was a contract out on him
there."

It was exposition without cant, complete and to the point. As
she did through all the years we were together, Leah spared me
her considerable fluency in the jargon of protest. She seemed to
sense that I was deaf to it. In fact I wonder now if the absence of

rhetoric in her explanation that day in Department 34 was the first signal she sent me.

"So he gets himself whacked out in Folsom instead." Not that I was surprised. A transfer from one state prison facility to another never really helped a convict with a snitch jacket. The inmates at the new institution always knew. The manner of the Canary's death was a statement in itself, an elaborate warning.

"A snitch gets what's coming to him."

Are you always this unfeeling? I wanted to say, but I didn't, because of course she was right. From the day she first began the practice of law, Leah was a scholar of the constitution of the underworld. "A snitch gets what's coming to him" was in the preamble of that unwritten document.

She put the Burberry over her arm.

"Let me ask you something." I was thinking aloud, trying to delay her departure. "If seventeen people . . ." I searched for the proper hypothetical wording. ". . . are alleged to have urinated in someone's mouth . . ." I paused, contemplating the question. ". . . then how do you know whose piss was actually responsible for drowning him?"

She smiled, a teacher to a slow student who had somehow managed to synthesize a difficult proposition. "You don't."

I played it out. "But what about the pencil?" That number three soft Dixon Ticonderoga stub. I abandoned the hypothetical. "How do you get your guy out of that?"

"There are seventeen defendants." She picked up her briefcase and started down the aisle. I trailed behind her. "And only one pencil. Who's going to snitch?" At the door, she stopped and switched off the lights in the courtroom. It was the instinctive reaction of a well-bred young woman brought up to conserve electricity whenever possible. Then she turned to face me. "Look what happened to the Canary."

I tried to discern a connection between the energy conserver and the woman who seemed perfectly content with the notion that Lionelle Partridge's murder served the entirely useful purpose of ensuring that no one would testify against Mercury Baker when he stood trial for the commission of that murder.

"Listen." Leah Kaye paused at the door. "Do you really think a

jury, a largely white jury, is going to care how seventeen niggers
killed another nigger?" She used the word "nigger" as if it were a
poison dart. "Or which nigger actually did it? Do you really
think that?"

I could not contest her logic.

"No one's going to take the fall for the Canary," she said. "You
can bet on it."

A cinch bet, as it turned out.

I followed her out into the corridor. I remember now that as we
walked toward the elevator she suddenly stopped and tried to
open a door that was plainly marked JURY ROOM—NO ADMIT-
TANCE. The door was locked. I point this out only because all her
adult life Leah was almost constitutionally incapable of passing
any portal marked NO ADMITTANCE or STAFF or EMPLOYEES
ONLY without at least trying the doorknob. She did it in hospitals
and jails and police stations. She did it in government offices and
private buildings and at airports and municipal arenas and sports
complexes. It was as if the signs abridged what she considered her
right of free trespass and for her not to at least try the door would
be to exhibit some private failure of nerve. If the door happened
to be unlocked and someone inside, she would demand, in the
voice of a testy supervisor or a regional inspector, "Who are you?
And what are you doing here?" More often than not, she would
receive a stammering answer, a totally unexceptional explanation
of some clerical function or technical task, the scheduling of air-
line flight attendants, say, or the cataloging of stool samples or the
allocation of season tickets. I once asked her if she had ever discovered anything useful behind those closed doors and she replied, "No, but I might."

This was the woman I was to marry.

A woman so absorbed by autopsy reports that I often thought
that medicine rather than the law was her true calling. She au-
dited courses in forensic pathology at UC Medical Center in
order to be more conversant with organic malfunctions and
therapeutic misadventures and pathognomonic signatures and
hence less willing to accept on faith the findings of a medical examiner's postmortem. She would always anticipate with pleasure

the opportunity to cross-examine a coroner, confident that if she displayed enough familiarity with cyanosis or retropharyngeal abscess or petechial hemorrhages of the pericardium or lower nephron nephrosis or pulmonary thromboemboli or the minimum lethal level of ethchlorovinyl she might be able to shake a medical examiner's professional calm and resolution, perhaps trapping him in a misstatement that might lead to the admission of a faulty diagnosis.

A woman, I might add, who was once reduced to tears when I noted that she always made three right-hand turns in order to circumvent the necessity of making a left turn in traffic.

Who always waited for the light to turn green before she crossed the street.

Who diligently worked out a seventeen percent tip on her pocket calculator before adding it to every restaurant bill, never rounding the sum off, which often resulted in such whimsical gratuities as $6.98 or $9.01.

A woman who as we approached the elevator that first day we met was suddenly accosted by a meter maid, a short stocky black woman bulging out of her blue uniform. She seemed to materialize at Leah's side from the ranks of those invisible people who inhabit courthouse corridors, the defendants and victims and survivors and friends and relatives and witnesses to the most abominable acts. Her eyes wild and popping, she thrust her face next to Leah's and for what seemed an eternity spat sexual and scatalogical abuse at her. No one, myself most especially included, moved to stop the outburst. An off-duty policeman with a badge and ID card pinned to his war surplus leather flight jacket observed the scene for a moment and then returned to the sports section of his newspaper. A few spectators occupying the benches along the corridor wall stared blankly at the scene and then disappeared back into their private embarrassment at being in such a place. A marshal walked by without a glance, massaging his crotch. It was as if the meter maid's outburst was the accepted diction of this corridor.

Even Leah seemed no more than perplexed. She looked at the meter maid as if she were only trying to find an acceptable translation for the text of the diatribe. By now the meter maid had found her second wind and the abuse began all over again, this time accompanied by spittle that she sprayed all over Leah's face and white silk blouse. Motherfucker, kike, cunt, lawyer, Jew, dyke. The words were the same, the combinations different. My baby. You done it. You swallowed his come. You're the one. He fucked you up the ass. My baby.

The effort expended finally caused a button to burst from the meter maid's pale blue uniform shirt and in a gesture I will never forget Leah bent over, picked the button from the floor and handed it back to the other woman. At that moment, the elevator door blessedly opened and followed by the torrent of obscenity we entered. We rode without a word to the ground floor, objects of the silent scrutiny of our fellow passengers.

"Who in the name of Christ was that?" I demanded in the lobby.

Leah affected unconcern. "I have no idea. A crazy woman. You meet them here."

"She knew you."

"I don't know her."

"She knew you were a lawyer. There was something about her baby."

Leah picked up the note of disbelief. Her voice was cold, dismissive. "I have never laid eyes on that woman in my life."

And with that, she turned abruptly and walked out the revolving door into the street.

I never did discover who the meter maid was. Later, after we were married, I would sometimes ask Leah about the incident. Could the meter maid have been the victim in a case she was defending? The relative of a victim? A witness subjected to a particularly exacting cross-examination? To every question Leah was indifferent. Indifference was her heat shield against the peculiar psychic demands of the criminal bar.

The woman was crazy.

She said.

In every felony, there were bruised survivors.

She said.

The courthouse was a place where the victims of suffering and misery attracted the groupies of suffering and misery.

She said.

Life itself was a risk.

So what?

If I persisted, she would ask how often I recognized the people I wrote about after they had fulfilled their purpose of supplying me seven hundred words of copy for my column.

She filtered out the extraneous. She defined as extraneous whatever did not promote the interests of her clients.

The meter maid was extraneous.

That seemed to be the lesson of the incident. The one I worked out while watching the news at five, six and eleven with Wendy Chan. You see the problem. I am by disposition one of life's neutrals, a human Switzerland. Leah Kaye was the exact opposite, a woman who promised only trouble.

One to avoid.

Because opposites attract.

Although opposites attract.

I did not see her again until I introduced her to Bro in the parking lot at San Quentin.

BOOK THREE

AN EXECUTION

DEPARTMENT OF CORRECTIONS

INSTRUCTIONS
FOR OPERATING AND CLEANING
LETHAL GAS CHAMBER

Ventilating fan in witness area should be kept running. All adjacent exterior doors and windows should be open during the entire procedure. After determining that Chamber is airtight, proceed as follows:

1. Place portable electric fan in Chamber, plug in and be sure it operates when exhaust fan switch is turned on.
2. Prepare a cheesecloth bag of proper size, placing one pound of lead weights or small stones in bottom of bag. Put 15 one-ounce cyanide eggs in bag and tie securely.
3. Have on hand two gallons ammonia solution, equal parts ammonia and water, in corked bottles. Cover iron drain plug tips with Vaseline and seat firmly in drain hole of pots.
4. Place two quarts of clear water in sink, first being sure drain plugs are firmly in place. Iron plugs should be daubed with Vaseline.
5. Pour two quarts of concentrated sulfuric acid into the water, stirring slowly but constantly with a glass rod or clean hardwood stick.
6. Secure prisoner in chair. Attach stethoscope to prisoner. Remove plug from outer end of stethoscope tube and attach earpiece of stethoscope.
7. Attach bag of cyanide pellets to hook on release mechanism. Wipe a film of Vaseline on rubber gasket, close and tighten door. Open exhaust valve, start exhaust fan. Close fresh-air intake. Open water-gauge valve and observe water gauge. When water level begins to lower slightly, chamber is airtight and ready. Close all valves. Switch off Chamber fans. Pull iron plug in sink, allowing acid to flow into iron pot. Replace plug tightly and run an inch of water in sink to ensure seal.

101

8. Warden selects switch on selector panel, turns switch to ON. Switches on control panel are tripped, releasing acid pellets in bag. (Circuit has delayed-action relay. Hook does not drop until 15 seconds after switch is thrown.)
9. Doctor is in place with stethoscope. As soon as prisoner is pronounced dead, open exhaust valve, start exhaust fan. Pour contents of ammonia solution bottles into sink, pull iron plug allowing ammonia solution to flow into pot, covering and neutralizing acid in pot. Replace plug, fill sink with water. Open fresh-air intake and allow Chamber to clear for at least 20 minutes.
10. As soon as Chamber is opened, pull iron drain plug in pot, empty pot, replace plug and fill pot with clear water.
11. After each execution, sinks, plugs, pot and entire inside of cabinet should be washed down with warm water and a detergent. Add 2 ounces of agua ammonia to each gallon of water. Rubber door gasket should be scrubbed free of Vaseline with suds of kitchen detergent.

I

ON A TUESDAY MORNING the following August, Bro and I drove from Bohemian Grove to San Quentin to witness the execution of Germany Baker. We left the Grove shortly before six in my black Porsche. The sun was just coming up, filtering through the redwoods, dappling the narrow, curvy two-lane road. Bro insisted on driving, and he drove as he always drove, like a madman, cornering at speeds so fast I thought we would end up in the Russian River, secure in some misplaced belief that no highway patrolman or cow county sheriff's deputy would ever give a ticket to a priest.

He was not dressed like a priest. Top-Siders with no socks. White duck pants. A sailor blue cashmere sweater. No shirt. Not the usual clerical uniform for a chaplain officiating at an execution. That was to be Bro's role. I cannot say I was really surprised. Nothing Bro did ever really surprised me. He had no connection with San Quentin nor was Germany Baker even a Catholic, but these were facts of small concern. He was a Broderick, one moreover intimately connected with the president of the United States. A Broderick who could call the governor and the governor in turn would call the warden. The warden was de-

lighted to accommodate the governor and even more delighted to
accommodate Bro, delighted in the way that association with the
Brodericks in even the most tangential way seemed to make so
many people. The regular prison chaplain was scheduled for va-
cation and now there was no need to have him return for such an
unpleasant errand. Bro would be a more than adequate stand-in.
He would give Germany Baker the last rites in the holding cell.
He would escort Germany Baker from the holding cell to the oc-
tagonal gas chamber. He would make the sign of the cross with
holy oil on Germany Baker's forehead while the guards belted
Germany Baker into the seat nearest the stethoscope tube. He
would intone the prayers for the dead while the guards taped the
stethoscope to Germany Baker's chest. He would offer Germany
Baker reassurance while the guards then checked with the attending physician to make sure the stethoscope was working so
that Germany Baker might be pronounced dead before the fumes
were blown away and the walls flushed with water and the body
of Germany Baker sprayed with liquid ammonia to neutralize the
cyanide gas in his clothes. He was the last friendly face Germany
Baker would see before the door to the gas chamber was sealed
shut—and he was dressed like an extra in *Madame Butterfly.*

"You look like a pansy," Leah said when I introduced her to
Bro in the parking lot outside San Quentin.

One thing Bro shared with Leah was a passion for organization
and logistical order. How much so I did not fully appreciate until
after he died when I began rummaging through the papers in The
Augustine Broderick Collection at Harvard. Until I was named
executor in his will, I had not even been aware that he had established, long before his death, a Broderick repository at the Widener Library. That was Bro. Always secretive. The official
papers were consequential only in their thoroughness. Hearing
transcripts. Commission reports. Letters of transmittal. Flowery
and insincere acknowledgments from several presidents. Cables.
Telephone logs. Privileged communications so unexceptional that
their contents could have been chiseled on the pedestal of a mon-
ument. Invitations: "The Ambassador of the United States of
America requests the pleasure of the company of Dom Augustine
Broderick, O.S.B., at a luncheon honoring . . . Dress: Casual."

I learned, in those weeks I spent in Cambridge, that it was Bro's habit, after each official mission, to deposit in the Widener a copy of the diary he had kept during the course of the assignment. I suspect these diaries were meant to be the basis of his autobiography, had he lived to write one. What surprised me about them at first was how unlike Bro they actually were. It was as if he had deliberately purged them of the irony and sardonic humor that so characterized him. As an insight to Bro, and I would think also as an insight to the events he describes, the diaries are worthless, written in a kind of semi-officialese, the guarded and dead cadences of someone trying not to offend:

> Up at five, Mass at 5:30, offered for the repose of the souls of my beloved mother, Gertrude Mary Mahoney Broderick, and my dear sister, Priscilla Broderick Finn, then off to the airport in the limo of Senator Domingo Coolidge (R., N.M.). Mingo and I are on our way to the annual Pugwash Conference in Nova Scotia and I am really looking forward to it. Good talk is always at a premium. World hunger is on the agenda this year, and nuclear proliferation, two hard ones not offering easy solutions. Mingo said his daughter Beth (she's married to Art Underwood, who works out at Langley) is expecting, his first grandchild, and he's pleased as punch. It's always good to see Mingo and have the opportunity to listen to that straight-shooting New Mexico common sense.

"Who works out at Langley" was a nice bland construction. In case there was anyone sentient who did not know that Langley was a single-industry suburb, the industry being the DELETED DELETED DELETED, an affirmative action and covert activity employer. I also knew Bro thought Mingo Coolidge was an idiot, an opinion he was never leery about ventilating, which was why I was not terribly surprised when a second, unofficial, diary showed up among his papers, available not even to the librarian at the Widener but only to the executor of The Broderick Collection. In other words, me. There were no instructions on how this second diary should be disseminated, if at all, beyond the single caveat that I and I alone would make the final decision on whether it would be distributed, and if so, in what form and to

whom. It was so like Bro, an expression of trust I never would
have discovered if he had not been killed. Each entry was hand-
written, in the calligrapher's script he had picked up in the seminary at Portsmouth Priory, and here was the essential Bro,
pointed, funny, perceptive, occasionally nasty. There were two
additional colors, and I knew it was because of these that Bro had
entrusted the unofficial diary to my charge, the first a sense of
doubt at odds with his public persona of effortless detachment,
the second a sadness almost to the point of melancholy. Here is
that Bro on Leah, an undated entry sometime after their first
meeting at San Quentin:

> I think we were meant for each other, Leah and I. Who is the
> real criminal—the prisoner or the society that imprisons
> him? I like that. It's the kind of glib paradox that appeals to
> me, talk show stuff, think tank stuff, lots of heavy nodding at
> the weekend seminar and on the prime-time news special, I
> think you've got something there, Father Bro. Thank you,
> Senator. Let's take it up when the committee on goals meets.
> No, the committee on urban consensus, that's my gig this
> week.

> Let's face it. Mine is a history of trying on and discarding
> social fashions, as if each one were a Mao jacket or a Nehru
> suit, *mea culpa, mea culpa, mea maxima culpa*. Something I
> abandon when a new line comes in, *mea et cetera*. But she is
> something else, Leah. I am absolutely transfixed by her. The
> metaphor of society as a prison is appealing. And so is the
> notion that man outside the law can not only redefine the
> social contract, but also the moral frontiers of society itself.
> Leah Kaye, pure and simple. The con in the slammer as the
> point man of social upheaval, ta-ra. And if the prisoner has a
> commitment to crime, then crime is only a left-handed form
> of human endeavor, as John Huston has someone say in *The
> Asphalt Jungle*, the crooked lawyer, I think. Not something
> I will mention to Leah, that. And if the innocent are hurt,
> aren't the innocent only the sleepwalkers of a corrupt so-
> ciety? In any event, who defines the innocent?

> It's not so much that I buy the package. Let's face it, I know
> where the holes are. Forget that. Just imagine finding an in-

choate new ten commandments in the cell block. And to the mix of crime and punishment, Father Bro will add redemption, as if it's a kind of seasoning salt. Now let's get to the negatives. She's volatile. I have a feel for the possible and she for the rhetorical, and the two are not often compatible. On the upside, she offers me a visa into this uncharted world beyond the perimeters of the law and I in turn can give her a legitimacy she's never had. The architecture of the Broderick name, the scaffolding of my reputation, such as it is, propping up her fucking self-righteousness. Why is she so often so needlessly lethal?

I had not realized how much he loved her.

II

HE HAD ALREADY BEEN on the cover of *Time*. That issue of *Time* was included in the papers he bequeathed to the Widener Library in his will. The slash line on the cover read, CATHOLIC CHURCH IN TRANSITION—FATHER AUGUSTINE BRODERICK & THE "NEW CLERGY" MEET THE CHALLENGE. And there on the cover of the magazine was Bro in what *Time* seemed to think was the habit of the new clergy, blue jeans and a green Lacoste shirt, in Bro's case with the little green alligator carefully removed. Father Augustine Broderick, O.S.B., listening intently in one photograph to a cadre of inner-city revolutionaries in ski masks and camouflage fatigues and in the next picture interpreting their point of view to Sammy Davis, Jr. There were also photographs of Bro with the Duke of Edinburgh and Bro with Henry Mancini. And of course Bro at the White House.

Fritz Finn was not a president given to prayer breakfasts, but with Bro offering thanks as presiding clergyman he would often make an exception. They meshed easily together. Bro as a photo opportunity was almost as glamorous as Fritz himself, a rich young American priest with a taste, although not a glutton's appetite, for liberation theology. In this role, Fritz found Bro a useful emissary to some of the more truculent Catholic enclaves in the Third World, and the Benedictines were more than willing to second him to the Finn administration for such missions. And the fact that Bro was Hugh Broderick's son protected Fritz from that element in the Congress who thought the Big Stick was there to use, particularly on those who did not subscribe to the notion that they were the white man's burden. The man of action meets the man of God—the equation was advantageous to both Fritz and Bro, and who made better use of whom I suspect was a matter of complete indifference to each, an attentiveness to the situational being the governing principle of their relationship.

The part Bro played in the affair between Fritz and our sister Priscilla being a case in point.

Fritz Finn's philandering was as much discussed privately among the army of the knowing as were his domestic policies and his diplomatic overtures, so much so that the trade in names of his various consorts had become one way of hinting at a spurious closeness to the seat of power. Another was to speculate on how much Fiona Finn actually knew. Fiona remained aloof from such speculation, aided by a definite and regulated schedule. July and August she was in Kennebunkport with the children. February and March she was in Hobe Sound. December was spent in Vail after the ceremonial lighting of the White House Christmas tree. The other seven months of the year she was the president's wife. The First Lady. The role seemed to amuse her. "Come dish with the First Lady," she would say to me or to Bro if circumstances allowed her a third vodka on the rocks. Fiona interrupted her routine only for the nominating conventions and for state visits by the more prominent allies or for summit conferences when Fritz petitioned her presence. She spoke perfect French, stayed away from the more obvious homosexuals who attached themselves like limpets to rich and attractive women with inattentive husbands and she visited Fritz's bed often enough to have had two miscarriages after his election to the presidency. "A miscarriage," she told me once "is good politics when the president's wife is forty-two." She and Fritz got along well in that offhand and ad-lib manner people who go their separate ways so often do. Theirs was the perfect political marriage. She and he and the two

children photographed well together and they took care never to
say anything about each other in private that could not be repeated in public. I sometimes thought Fiona was born to be a
First Lady, like some Ruritanian countess who from the cradle
was raised to be the wife of the crown prince. She was so secure
in her detachment that none of Fritz's indiscretions ever was a
factor upsetting her serene equanimity.

Even when the indiscretion was committed with her sister-in-
law.

In its cover story on Bro, *Time* had said, with a barely unac-
knowledged wink, that Fritz was "extraordinarily close" to
"both" Priscilla and Dickie Finn. The affair between Fritz and
Priscilla was conducted mainly at the Carlyle and at Camp David.
And at Priscilla and Dickie's house in Georgetown. Always when
Dickie was out of town on the president's business, as Fritz was a
stickler for certain proprieties when it came to cuckolding his
brother. Bro was occasionally the beard in Georgetown. I would
imagine this was a duty in the service of the state about which he
neglected to inform his superiors in the Benedictines. One best
saved for the seal of the confessional. If even then, as Bro was
nothing if not supple in his reading of what he considered the
least of the Ten Commandments. It was a measure of Bro's innate
confidence in himself that he weighted the commandments in his
own mind, and the strictures against the carnal transgressions
never rated particularly high in his pantheon of sins. He was celi-
bate by choice, but he was not a strict constructionist when it
came to the adultery of others, and certainly not his sister's adultery with the president of the United States. Such views of course
were never stated or even implied. They were just intuited,
mainly by the media constituency I often thought was Bro's only
congregation.

Two or three times a year, he blew into San Francisco like a
one-man wind of change, making a pit stop on his way to or from
some new battleground of the church militant. San Francisco was
home, a place of rest, a place of repose, a place to recharge his
batteries, and though I privately thought it inconsistent with his
avowed purpose of R&R, he invariably shared this disclosure,

as if it were a state secret, with the local print, radio and television interviewers, who invariably seemed to treat it as such. In the city's newspapers and by the city's television outlets, he was accorded the respectful attention of a municipal asset, a tourist attraction in a Roman collar who reappeared in the city every other solstice, schedule permitting. He had the Broderick name. He had access to the Broderick millions and by choice he had taken a monastic vow of poverty. A tabloid irony ensuring that the spotlight would seek him out.

And he did not blink in its glare.

In any event, Bro's idea of seclusion was relative. Repose was a matter of interpretation. On one visit, he said Mass in fluent Mandarin (mastered, according to the clips on file in The Augustine Broderick Collection at the Widener, at the urging of a granddaughter of Sun Yat-sen) at a temple in Chinatown to celebrate a truce ending a murderous feud over the numbers racket between competing tongs.

Top of the news.

Front page, above the break: BRO SMOKES PEACE PIPE WITH CHINATOWN MOB. The BRO seemed almost papal, as if his diminutive were as identifiable as PIUS.

BRO PRAISES PRESIDENT.

BRO APPLAUDS FREEDOM RIDERS.

BRO BACKS WAR ON CHOLESTEROL.

BRO: "BAY AREA BEST."

With every visit, another headline. And then, BRO BEATEN.

By assailants unknown.

An event that was a paradigm of Bro's style.

He had, on that occasion, moved into a decaying housing development in Hunters Point. It was some months before the execution of Germany Baker and he had the frosty permission of His Excellency, the archbishop of San Francisco, a cleric of the old school who detested the idea of the priest as soloist, but who at the same time was not immune to the pressures inherent in the Broderick name. "An urban missionary," Bro had described himself in all the appropriate media outlets. I had not failed to notice that "urban missionary" was less inflammatory than "worker-priest," a designation he had once favored. I mentioned this when

I visited him at the development. He had smiled, that smile like a baffle. He was wearing jeans and moccasins and a windbreaker. "More Maryknoll than Marxist this trip," he had said. "It's only a nuance, but nuances are important."

I did not write a column about my visit to the development on Hunters Point. I did not write that the plaster was already crumbling in the various buildings nor did I write that the bricks could be pried loose with a putty knife. I did not write that the rival gangs in the development used the bricks as weapons. I did not write that a putty knife was also an effective weapon. I did not write that a gang member was thrown down an elevator shaft the day Bro arrived. I did not write that the shaft was empty because the elevator had never been installed, a mute reminder of construction money gone into the wrong pockets. I did not write about the rats. The rats were the size of prairie dogs. One of the rats had bitten the nose of a slumbering infant the day before. The infant was four months old. He had just been nursed by his mother. The dried milk on his lips had attracted the rat. I did not write that Bro had driven the infant to the hospital. A tacit agreement between us. I never mentioned Bro in my column.

His altar stone was stolen the day after my visit.

A week later he was thrown down a flight of stairs. A crudely lettered note was attached to his windbreaker: "Get lost, honky," the note said.

He was chipper when I saw him in the hospital. "It could have been the elevator shaft," he said.

"You were lucky."

"God was watching over me."

Even in the hospital I had an uneasy feeling when Bro mentioned God. I always felt he had to repress an instinct to arch an eyebrow whenever the word passed his lips. It was as if the concept of God were embarrassing to him, on the level of Zoroastrian sorcery. Bro was always most selective around whom he used the word when he was not in the pulpit. Never in front of my father. My father thought God was reserved for those who believed in four-leaf clovers. Nor with Fritz after grace at those prayer breakfasts. Fritz wore God as he wore a blue service cap when he spoke to the American Legion convention. God was part of the attire of a presidency. Only occasionally with me would Bro mention the idea of God, and always, as here, in a way I can only describe as ironic. It was as if his faith, if that indeed was what it was, needed testing, and I was his chosen inquisitor, chosen in part because I embraced doubt as an idea, in part (and I suspect the larger part) because he considered me an inquisitor who might be easily routed, his faith then safely defended.

I did not rise to the bait. "He always has an eye peeled on you, Bro."

"That's what Fritz says."

He offered absolution to his assailants when he described his experiences to Walter Cronkite on the "CBS Evening News" after his release from the hospital. I remember that his arm was still in a cast and that he wore a red silk sling. An attention-getter, that red silk sling, making the sober black suit of his profession somehow dashing. He had already been to Washington. He had seen the president. The president had asked him to chair a bipartisan commission to study the permanent underclass of the urban poor and to make recommendations.

Top of the news.

Front page, above the break: BRO TO PREZ: "POOR NEED HELP."

III

—————————

"WHAT DID FRITZ REALLY SAY?" I asked when Bro returned to California several months later. It was the week after the Mercury Baker hearing in Department 34. We were having lunch in a small Italian trattoria across the square from Saints Peter & Paul, where Bro stayed when he was in San Francisco. He preferred the rectory to the house on Washington Street, even (perhaps especially) when our father was in town, as he rarely was (and was not on this occasion), the peripatetic being as much his style as it was Bro's. Bro liked to maintain a certain distance from Washington Street and the more obvious entanglements of the Broderick name, and the rectory allowed this relative freedom of action.

"He said he wished those darkies had killed me."

"Quote, unquote?"

"Of course." Bro smiled across the top of his wineglass. I noticed a thin white scar across the bridge of his nose. A legacy from the urban mission. "No votes in the schwartzes in the next election. Again quote, unquote."

It sounded like Fritz. The private Fritz.

"He also wanted to know if I knew another word for 'cocoon.'"

I cracked a bread stick and waited.

"N-nigger."

"The healer of the nation's wounds," I said.

"You know he's got a good side? His right. He's got that small mole under his left eye and he doesn't like it showing up in photographs. He goes over the contact sheets. I swear. Shoot the mole, you're fired. He's gone through three White House photographers already."

"He's also got girl trouble."

"Yes." His eyes moved around the restaurant. In case someone might be eavesdropping. "As a matter of fact, no longer. He decided on discretion."

"The way I hear it, he decided on no such thing. The way I hear it, Priscilla dumped him."

"Where did you ever hear that?" In a voice indicating that only a fool would believe such nonsense.

"Priscilla was here a couple of weeks ago."

"Oh, yes. I forgot. When she came out to see Hugh." Ever since taking holy orders, Bro had referred to our father as "Hugh." A small step in the process of distancing. "I thought she was more discreet."

"She is. I asked her." Priscilla had always shared her secrets with me. "It seems that Tuck Bradley is the new light of her life."

A pained expression crossed Bro's face. "Yes."

"It must be a new experience for Fritz. Pining."

"It's for the best. He was worried that Dickie might find out."

"Dickie always knew."

"So I told him."

"Priscilla could fuck a telephone pole and Dickie wouldn't care. He ever divorces her he won't get his chance to take over from the old man when he kicks off, if he ever does, which I doubt. That's all he cares about, Dickie, you know that. Who else in this family can manage those Broderick millions I get so tired of reading about every time I pick up a magazine? You're committed to a higher authority and I'm patently unqualified. Even if I were interested, which I'm not. That leaves Dickie, unless he gets weak at the knees every time Priscilla cuckolds him. He's got good knees, Dickie, they don't buckle. Even when Priscilla sleeps with his brother and his Benedictine brother-in-law's offering them both absolution the minute they jump out of the kip from the portable confessional he's set up outside the bedroom door."

Bro surveyed me from across the table, a bemused look on his face. Now that he is dead, I realize that in his presence I resorted to the obscene and the scatological far more often than I normally did. A combination of hostility and the faux bravado that cheeky adolescents sometimes affect in front of a priest.

"Colorfully put," he said after a moment. "Not necessarily accurate, but entertaining. You have a certain demotic flair that doesn't quite fit with all those Broderick millions you're so tired of." He glanced out the plate-glass window of the restaurant. My car was parked out front. "And which put you in that fancy black Porsche out there, if I don't miss my guess. Unless the newspaper business is paying better these days." He ran a long bony forefinger along the new scar on his nose. "In any event, I think Fritz is aware of the broad outlines of what you say."

"Broad outlines." I italicized the words. "I like that."

"I thought you would."

"You two must have a lot to talk about, you get together these days. This, that and the other thing. The broad outlines, as you call it. I bet what you two talk about, you don't pass the word to the attorney general or the secretary of state afterward." I paused and when he did not respond, I added, "One thing I've always wondered."

"What's that?"

"Was Cardinal Richelieu Louis the Fourteenth's confessor?"

"Louis the Thirteenth's actually. Mazarin was Louis the Fourteenth's." I received the wintry smile with which he devoured error. "Tell me," he said briskly, "how is Wendy?"

In other words, the subject of Fritz and Priscilla was closed.

"Still listening to the police band," I said.

"And that's it?" He had always taken a keen interest in the women in my life.

"Wendy has ambitions. I'm just a comfort stop on the broad highway of her life."

"You make me glad I opted for celibacy."

I shrugged. He played with the prongs of his fork while the

waitress cleared the table. She brushed away the crumbs. Bro did not take his eyes off her. She was tall and rawboned. The black plastic nametag on her uniform said LeAnne. We both ordered espresso. When she left, he suddenly said, "You know, I sometimes think if it weren't for divorce there wouldn't be any waitresses."

I looked at the retreating waitress, then at Bro. He always did have the capacity to surprise. To disarm.

"I suppose there's a grain of anthropological truth buried in there somewhere," I said. Carhops and waitresses had always incited a certain idle sexual speculation in me. In Bro as well, it seemed. I found the thought comforting. "Although not one likely ever to be found in a papal bull."

"No, I suppose not." He lined up the remaining silver. "How is Hugh?"

My relationship with our father was a subject Bro always treated with extreme delicacy and precision, as if it were a topic on the agenda of a disarmament conference.

"He never changes, does he?" I said.

"What's he doing in Rome?" Rome was our father's port of call that week.

"Probably trying to get you made a cardinal. If not arrange for you to succeed the pope. He talks about you a lot."

"You see him, then?"

"The obligatory lunch. The duty dinner when he's in town. We go to the Pacific Union. Neutral turf. The house gives me the creeps. It's so goddamn big and so goddamn empty. Like it's inhabited only by bad memories. I don't know why he keeps it. He's never here."

"Because it's home," Bro said. "He needs the bad memories. Like most of us do. They keep us honest."

Bro gave our father credit for a conscience. Which was more than I did. I was surprised. I was always brought up short when I realized that Bro had a larger sense of sin. Which conscience was there to acknowledge.

"You're about the only subject we have in common. He tells me who he set straight and where he put the fix in."

His expression darkened. The waitress LeAnne returned with

the two espressos. This time Bro did not look at her. While I wondered if there were stretch marks on her breasts. The silvery striations of use. LeAnne. Ah, LeAnne.

"I wish he wouldn't do that," he said when the waitress departed.

"That's like wishing the tide won't come in. It's what he does. He told me the last time he was here he'd made the archbishop a little testy. Something about a Mrs. Finbar Funicello. And a place in Balboa. There's also this boat that's tied up at the dock at the place in Balboa."

"*The Pink Lady.*" He wiped the lemon peel around the rim of his espresso cup and as he dropped it finally into the cup, he said, "He thinks I need his help."

"And you don't."

"No."

At least he didn't beat around the bush. There it was. He thought our father was over the hill. Past his prime. Even an embarrassment. The signs were clear enough. Bro calling him Hugh. And staying at the rectory at Saints Peter & Paul rather than at the house on Washington Street. I suspect my father was able to read the signs as well. He was not given to self-delusion. To my surprise, I was dismayed by Bro's attitude. There was an orderliness in my father's brutish efficiency that I found reassuring in a way. A standard against which to measure what he was quick enough to call my failures. But at least the standard was always there. And now, as if he were a paleontological fossil, Bro seemed quite prepared to consign him to some private museum of natural history. I admired his assurance but regretted that our father was the object of it. He was a fossil about whom I could become almost sentimental.

"What did he say to you about Hunters Point?"

"Oddly enough, he was more muted than I expected. He said I had made a chump's play. 'I didn't raise a son to be a chump,' he said. Fair enough. And then he said, 'I didn't raise a son to be a priest either, but that's over and done with now.' "

"To which you said?"

"Nothing, of course. My vocation is a subject I take pains never to discuss with him. Then he changed the subject. He wanted to know about Fritz."

"How is Fritz, anyway?"

"He's rather taken with the Shah these days." He held his espresso cup in both hands and sipped. "I think the idea of the Peacock Throne appeals to him. I always have thought Fritz wanted to be weighed in diamonds. He's put on a carat or two, by the way. A little plump under the chin. And his shirts buckle a bit around the buttons. So much so you can see the hairs on his stomach. The shirts are monogrammed. That's a new touch. FGF."

Fritz had a good side, Fritz was putting on weight, Fritz wore monogrammed shirts. As always, Fritz was much on Bro's mind.

"When do you have to deliver your report?"

He did not answer directly. "Oh, come on, Jack. You know why the government appoints bipartisan commissions as well as I do. It's a stalling operation. A lot of activity and no action. Hire staff, hold hearings. We go from city to city like a cut-rate package tour. If this is Tuesday, it must be Cleveland. Tomorrow, Detroit. Another opening, another show, in Philly, Boston, and Baltimo'. For what? To make a report. Graphs and Charts. Cases and Examples. Root Causes. Short-Term Remedies. Long-Term Solutions. In Summary. In summary, nobody reads the goddamn thing."

I was not prepared for the asperity of his reply. "So what's the answer?"

"The answer is to get something that will make people take notice."

Of course. He had a tropistic instinct for the next moral battlefield where he might place his standard. Dom Augustine Broderick, Order of Saint Benedict. Advance man for God the Politician, attracting hostile fire on the point. Bro, *coeur de lion.*

"Like Hunters Point," I said.

"Something like that." He seemed lost in thought. Finally he said, "You know I liked it there."

"You liked getting thrown down the stairs?"

"No," he said quietly. "I liked it *there.*"

"Then you must have aberrant tastes."

"I was anonymous."

"You were the only white face in the whole project."

"I was still anonymous."

I think now he meant that he was not a Broderick, but I did not question him any further. I was always too willing to take anything Bro said as stuff and nonsense.

"Do you remember me telling you about the baby?" he said. "The little boy. The one whose nose was bitten off by the rat?"

I nodded.

"I drove him to the hospital that day. For a rabies shot. They shoot you in the stomach for rabies. I didn't know that. I hate not knowing things like that. Because I'm supposed to sign off on root causes. And it seems to me when a rat chews off a kid's nose, that's a good definition of a root cause. And the shot in the stomach is a short-term remedy. If not a long-term solution. In summary. In summary, I don't know shit."

"That could be the beginning of wisdom, Bro."

He smiled. "It could also be self-absorption. A continuing pattern."

"I'll concede the possibility."

"I was sure you would."

"What about the child?"

"The doctors at Kaiser said he'd recover. A shot a day for twenty-eight days. His stomach would look like a dart board. But then he'd be all right. Except for the nose, of course. Reconstructing the nose promised to be a small problem."

"That's all you know?"

"I drove out there this morning. Not without a certain amount of trepidation, I admit. I checked around. They'd left. The child, its mother. There wasn't a father, of course. Grandmother and great-grandmother. Half-dozen other kids. All gone. With the wind."

"So," I said. "Something to make people sit up and take notice. Any ideas?"

"Bureaucrats have ideas."

Condescension came naturally to him. I wiped the damp bottom of the espresso cup on the tablecloth, waiting for the flash of irritation to pass. Out the window, I could see a meter maid ticketing a car across the square. For a moment I thought she might be the one from the courthouse. I stared at her until she came into plain sight, but then, with a sense of relief, I saw I was mistaken. I was not ready to match her story against that of the boy with no nose.

"I'm late." I rose and motioned for the check.

Bro looked directly at me. "Have you ever heard of a man called Germany Baker?"

IV

I REMEMBER that morning clearly.

The speedometer on the Porsche quivered at 110 mph. The sun glinted off the river-washed stones below. At the speeds we were traveling, we would easily make San Quentin by seven-thirty. In time for Bro to see Germany Baker change from his faded blue Death Row work clothes to a new pair of denim pants and a fresh white shirt and a pair of cloth slippers. The execution was set for ten. Time for the courts of last resort on both coasts to be in session in the event of a last-minute stay.

Bro drove with his left hand. With his right, he turned the radio dial, searching for a newscast. There was always a chance the governor might issue a reprieve.

There was no news from Sacramento. After a moment, Bro turned off the radio and to my relief he put both hands on the wheel.

We drove for a while in silence, on the freeway now, speeding south toward San Quentin. I checked my watch. By my reckoning, the executioner would be drawing two pounds of cyanide from the prison armory in a few more minutes. The cyanide pellets were egg-shaped. The pellets would be put in two gauze bags and a bag would be hung from a hook beneath both chairs in the gas chamber. Both chairs even though Germany Baker would be the only occupant. Standard operating procedure. The chairs were clearly marked. A and B. Germany Baker would sit in the B chair because the B chair was nearer the stethoscope tube. Ten minutes before Germany Baker was strapped into the B chair the executioner and his assistant would pour a gallon of distilled water into two jars and then they would add sulfuric acid to the water. Tubes ran from the jars into the vats beneath the A and B chairs. The tubes were sealed and would remain so until Germany Baker was alone in the gas chamber. The first sound he would hear when the door was shut would be the acid and water mixture sluicing into the wells beneath the two chairs. He would be able to see the witnesses through five of the seven windows in the eight-sided cabin. The other two windows had venetian blinds drawn so that he could not see the executioner. At a signal from the warden, the executioner would push a red lever forward and the egg-shaped cyanide pellets would drop into the acid-filled vats.

"Check the radio," Bro said.

Still no report from Sacramento. The top story of the news update was the arrest of a rock star in Phoenix. I started to turn off the radio, but Bro leaned over and turned up the volume.

The rock star had been put off a DC-10 which had made an unscheduled stop in Phoenix so that he might be arrested. A stewardess had asked him to buckle his seat belt when the sign went on over the Grand Canyon. The rock star had refused and then had stood and flashed the other passengers. "Bared himself" was the way the newscaster described the scene. The rock star was said to be in a highly agitated state, and when he would not return to his seat, the pilot radioed Phoenix. The police were waiting at the gate. The DC-10 then continued on to New York without further incident.

Bro turned off the radio. A road sign on a freeway overpass said we were ten miles from the San Rafael Bridge. The prison was in the shadow of the bridge.

"He was at the White House last year," Bro said. He had put on aviator sunglasses, which heightened the *Madame Butterfly* effect. "Fritz wanted to open lines of communication to the young. His phrase. I told him to get this guy . . ."

It was only then that I realized Bro was talking about the rock singer who had been busted in Phoenix. Germany Baker did not seem to be much on his mind. Or distilled water and sulfuric acid and cyanide pellets. I wondered if I would get sick. Bro had eaten breakfast at the Grove before we left. I had not.

" 'An authentic voice of the young,' I think I said. 'I hope we're talking about the same young,' Fritz said. 'I mean the young who'll vote for me next year.' 'Then he's your man,' I said.

"So he shows up at the White House. Fritz was very good about the diamond in his front tooth. It was like he sees one every day. Then after dinner this guy disappears. Nobody can find him. One of the marine guards finally discovers him in a bathtub in one of the cans. With the shower curtain drawn. He'd OD'd.

"Now it's a little too public to call an ambulance for someone with an inlaid diamond in his right incisor who just happened to OD at the White House. It causes talk. So they bring him upstairs to Fritz and Fiona's private quarters. When he wakes up, the first thing he reaches for is the sparkler. In case Fritz copped it, I guess. And he looks at Fritz and he says, 'Hey, motherfucker, I guess I made the head pig shit his pants.' "

I could see the bridge. We were almost there. "What did Fritz say to that?"

" 'Fuck the young,' as I recall."

I am not as sure now as I was then that Bro was as insensitive to the occasion as he seemed, that the execution of Germany Baker was only another media spectacular for him. The rock singer—it was Ferdinand Flash, and since he died, choking on his vomit in his suite at the Crillon in Paris after some bad smack, that diamond (although in fact it was not a diamond at all, but paste) turns up occasionally at auctions of rock-and-roll memorabilia, where it is sold and resold as if it were a golden oldie—belonged to a world that Bro claimed to understand, a world where deals were cut and bargains struck and where everyone had a role, even Ferdinand Flash, whose role was to be a spokesman for the constituency of the young (and not coincidentally to arrange a se-

ries of concerts, the proceeds of which would go to Fritz's re-
election campaign). That Ferdinand Flash was not cut out to be a
role player never seemed to have occurred to Bro or to anyone
else at the White House, but nothing ventured, nothing gained.
In any event, it seemed to me that morning that Bro considered
Germany Baker as just another role player, as Ferdinand Flash
was intended to be, one whose death would serve some higher
purpose, focusing attention in a spectacular and dramatic way
on the agenda he was promoting for the relief of the permanent
underclass. And so as we turned into San Quentin not three
hours before the Marin County medical examiner would pronounce Germany Baker dead, I found myself furious, less at Bro
actually than at myself for being there.

Of course my being there was Bro's idea.

He had made me a proposition.

I had accepted.

I was bored.

I was particularly bored with my column. Bored with the little
fellow to whom I was supposed to give a pat on the back for a job
well done. Bored with celebrating testaments to the human spirit.
Bored with what the promotion department publicizing my column insisted on calling the infinite variety of life in our city. Instead I was becoming more and more attracted to the grotesque. I
wrote about the man who kicked a vending machine when the
exact change mechanism did not return the twenty cents he was
due from the two quarters he had deposited to buy a package of
crunchy Laura Scudder potato chips. The machine had tipped
over on him. The package of crunchy Laura Scudder potato chips
was still clutched in his fist when his body was discovered. I
wrote about the teenager with braces and rubber bands on her
teeth who had disappeared with her married, forty-year-old alge-
bra tutor, leaving behind a note to her mother that said, in part, "I
may be thirteen physically, but mentally I'm fifty-six. Please take
care of Elvis." Elvis was her goldfish. I wrote about the 240-
pound bouncer at the topless bar in North Beach. He had died
while fornicating after hours with a dancer from the show on top
of the club's white-spangled grand piano, an elaborate prop
which rose and descended from a hole in the ceiling, enabling the

star topless attraction to make her entrance and exit standing on it. The bouncer had apparently tripped the switch elevating the piano with his foot when in the throes of passion, and both he and his partner were unaware that it was ascending until he was pinned to the ceiling. He finally expired of asphyxiation because his chest was unable to expand enough for him to breathe. The dancer, who was naked (unlike the bouncer, who was fully clothed), was trapped beneath him for three hours, her legs over his shoulders (a position that police said made it impossible for her to have been responsible for activating the elevator), and was given breathing room, according to the attending paramedics, by the silicone implants in her breasts.

I was also bored with Wendy.

"Tell me about Saigon," I said. She had just returned from a weekend in Vietnam with an Air National Guard medevac 707 out of Travis AFB, between Oakland and Sacramento. The ANG officers and crew fulfilled both their flight pay and one weekend a month reserve requirements on these trips, and by sending Wendy along, her channel was able to put a local spin on the war. Travis to Anchorage. Anchorage to Yokota AFB in Japan. Yokota to Tan Son Nhut. Total flying time Travis to Saigon nineteen hours. A nine-hour turnaround. Time for a taxi to Cholon for dinner and five hours in the rack. Then head back to Travis with a load of wounded. Five nurses and two doctors on board. In-flight movies. There was one DOW on Wendy's return trip. Ambulances on the tarmac at Travis to take the wounded to Letterman Hospital. Forty-nine hours and forty-one minutes from takeoff to touchdown. "Tell me what it looks like."

"It was the wrong time of the month," Wendy said. "I got my period on the way back."

"Oh."

"And I forgot my Naturetin."

"Oh."

"So I looked bloated during my stand-up. I couldn't find a diuretic anyplace. I asked this cunt nurse if she had one and she said she had other things to worry about."

"And that's it?"

"I got some great grass."

It was Bro's idea that I write about the execution. About the life and death of Germany Baker. About the crimes he committed and about the victims of those crimes. About the policeman he had killed. About the policeman's widow and their two children. About the logistics and minutiae of an execution.

I was bored enough to be interested.

I was tempted by the pornography of violence. Tempted by a Roman Catholic priest. Tempted by my own brother.

Who knew his man.

"He's a thug, Bro," I said. At least I could chalk in the boundary lines of the discussion.

"A murdering thug, to be precise," Bro said.

"Oh, that's rich," my father had said. We were sitting in the library of the house on Washington Street after one of our infrequent dinners together. The dinner was Bro's idea. And, as I reconstruct that evening, a clue to the way Bro operated. He knew our father would ridicule any suggestion that I write about Germany Baker. And he also knew that the ridicule my father heaped on the idea would make me more inclined to consider the proposition. "That is really rich."

"Why is that, Hugh?" It was Bro at his most insufferable. If my father knew he was being humored, he gave no indication.

"At least you're calling him a murderer now," my father said. "I've been sitting here, I thought you were talking about a dinge Saint Francis of Assisi that was good to the animals, the rabbits and the chipmunks and them. It's like I been listening to a couple of elves, from Brigadoon. You, at least, I thought you had a grain of sense." He was talking directly to Bro, as if the thought I might have a grain of sense had never entered his head. "But you're softer than a Halloween pumpkin that's been left out on the porch till Thanksgiving. It must be all that running around you do these days. Popping around the world on your American Express Gold Card, bringing the word to underprivileged short people. Have faith, will travel. Sanctifying grace and watermelon seeds in your old kit bag. Well, just between you and me, those midget darkies prefer the watermelon seeds. Better yet, the moolah to buy the watermelon seeds with. They got medicine men for the other thing." He shook his head. "You been out in the sun

too long, Bro. It's done something to your bean. You're going to
start telling me the poor are God's chosen next. Well, you can
save that malarkey for that Carmelite nun over in Holy Trinity
Parish that thinks she's Our Lady of Fatima."

"Actually I wasn't going to tell you that at all," Bro said pleasantly. "Because I don't really believe it." He went to the bar,
poured three snifters of Hennessy Three Star, kept one for himself and handed the other two to my father and me. "Most priests
believe it, of course. If they didn't, they wouldn't have a constituency. And the rich find it useful to think that. It justifies their
making sure the poor remain poor. They don't mind at all the
meek inheriting the earth, just so long as they're not around to see
it. You're a refreshing exception, Hugh." He raised his glass in a
mock salute to my father. "You never hear a poor person say that,
though. You never hear a poor person say hallelujah, he's so glad
he's poor because when it's all over, he's going to sit at the right
hand of God and suck on that big lemon-lime lollipop in the sky. I
didn't hear that once in Hunters Point when I was there. No one
ever said to me"—and here his voice became harsh, accompanied
by a spray of saliva—" 'When this motherfucker's all over, man,
that's when it's my motherfucking turn, and the rest of you
honky motherfuckers can sit on this.' " He shot up the index finger of his left hand. My father started to speak, then uncharac-
teristically shut up. I think he was as surprised as I was by the
sudden savageness of Bro's tone. The three of us were silent for a
moment. Then Bro said quietly, "It would be nice if they did believe it. Maybe then the natives wouldn't be so restless."

My father contemplated Bro. "So that's what that deadbeat in
San Quentin was. Restless."

"No, I said he was a murderer," Bro said evenly. And as he said
it I thought of Leah Kaye. He had the same way of making murder seem like a misdemeanor, a moral traffic ticket that could be
fixed. "Not all the restless become murderers. Just some of them.
A statistically higher percentage than the Benedictines."

"I bet they didn't know they were getting Chairman Mao when
they got you," my father said. He gave a short unpleasant snort
that passed for a laugh. "Maybe I'll have the last laugh on those
chowderheads yet."

"It won't be the first time you've had the last laugh," Bro said. I had the distinct feeling that he was going through the motions of filial deference when in fact my father bored him. That was an essential difference between us. I was never bored by my father.

"You can bet your life on that," my father said. "And the life of that dinge, too. Not that his life is worth even the arsenic it takes to put him away."

"Cyanide," I said.

My father stared at me as if he had forgotten I was in the room. I felt like a butler who had entered without knocking. Then he turned back to Bro. "You going to convert this coon? Like that overrated harp Fulton Sheen used to do with all the big shots that wanted to hedge their bets? In case there was a heaven after all. He gets Clare Luce and you get this baby? Although maybe you got yourself a deal. She's the world's champ when it comes to trading on someone else's name, but then I never did think Harry's elevator went all the way to the top floor. The only one who ever listened to him was the golfer, and his golf score was higher than his IQ . . ."

As always I was amazed at my father's capacity for slander. It was like a rich vein of high-grade ore that ran through his speech, a nugget in every clause. When he paused for breath, Bro interrupted smoothly.

"I don't think conversion's in the cards," he said. "The only thing I can provide is a certain . . ." For a moment he hesitated, and I had the sense that the phrase he had in mind was not precise enough in the face of my father's implacable resistance to the rhetoric of the priesthood, but then he plunged forward. ". . . a certain moral sustenance."

My father pounced. "You make it sound like a chocolate chip cookie."

Bro smiled, as if the rebuke were less than he had expected. He nodded almost imperceptibly at my father. The nod was like the ceremonial offering of incense to the archbishop presiding at High Mass.

My father persisted. "When all you've got there with that number is a darkie trying to hop a ride on the salvation train."

"That's a given of Death Row, Hugh," Bro said quietly. "Salvation has a certain appeal for terminal cases. Whether life is terminated by cyanide fumes or cancer or congestive heart failure."

My father snorted again, but in that instant, listening to those words so softly spoken that I had to strain to hear, I knew I was going to enlist in this folly of Bro's no matter what my reservations, no matter my conviction that his words existed only to convince himself, an imprimatur granted by him to himself. Here was a story with a beginning, a middle and an end, an ending so final, so absolute that I knew I would be disappointed if there were a reprieve. I had a passion for the vicarious and being a witness at the official legal extinction of another human being would satisfy that passion as nothing else ever would. I was born a professional scorekeeper. I had a lifetime sideline pass. Pencil sharpened, scorecard in my lap, I would get it down, I would get it right, I would not get involved. Which of course was why Bro had asked me to write about the execution of Germany Baker.

"What happens if he gets himself a reprieve?" my father said. "You never know with this nitwit." The nitwit in question was the governor, one of his favorite hobbyhorses. When he was elected, the governor had paid a courtesy call at the house on Washington Street with his wife and two small children, one of whom threw up on a Meissen plate of macaroons while the other broke a Val St. Lambert goblet filled with 7-Up. The governor had not been invited back. "He's such a lightweight, if he fell out a window he'd go up. Imagine what he'll do with this. Check it out with Marshall Rutland probably." Anabel's grandfather. And another nemesis of my father's. "He sits on Marshall's knee like he's Mortimer Snerd." Marshall Rutland had spent more to get the governor elected than my father had given to the Finn campaign for the presidency. "The reason he combs his hair so funny is so you won't see the little white string coming out the back of his head that Marshall pulls when he wants the dummy to say something."

"If he gets a reprieve, then I guess he hops off the salvation train," Bro said. " 'Adios, Padre Bro.' " He stood up and put his brandy snifter on the sideboard. "Speaking of adios, Padre Bro, I've got to go." He went over and kissed my father. It was a gesture that always seemed to make my father uncomfortable. I never did anything more than shake his hand.

I drove Bro to the airport. He was taking the Broderick family jet to Philadelphia, where the commission on the urban poor was holding hearings the next day.

"Just a photo opportunity for me," Bro said in the car on the way to the airport. "Charley PentAngeli does the real work. The commission counsel. Loyola and Fordham Law. Drip-dry suits and forty-pound shoes. But he works like a son of a bitch. While I get my picture taken in front of the Liberty Bell with a bunch of local dignitaries with their hands in each other's pockets, and look concerned. If anything comes out of this commission, they'll want a piece of the action, Philadelphia branch. Dom LoBianco will be there, I bet. You know Dom?"

I shook my head.

"A hood gone legit. Or what passes for legit in Philadelphia. Son at West Point and he's head of United Way. You better give or you might end up in an industrial paper shredder. Fritz was in the Justice Department when his Uncle Guido kicked off. Dom's Uncle Guido. There are no Guido Finns that I've heard about. Remember that funeral?"

Again I shook my head no.

"More upscale hoods than at Apalachin. Not to see old Guido off. He was about a hundred and twelve, he hadn't whacked any-one out since the Risorgimento. But there they all were anyway, and the FBI had photographers hanging out of every tree snap-ping away, shots of all the boys. It turns out the boys had planted Carmine Lucci, or what was left of him, in Guido's hole the night before, covered him with dirt and then put a layer of black pepper on the dirt in case any stray dogs came sniffing around, looking for old bones. Then the next morning they set old Guido's casket right there on top of Carmine and his pepper blanket. And that's what the boys had really come to see. They wanted to make sure Carmine was in there.

"It was Fritz who figured that out. He was in the Organized Crime Division at the time. A young lawyer trying to make a name for himself. Well, he looked at all those photographs and he looked at them some more and finally he said, Guido doesn't draw that kind of traffic on his own, there's got to be another reason why the boys are all there. So he gets a court order to get Guido disinterred. Bingo! That's why Fritz has a soft spot for Dom

LoBianco. It was Dom's Uncle Guido who put him on the map."

And ultimately into bed with Priscilla, I thought. Priscilla did not mess with men who were not on the map. I wondered who had told Bro the story. Fritz was never the sort who would credit Guido LoBianco with putting him on the map. My father, probably. It was the sort of thing he knew.

"Poor Hugh," Bro said after a moment. It was as if he had been reading my mind. "I think what he wanted more than anything else in the world was a dynasty. I can almost picture it. It was a Tuesday morning, it was snowing, he was playing solitaire and he said to himself, I think I'll buy myself a dynasty. The taxes I pay, I'm entitled. And what he got was me getting my picture taken with Dom LoBianco and you with a likeness on the side of a bus. I don't think that's what he had in mind."

I wonder if I detected the same sense of regret that night on the way to the airport as I do now, remembering. Am I reading too much into it? It is the only time I can ever recall Bro even hinting at any reservation about the path he had taken.

Is my memory absolutely clear?

We drove in silence for a while, each lost in our own thoughts. Finally Bro said, "You're going to do it, then?"

"Yes."

"I know somebody at *The Saturday Evening Post.*"

Manipulation was as natural to him as breathing. "I don't need your help to place it, Bro," I said sharply.

"Sorry."

It began to rain. I turned on the windshield wipers. Time to make amends. "I've never seen an execution."

"I have."

Of course. And of course the revelation irritated me. Bro always did have a way of making one's own experience seem insignificant when compared to his own.

"In Mindanao last year," he said. "A hanging." His face was suddenly lit by oncoming headlights. He was looking straight ahead out the window and not at me. "Eastern Mindanao, to be precise. A place called Tagum."

"You were there on a mission of state?"

"Officially for The Society for the Propagation of the Faith. Someone in the Vatican thought I might be useful."

"You speak Tagalog?"

"A word here, a word there. The conference was in English, actually."

"In Tagum?"

"Manila. I went to Tagum afterward. I was told the native artifacts were interesting. Especially the fertility symbols. To touch one was to make one tumescent, according to the local lore. I thought it best not to. The flesh is willing, the spirit unfortunately weak . . ."

It was a laugh line. I waited and then offered him a perfunctory smile.

"There was also some sort of unrest in Mindanao. Small brown people with Kalashnikovs, the spooks at Langley said. Springfield ought-threes, it turned out. Left over from the days when Mac-Arthur was walking on water. Fritz said as long as I was going out there anyway I might have a look. That was the unofficial reason I was there. He sends someone from the Asian desk, one of those Back Bay Porcellian types who wouldn't let us into the Somerset Club, let alone the Kennedys or the Finns, it would be like putting SEATO on red alert. The bishop of Tagum was my beard. He was something to look at. Eighty-three pounds soaking wet. Before he was consecrated, he was financial secretary to the cardinal in Manila. So he knew where all the bodies were buried, and that's not just a turn of phrase in the Philippines. Plus the numbers of the secret bank accounts. That's one way to become a bishop. Although Tagum is a rather heavy price to pay for a little scarlet piping on your cassock. On the whole, I think I'd rather be a simple Benedictine monk."

"I think you're about to favor me with that famous self-deprecating smile."

"I only use it when it's effective, Jack. It never is with you."

True enough.

"Anyway the shooting wasn't much. Local thugs. Not Moscow's. Nothing the locals couldn't handle. No reason to send in the Seventh Fleet. So I decided to hang around a bit and loot some of the native art treasures if the price was right."

The rain was pelting now. The overhead freeway signs indicated the airport exit was a quarter mile ahead.

"That's how I got mixed up in this hanging. I was in the wrong place at the wrong time."

"One of the local shooters?"

"No. Just a murderer. He cut up his woman. The dead woman was the sister of the local priest and he wouldn't give the man the last rites. I was there, so I read the words and gave him extreme unction. The executioner botched the job. He sprung the trap but the poor man's neck wasn't broken. The noose wasn't on right and the fall wasn't long enough. You could see him swinging under the gallows, choking to death. Two men crawled underneath and pulled on his knees. I went with them. There wasn't enough room for them to grab and pull. The poor bastard's eyes were open and he made this terrible noise, as if he had a piece of meat stuck in his windpipe. When they cut him down finally, he was still alive. Just barely. I held his hands. There was nothing else I could do. The smell was terrible. He was wearing cheap white spun cotton and he had shit his pants and the stain spread down his legs. That's what I remember most. I remember I couldn't stand the smell and I crawled out from underneath the gallows before he died."

"Jesus." I could not think of what else to say. I drove into the airport through sheets of rain, thinking how effortlessly Bro seemed to bridge the gap between Tagum and Dominick Lo-Bianco. At the civil aviation terminal, I was passed through the gate and allowed to drive onto the tarmac to where my father's Lear was parked. There were three or four people huddled under umbrellas at the door of the plane, as if they were guests unwilling to get on the plane until Bro arrived.

"Mingo Coolidge," Bro explained. Domingo Coolidge. The senior Republican senator from New Mexico. "And a couple of his boys. He was out here giving a speech. Modesto, I think. He asked if he could hitch a ride back."

I thought there was probably more to it than that, but said nothing.

After a moment, as if he intuited what I was thinking, Bro said, "Fritz wants me to chat him up on the plane. Amidst all that

Broderick plush and splendor and Havana cigars no one is supposed to have. A real beanbag, that one. He's one of those birds in
the Congress who thinks democracy beyond the continental
limits is best maintained by electrodes selectively applied to selected genitals."

He made no move to get out of the car. I think he was quite
content to sit there watching Senator Coolidge get wet. And then
to my surprise he did something he had never done before and
never did again. He raised his hand in a blessing, forefinger
touching his thumb, the consecrated digits, his sign of the cross so
constricted it might have been in shorthand. When he was finished, he quickly opened the door of the Porsche. "I'll tell Fritz
you were asking for him," he said. With that, he was out of the
car and loping through the rain to the Lear. At the door of the
plane, he turned and waved, as if to a TV camera.

There was so much about Bro that I never knew, that he never
allowed me to know. He was always the enigma wrapped in a
paradox and that pretense of mystery seemed, in some way I
could never fathom, to please him. I can imagine the pleasure he
would have taken at my total surprise when I read in his diary
that only a few months before his death he had petitioned the
Vatican to be released from his vows. The entries are sketchy, almost enciphered, as if he did not wish to commit too much even
to this private chronicle. On my own, I made discreet inquiries—
in Rome, to the Benedictines, finally to a friendly Maryknoll father, a student of both church politics and ecclesiastical blood
sports who has always looked benignly on my agnosticism as a
temporary addiction—and in time I was able to fill in most of the
blanks.

With regret, the abbot general of the Benedictines had recommended that Bro be granted the dispensation, but Rome had
balked. In the papacy of the current pontiff, the rules pertaining
to laicization have been tightened in an effort to stem the hemorrhage of priests leaving holy orders for no other reason than their
wish to marry. Curia bureaucrats indicated the Vatican thereafter
would consider a request only if the petitioner claimed, and had
the medical documentation to prove, a psychological disorder, or

maintained that he had been forced into the priesthood by pressure from a family determined to give a son to God.

There was no evidence that Bro wished to marry.

A reason which in any case was a nonstarter.

He claimed no psychological disorder.

And even had he been willing to offer it, the proposition that my father had forced him into the Benedictines would not have been swallowed by even the most gullible of prelates.

He was summoned to Rome.

He was after all Dom Augustine Broderick, O.S.B.

A figure in the Church.

He stayed at the Hassler.

"The TV boys are blocking the front door of the hotel," the diary said. "For a terrible moment, I thought they were there for me, that they knew why I was in Rome. I guess that's as good an explanation as any as to why I am here. I have led, I lead, a secular life. I am cheating God. It turned out the cameras were for Hussein and Queen Noor."

God and King Hussein.

Bro's parlay.

"I saw Queen Noor at lunch," the diary said the next day. "In a sea-spray green gabardine suit. She was by herself. Her bodyguards were all at the next table. Not the safest way to protect a queen. An easy hit with that kind of security. Is that the direction my mind is running? I guess it keeps it off Thursday. Anyway. She was scarfing down an eclair. Then she scarfed down another. I almost said we had met in Amman with Phil Habib, but let it go."

The interrogation took place on a Thursday in July.

The night before, he moved from the Hassler into the Benedictine mother house.

"The most miserable day I have ever spent," the diary said.

"I feel brain dead," the diary said.

"All I want is to be unhooked from my spiritual life-support system," the diary said.

"Bronzini was the interrogator," the diary said. "His pectoral cross was resting on that huge stomach of his so that it was pointing straight at me. I couldn't take my eyes off it. The feet of

Christ appeared to have been broken off in some way. I wanted to
ask if he was going to get it repaired, but under the circumstances
it would have seemed a frivolous question. My mind kept wandering like that. It occurred to me at some point during the
morning that one reason I'm here is that all of a sudden I'm at an
age where I've started to pee in the bathtub. The little dribble I
can't hold back. And I need a couple of extra shakes now when I
take a leak. I wonder if I should have said that to Bronzini. Explained how the onset of incontinence might be construed as the
first outward sign of clerical midlife crisis. I was getting off on
that when I heard him say, in Italian, 'We can never accuse you of
being a bad priest, Dom Augustine.' By his standards I suppose
not. I've never been soft on altar boys and I've kept my paws off
the mother superior. I should have left it at that. Not my style, of
course. And so I said, 'My lord archbishop, you sound disappointed.' That was it. He offered his ring. I was dismissed. Now I
wait. Benny Filicchio in the Holy Office says these things take
time."

I had the sense he was humiliated.

He had not written down the substance of the interrogation.

Nor was there a copy of his request for dispensation among his
papers at the Widener.

The Benedictines refused to release their copy for my perusal.

And the responsible authorities in Rome would not even acknowledge receipt of the original.

In any event, his death made the matter moot.

"What if it's turned down?" That was the penultimate entry
on the day of the interrogation. The last was, "Dinner at Il Buco
with Dino Pecci."

V

A WEEK AFTER Bro and I had dinner with our father, I drove over
to Oakland. I had called Leah Kaye a dozen times but the calls
were never returned. She was busy, she was in conference, she
was out of town, she was in court, she was meeting with a client,
does she know you, what is this in reference to, she'll get back to
you, tomorrow, Wednesday, Friday, listen, you ever consider
she's got better things to do, then blow it out your ass. *The Saturday Evening Post*, as I had expected, was enthusiastic about my
covering the execution of Germany Baker (how about pictures,
can you sneak a camera in) and now I needed her help. She could
open doors, provide access, get me the trial transcript, keep me
posted on the legal maneuvers to delay or stop the execution, perhaps even arrange an interview with Mercury Baker for the purpose of talking about his half brother, provide a radical
perspective.

Or so I told myself.

Actually I was quite capable of making all the necessary arrangements myself. Except for providing a radical perspective
(and that was hardly difficult to unearth in San Francisco at the
time), she would in point of fact have been a hindrance to my re-

search, a name that would close rather than open many of the doors I needed to enter.

I wanted to see her.

Simple as that.

Although I didn't admit it.

Even to myself. Especially to myself.

I wanted to find out who she was.

I wanted to get to the bottom of her.

I wanted to know what made her tick.

Notice the repetition of "I wanted."

Which is really why I drove over to Oakland without an appointment to see Leah Kaye. I thought my chances were better if I arrived unannounced.

The new storefront offices where The Justice Department had moved after being burned out of its old quarters by the Abruzzos were in a neighborhood of cheap hotels, three-dollar tax advisers, spiritualists and palm readers. Madame Magda was down the street, Voodoo Rose at the corner. The office itself was flanked by a bowling supply store with (I had been told by Joe Kenna) a numbers operation in the back and by a Finger Lickin' Good rib franchise that had been closed down, according to a weathered and peeling notice tacked to the front door, by the city health department. Around the corner was the shabby old Oakland draft board. Although it is irrelevant to this narrative, I should note that young men refusing induction—usually students, always white—had composed the larger part of Leah Kaye's practice when she first passed the bar. As an obiter dictum, I should also note that it had hardly escaped her attention that few blacks tried to avoid induction. While she would never admit it, I suspect it was this fact that led her after a time to refer selective service cases to other radical attorneys.

The plate-glass window of the storefront occupied by The Justice Department that week was spray-painted with the slogan, THE SNIPER IS WATCHING. I could not help but wonder how that sentiment would appeal to the Abruzzo brothers. I thought it would probably have the same effect as Harriet Hecht's FELLATIO IS FREEDOM T-shirt. It was like a request for another firebomb. Inside the office hard-eyed young women tried to turn me away. Ms. Kaye was unavailable. I said I would wait. Ms. Kaye was busy. I said I had plenty of time. The hard-eyed women typed and filed and drank instant coffee spiked with Coffee-mate and pretended I was not there. Ms. Kaye had been called away. I said I would wait until she returned.

And I waited.

I read a mimeographed pamphlet that said, "Socialism has a tough row to hoe in San Luis Obispo."

On the face of it, a declaration that appeared to be incontrovertible.

I tried to make conversation.

"Who's the sniper?" A question I addressed to the room at large.

No one answered.

"Perhaps he's an abstraction," I said.

Still no response.

"A philosophical idea."

It was as if I were conducting a Socratic dialogue with myself.

"Or perhaps no one knows."

That did it.

"Those who know don't say, those who say don't know."

The speaker wore glasses and was the only one of the women working behind the counter who I would not describe as hard-eyed. She was plump. Not fat. Plump. With baby fat and a round open face that seemed ready to burst into a smile at the slightest provocation. When I looked at her, she turned away quickly and actually blushed, then began to clean her glasses with the tail of her brand-new denim work shirt, which she wore outside her equally new blue jeans, still stiff with sizing. I noticed that her glasses were broken and glued together with a piece of adhesive tape. The signature, in all the years I was to know her, of Phyllis Emmett.

A second woman leaned on the Formica counter and stared me down. She was wearing a T-shirt on which were printed the words DIAL 911—MAKE A COP COME. The inimitable style of Harriet Hecht, I was sure.

"Sniping is a revolutionary act," she said.

"Doesn't it depend on the sniper?" I said.

"Pig," the woman I thought was Harriet Hecht said. And then a moment later, "Shithead."

The woman who turned out to be Phyllis Emmett looked embarrassed.

"Hey, listen, buddy, Leah's not here, okay?" Harriet Hecht said.

"Okay, Harriet," I said pleasantly.

A shot in the dark that struck home. Harriet Hecht fell into a sullen silence, not willing to acknowledge that I had guessed her name.

I waited.

I pored over the pamphlets and underground newspapers that littered what I suppose passed as The Justice Department's reception area. I read that if men refused to shave and women let the hair grow on their legs and under their arms the razor blade companies would be forced into bankruptcy, and a further result would be that Gillette would no longer be able to sponsor the World Series, tranquilizing the proletariat with its subliminal message of beardless middle-class conformity. I read that if the masses blew grass instead of smoking cigarettes they could humble The Tobacco Trust (and indeed the words were uppercased in the flyer) that kept all those racist senators and congressmen in the positions of political power from which they systematically denied the civil rights of our black brothers. I read that the R. J. Reynolds Tobacco Company had secretly acquired, through bribery and sexually compromised intermediaries, thousands of acres of prime marijuana-growing land in Mexico as a hedge against the possibility that pot might one day become legal.

The ink from the pamphlets came off in my hand. I wondered if broadsides had always been so crudely printed. I wiped my hands clean with a handkerchief and looked around for a washroom, but did not ask if I could use it. I knew it was a matter of who could outwait whom.

I waited.

And then an argument broke out among the hard-eyed women beyond the counter who were trying so hard to ignore my presence.

"Karate as a form of self-defense is bourgeois bullshit," Harriet Hecht said.

"Shooting is what we should learn." A voice to which I cannot put a face or a name. Memory only dredges up Harriet Hecht and Phyllis Emmett. So bear with me if I let the other women behind the counter go unidentified.

"The brothers could teach us."

"Right on," Phyllis Emmett said. I remember her round face, the pleasure she seemed to take in putting those two unexceptional words together.

"For all that good head we give them," Harriet Hecht said.

Phyllis Emmett blushed a deep pink. I had the sense that this entire conversation was being conducted solely for my benefit and that she had not been let in on the joke, such as it was.

"The house pets of the oppressor rich . . ."

"What about them?" Phyllis Emmett said.

"We shoot them."

"Why?" Phyllis Emmett looked stricken. As I look back now, I doubt that her face had ever failed to register a single emotion she felt.

"Target practice," Harriet Hecht said.

"Why not bottles?" Phyllis Emmett said. I thought she was going to cry. "Or tin cans."

"Siamese cats," Harriet Hecht said.

"Persians . . ."

"Poodles . . ."

"Right on."

"Shooting in self-defense is a radical act," Harriet Hecht said. She pulled up her DIAL 911 T-shirt and examined a bare breast. A display that I knew was intended only for me, I suppose to see how I would react. "I've got a zit on my tit."

Only Phyllis Emmett averted her eyes.

I watched.

Harriet Hecht squeezed the pimple and lowered her T-shirt. "Shooting in self-defense is a radical act," she repeated. "Shooting the pedigreed dogs of the oppressor class is a revolutionary one."

"Right on."

"Phyllis?"

"Right on," Phyllis Emmett said.

I cannot tell you why the mood suddenly seemed to change. It just did. Perhaps they simply tired of the sport. Or perhaps they had work to finish. At any rate, one minute I was a threatening presence and the next I was not. I settled back to wait for Leah Kaye as if I were a patient in a doctor's office, doctor was delayed, please excuse the inconvenience.

Phyllis Emmett made the first friendly overture. "Is it really true that you're Augustine Broderick's brother?"

I was so surprised that I almost failed to recognize his name. The Justice Department was the last place I expected to hear Bro mentioned with any reverence. He was a man of many bizarre venues, but I would have bet he was not familiar with any where a young woman might squeeze a hickey on a naked breast as a political statement.

"Yes," I said. "It's really true."

Phyllis Emmett stuck out her hand, pumped mine enthusiastically and introduced herself. "You're such a lucky man having a brother like that."

"I suppose I am."

"You read that article in *Time*, then?"

"Oh, yes."

"Such a wonderful article. I didn't realize the president depended on him so much."

I wanted to say that Fritz never made a move without Bro, but the sarcasm would have been wasted on Phyllis Emmett. In her earnest innocence she would have believed me. "He does," I said.

"And a sister related to the president by marriage," she said. "You must be so proud."

"I suppose I am." She made me feel like the odd man out. A Broderick without a White House connection.

"I met him once, you know," she said.

"Bro." I could not conceal my surprise.

"Oh, I'd never call him that." Again that becoming blush. "He'll always be Father Broderick to me."

It occurs to me now that Bro might have been better off if more people had called him "Father" instead of his diminutive. "Where?"

"When I was in the convent." She glanced furtively back over her shoulder. I think she thought that Harriet Hecht might be eavesdropping.

"I didn't know you were a nun."

"A Sister of Mercy."

That explained the blushing. It was a long way from the noviatiate to The Justice Department.

"Father Broderick gave a retreat for the postulants. He was such a wonderful retreat master. He was so powerful. I'll never forget."

"Really." Bro as a retreat master was just the man to set virgin hearts aflutter. I wondered if postulants had wet dreams about their retreat master. And thought them a religious experience. An ignoble thought I regretted as I looked at Phyllis Emmett's sweet open face. She was a young woman born to be called "Sister," and I wondered what she was doing here.

Her voice lowered to a conspiratorial whisper. "It was after, you know . . ."

I did not know.

"He was . . ." She arched an eyebrow, then cocked her head quickly back in the general direction of Harriet Hecht. She had that maddening indirectness I remembered so well from the parochial school nuns of my childhood. The wink, the arched eyebrow, the shake of the head. These were meant to convey meaning without words.

"He was what?" I spoke more sharply than I had intended.

"Set upon," she said nervously, shielding her mouth with her hand. It was as if she expected a squad of thought police to pounce on her if she articulated clearly.

I still did not understand.

Again Phyllis Emmett peeked surreptitiously around to check the exact whereabouts of Harriet Hecht. There seemed no cause for concern. At the other end of the room, Harriet Hecht was preoccupied nailing up a poster that said, AMERIKA SUCKS. What Amerika was sucking was not spelled out, an oversight that I was sure filled Phyllis Emmett with gratitude. Silently she mouthed the word, "Mugged."

Ah, yes. "Mugged" did not seem quite the way to describe what had happened to Bro in Hunters Point, but it was closer to the mark than "set upon." I think he would have been amused. The Church always did set great store in nonthreatening, nonflagellating euphemisms. In the days when I was still going to confession, I would always mumble that I had committed "lewd actions" when I admitted to masturbation. "Self-abuse" and "self-stimulation" were too humiliating, "beating off" out of the question.

"Mugged," Phyllis Emmett repeated softly.

"Yes, I remember."

"He was still wearing the cast when he gave the retreat. He must've been hurting so . . ."

"Yes." I wondered if Bro had worn his red silk sling. Catnip for the postulants.

"He inflamed me."

Good God, he had worn it. "How?"

"I had given my life to the convent, you see." Phyllis Emmett glowed. "I truly was a bride of Christ, I can say that to you, you're a Catholic, too, like Father Broderick, you'll understand, but when he spoke, your brother, I realized my vocation wasn't enough, I had to venture out into the real world . . ."

The words tumbled out. Her cheeks reddened, as if with fever. Behind her I saw Harriet Hecht watching us. She began to slip closer so that she could hear more easily what Phyllis Emmett was saying.

". . . there was a real world outside and I was missing out on it in the convent, I couldn't be true to myself if I just remained there, teaching first grade, that's what I was slated to do, at Saint Dominick's in the city. There was poverty, there was oppression, and he opened my eyes to it, your brother, he's the reason I'm here, really, I said to Reverend Mother, 'Reverend Mother, I want to work in the real world, like Father Broderick . . .' "

The real world. She had no idea that the real world inhabited by Bro was the world of Mingo Coolidge and Dominick LoBianco and eighty-pound cardinals who knew the numbers of all the se-

cret bank accounts and a sister who committed adultery with the
president of the United States, who considered cocoon a synonym for n-nigger. Phyllis Emmett was spectacularly unequipped for this world, which was perhaps why she ended up in
the red clay of Chalatenango Province, Cristo Rey, C.A., her Lily
of France cotton bikini bottoms inside out and backside front
around her ankles. Poor Bro. I always did think that he gave re-
treats and went to places like Hunters Point as a penitential offering for the absolution he dispensed in the real world to people
like Fritz. He had seduced this child with his silver tongue and
his red silk sling and in so doing had only anointed another
victim.

"That pious honky fraud." The voice of Harriet Hecht. She
had slid up behind Phyllis Emmett. Her face was mottled with
fury. Anger seemed to make her tumescent, for her nipples had
hardened and were protruding against the lettering of her DIAL
911—MAKE A COP COME T-shirt. It took me a moment to realize
she was talking about Bro and only indirectly, as I was a blood
relative, to me. "A wine-and-cheese liberal. An altar-wine-and-
cheese liberal."

Phyllis Emmett looked as if she had been struck across the face.
"Harriet. Father Broderick's not like that at all . . ."

"A member of the oppressor class," Harriet Hecht shouted. I
could not take my eyes off those protuberant nipples. They
seemed the size of new potatoes. "A member of the oppressor
class who . . ."

"Harriet, please . . ."

". . . presumes to offer the oppressed forgiveness, that asshole . . ."

Phyllis Emmett grabbed my arm. "Mr. Broderick, I think it
would be better if you left . . ."

"Our black brothers don't want the white man's forgiveness . . ."

Phyllis Emmett steered me to the door. "Nice to meet you,
Harriet," I said.

"Butt out, asshole."

In the street outside, Phyllis Emmett said, "You have to excuse
Harriet."

"Why?"

The question seemed to startle her. "Because she's a soldier."
Her sweet dumb earnestness was appealing. "For the cause."
"Yes."
" 'Soldiers of Christ arise, and put your armor on . . .' " A
hymn dredged from the memory of parochial school.
"Something like that."
"The cause is different."
"Oh, not if you believe in the new church, Mr. Broderick. Like
your brother."

Through the window I could see Harriet Hecht staring out at
us. She gave me the finger. And again. And still again. And a
fourth time.

"By the way, where is Miss Kaye?"
"Oh, she's in Beverly Hills. With Alex. Mr. Fahr. His father's
the comedian, you know. They're at a fundraiser. The people
down there really open up their hearts to us. You should've called
first."
"I did."
"We're really not very good about returning calls. We think
our lines are tapped. The pigs." She blushed furiously, as if the
word embarrassed her. "My uncle Eddie Dalton is a policeman.
Over in the city. I can never think of him as a pig. Don't tell Harriet."
"I promise."
"I'm afraid they'd make me leave if they found out."
"Your secret's safe with me, Sister."
"Phyllis." She touched my arm and scurried back inside the
office. For a moment I watched her, my view partly obscured by
the THE SNIPER IS WATCHING slogan. Then I saw her wave discreetly, through the P in SNIPER.

I hesitate.
Perhaps you discern the problem, the reason I seem to hesitate,
the reason I do not follow the rules of narrative convention and
cut to the execution of Germany Baker. ("Cut," of course, belongs to the screenwriter's vocabulary, and that vocabulary de-
fines the narrative conventions with which I am most familiar.) I
hesitate because I know how this story turns out.

This is the eternal problem of the first person narrator, he who in the first line would tell you that this is the saddest story he has ever heard. The knowledge of what happened is an almost intolerable burden for the narrator. I after all did leave the country when the trial began, so I cannot let the narrative simply unfold, pretending that I am unaware of its surprises and permutations. I ask your indulgence. I need to allow for memory. To measure memory's angle of distortion. I am after all an interested party. I carry my own psychic light meter.

An example.

I know who the sniper was of THE SNIPER IS WATCHING. I found out years later. From Leah. Who he was is less important than how I found out. How I found out is important to my conception of Leah. However I try, I cannot think of her as frozen, a figure in a snapshot. I can only think of the woman complete, the woman who died, the woman whose story in all its complexity is finished. The end. Her dates chiseled on a tombstone. Freeze Leah at any given instant of her life and I will always say, "Yes, but . . ."

THE SNIPER IS WATCHING.

Bear with me.

I slept with Leah often the year before she died. We were two formerly married people, contentedly divorced, who in the avuncular passion of middle age found it easier to review their volatile life together than it was to live it when it was actually happening. Let me set the scene. Leah would be smoking. She would always light a Lark immediately after we untangled and would lie back and blow those perfect smoke rings toward the ceiling. For years I tried to break her of this habit of smoking in bed. I told her she would burn up in her sleep. I told her it would be a horrible and disfiguring death. I told her that her last expert witness would be the dentist who would use dental charts to positively identify her. I told her that her last humiliation would be the public disclosure that this vocal spokesperson for the underprivileged had a mouthful of platinum crowns.

The admonishments would only make her smile. I would always notice that the tufted moire headboard was dotted with cigarette burns. As always, I would wonder how many others she had taken to this tiny child's bed. The bed had been hers when

she was a little girl. After we were divorced, she had rescued it
from her mother's house in the San Fernando Valley, and from
then on, wherever she lived, there too was the bed, its ostentatiously diminutive size a warning in itself that here was a woman
whose life did not accommodate permanent sexual alliances. It
was the kind of aggressive understatement at which Leah ex-
celled.

I can recall her arms thrown back over her head, stretching her
breasts nearly flat. The cigarette pinched between her fingers was
already beginning to singe the headboard. Her underarms needed
shaving. An unnecessary detail I include only because Leah once
remarked that she had never seen a woman in bed with a man in
any American movie whose armpits were not smoothly shaved
and freshly powdered. It was as if, she had mused, foreplay had
begun with a cordless Lady Remington. This was the sort of detail that Leah, with her lawyer's eye for the potentially significant
trifle, was quick to spot in a movie, and the running commentary
it provoked often made our occasional evening out at the neighborhood theater a trial to endure. Why was Carlotta French
wearing a brassiere under her nightgown in *January, February*?
Doesn't she like her tits? Why do people in the movies always
wake up in the morning and begin to fuck without first brushing
their teeth? Maybe there's some mouth spray on the bedside
table. But don't they need to take a leak? Brush their hair? Wash
the night gook out of their eyes? By this time the people in the
adjoining seats would have begun to complain about Leah's sotto
voce monologue, and I would shrink down in my chair, pretending she was a stranger I had nothing to do with. Fuck off, she
would answer back under her breath, loud enough so that only I
could hear. It was as if she were working in those darkened movie
houses, perfecting her skills, each incongruity up there on the
screen grist for the cross-examination she always seemed to be
conducting in her mind.

I remember.

Remember the way we would talk in bed that last year before
she died.

New twists on old stories.

Picking at old scabs not allowed.

Such being the wisdom of middle age.

"Why did you call your firm The Justice Department, anyway?"

"Why not?"

"It didn't strike you as a little grand?"

"Maybe you think people would've come flocking in off the street for 'Leah Kaye, Attorney-at-Law, Age 27.' Or maybe 'Leah Kaye, Recently Admitted to the Bar.' The second time around, I might add. I flunked the bar exam the first time."

Something I had not known until that year before she died. A new twist on an old story.

"You always were practical."

"You married a Jew, remember?"

I remembered. As if my father would have let me forget. But then Leah had always liked my father. Even before she fucked him.

Which of course I did not say.

As picking at old scabs was not allowed.

"What about that meter maid?"

"How often do I have to tell you I don't have any idea who she was. It was what, fifteen years ago? If I was going to lie to you, the statute of limitations has run out, there'd be no point to it. You know the kind of people I was defending."

I was always trying to set the record straight.

"What about the sniper?"

"What sniper?"

"THE SNIPER IS WATCHING." My finger traced the swell of the abdomen between her ilia. "It was spray-painted on your office window in Oakland."

"A wacko," she said presently. Her legs parted slightly, allowing further examination of the southern terrain. "He'd been in the bin for twelve years. Something like that. Anyway a long time. Napa, I think. Some shrink said he was cured. He bought the rifle the day he got out."

"Who was he shooting at, then?" My fingers fanned toward the pubic symphysis.

"The little green people."

"It wasn't a revolutionary act, then?"

"Not even a radical one."

You see what I mean. My light meter picks up shadows yours might miss. Memory confounds the demands of narrative, certainty is a casualty of memory.

VI

THE FIRST LIVING THING killed in the San Quentin gas chamber was a thirty-pound pig. The year was 1938. Hanging was the mode of execution in California prior to the purchase of the two-ton riveted steel cell from a company in Denver. The cost of the gas chamber was $5,016 and the state paid another $10,000 to have it installed at San Quentin. The chamber was jade green and eight feet wide. Prison officials said the pig had died swiftly and mercifully.

Eight months later, on December 2, 1938, the first two human beings were put to death in the new gas chamber. Their executions were simultaneous, one man in each chair. There were thirty-nine spectators looking through the windows of the new gas chamber. Twelve minutes after the cyanide pellets were released and the gas had begun to attack their respiratory organs, Robert Lee Cannon was pronounced dead by the attending physician listening to the stethoscope attached to Cannon's chest and three minutes later so was his companion in crime, Albert Kessel. It was two hours before the chamber was fumigated and judged safe enough for the bodies to be removed. Between them, during a riot at Folsom Prison, Cannon and Kessel were responsible for four murders, the victims being the warden, a guard and two other prisoners.

Four women and 188 other men had since been put to death in the San Quentin gas chamber. The last words witnesses outside the chamber heard shouted by Warren Cramer, a murderer, were that the fumes smelled like rotten eggs. Leandress Riley, another murderer, was so slight that he was able to slip free from the restraining straps that bound his arms and legs. The chamber was unsealed and guards belted him tightly back into his chair. The first woman ever executed in California was Ethel Leta Juanita Spinelli, a murderess nicknamed "The Duchess," who went to the gas chamber wearing a new green dress and with snapshots of her three children and one grandchild taped over her heart. Barbara Graham wore a black mask over her eyes so she would not have to look at the witnesses who had come to see her die. Farrington Hill listened to a recording of "Tales from the Vienna Woods" made especially for him by the San Quentin prison orchestra and played over and over throughout the night before his death. At his request, the recording continued to play even after he was sealed in the gas chamber. John Sarrassawski consumed a last meal of salami, smoked kippers, rye bread, dill pickles, radishes, onions and coffee and topped it off with eggs and fried onions for breakfast.

These and other facts I gleaned before the execution of Germany Baker. I read the newspaper clippings and the biographies of retired wardens. I interviewed guards and officials in the Department of Corrections and witnesses and lawyers whose clients had died in the gas chamber. I knew that the average cost of an execution was $900 in materials and bonuses. I knew that the executioner and the chief of the guard detail would be paid $150 each for an execution and their assistants $75 each. I knew that the federal government paid the state of California $300 each time it rented the gas chamber to execute any of its own condemned prisoners incarcerated in Alcatraz. I knew that the warden of San Quentin was paid one dollar a month more than the wardens of California's other state prisons because his was the only gas chamber in the state penal system. I knew if there were three executions scheduled for one day, the third was always a solo and took place three hours after the first two.

I still have the black French graph-paper notebooks in which I wrote down these details for that piece *The Saturday Evening Post* commissioned on the execution of Germany Baker. Bro used to order those notebooks two dozen at a time from a small *papeterie* on the rue de l'Ancienne Comédie in Paris and send them to me twice a year as birthday and Christmas presents, knowing how much I liked them. This *papeterie* was just one of the network of perfect small shops around the world where he kept a standing order for perfect annual remembrances to friends and relatives. I also still have the Zippo lighter into which I had a custom metalworker install a Minox camera with which I proposed to snap surreptitiously, through the windows of the gas chamber, a last photograph of Germany Baker, which in the turmoil surrounding the bloody finale I neglected to do. The fake lighter I am embarrassed to say was a touch I appropriated from the photographer played by Eddie Albert in *Roman Holiday* and once, years later, at a party given by Marty Magnin in Beverly Hills, I contemplated telling Audrey Hepburn and Willy Wyler the story of my lighter, but thought better of it. The story, however, or some distorted version of it, did not escape the ears of Marty Magnin.

"Make it a woman instead of a schwartze, kid, someone with nice tits, we need a vedette, I can get Lottie, I hear her marriage is in tap city, she needs the job, she's the right age, she'll work with Reggie Poland, she used to fuck his ex-wife, no problem, he needs a hit, his phone hasn't exactly been ringing off the wall lately, I'm on the horn to Lew and Sid in the morning and with that ending, it's 'The envelope, please, and the winner is . . .' "

"No, Marty."

"Teedeo, tedium," Marty Magnin said, patting his lips in a pantomime yawn. "Little Sheldon Sensitive."

"That's it." Definitely. Little Sheldon Sensitive, that's me.

And no wonder.

I have always taken precise and voluminous notes and even after so many years it is easy to reconstruct the events leading up to that bloody morning in San Quentin. I can look at each entry and a scene comes back. "Hair rollers & plastic furniture covers." That would be the widow of the policeman shot by Germany

Baker. She lived in a tract house in South Sacramento and what she called the "settee" and the "living-room suite" were covered with plastic to keep them clean, plastic covers on which I slipped and slid and noticed the cigarette holes burned through them. She was wearing a yellow muumuu and her hair was in white rollers which were covered by a lemon chiffon scarf. The only thing this heavyset woman with thong sandals and thick legs already knobby with varicose veins had to say about her late husband was, "Ed was nice." I could not, however, see a single photograph of Ed anywhere, perhaps because her new husband-to-be was sitting at the Formica kitchen table drinking Coors from a can, one can after another, a package of Salem's wrapped in the sleeve of his T-shirt, a one-word tattoo on his arm that I could not read. Ed's widow—her name was Maye ("With an e," she had said)—had not introduced us and the only words I heard him utter in the silence-filled half hour I was in the tract house in South Sacramento were, "Hon, where's the church key?" There was a time when I thought the social observation inherent in "Hair rollers & plastic furniture covers" useful and valid, but now that I am older, a relative of two victims, I am less sure. I also detect a pernicious sense in the entry that Ed was a victim less of Germany Baker than of his own bad taste.

"George Cahalan, Esq./O. W. Holmes." George Cahalan, Esq., or as his card said, "V. George Cahalan, Esq.," was Germany Baker's lawyer and he looked like Oliver Wendell Holmes, but there the resemblance ended. He told me, running long fingers through his flowing white hair, that he had seen six people—five men and one woman—die in the San Quentin gas chamber, "all clients of mine," he added, without a shred of embarrassment. He always had dinner with the warden the night before an execution and the warden would always serve the same last meal that the condemned man had requested. I had the distinct impression that V. George Cahalan, Esq., remembered the menus better than his clients, each menu hinting at the ethnicity of the condemned. "Chiles rellenos, that was Manuel Perez, uh, Mendez, collard greens and ham hocks, that would have to be that big colored fellow, the one that did the fingertip push-ups in his cell and his arms got so big he couldn't fit them through the bars, Leo Lewis, that was his name, and then there was the double cheeseburger and nacho chips, that was just last year, Wally Wilson, no, Wilson Wallace, and then there was Sue Lennon, all she wanted was her rib-eye lamb chops, when they transported her from Frontera up to Q, all she wanted to know was if she was going to get her rib eyes. Now this fellow up there now, he seems to want a few bottles of Dr Pepper and some shrimp, but the shellfish won't be good that time of year with the red tides and all, although if he gets himself a bad shrimp, I don't think it would matter all that much, do you?"

I noted that the cells on Death Row were 54 inches wide and 128 inches long and that this was less room than was allocated to a single stray dog in the pound maintained by the San Francisco Society for the Prevention of Cruelty to Animals. I interviewed the guard who would be at the cherry-red lever when Germany Baker was executed and he maintained that the state of California was the actual executioner and he only a servant of the wishes of the people. The warden saw me in his office and said he was a firm believer in free choice, free will and the free enterprise system. "You take your normal inmate," he said. "When your normal inmate is separated from this institution, there's nothing to ensure that when he gets home, he won't stop by at the local Bob's Big Boy and stick it up. That's basic to America, the opportunity to make free choices." The warden smoked a pipe and had a degree in penology.

"Cynical????" I had written in my notebook.

"Have you met Irene yet?" the warden asked. Irene Kinsella, a transvestite inmate born Ivan Klimchok. Irene was a stop on the San Quentin tour, along with the gas chamber and Death Row on the sixth tier of the north cell block and the wire-enclosed exercise yard used exclusively by the condemned on the roof just above their cells. Irene Kinsella worked in the shoe factory. She—I called him "she"—wore bright red lipstick and her long fingernails were painted inside and out. Her tinted gray hair was in a pageboy cut and held in place by a tortoiseshell barrette. Irene French-inhaled, drawing the cigarette smoke up through her nose and then blowing it out in doughnut-shaped smoke rings. "I bet I've fucked everyone on the mainstream population,"

Irene said, "but everyone says I'm a terrible cocksucker." I under-lined the quote three times in the graph-paper notebook from the *papeterie* on the rue de l'Ancienne Comédie, for what reason I cannot remember unless in some delusionary state inspired by Wendy Chan's stash of imported narcotics I thought I might somehow slip it past the editors of *The Saturday Evening Post* under the heading of prison lore or local color.

To be honest, I was exhilarated by the assignment. I even found my column less onerous. I would dash it off in the morning, sailing with a garbage scow on the Bay ("mud work," in the tugman's argot, and it was an article of faith among them that the sweet rotting scent of sewage smelled like sex) or talking to a fisherman named DiMaggio who was not related to Joe. The rest of the day was free for the research I was doing. In the evening, I would fuck Wendy. She found my sudden attention to her charms suspicious. One night I woke up and found her smoking and poring over my neatly typed notes. She was unrepentant. "Is there an angle in this for me?" she asked.

"What kind of angle?"

"Human interest."

"He killed a cop. That tends to limit the human-interest angle."

"Maybe I can spend the day of the execution with his wife."

I could hardly object on the grounds of invasion of privacy. "Her boyfriend will be there."

"He a cop, too?"

"He drives some kind of rig. An earthmover, I think. He's on unemployment."

"Shit."

"Why 'shit'?"

"If he was a cop, that would be a nice human-interest angle. 'Colleague Waits with Widow of Hero Officer.' "

"He lives there."

"You sure?"

"His jockey shorts were in the load of laundry she was doing."

"Maybe he doesn't have a washing machine of his own."

"There were also two boxes of rubbers in the medicine cabinet.

Sheiks." I did not add that there was also a used one in the waste-basket wrapped in Kleenex.

Wendy was impressed. "You really checked out the medicine cabinet?"

"Yes."

"I mean, how'd you do it?"

"She asked if I wanted to use the facilities. That's what she called it." I felt tainted telling Wendy this. "And the rest room."

"You think she'll talk to me?"

"She might be a little embarrassed."

"Why?"

"My impression is she was fucking the other guy before Ed was shot."

"Who's Ed?"

"The hero cop."

"You sure?"

"I looked at the homicide report. The usual stuff. Name. Date. What happened and where. Date of birth, address, Social Security number. It all seemed straightforward enough, except for one thing. I didn't catch it at first. I don't think I would've caught it if I hadn't been struck by her address when I went out to see her. Nine Thousand Wilson Way. You know the way you always remember an address in round figures. Two thousand, four thousand. Or one where all the numbers are the same. Five-five-five-five. Anyway. Nine Thousand Wilson Way. I didn't remember what his address was on the report, but I knew it wasn't nine thousand anything. So I checked out the place that was listed. It turns out he'd been there a couple of months, according to the landlord. Alone. Never with a woman. It cost me twenty to find that out. There was an unpaid utility bill and the telephone had been turned off the day before he was killed. Nonpayment."

"Terrific," Wendy said.

I thought she meant my detective work. I affected modesty. "It wasn't that tough."

But of course she was only interested in how she could use the information. "Maybe that's why he forgot to duck. He was all broken up by his wife balling his best friend." Then I realized that she was sketching out a story line. "Best friend" was an addition of her own. "He'd lost his will to live. He didn't take the proper precautions." She made it sound as if he had failed to use a contraceptive. "It's all there."

I tried to make a joke. " 'Wife's Love Nest Makes Hero Officer a Victim.' "

"Hey," Wendy Chan said. A joke was always risky business with one who had so literal a mind. "Out of sight." She threw a leg over my chest. "You want to fool around?" I felt as if I were being rewarded, like an employee in a factory who had won the Suggestion of the Month Award, her tight little quim the prize. She whimpered when she made love, an obbligato of small musical squeals that never seemed to capture the tempo of her movements. When she assumed the superior position, I always felt as if my member were the pommel of a saddle and I a horse to be broken. She copulated vigorously, but not always to the point. I had the impression that she preferred the top because it allowed her to think. "Shit," she said as she finished.

I was a beat behind. "What's the matter?"

She was already lighting a joint, pulling furiously in short, sharp intakes of breath. "That's a Sacramento angle, the love nest."

One day at the paper, I also received a telephone call from Alex Fahr.

"Broderick . . ."

I dislike being called only by my last name. It is as if the other person thinks it gives him an advantage to address you like a butler. "Who is this?"

"Alex Fahr."

"Who?" As if I did not recognize the name.

"Alexander Fahr," he said impatiently.

"Oh. Pluto Fahr's son." I thought it would be some time before he addressed me as "Broderick" again.

"I'm told you were snooping around Leah's office."

I ignored the remark. He never had the capacity to be rude with brio the way Leah could. "Who gave the fundraiser in Beverly Hills?"

The question surprised him. "What fundraiser?"

"The one where they opened up their hearts."

"I'm not at liberty to say," he replied stiffly.

"Because you think your line is tapped."

"Who told you that?"

"Those who know don't say, those who say don't know."

Alex Fahr laughed nervously, a dry little tic I could hear on the other end of the line. "This is a safe phone." I waited. He had called me after all. I knew the call was not going quite the way he had anticipated. Alex would always be disappointed in any attempt to be the master of a given situation. He existed to be tormented as my silence was tormenting him now. Finally he said, "What is it you want?"

I explained about my assignment and said that I wished to interview Mercury Baker about his brother.

"What's your angle?"

He sounded like Wendy. The Sacramento love nest angle. Now kaput. "If you mean does it have anything to do with socialism's tough row in San Luis Obispo, the answer is no."

"What's that supposed to mean?" he said suspiciously.

"A private joke. I'm sorry."

"Well, you can't see him."

"I was only being polite. There are other ways to get in to see him."

"That's where you're wrong, buddy." He sounded like Harriet Hecht. I would probably be "buster" next. "Asshole" exceeded the limits of his nerve. "You want to see Mercury Baker, you've got to see us. We've tied up all publication rights. Book, serial and dramatic. That includes stage, screen and television."

I pondered this for a moment. Alex Fahr had said "we." That meant Leah Kaye. And possibly someone at that fundraiser in Beverly Hills. From my present vantage point, I marvel at the way Leah could see in Mercury Baker the stuff of legend. She was like a baseball scout who can see a teenager's swing and project Lou Gehrig. In Mercury Baker, I could only see an inventive thug.

Alex Fahr seemed pleased with himself. "Why should we give it to the enemy for free?"

"What enemy?"

"The straight press."

"Oh."

"The only way we would let you interview Eugene is if we had the right of approval over your copy."

"I thought you were against censorship."

"Listen, buster, you can write anything you want in the pig press," Alex Fahr said.

Periodically I would bring Bro up to date with what I was doing.

"A pig?"

"That's what it says." I read the copy I had made of the AP clip I had found in my newspaper's morgue. "March 22, 1938."

"I wonder what happened to it."

"The pig?" The detours that Bro's mind was capable of taking were always a source of amazement.

"Was it butchered afterward? If so, who got it? The guards? The executioner? Maybe you can't butcher a pig that filled with cyanide."

The possibility did not engage me. "I think I'll see Germany now."

"No problem," Bro said. "He's thinking of converting."

"I thought you said it wasn't in the cards."

"I'm trying to stall. I know all souls are equal under God, but he's a feather in my bonnet I'd rather not have. Although he does have a rather interesting view of the Church. 'That Catholic shit is good shit.' As doctrine, it has the virtue of being unequivocal. And simply stated. You should ask him."

Germany Baker assured me that he had never been with Irene Kinsella. "I don't even take things in my own hands, so to speak," he said, peering at me beneath heavy lids to see if I had picked up his jape. "There's them that homo and there's them that take things in their own hands, if you get what I mean." He showed me the pink underside of a large black hand and began moving it up and down. "I found Jesus."

A thick clear plastic screen separated us. "With Father Broderick . . ."

"He the one." Germany Baker examined me through the screen. I wondered if he saw the resemblance. "You know that dude?"

I nodded.

"He don't talk about Jesus much. I ain't much on that Jesus shit."

A perfect convert for Bro. One who preferred God on the back burner. "You have a brother . . ."

"My brother Merc. He's in Folsom." A grin split his features. "He drowned that dude."

"You keep in contact with your brother Merc, then?"

"Shit." He stared at me with incomprehension, as if I had asked if he kept in touch with the man in the moon. "He's in Folsom."

"You ever write?"

"Shit."

"When was the last time you saw him?"

"Never seen the Merc."

Here was a possibility I had never considered. But of course. Same father, different mothers. I knew that from the files made available to me by the Department of Corrections. I studied Germany Baker through the screen. He was, if anything, even more massive than his brother. He had the dimensions of a trailer on an eighteen-wheeler. That brothers could live their whole lives without ever meeting seemed to him not at all untoward. Not even a source of concern. I felt like an innocent, a baby unequipped to survive in the world inhabited by the Baker brothers. "Never," I said.

"I was on the move."

On the move from prison to prison. I had Germany Baker's jacket in the manila folder on the floor beneath my foot. As well as the psychiatric profiles drawn up at every institution in which he had been incarcerated for all but seven months and three days in the twenty-one years since his first conviction. "Extremely angry . . . A long-standing thought disorder." That was from the stockade in Germany from whence came his nickname and where he had been sent after stabbing a corporal who had been "crowding" him. "Capable of sudden violence," said the psychiatrist at

Joliet. "Has never developed the ability to interface socially with others," read the report from the Bureau of Prisons Psychiatric Center in Butner, North Carolina. I do not think I would have used "interface" to describe any encounter with Germany Baker.

"And then the Merc, he was on the move," Germany Baker said. Same moves, different institutions. They had never served time together.

"How do you keep in touch, then?"

"You hear the word in the joint."

Which was true. The prison grapevine was almost instantaneous. Sneeze in Folsom and someone reached for a handkerchief in San Quentin.

I nodded sagely. At what I was not sure. I felt completely disoriented. Nodding gave me time to collect my thoughts. As if they were worth collecting.

"You know the bitch?"

I shook my head. It seemed better than saying, "What bitch would that be?"

"The Merc's lawyer."

"Oh, yes."

"She some kind of bitch, right?"

I nodded.

"You know my lawyer?"

I nodded again.

"I wish I had the bitch."

He said it without rancor. I suspected that the bitch would not have spent much time planning a last menu. Last meals did not figure in Leah Kaye's scheme of things.

"You were a Baptist?"

"I was a sinner. I'm going to be Catholic now."

Unless Bro could prolong the period of instruction, extreme unction would be the only sacrament he would visit on Germany Baker.

"You Catholic?" he asked.

"Yes."

"Good shit. None of that nigger music. I be a priest, I ever get out of the joint. I like that wine in the morning." A giant conspiratorial wink and a smile that showed a tongue like a pink glacier and a mouthful of shiny white teeth. "That wine Ripple?"

I was suddenly disconcerted. Here was a man who was going to die at a day and time set by the state of California in the manner prescribed by law in front of the twelve witnesses mandated by law, five of whom he could, if he wished, select himself, as long as they were not convicts currently incarcerated within the penal system, and as many other unofficial spectators as the warden and the state director of corrections allowed, and he was grinning ear to ear, showing me that tundra tongue and those teeth like icebergs. The smile, the wink—I had the uneasy feeling that somehow, in some way, I was being put on. The black face on the other side of the plastic screen was a relief map of grooves and pockets and scar tissue, a map of terra incognita. It was a map I knew I could never read and that seemed, for a flickering instant, the message the wink and the smile were ordering me to acknowledge. I shook my head, more to rid myself of this thought than to answer the question about the Ripple.

"I like that Ripple. They got some rule say it can't be no Ripple?"

"I don't think so." I tried to erase my uneasiness by imagining Bro sipping Ripple from his gold chalice. "Do you ever go to Mass?"

"Mass?" Germany Baker seemed perplexed.

"The service."

"Mass what they call it?"

"Yes."

Germany Baker nodded agreeably, his huge head moving up and down like a metronome. "He say that mother up here once, the preacher."

"In the cell block here?"

"Right here."

There were times when I wondered if Bro ever said Mass on an altar. In a church. With a pulpit. And confessionals and a baptismal font and the stations of the cross. Death Row was only one more of the extraordinary cathedrals where he had set up his altar stone. I stared through the clear plastic at Germany Baker and suddenly I could locate the source of my unease. Not Bro. It was this interrogation itself, so much like the captain's masts I had conducted occasionally when I was in the Marine Corps. In any set of circumstances, there were those who asked questions and those who answered them. Germany Baker had spent a lifetime answering questions. "Do you have any enemies here?" he had been asked when he checked into Death Row. And then: "Who is your next of kin?" The interrogator would hear the answers; he would never know what it was like to be questioned. Even as Germany Baker was on death's countdown, I was asking, he was answering, the white hand once more taking the black pulse. And in this instance I was a surrogate pulse-taker. Germany Baker was not even my patient. He belonged, in some way perhaps only Bro understood, to history. He was just another symbol.

He considered me with his large watery bloodshot brown eyes. I had the sense that he was bored with me. "You know the cookie?"

I shook my head. The conversation was becoming more bewildering. "What cookie?"

"The one he hands out. The preacher. In the service. He give you some kind of cookie."

I allowed that in certain circumstances a communion wafer might be called a cookie. *You know the cookie?* I wrote in my notebook, as if it were a dialect joke, on the order of Fritz Finn's synonym for cocoon.

"How come he only give out one cookie, that preacher?"

It was a question I could not answer.

"Some nigger church passed out them cookies, you take a whole shitload full, you want."

It was a point of comparative religion that seemed on the verge of making him belligerent. I wondered how he interfaced with Bro on this subject. I looked at the guard. He was clipping his nails, three snips to each finger. I wanted to leave this place, but I knew I had to ask Germany Baker his version of the events that had put him on Death Row.

"It weren't no damn murder," Germany Baker said. His tone was agreeable, as if he were relieved that I was interested in something other than his possible conversion and his renewed allegiance to Jesus, two subjects about which he seemed as painfully uncomfortable as I. "I was set up. Just some damn cop don't like the nigger. Always crowding the nigger, I know his damn type. Just wanted to whip my nigger ass, leave me by the side of the road. That's his type, I know that type . . ."

I had read the trial transcript in the office of V. George Cahalan, Esq., an office filled with photographs of V. George Cahalan, Esq., on the bridge of his thirty-seven-foot Chris-Craft Commander, his generous, veiny nose snowcapped with white sunscreen. The transcript contradicted Germany Baker's version at every turn. His Trans-Am was stalled by the side of highway 99 outside Sacramento. The hood was up and he was under it. Ed the policeman, husband of Maye with the white hair rollers and the yellow muumuu, Ed the cuckold, had stopped to offer assistance. Germany Baker came out from under the hood shooting. The Trans-Am had been stolen the day after his release from his previous stretch in Soledad.

I took a deep breath. "It was a hot car."

"It be night. How he know it was some damn hot car, that dude?" He smiled as if he had scored a point. "It been someone else got snuffed, 'stead of that dude, you think they charge me? You thinking shit, you think that shit. They got some peculiar damn view in this country, a pig gets himself offed, it some kind of big damn deal. They don't want to hear no facts, like who the damn dude was began shooting first. They just want to put some nigger in the damn gas chamber . . ."

I wrote it all down, every word, making sure I got his grammar precisely right. "Nigger talk": the underlined notation still condemns me after almost twenty years. It was as if I thought the assaults on the mother tongue by Germany Baker somehow made him and the crimes he committed not only explicable but perhaps even inevitable.

There was also another code contained in the private cipher of my notebook, a subtext, as it were, and I was its only exegete. Even as I tried so assiduously to parse the rich rhetoric of Germany Baker, I was at the same time searching my memory for some tenuous connection between us, a specious personal bond between the journalist-recorder and the soon-to-be dead man on the other side of the thick plastic screen. I remembered the other men I had seen die violently, and I wondered if I could draw parallels, make an analogy which, implicitly at least, would give the personal journalist equal billing with the state's star attraction. "29." I had written and circled the number in the midst of the so carefully transcribed Germany Baker monologue. Twenty-nine what? Cents? Dollars? Women I had fucked? Shirts? No. "29" was the Marine Corps depot at Twenty-nine Palms in the Mojave Desert where I had served for a time when I was a callow subaltern with a swagger stick. As I said, I was only in the peacetime Marines, but I did see a full complement of body bags at Twenty-nine Palms. Desert automobile accidents with broken bodies strewn over the highway. The explosion of an oil truck in the motor pool that had incinerated six enlisted men.

And the gunny.

I was officer of the day when a gunnery sergeant faced with retirement put a BAR he had drawn from the supply room into his mouth and triggered it with a broom handle. There was nothing much left of his head, which was splattered over the beaverboard walls of his quarters. There was, however, a complication. The bullets from the Browning had gone through one thin wall and riddled the two corporals who shared the NCO room next door in the barracks. They were found by me in what the board of inquiry later delicately called "a compromising position," meaning they were stark naked, their position on the cot "indicating," as I told the board under oath, "the possibility of mutual oral copulation." It was the finding of the board of inquiry that the possibility was strong enough to deny the two corporals, as well as the gunny, their death benefits and government life insurance. "Relevant?" I had written and underlined in the notebook under "29." And then: "Possible lede? Compare?" That was the subtext. Always the story. Never let the story get out of focus.

It was time to go. There was nothing more I needed. I put the notebook in my jacket pocket and without thinking straightened my tie in my reflection on the plastic screen that separated us. I stopped, embarrassed, when I saw him looking at me.

"You think that sucker listening?" I did not write this exchange down, but it is etched as with acid on my memory.

I said I was not sure what sucker he had in mind.

"That sucker upstairs. The one that preacher always talking

about. I got myself a date next door coming up." He took a few deep gasping breaths as if I needed reminding what date he had in mind and then he flashed that terrible smile that slashed his face from ear to ear. "I say to him, I say, 'Sucker, that one date I don't want to keep.' I hope that sucker listening."

I suddenly realized that God was the sucker to whom he was referring.

"You know the Merc?"

I shook my head. There seemed no point in telling him I had once seen his brother in Department 34 in the same kind of prison fatigues he was wearing himself.

"That sucker not be listening, then I want the Merc be there. I got the right. I got five witnesses. That's my right. That's the real shit, that's what the man say. I want the Merc. I want my baby brother there. 'Hi, Merc,' I'll say. 'Hi, Germ,' he'll say. That ain't much to ask, see your baby brother just once in your life. 'Hi, Merc.' 'Hi, Germ.'" The fantasy greeting seemed to soothe him. "They say no. They say the Merc drowned that dude. He some kind of crazy motherfucker, the Merc, if he drowned that dude. In *Folsom*." Germany Baker began to cackle with laughter. "I just want to meet that crazy motherfucker, that's all. Just once! 'Hi, Merc.' 'Hi, Germ.'"

In fact, the two brothers never did meet. As expected, the warden and the state director of corrections excluded Mercury Baker from the execution of his half brother. Of the five witnesses he was allowed, I was the only other one he selected to watch him die.

VII

IT WAS BRO'S IDEA that we spend the night before the execution
at Bohemian Grove. We were both members of the Bohemian
Club, in itself a rarity because of our relative youth, most members being of an age generally associated with captains of industry. But our father was a member and our grandfather, and our
father, with the arrogance that a sizable fraction of a billion dollars generates, insisted that we join. He further insisted that on
our application forms we list, as the five club members known to
us who would personally vouch for our good character and all-
around clubmanship, two former presidents, Herbert Hoover and
Dwight Eisenhower, and one former vice president, Richard
Nixon. The other two we listed were the board chairman of the
Bank of America and the current president of the Bohemian Club
itself, these dragooned references being the sort of private game
he liked to play, just to see how far he could bend other men to
his will. I should also note that all five were Republicans while he
remained all his life a nominal Democrat.

All five of these worthies replied with the most fulsome letters
of recommendation for both Bro and myself. My Marine Corps
service stood me in good stead with Nixon ("a dedicated Ameri-

can . . ."), while Ike's evaluation was considerably more cagey ("Lieutenant Broderick is everything a junior officer should aspire to be . . ."). The most Delphic and meaningful reference came from Mr. Hoover, who wrote that I was "indubitably a Broderick," those three words implying volumes, leading even my father to say, "That sour old prune has a better sense of humor than I thought."

In fact, my father rarely went to the Bohemian Club when he was in San Francisco. He preferred the Pacific Union if he ate at a club at all, and he never visited the annual summer encampment at Bohemian Grove, his considered opinion being that the putative captains of industry who made up the club's membership were, in his words, "caddies and ballboys," or again, "corporate ribbon clerks with stock options." I confess this was one of the few views I shared with him. I have never been able to take seriously the radical contention (so vigorously embraced by Leah when we were married) that the Grove was headquarters for the junta of American business, a dark Masonic lodge of interlocking directorates conspiring there in the redwoods to decide, beyond public scrutiny, the economic and political fate of the nation as it best benefited them.

My own attitude toward the Grove, on those few occasions when I visited the summer encampment (usually in the company of Dickie Finn, who seemed to think his appearance with any Broderick, even me, would lay to rest the rumors that my sister Priscilla was cuckolding him again), was composed of equal parts boredom, dread and amusement. It always struck me as being approximately as sinister as reunion weekend at Princeton, a convocation of middle-aged and old men with pink faces and broken blood vessels and dewlaps and pacemakers and quadruple bypasses and fading memories of terrific hard-ons. These were men who called women "gals" and each other too often by their first names in the manner of people who really did not know each other too well ("How's the writing game, Jack, keeping you busy, is it, Jack, you know the vice president, don't you, Jack, I hear Jack's doing well in the writing game, Mr. Vice President, right, Jack?"). In the sylvan shadows, they drank too much, their fists always wrapped around a glass, exchanging heavy badinage about warming up the ice cubes and building another highball, and when they had to relieve themselves, they pissed against the redwoods as if it were a revolutionary act, the good fun of the alfresco leak marred only by the incontinent dribble that sometimes stained a pant leg even after an energetic shake. These were men who dealt with the gross national product on a daily basis and who were—or their companies were—those entities the newscasters called "economic indicators" and they spoke in a kind of fancy diction that seemed the special dialect of the upscale executive suite. It was never enough to ask for butter to lather on the breakfast hotcakes, it was on the order of, "How about sticking a jib in the butter down there and sailing it up to this end of the table." Their musings were of the country club locker room, Republican and profit-oriented, their jokes of the ethnic variety: "Jack, you know why so few Polacks go elephant hunting?"

I was always a good straight man at the Grove.

"Because they get so tired carrying the decoys." Laughter and backslapping and general agreement that there was no finer bunch of men in the world than the fellows right here in the Grove. "Tell that one to your dad, Jack, if there's one thing your dad loves, it's a good story," a misreading of my father so absolute as to banish any idea I may have entertained that the storyteller might actually have known him.

Every day at the Grove there was an informal lakeside talk given to the assembled Bohemians by a fellow member or a guest at the club—an astronaut, a senator testing the presidential waters, an economist, a member of the cabinet, an educator—on subjects ranging from the political and economic structure of the twenty-first century to how best to recover from a hangover, the latter being in a category that club members invariably called "a humorous-type thing." It was to this forum that Bro had wangled an invitation to speak that day before the execution. We checked into the Grove a few hours before his talk and at Mandalay, the hillside camp where we bunked in log cabin splendor with assorted bankers and brokers and industrialists, we were assaulted with bonhomie. This was a constituency to which Bro and I belonged by birth and however suspect politically the men of Mandalay might have found Bro (and by extension me), we were

Brodericks and thus entitled to the benefit of any doubt. Even though it was before noon, glasses of Chivas Regal over ice were pressed into our hands.

"What do you think of those damn Berrigans, Bro?"

"What Berrigans would you be speaking about, Charlie?" His Grove banter was as fluent as his French.

"A pair of damn socialists, you ask me."

"So's the German chancellor, Bob. And he was here at the Grove last weekend."

"I just think the pope ought to look into that pair."

"Like the SEC's doing with you, you mean."

"As a matter of fact, Bro, that's a damn fine analogy. Sure, the SEC's looking into us. I only wish those Berrigans would come out of an investigation as well as we're going to."

"Oh, I thought you were practicing up on your Latin, Bob."

"Why would I be doing that, Bro?"

"Well, I heard you were trying to find out what nolo contendere means."

"Goddammit, you've got your dad's sense of humor, Bro. A chip off the old block. Both you boys. You, too, Jack. You're the deep one. Just taking it all in. A little more Chivas, Bro. It's good for what ails you."

"Well, in that case, Bob, just a touch. I can always tell His Eminence it was for medicinal purposes."

"That's one old boy who can handle his Chivas, Bro, that cardinal. A goddamn wooden leg, you ask me."

"I think that comes under the same heading as secrets of the confessional, Charlie."

"Dick Nixon's playing the piano up at Stowaway, Bro. You want to walk up there?"

"Not even to hear Harry Truman, George."

"Can you imagine Harry Truman at the Grove?"

"Isn't that the goddamn end, Bro?"

"Bro, let me ask you something."

"Fire away, Burl."

"What's six miles long and goes four miles an hour?"

"You got me there, Burl."

"A Mexican funeral with one set of jumper cables."

"On that one, Burl, I guess I better take a leak."

"You do that, Bro."

"Just pick a tree, Bro."

The lake where Bro spoke later that afternoon was one of the few places at the Grove where the sun was not concealed from view by a canopy of redwoods. I sat near him in the clearing, soaking up the sun, light-years away from San Quentin. On the slope leading gently back up from the lake into the ominous cathedral of redwoods I spotted the secretary of the treasury and the governor of New York and the chairman of Chrysler and two Nobel laureates.

Bro was introduced by Dickie Finn. Always the cuckold, always the introducer, I thought. The applause was sporadic and polite. Bro waited until it had completely died down.

"How many of you went into Monte Rio last night?"

An appreciative chuckle crawled up the slope from group to group. Monte Rio was the nearest town. There were girls who worked the two bars in Monte Rio during the encampment. The girls came from Reno and San Francisco, a few from Vegas. The price was right, the motels kept rooms available. The sheriff made sure that there was seldom any trouble.

"For those of you who may feel the need," Bro said after a moment, a small smile on his face, "I will be available later for confession." There was more laughter. "And for those of you not fortunate enough to be Catholic, let me explain confession." He paused. "Confession is essentially a form of plea bargaining with yourself. Most people, when they examine their consciences, will plead their mortal sins in Monte Rio last night down to venial. Then if they still have a bad conscience, they add lying to the list."

This time the applause was spontaneous. Members rose and clapped, a few trying in vain to whistle through their teeth or dentures. Bro stood there, still smiling, an incongruous and worldly cleric in blue espadrilles and white ducks, a red-and-white polka-dot handkerchief knotted around his neck. I could see why Fritz found him useful.

"Tomorrow morning," he said when the noise finally died down, "my brother Jack and I are going to see a man die." His tone was the tone of a man who knew what was six miles long and went four miles an hour. "His name is Germany Baker and in approximately twenty hours or so he is going to be executed in the gas chamber at San Quentin. He killed a policeman. He was found guilty by a jury of his peers. I have no reason to doubt his guilt. Germany Baker is not a very nice man . . ."

He had them. In just those first few short sentences. He did not hector. Nor did he plea for understanding or appear to be making any special case. His voice was low, barely audible, so that they had to strain to hear him. I suddenly thought, Friends, Bohemians, Countrymen, lend me your ears. He was Marc Antony, coming not to praise Germany Baker but to bury him. He talked about the thirty-pound pig. He talked about the smell of rotten eggs. I should not have been annoyed that Bro remembered so well what I had told him, but I was. He talked about the salvation train and Commutation Station and he said that Germany Baker called the communion host a cookie. He described Germany Baker's cell on Death Row. The only decoration was a picture postcard of a sailboat at sunset off Maui. He said that Germany Baker liked to watch "General Hospital" on the television set mounted on the wall outside his cell. He said he had given Germany Baker a bible to read, although his reading skills were only at a third-grade level. The bible had pictures and Germany Baker liked the pictures. He said that Germany Baker could do one hundred chin-ups on the bar in the wire-enclosed rooftop exercise yard above Death Row and that he splashed Mennen Skin Bracer in his armpits on those days when he was not allowed to shower and that every morning he was handed a Schick injector razor which the guard retrieved immediately after Germany Baker shaved.

His audience was transfixed by this recital of the mundane. A Common Market ambassador made notes, the governor of New York cupped an ear so he could hear, the Nobel laureate nearest me on the slope kept his eyes closed, as if in prayer, periodically shaking his head, I thought perhaps in dismay at the idea that chemistry and technology could be put to such a use. Burl and Bob and Charlie let the ice melt in their glasses. And yet I could not help but wonder what point Bro was trying to make. He had succeeded in making his listeners uneasy, but I doubted that he had changed anyone's mind about the necessity of doing away with Germany Baker. There would be no flurry of telegrams to the governor from the Grove asking that Germany Baker be spared. The next morning when the walls of the gas chamber were being washed with ammonia, this group of the finest fellows on the face of the earth would still be drinking Chivas and comparing handicaps and asking what was white and twelve inches long and answering, "Nothing." Perhaps Bro was only showing the flag to the hostiles. Telling them things they did not wish to hear. Perhaps the next time they would be more willing to listen. Perhaps they might even be useful.

Useful to whom? That was always the question with Bro. He collected useful people the way some people collected stamps.

It was something to do.

SAN QUENTIN—NEXT EXIT.

What neither Bro nor I nor the state of California could have anticipated, however, was the melodrama that awaited us when we finally adjourned to the witness room outside the gas chamber.

VIII

"YOU LOOK like a pansy."

Imagine the scene first.

The early morning cold rolled in off the Bay through the San Quentin parking lot. Gray day, gray prison walls, puffs of fog like cigarette smoke. A San Francisco radio station on a transistor radio. Early morning cloudiness burning off by noon. The St. Louis Cardinals led by former Giant Orlando Cepeda, Roger Maris, Bob Gibson and company will be at Candlestick today at 1:05, probable starters Ray Washburn for the Cards and former Redbird Ray Sadecki serving up his southpaw slants for the Giants, the hometowners were victorious last night seven to two, Marichal over Larry Jaster, with home runs by Jim Hart and Downtown Ollie Brown for the Giants and a two-run shot by the Cardinals' Mike Shannon accounting for all the scoring off Marichal, Juan otherwise near perfect in his six-hit victory, his third of the campaign over the Cards and his twelfth overall, Lindy McDaniel picking up his fourth save after El Señor ran out of gas with one out and two on in the visitors' ninth, Lindy throwing a double-play ball to pinch-hitter Bobby Tolan to wrap up the Giant victory. And at San Quentin this morning, all is in readi-

176

ness for Elrod Baker, who has a date in that institution's gas
chamber approximately two hours and thirty-seven minutes from
now, our reporter Wilbur Horton is at the scene in case of any
late-breaking developments, there have been reports of possible
demonstrations outside the Marin County facility by sides both
favoring and opposing capital punishment, it's a knotty question
indeed, and that's the latest from KSFO weather and sports, all
the news that is the news, at the tone the time will be . . .

I remember the cold.

I was wearing a Brooks Brothers seersucker suit and a white
shirt and scuffed-up brown loafers and bright red socks I had
borrowed from someone at Mandalay who told me he had bought
them in the pro shop at Augusta National the year Arnie won his
first Masters, and when I got out of the Porsche I put on a black
knit tie because I thought it disrespectful to see a man die if I
were tieless and wearing red socks. Bro looked even more louche
and inappropriate than he had in the car coming down from the
Grove. Of course he did not shiver in the cold. He never gave any
sign anywhere of acknowledging the elements. From the back of
the Porsche he took a small Mark Cross leather case containing
his stole and breviary and the oils for the last rites. My Porsche,
the Mark Cross case, the Top-Siders without socks and the blue
cashmere sweater and the red bandanna knotted around his neck.
The accouterments did not seem what God had in mind for the
giving of extreme unction. In the foul mood I was in, I remember
thinking he was decked out in rough trade duds.

The same thought seemed to have occurred to Leah Kaye.
"You look like a pansy," she said when I brought Bro over to
meet her.

"And you don't look at all like your pictures," Bro replied, as
always unruffled. It was a lifetime pattern. He ignored what he
chose not to hear. "The Benday dots in a newspaper photograph
don't do you justice." Leave it to Bro to use Benday dots to deflect her calculated hostility. "I was expecting a virago. Finger
pointing, head cocked, all the veins in your neck like hawsers
stretched taut, that knob of muscle in your jaw contorting, eyes
like coals." He was making fun of her and she knew it. "Actually
your eyes are quite blue. I wasn't expecting that."

"Jews do have blue eyes," she said.

"And occasionally priests look like pansies," Bro said. "Some are."

Then she smiled. There in the San Quentin parking lot she seemed slighter than I remembered. She was scarcely more than five feet tall (I would learn later that she claimed five-two on her driver's license and passport applications, an affectation I would never let pass unmentioned), she was wearing a khaki skirt (I did not yet know she always wore a skirt or dress and never trousers or even underwear because of that stubborn yeast infection) and a safari jacket with the belt tied in back. I remember her hair was short and tightly curled (the curls were naturally so unyielding that she would sometimes threaten to get her hair conked, as some of her black clients did) and there was a hint of what I later knew was Joy, expensive perfume being another affectation she did not like to admit. There were too many sharp planes for her to be beautiful—even her breasts were like pointy triangles against her pink polo shirt—but in repose she was less severe, less intimidating than I had remembered from that day outside Department 34.

She shook Bro's hand. Hanging from her left arm was a black motorcycle helmet with a tinted plastic face shield.

"Do you ride a bike?" Bro asked. "I have a Kawasaki in Washington."

"Oh, you poor baby." She started to laugh, not unkindly, but as one would at a child who flops down when trying to walk.

Now it was Bro's turn to appear confused. But only for a moment. "Oh, I see," he said. "It's to protect your head."

"From the pigs," Leah said. It was as if she thought "pigs" was a rhetorical touch that was expected of her.

"In case there's trouble," Bro said. "Well, I hope there isn't any."

"I don't," Leah said. I never knew anyone, even Bro, who could be quite so matter of fact. She would not look for trouble, but neither would she go out of the way to avoid it. The motorcycle helmet to cushion her head from any possible blows from a policeman's baton and the touches of Joy applied to the wrists and behind the ears—Leah was a compendium of opposites.

"Jack."

Another voice from across the parking lot drew my attention reluctantly away from Leah and Bro. It was Wendy Chan getting out of a white van with her station's call letters and channel number painted in ostentatiously large red letters on its side. In the reflection of a side window, she ran a large blue comb through her long, lustrous dark hair as her camera crew unloaded its gear. (How Leah, her head imprisoned by its tangle of tight curls, hated Wendy Chan's hair. Once she even importuned me to tell her about Wendy's bush; was it long and silky, too?) I started to kiss her on the cheek, in a pro forma way, but was frozen by her look. This was a professional encounter.

"Do you have the Minox?" All the time we walked, she never stopped looking at herself in the small vanity mirror of her Chanel compact, running her tongue inside her lower lip to inspect her skin for pits and crevices, checking the straightness of her lipstick, the line of her eye makeup.

I felt for the Zippo lighter in the pocket of my seersucker jacket. I had told her about putting the Minox in the lighter and had immediately regretted it. "Yes."

"Anyone else know about it?" She smoothed a ridge of powder on her nose.

"No."

"Jack, if you let me have that picture . . ."

"No."

"I'd do anything if you let me use it on my story. Exclusive." She looked at me over the mirror. "Anything."

I tried to make a joke. "We've already done everything, Wendy."

Now Wendy was checking her teeth in the mirror. "I'd sit on your face for a week."

All the news that is the news. I made another joke. "Two weeks?"

"Fuck you." She smiled, a dazzling on-the-air Chinese smile, but I knew she meant it. Wendy was a woman who was going places. She had no room for excess baggage, and anyone she was sleeping with qualified as excess baggage if a favor asked in return for her favors was not forthcoming. She would have been surprised if I had not felt exactly the same way. I shrugged. At least we understood each other.

"Hello, Wendy."

"Bro." She offered a cheek so as not to smudge her makeup. "Mmmmm. Jack's being a pain in the ass."

"He often is."

"He has something I want and he won't give it to me."

"Correction," I said. "I might have something she wants and I won't give it to her."

"Jack likes to keep the record straight," Bro said.

"Jack's an asshole," Wendy said. "How about an interview?"

"Of course," Bro said. "You want to do a sound check first?"

Another TV van pulled in alongside Wendy's. The parking lot was beginning to look like an asphalt demilitarized zone. Leah and her group were on one side, perhaps thirty of them. Everyone was in jeans and chinos and work clothes except Leah herself. And of course Alex Fahr. I saw him at the edge of the parking lot. He was wearing a suit and talking to reporters, as if he did not belong to the demonstration that was setting up. Most of the men with Leah had beards and some wore their hair in pigtails. Two of the women were nursing infants. The group was forming up in what looked like a conga line, at the front of which I spotted Harriet Hecht. She was wearing a T-shirt that said, SAN QUENTIN IS A POW CAMP. From inside a battered Day-Glo pink Volkswagen bus minus a fender, she was pulling signs and ordering Phyllis Emmett to pass them out. Those who already had signs were beginning to wave them in the direction of the television cameras. I wrote down the slogans in my notebook: FREE THE POLITICAL PRISONERS. CAPITAL PUNISHMENT IS JUDICIAL MURDER. ALL CRIME IS POLITICAL.

Phyllis Emmett tried to thrust a placard into my hand.

"I'm afraid not, Sister Phyllis."

"Oh, Mr. Broderick. I'm sorry. I didn't recognize you."

In her confusion she dropped her armload of signs. I helped her pick them up.

"Oh, I'm so thrilled," she hissed into my ear. "I saw your brother a minute ago. Father Augustine Broderick. He'll be such a comfort to the condemned man, may his soul rest in peace."

I gathered the placards and placed them in her arms again. "Would you like to meet him?"

"Oh, no. I wouldn't want to disturb him when he's carrying the sacraments."

"I understand." I could see Bro finishing up his interview with Wendy. The sacramental paraphernalia in his Mark Cross case did not seem to burden him unduly.

I looked around when Phyllis Emmett scurried off with her signs. On the far side of the parking lot, separated from Leah's band by a thin line of Marin County sheriffs, was another gathering of thirty or more people, who had begun to walk in a neat circle, like Indians around a beleaguered wagon train. The women wore dresses, the men were clean-shaven and many had pinned to their jackets the badges of the various police agencies they represented, as if to emphasize the solidarity of police officers with Germany Baker's slain police victim. This group was also carrying signs, hand-lettered and more truculent than those across the parking lot. TAKE A LITTLE BICARB FOR THE GAS IN YOUR STOMACH. NEED GAS, GERM? FILL 'ER UP. TOO MUCH GAS? THEN FART CYANIDE. The news cameras zeroed in on the placards and I had no doubt, suddenly, that the trouble Leah had seen little reason to avoid would sooner or later erupt. This was an event made for the evening news.

Bro was now surrounded by interviewers and their equipment as he moved slowly toward the door in the prison gate. As I watched I was struck by the thought that wherever he ventured the warping element of his celebrity was also ever present, distorting the actual event, sending it out of focus. Father Augustine Broderick, O.S.B., was always the star attraction.

"What did he have for his last meal, Father?"

"I'm still hoping it wasn't his last meal."

"Was it soul food, Father?"

"Sanctifying grace is the best soul food I would have to say." And say it, he did.

"Have you talked to the governor, Bro?"

"No, I have not talked to the governor. To reprieve or not to reprieve is a decision the governor will make in the solitude of his own heart."

"How is Germany, Father?"

"I would like to think he is at peace with God."

"Have you discussed this case with President Finn?"

"I think the president is aware of the circumstances attendant on my being here this morning."

I knew exactly how much Fritz would enjoy being linked with Germany Baker, however indirectly, when he tuned in to Walter Cronkite that evening. As long as there were two seats in the gas chamber, he would wonder why Bro was not strapped in the other one. Black was definitely not beautiful until after his re-election. Then he would hoot and holler and learn to tap-dance, if necessary.

There was a smaller gathering of reporters around Leah. She was not the beneficiary of the respect accorded Bro's celebrity, but she was calm and patient in the face of the almost palpable hostility.

"So why are you here?"

"Mr. Baker's brother is my client."

"Who did he murder?"

"He has not been found guilty of any violation of Section 187 of the state penal code."

"And you think Baker should get a reprieve?"

"No, I think he should be freed."

"Freed?"

"Mr. Baker is a political prisoner."

"He killed a cop."

"All crime is political."

"Then you think everyone inside there should be freed?"

"I said all crime is political."

"Even cop killers?"

"A life is a life. The life of a policeman has no more value than yours. Or mine."

"But you want cop killers freed, yes or no?"

"Four months ago, the adult authority . . ."

"What's the adult authority?"

"The parole board."

"Why the fuck doesn't she call it that, then?"

". . . the adult authority freed a man who hacked his wife to death with a hatchet, then stuffed the pieces into the trunk of a car and reported her missing . . ."

"Yes or no?"

"Last year the adult authority granted parole to a man who beat a deaf and dumb night watchman to death with a claw hammer during the commission of a burglary . . ."

"Yes or no?"

"Does the life of a policeman have more value than that of a night watchman? Or a wife who's been cut up into little pieces?"

Her voice was drowned out as she seemed to disappear in the middle of the wave of shouting reporters. The Marin deputies moved toward the protective cordon of the off-duty police marchers, as if they were reinforcements and not part of the brewing demonstration. Now the two separate groups on either side of the parking lot were beginning to yell at each other.

"Pig."

"Don't you ever take a bath?"

"Oink, oink."

"Faggots."

I saw Bro duck into the prison and with a sense of relief I showed my identification to the guard and moved inside the gate after him.

"I'm going to the holding cell," Bro said. "There's a waiting room for the witnesses. They'll bring you up just before . . ."

I nodded and he was gone, a priest in white ducks and a Mark Cross case holding the oils of extreme unction, strolling across the prison yard with the languid stride of the entitled. I glanced at my watch. It was just eight o'clock. Two hours to go. A guard gave me directions to the waiting room. He said there was coffee available and asked if I would like a doughnut, he had an extra, a crumb doughnut and he liked glazed, the wife must be coming up on her monthlies, like forgetting the thing about the doughnut, although what the hell, a doughnut's just a doughnut, you get right down to it. I thanked him and said no. As I walked across the yard, I could see the chimney atop the gas chamber through which the gas would be dispersed.

V. George Cahalan, Esq., was already in the waiting room.

"He had the shrimp," V. George Cahalan said. "Even though it was off. I hear he had the Mexican two-step all night long. The shits," he added, in case I could not translate Mexican two-step. "Imagine having the shits your last night." He shook his head. His flowing mane of white hair sat on his scalp as if it were sculpted in white concrete. "The warden and I had the prime rib. Yorkshire pudding and strawberry shortcake." He became confidential. "I see many more of these things, I'll have to go on a diet. Last meals. It would make a hell of a cookbook, you ask me. A big seller."

Soon there were too many people in the small enclosed space of the waiting room. Witnesses, reporters, law enforcement officials, representatives of the Department of Corrections. The air conditioner was on the blink and the room grew sour with the smell of sweat and stale cigarette smoke. Small groups talked softly among themselves, urgent talk of fishing and off-track road racing and the merits of RV parks at Tahoe versus RV parks at Mono. V. George Cahalan, Esq., was explaining the Mexican two-step to his former courtroom adversary, the assistant district attorney who had prosecuted Germany Baker. An appointed member of the Department of Corrections laboriously spelled his name out for reporters, Dewey Peete, that's P-E-E-T-E, all the letters rhyme, and he said the state was just doing its duty, unpleasant as that duty sometimes was, but the law's the law, as we always say in my business, that's the franchising business. Three policemen from South Sacramento stood apart from the rest of the witnesses, hands clasped in front of them, each wearing a sport coat with piping on the lapel and a high-school class ring. They said they were brother officers of the victim, come to see justice done. Two said they had not known Ed real well, the third said Ed was a real pisser and the other two said they had heard that. The reporter covering the execution for the *Los Angeles Times* asked if I thought it might be too grandiose to call the gas chamber a cockpit of death.

I was trying to frame a suitable answer when I realized that something was afoot. There was a sudden flurry in the waiting room. Prison officials kept hurrying in and out of the door to the corridor leading to the gas chamber, whispering among themselves. Then a deputy warden grabbed Dewey Peete, who was spelling his name to still another reporter, P-E-E-T-E, all the letters rhyme, and they both bolted for the door, slamming it behind them. A guard planted himself squarely in front of that door so that no one could follow. The voice level in the crowded room rose.

Did you hear?

What did you hear?

I heard.

Piece by piece, overheard whisper by overheard whisper, the rumors began to take shape. Germany Baker had tried to kill himself. No one was quite sure how he had done it. The guard would offer no information. I have my orders, the guard said. No one is to leave this room. This is the United States of America, someone shouted. You can't keep us here. It was probably a pill, someone said. A pill's easy to hide. It happened in the can, someone said. The babysitters had taken him to the bathroom. He had the shits, V. George Cahalan, Esq., said. The Mexican two-step. It was the bad shrimp. There's nothing like a little tainted shellfish for loosening up the bowels. The warden was on the telephone to the governor, someone said. The governor had ordered that if Germany Baker were still ambulatory he wanted the execution to continue, someone said. It was in the hands of the warden, someone said. It was in the hands of the doctors, someone said. The governor was keeping in close contact, someone said.

Then the door leading to the gas chamber opened and Dewey Peete and the deputy warden came back into the waiting room. Give them a little room, someone said. For Christ's sake, someone said. Let them talk, someone said. Neither Dewey Peete nor the deputy warden seemed willing to begin. What the fuck, somebody said. What the fuck happened? Dewey Peete cleared his throat. The deputy warden interrupted. Yes, Germany Baker had tried to commit suicide. No, it had not been a pill. Then what the fuck was it, someone said. The deputy warden cleared his throat. He tried to cut his throat, Dewey Peete said. In the bathroom. He had the shits, V. George Cahalan, Esq., said. The Mexican two-step. From the shrimp. How serious is it, someone said. Serious, the deputy warden said. Very serious. Will the execution con-

tinue, someone said. The doctors are confident, the deputy warden nodded, and then, as if reconsidering what he had just said,
retooled his sentence. The doctors think. His voice trailed off.
He'll go, Dewey Peete said. How'd he do it, someone said. With
a jagged piece of glass, the deputy warden said. How'd he
get a piece of glass, someone said. From a pocket mirror, Dewey
Peete said. Wasn't he being watched, someone said. It was hidden, the deputy warden said. Where? In the holding cell. The
answers were being pried from him. Where in the holding cell,
We don't know. How did it get there, Maybe the inmate cleaning
crew, the deputy warden said. We're investigating, Dewey Peete
said.

The door opened once again. A guard whispered to Dewey
Peete and the deputy warden. We elbowed closer, trying to hear.
Gentlemen, the deputy warden said. The doctors say. He cleared
his throat. The governor has indicated. The deputy warden could
not seem to finish the sentence. It's on, Dewey Peete said. The
doc has patched him up. It was touch and go there for a while, but
it's on. So said Dewey Peete. P-E-E-T-E. We can go over now,
the deputy warden said. Dewey Peete clapped his hands like a
football coach leading his team out of the dressing room. We
crowded through the door, pushing and elbowing and shoving.
No one held back. Everyone wanted to be first. It was only a
short walk. And then we were there.

The gas chamber looked like a green space gondola set incon-
gruously down in this sterile beige room. Its steel door was open.
Inside, guards were checking the stethoscope tube and the rotary
mechanisms that held the cyanide pellets and the red cloth restraining straps that were folded like seat belts in each of the two
square metal chairs. As I passed by, I could see the honeycomb of
holes in the seat and in the base of each chair through which the
gas fumes would rise. A sign warned, KEEP OUTSIDE OF RAILINGS
AT ALL TIMES. All the places at the railing were immediately
taken. I quickly climbed to the top step of the two rows of
wooden spectator bleachers and from this perch, standing up and
utilizing my height, I could look down directly into the gas chamber and watch the guards perform the last and most eerily domestic of their pre-execution housekeeping chores.

Bear with me for a moment while I try to describe these chores, which even today I have more difficulty contemplating than the grisly finale that would almost immediately follow. Two of the guards began to unroll a red carpet leading from the heavy bulkhead door of the chamber to the door into the holding cell area. At the same time, a third guard lowered the venetian blinds on the two windows in the chamber nearest the executioner's post. Twenty years after the fact, I am still not sure whether the blinds were intended to shield the executioner from any sight of the condemned man, and the concomitant possibility that he might hesitate even for the flicker of an eye in the performance of his task, or whether they were to ensure that the condemned convict would not see the physical maneuver that would bring, after a few last terrifying seconds of holding his breath, unconsciousness and then death. The red carpet and the venetian blinds—the first a symbol of status, the latter an emblem of bogus respectability. I wondered and still wonder by what alchemy of bureaucratic reasoning these artifacts were selected. A touch of refinement? An attempt to vitiate the impact of the deed? Why not flowers and chintz curtains? Such were my thoughts when the warden suddenly appeared, alone, like a stage manager announcing a cast change for that evening's performance.

The bowl of a meerschaum pipe stuck out of the breast pocket of his gray tweed jacket. Emory A. Schatzeder was always described as an eminent penologist, as in Emory A. Schatzeder, the eminent penologist and warden of California's San Quentin Prison, and it was in the stilted language of the penologist's trade that he spoke to the assembled witnesses and spectators. Yes, Mr. Baker had made an attempt on his life. The attempt was life-endangering. Mr. Baker was saved by the prompt action of his guards and by the valiant efforts of the institution's medical staff. Mr. Baker had suffered a serious loss of blood, but there was no interference with his major arterial systems. Mr. Baker was not currently in a life-threatening situation. Emory A. Schatzeder, the eminent penologist, suddenly seemed to realize that this last remark needed some qualification. Mr. Baker, Emory A. Schatzeder corrected, was currently not in a life-threatening situation as it applied to the injuries sustained on his neck by the piece of glass from the broken pocket mirror. The injuries, Emory A. Schatzeder said he felt compelled to add, incurred by Mr. Baker in his unfortunate attempt to circumvent the verdict of the court. Emory A. Schatzeder said that he had been in constant communication with the governor since being notified of this unfortunate and, it needed to be said, unlawful incident. He had told the governor that the medical staff had certified the condition of Mr. Baker as stable. He had told the governor that in the opinion of the medical staff Mr. Baker was able to walk and could navigate the distance between the holding cell and the gas chamber on his own two feet. Emory A. Schatzeder said that the governor was the final authority on this matter and that the governor on the basis of the information supplied by the San Quentin medical staff had ordered the verdict of the court to be carried out. Acting on the orders of the governor, Emory A. Schatzeder said that the execution of Mr. Baker could now proceed.

I remember reaching for the Zippo lighter that held the Minox camera, but in my haste the Minox slipped from my sweaty palms, dropped between the steps of the bleachers and smashed on the floor below. I remember Bro. His white ducks and his Top-Siders and his sweater and his funeral stole were all caked with blood, but his voice never faltered as he read the prayers for the dead, I am the resurrection and the life. I remember Germany Baker. If he could walk, he did not. He was dragged along the red carpet by four guards, blood spurting from his neck over himself and them. His face was ashen from loss of blood and I am sure fear. His legs stuck out behind him stiff as boards, his head lolled on his blood-drenched white shirt. His voice was weak and I could only barely make out what he said. Motherfuckers, he said. Where's the Merc? he said. I want the Merc. Motherfuckers. His large damp brown eyes fixed me just as the guards half-dragged, half-carried him over the threshold of the gas chamber and then placed him in the B chair. As the guards began strapping him down, a doctor tried to place a bandage on his neck to stanch the flow of blood. With his one free hand, Germany Baker tore the bandage off. Emory A. Schatzeder jumped back, knocking down a guard, as a shower of blood stained his gray tweed jacket. Bro placed his hand on Germany Baker's head. Another bandage was hastily slapped over the wound. Then the chamber was cleared.

Emory A. Schatzeder was the last to leave. He stood for a moment in the doorway and I could hear him say, Are you all right, Mr. Baker?

Through the rear windows of the chamber I saw Germany Baker nod. His bandage fell away and the blood began to spurt, as if in rhythm with his weakening pulse. Two guards closed and sealed the steel door shut, spinning the wheel tight. A doctor adjusted the earplugs of the stethoscope and checked through the window to make sure the endpiece was still taped to Germany Baker's chest. The executioner waited by the venetian blinds. Emory A. Schatzeder took the meerschaum pipe out of his jacket pocket, slapped it distractedly in his palm, blew through the stem and then replaced it in his pocket. At a nod from him, a guard turned the valve that sent the acid mixture sloshing into the wells beneath the chairs. The seconds ticked away. I was glad the camera had smashed. The only sound I heard was Bro's voice, Glory be to the Father and to the Son and to the Holy Spirit, as it was in the beginning, is now and ever shall be, world without end, amen. Emory A. Schatzeder nodded at the executioner, who pushed his lever forward, releasing the cyanide pellets into the lethal solution. The clock on the wall said 10:27. I could see the fumes begin to rise. Germany Baker threw his head back. Blood dripped down the back of his chair. It was over in seven minutes.

Of course there was an investigation. The first casualty of the investigation was Emory A. Schatzeder, who was fired by the governor for an acute lack of judgment in allowing the execution to proceed as scheduled. The governor maintained that at no time had he ordered Emory A. Schatzeder to carry out the verdict of the court and in corroboration he produced his chief of staff, his appointments secretary and the director of the Department of Corrections. The director testified before the investigating committee in the state assembly that the governor had in fact delegated the authority to make this decision to Warden Schatzeder because he was on the scene and in the closest possible communication with the medical personnel treating Mr. Baker and therefore in the best position to make the final determination on the fate of Mr. Baker.

Emory A. Schatzeder did not go down without a fight. He

produced transcripts of three of his four conversations with the
governor on the morning in question, which he had the foresight
to have his secretary take down secretly on an office extension
after his first conversation with the governor that morning had
seemed to him indecisive and unsatisfactory. The governor said
that it was unconscionable that a subordinate would secretly
monitor the telephone conversations of the state's highest elected
official, and that in itself was ground for the immediate dismissal
of Warden Schatzeder, not that the transcripts, as they appeared
in most of the state's newspapers, showed Emory A. Schatzeder
in much better light than the governor himself.

Well, what do you think, Warden?

The final decision is up to you, Governor.

Well, how serious is it, for Christ's sake.

Well, the wounds weren't deep enough to sever the deep ar-
teries in the neck, although the bleeding is certainly profuse, it
was like an abattoir in there, you want to know the truth. . . .

Of course I want to know the goddamn truth. Can they
patch him up or can't they patch him up?

The indications are, Governor, that they can patch him up,
but I think we ought to consider the possibility of a postpone-
ment.

I think that's all that son of a bitch wanted was a postpone-
ment.

Does that mean, Governor, that you don't want a postpone-
ment?

You're on the scene, Emmett . . .

Emory . . .

Hell, yes, Emory. I'll rely on your good judgment.

Then you want me to proceed, Governor?

Whatever you decide to do, Emory, I'll back you to the hilt.

Now, Governor . . .

As long as I'm governor, I'm not going to let every Tom, Dick and Harry think he can evade the verdict of the courts of this state. You understand me, Emory?

I think I understand, Governor.

I'm glad we're on the same wavelength, Emory. We've got to take a stand, goddammit.

I see, Governor.

I thought you would, Em. You can count on me, you know that.

Bro was not called to testify. Nor Leah. Nor I. Nor the AP photographer who won a Pulitzer Prize for his shot of Leah being pummeled around her helmeted head by the off-duty policeman carrying the sign that said, TAKE A LITTLE BICARB FOR THE GAS IN YOUR STOMACH. He was the policeman I hit when the riot broke out. That was at the impromptu parking lot press conference outside the main gate of San Quentin after the execution. Wendy Chan was waiting for me when I walked out of the prison. "Asshole," she said when I told her I had dropped the Minox and did not get the pictures of Germany Baker's death. Then the press conference started. Bro did most of the talking. His hair, his hands, his clothes were caked with dried blood. And over his blue cashmere sweater he was still wearing the blood-spattered funeral stole he had worn in the gas chamber, whether because he had forgotten to take it off or out of a sense of the dramatic I am not sure. I had to hand it to Bro. His résumé of the morning's events was as precise and concise as a staff briefing. Nothing was added, nothing was left out. He described Germany Baker's last cigarette. He had held it between his own fingers while Germany Baker smoked, held it until the butt was too blood-soaked to inhale anymore.

"What about Mercury Baker?" The shouted question came from Leah, at the edge of the throng surrounding Bro. It was, she told me a long time later, a calculated attempt to get something going. "What did he say about Mercury Baker?"

"He said, 'Where's Merc? I want the Merc.'"

"Murderers," Leah screamed. It was as if she were leading a cheer. "Pigs."

And then the riot started. You saw it on television that night. The story of Germany Baker's execution and the riot outside San Quentin led off all three network newscasts. It was the first time Leah had gone nationwide. Each network also had a sidebar about Mercury Baker. The drowning of an adversary in a waterfall of urine was too good a story to pass up. I think the coverage that day was the beginning of his legend. Mercury Baker owed that at least to the half brother he had never seen. The melee swirled around Bro. No one even touched him even though he made no effort to move. Leah was a more inviting target. Leah in her motorcycle helmet with its tinted plastic face shield. The cop with the sign was raining blows on her head and shoulders when I finally reached her side. I dropped the cop. Nothing fancy. He wasn't looking and I chopped him in the back of the neck. Bro bailed me out that night.

The next summer I went to Bohemian Grove not with Bro but with Tuck Bradley and Dickie Finn. It was while we were there that my sister Priscilla suffered the stroke that killed her.

IX

"YOU HAD TO SEE HIM," Fritz Finn said that morning after Priscilla died, "he had one of those department store names, Saks, no Magnin, that was it, although I assure you he was no relation of Cyril's." He turned to Dickie Finn. "I imagine Cyril will be at the funeral, by the way, right, Dickie?"

"I'll make sure he's asked," Dickie Finn said. The bereaved husband. He wrote Cyril Magnin's name on a card and placed the card by the telephone. In whatever the circumstances, even these, Dickie always did Fritz's bidding. Dickie's a good detail man, the best, Fritz Finn would often say about his brother. It was the only value judgment I ever heard Fritz offer about Dickie.

"Martin Magnin, that was his name," Fritz continued. " 'Call me Marty, Mr. President,' he said. I'd sooner call De Gaulle Chuck. And he had this hair transplant. Have you ever seen one?"

We—Dickie, Tuck Bradley and myself—shook our heads.

"Well, he had these little clumps of hair planted in his bald head like a bunch of oleander bushes, and he said to me, 'Mr. President, Mr. President, what's a Jewish-American princess's favorite position? I mean, when she's balling, Mr. President?' "

Fritz paused, the politician's practiced and almost imperceptible pause, indicating that applause or laughter was called for. Dickie Finn laughed. Tuck Bradley smiled. I pretended to clear my throat. Fritz's gaze fastened on me for a moment before he continued.

"Now this is Beverly Hills, remember," Fritz said. He was directing the story at me now, almost as if this were a clash of wills. "And these people had all ponied up four grand each and got decked out in black tie just to get a gander at my patrician gentile features." He arched an eyebrow slightly. "Using the term loosely, of course, Jack." I nodded in return. "And there's this guy with a head full of oleander bushes saying, 'What's a JAP's favorite position, Mr. President?' And before the Secret Service detail can cart him away, Mr. Magnin says, 'Facing Rodeo Drive, Mr. President.' "

Dickie Finn laughed. Tuck Bradley chuckled. It would not do to remain stone-faced a second time when the president of the United States told a story. I smiled.

"Hollywood," Tuck Bradley said.

"Rodeo Drive's the main shopping drag in Beverly Hills," Dickie Finn said. I had never known him not to explain the punch line of any joke he had ever heard.

"Dickie, why don't you call Cyril Magnin?" Fritz said.

"Right away," Dickie Finn said. He left Fritz, Tuck Bradley and myself alone in the living room. In the hallway outside, I could see the unobtrusive shadow of a Secret Service man.

"It's good to keep him occupied," Fritz Finn said. "At a time like this. How old was Priscilla?"

"Twenty-nine," Tuck Bradley and I said simultaneously.

"Of course," Fritz said. "In May."

"May twenty-fourth," Tuck Bradley said. Priscilla's last love. Or the last I knew about. Priscilla kept busy. "We had lunch at the Clift."

"With Dickie?" Fritz said. The logistics of illicit love affairs always fascinated him.

"No," Tuck Bradley said. "He sent champagne, though. Perrier-Jouet. He was in New York."

"Setting up the rally in the Garden," Fritz said. "For my

birthday. We cleared nearly three-quarters of a million. Frank sang 'Happy Birthday.' "

We lapsed into silence. It did not seem the most opportune moment to make small talk about liaisons with Priscilla or the party's war chest for the next election.

"Your mother died the same way, didn't she, Jack?" Fritz asked.

I nodded.

"It must run in the family," Tuck Bradley said absentmindedly, as if he were talking about freckles or red hair. He seemed distracted. We had been at Bohemian Grove with Dickie when we received the news of Priscilla's cerebral hemorrhage. The Secret Service contingent attached to Dickie because he was the president's brother had driven us through the rain and fog back down to San Francisco. As always, Dickie was the perfect advance man, asking questions, getting answers. The sudden death of a wife offered a new set of logistics to be dealt with. Even before we left the Grove, Dickie had given his permission for an autopsy to be performed on Priscilla. On the trip down, Dickie sat in the front seat, Tuck and I in the back. We listened to Dickie question the Secret Service driver. Yes, the driver said, the president had been informed at the fundraiser at the Beverly Hilton in Beverly Hills and he would be arriving in San Francisco on Air Force One in approximately seventeen minutes. His motorcade would proceed directly to the home of Mr. Hugh Broderick on Washington Street. Mr. Broderick had asked the president to stay at the house as his guest and the president had accepted. His superiors weren't too crazy about that deal, the driver said. They wanted the president to stay at the Presidio, it was only a few blocks away, it was secure, the commanding general would surrender his quarters to the president, it was his ass, he didn't, you could hook up the whole communications setup, it was no big thing. I could see Dickie nod as if all this information was new to him. He was always so perfectly accommodating. Of course he had already talked to my father. It was Dickie's decision to have the funeral out of the house on Washington Street. It was bigger than his own house on Broadway, the security was good, if not up to the level of the Presidio, and his two little daughters, Daisy and

Dinah, would not have to be so intimately involved with the preparations for their mother's funeral.

"Jack," Tuck Bradley had said quietly in the backseat. The Secret Service man was still talking, occupying Dickie's attention, comparing San Francisco to Denver, his previous posting, each was a hell of a town, you had the ocean in one and you had the mountains in the other, it kind of depended which you liked better, he was a hiker himself, that Pikes Peak was something else. "I wrote some letters to Priscilla. I'd prefer they not turn up. Would you know what she did with . . ." He took a deep breath. ". . . with things like that?"

I stared at him in the darkness. He had the look of a man who kept in shape by playing endless sets of strenuous tennis. His ambassadorship to Sierra Leone had just been confirmed in the Senate. I suspected his major appeal for Priscilla was that he had been Fritz Finn's roommate at Princeton and that they had been more or less best friends ever since, or as friendly as Fritz ever got with anyone. Leaving the president for the president's best friend was the kind of thing Priscilla would do.

"I don't imagine she kept them around," I said. "Priscilla was always very discreet."

If he caught the slight emphasis on the "always" he did not acknowledge it.

"I wouldn't like Dickie to see them."

"Or my father," I said, and regretted it immediately. The jibe was silly and unnecessary, provoked more by my dislike of Tuck Bradley than by any insight into my father. One thing I knew: Hugh Broderick would not need clandestine love letters to browbeat the likes of Tuck Bradley.

"I like Dickie," Tuck Bradley insisted, his voice rising just slightly enough to be heard in the front seat.

"Thanks, Tuck," Dickie Finn said. I had no idea what he had heard of the rest of the conversation. Not that it really mattered. Tuck had been Dickie's guest at Bohemian Grove. Most of Priscilla's lovers had in fact been friends of the family. I think it was only the stranger he did not know who truly frightened Dickie. "I'm glad you were here tonight. And you, too, Jack. It makes it easier when friends are around."

The Secret Service had already surrounded the house on Washington Street by the time we arrived. It was well after midnight, a soft cool evening, and there were still people behind the police barricades outside the house waiting for the sight of a familiar face. We went into the house in the glare of the television lights. Fritz was in the living room with my father. I shook Fritz's hand and then embraced my father awkwardly. It was the first time since my mother died and it would be the last until the day Bro was killed.

"Hugh is taking this hard," Fritz said that morning after he had dispatched Dickie to invite Cyril Magnin to Priscilla's funeral.

"Yes." My father had been upstairs alone all morning. I could not explain to Fritz, even if I had been disposed to do so, what I then only dimly understood myself. Priscilla had always been the most pliable of my father's three children, the only one to sail the course he had navigated for each of us in advance, less a daughter than a surrogate son, her infidelities attaching her to the world of command and affairs he had craved for Bro and perhaps even me. But I was a none-too-committed journalist and Bro could not get back from the Eucharistic Congress meeting in Quito in time for the funeral. And now Priscilla was dead and my father was upstairs alone. He could not manage Bro and he did not think I was worth managing, and so I think he was more comfortable alone, without the illusion of family.

"Dickie wondered if you'd say a few words at the funeral," Tuck Bradley said.

"Under the circumstances, I don't think it would be seemly," Fritz said. As always with that serrated edge of self-mockery. In his hands, the art of being disarming was a weapon.

"What should I tell him?" Tuck Bradley said.

"You'll think of something," Fritz said.

Tuck Bradley stared out the window for a moment. "What if I said it's too private a tragedy and if you spoke it would necessarily intrude the political."

"I think Dickie will buy that," Fritz said. "I *know* Dickie will buy that." He looked at me. "Right, Jack?"

I knew that what Fritz wanted to avoid was the arched eye-

brow of the more sardonic of the network anchormen, all of
whom I was sure had at least heard the rumors about him and
Priscilla. "Will Fiona be coming?"

"Fiona's in Kennebunkport," Fritz said, as if that explained
why his wife would not attend the funeral, and then extra-
neously, "She always liked Priscilla."

I wondered on how many of Fritz's girlfriends Fiona Finn had
expressed an opinion, and if he thought her liking of Priscilla was
absolution for his adultery.

"Actually I wish Bro were going to be here," Fritz said. "You
can always count on Bro to be appropriate. Which this situation
seems to call for." His voice was even, filtering out any condescension that I might have construed. He picked up the cable Bro
had sent from Quito and read it again. " 'Holy Father also asked
me to extend papal sympathies to Dickie and all the Brodericks
stop And of course to Fritz as well stop Vaya con dios stop.' "
Fritz laughed. "I'm surprised he didn't work in Mao and
Khrushchev. Maybe he couldn't get through to them from
Quito." He put the wire back down on the Chinese ebony desk.
"What's ever happened to that lawyer, Jack?"

I played dumb. "Lawyer?"

"You know the one."

I did, and knew he did, too. I was not going to help him out. I
shook my head slowly. "No."

I waited. Fritz snapped his fingers. "Kaye," he said finally.
"Leah Kaye. That was her name, wasn't it?"

I do not know why I thought it a small victory to get him to
say Leah's name. "Oh. Her. Yes. She's with the farm workers
now."

"Onyx Leon . . ."

"Yes. In Hermosa. Up past Bakersfield."

"As a matter of fact, I had heard that." I was sure he had. Tuck
Bradley handed him a second cup of coffee. Fritz held the cup
extended until Tuck dropped two cocktail cubes of sugar into it.
An imperial gesture I suspect Fritz made for my benefit. He
stirred the coffee for a moment. "She knows how to pick them,
doesn't she?"

I did not answer. I was quite certain that Fritz knew more
about Leah Kaye than I did.

"That fellow. The pisser. The brother of the one at San Quentin. She got him off, didn't she?"

Exactly as she said she would get him off. The jury was out only four hours.

"On the murder charge. He still has to finish his original sentence. He's up for parole this year."

"Do you ever see her anymore?" The disposition of any case against Mercury Baker was of little interest to him. Leah was the object of his attention.

I made a noncommittal shrug. But of course I had seen her since that day at San Quentin. The occasional guarded lunch in the cafeteria of whatever courthouse where she was appearing, the greasy Big Mac near the demonstration she was monitoring, the sit-in where she sat. The pose was strictly professional. Interviewer-interviewee. On my part proximity without commitment, on Leah's (I know now) amusement at the transparency of my pose. I suspect Fritz knew of these meetings, because he made it his business to know things like that, and I suspect also he would have called them clandestine.

"I read your piece. *Life,* wasn't it?"

"The Saturday Evening Post."

"Of course. It was stirring." He favored me with the presidential smile. "And altogether orthodox."

I returned his smile without comment.

"A terrible thing, of course. I mean the way it ended. The blood leaking down the back of the chair. That was a nice touch, Jack. You were the only one who had it."

Which meant he did not believe it. He thought I had made it up. A recurring theme with Fritz. When I want to read a novel, he once said at the Gridiron Club dinner, I read *The New York Times.* Creative journalism, he often said when a story displeased him. Faction was another favorite.

"You spent a night in the clink, I believe," Fritz said. The thought of my incarceration in the Marin County jail seemed to put him in good spirits. Although I had the feeling he thought it less than I deserved. If only on general principles. "We're in the presence of a dangerous felon, Tuck."

Tuck Bradley laughed heartily. The sycophant's tic. "I'll alert the Secret Service, Mr. President."

"Not to worry, Tuck," Fritz said. "The Secret Service knows all about our friend Jack here." He smiled his executioner's smile. "Including his mandarin tastes."

I acknowledged the remark with a blank fuck-you stare. Fritz seemed quite pleased with himself. Innuendo was his natural métier. It was scarcely a secret about Wendy and me, but at the same time I did not appreciate having the information in a dossier available for light bedtime reading in the private quarters at the White House. This was the sort of game Fritz liked to play. Any conversation with him was a series of veiled warnings. He was more than a practitioner of don't get mad, get even. He liked to let people know that he had, and would use, the means to get even. I think there was a pleasure principle involved. It was otherwise pointless to allude to an affair dead for some time of my inertia and Wendy's ambition.

"Bro bailed me out," I said evenly.

"And then I bailed Bro out."

In a manner of speaking, yes. So that Bro might be preserved as a valuable ex officio member of the Finn team. Four days after the execution of Germany Baker, four days after the riot in the San Quentin parking lot, Bro was on his way to Africa. Special presidential envoy to the signing of the new constitution in Ng'wana. An emerging nation. An addition to the democratic West. In the San Quentin parking lot, Bro was an embarrassment to the administration. His ties to Fritz were too strong. And so out of sight, out of mind. Which translated into Ng'wana.

"I've been told to bring my rather faded charms to some new venue," Bro had said over the telephone the night before he left Washington. "They've even given me a brand-new diplomatic passport. In the event I need diplomatic immunity, I suppose. Ng'wana. I like the apostrophe. I think if there'd been something going on in Antarctica, Fritz would have sent me there. Without a snowsuit. A conference on polar fishing treaties, say. But Ng'wana it is. The African schwartzes are the good schwartzes this year. They've got Swiss bank accounts and Mercedes-Benzes. All our darkies have are Molotov cocktails and room temperature IQs. That's the word from the White House. From a top White House source. From *the* top White House source. If you need another clue, Jack, his wife's name is Fiona. And his old girlfriend's a close relative of ours. And so I'm off to the Dark Continent. I feel like Lord Jim. Or is it Mr. Kurtz? He dead. Ng'wana's my purgatory. Where I can redeem my good name. Although the recent events at Q are supposed to make me marketable with my host, Mr. Mbela, who has done time in several of the more primitive slammers maintained by his former colonial oppressors. Mr. Kwame Mbela. Without the apostrophe. The revised histories say he was a patriot those days in the slam, Ng'wana's George Washington, Mohandas K. Gandhi in blackface, strumming on his old banjo. The unregenerate say he's a fucking cannibal."

Not to put too fine a point on it, Bro was plastered. Blotto. Shitfaced. There he was, sitting in the first-class lounge at National, Dom Augustine Broderick, O.S.B., decked out in his priestly tropicals, staring at a twenty-eight-hour flight, Washington to London, London to Cairo, Cairo to Nairobi, Nairobi to Mbela, which is what Ng'wana's George Washington had renamed his capital city, and the London leg of the trip was already delayed five hours, and so he proceeded to get systematically and deliberately ossified. I think he called me because he had been hustled and he was embarrassed. Embarrassed that he had accepted the sentence of this face-saving mission. "Penance in the heart of darkness," he called it. "The word is lay low. Lie doggo. Become an expert on famine and drought. On rickets and malnutrition and pickaninny babies with distended bellies and a life expectancy of eighteen months. That's a black problem you can get behind. No need to say the best thing about the bugger is it's eight thousand miles away. It's the stuff of programs. Commissions. Studies. White papers. Sunday fucking supplements. Color spreads. Look concerned. Feel bad. Ignore the sucker."

Of course it did not quite work out that way. Lord Jim turned out to be Lucky Jim, Ng'wana the right place at the right time. Bro's luck. Until he ran up against Richie Kane outside Glide Memorial, Bro was one of those rare people always blessed with perfect timing. Even in Ng'wana. Seventy-two hours after his arrival, President Mbela dismantled the constitution he had just signed, dissolved parliament, hanged the two scholars from the

University of Chicago who had written the constitution and de-
clared himself rex. Not king. Rex. Rex Kwame. The rex of
Ng'wana. He also called himself The Divine Light. And as the
two constitutionalists from the University of Chicago swung
from one of the fourteen telephone poles in the capital city of
Mbela, Rex Kwame wrote a new constitution himself, one sentence, eight words, grammatically imperfect but unmistakably to
the point: "The Divine Light, He Rule by Divine Right." The
death toll was a matter of some debate. *Time* said 4,000. The *New
York Post* said a quarter of a million. *Le Monde* put the total at
914. Tass said two. Bro escaped across the Ng'wana River in the
bottom of a dugout canoe. There was nothing like being an artic-
ulate living eyewitness to a bloodbath for refurbishing the reputation. San Quentin was absolved.

"Actually Bro is a saint," Fritz Finn said. "A pain in the ass at
times, but a saint." I received the uncomforting benediction of his
cold smile. Without looking at Tuck Bradley, he said, "Right,
Tuck?"

"I read his report on Mbela," Tuck said carefully.

"Good for you, Tuck." Fritz turned and perused Tuck Bradley. "And I bet you thought it was sound."

"Very sound."

"Measured."

"Very measured."

"Better than the crap we get out of Langley."

"In many ways, Mr. President."

I tried and failed to work up a sliver of sympathy for Tuck
Bradley. The way Fritz was toying with him was a kind of water
torture I had seen him perform many times. It was the price he
extracted from those who would get too close to him. I wondered
suddenly if perhaps Fritz really had been irritated when Priscilla
left him for Tuck Bradley. That might explain his performance.
He turned back to me. "So she's in Hermosa now, is she?"

It took me a moment to realize he was back to Leah Kaye.
"Helping Onyx Leon organize the grape pickers."

"I can't say she's a saint. At least according to the standards of
our more rigid moral guardians. Edgar and Clyde. They have
naughty minds, those boys. Right, Tuck?"

Tuck Bradley looked pained.

"At least Bro's a private saint," Fritz said. "Onyx is a public one. That's the nervous kind." He ran his spoon through his cold coffee. "They're this year's fancy crusade, those farm workers in Yerba Hermosa. Onyx's boys. Devoid of all the ambiguities of that inner-city shit Bro was so hipped on. The mugging down the block, the rape across the street." Again the Finn smile. "A good cause. The nobility of the soil. Simple Mexican peasants with noble agrarian ideas. All that Gandhi crap. The mysteries of the East flowering outside Bakersfield. Bakersfield, for Christ's sake." He raised his coffee cup and examined the maker's marking on the bottom. "Limoges," he said, as if to himself. And then to me: "All the smart people are boycotting grapes this summer. The ones who read *Women's Wear*. Fiona's even struck them off the menu at the White House." He permitted himself still another small smile. "I had that leaked to Jack Anderson. A small step toward shoring up my sagging reputation with my constituency on the left." He handed the coffee cup back to Tuck Bradley. "Fasting, nonviolence and a midget sister." Fritz shook his head admiringly. He had a politician's appreciation for the marketable. "Christ, it plays."

How well it played we saw that very afternoon when Leah and Onyx and fourteen demonstrators from Hermosa were arrested outside the house on Washington Street. I think even Fritz was impressed with the way Leah operated. She knew that his presence at my father's house, even on what was supposed to be a sad private occasion, guaranteed maximum press coverage and offered an opportunity for Onyx and his strikers to get prime network airtime. Leah was nothing if not thorough. She had searched land titles and discovered that my father, through a network of holding companies, owned several thousand acres of the very vineyards in Hermosa that Onyx and the farm workers were striking. Always cautious, however, Onyx did not want to come to the house on Washington Street. It is a time of sorrow, he told Leah. You'll never get a chance like this again, Leah told Onyx. No, said Onyx. *No cojones,* said Leah.

The demonstrators came.

I watched them from the second-story window. First the grape

pickers, fat brown women in shapeless dresses and men in ragged
work clothes, bent low and pretending to plow a furrow with
short-handled hoes on the sidewalk across from the house. Behind
them, nuns and priests in clerical habit knelt and sang over and
over, as if it were a broken record, "Nosotros Venceremos."

"Is that song what I think it is?" Fritz said.

" 'We Shall Overcome' in Spanish," I said.

"Oh, shit," Fritz muttered.

Then there were the placards, all of them caricatures either of
my father or El Presidente Finn. My father was drawn wearing a
wide planter's hat and sunglasses and he was smoking a fat cigar
and carrying a bullwhip and his foot was planted on the back of
his stoop labor. El Presidente sat on a picker's back and dropped a
bunch of grapes in his mouth.

"Oh, shit," Fritz repeated.

Onyx held a bullhorn. Leah whispered into his ear. "El Presidente Finn," Onyx shouted.

"*Viva la huelga,*" the demonstrators shouted.

"You ban grapes from the White House." Onyx Leon's amplified voice carried across Washington Street. "*La Casa Blanca.*"

"*Viva la huelga.*"

"Yet you stay in the *palacio* of the miserable *patrón* Broderick."

I suddenly wondered if my father were watching from his
window upstairs.

"The miserable *patrón* who will not give his workers dignity . . ."

"*Viva la huelga.*"

"The miserable *patrón* who will not give his workers security . . ."

"*Viva la huelga.*"

Again I saw Leah whisper into Onyx's ear.

"The miserable *patrón* who thinks we are short, happy and
built close to the ground . . ."

A chorus of *vivas.*

"*Viva la huelga.*"

"*Viva la causa.*"

"*Viva.*"

I watched spellbound through the window. The performance was so simple. *Huelga. Palacio.* Miserable *patrón.* My father had been called many things in his life, but I would wager never before a miserable *patrón.* Fritz caught my eye. "Agitprop," he said. "Effective," I said. "Crude but effective. And the timing's not bad either." Tuck Bradley said, "Whose side are you on anyway?" I said, "Christ, you're an asshole, Tuck." Fritz said, "Jack's just being an objective observer. Like the good journalist he is." And to me he said, "Fuck you." The sardonic smile was stitched to his face. "Disgraceful," Tuck Bradley said. A Secret Service man moved to my side and ordered me away from the window, it was a danger to the president. I told him to bugger off, it was my house. He then tried to wrestle me back, but Fritz intervened. "It's all right," he said. "Jack likes street theater."

"But, Mr. President . . ."

"I said it was all right."

I nodded my thanks.

"What are we going to say?" Tuck Bradley said.

"We're going to say the president was in mourning for his sister-in-law and was not aware of the demonstration. We're going to say the president is an active and vigorous supporter of all of society's dispossessed. We're going to say that the timing of this particular little event was perhaps unfortunate despite what the fuck Jack thinks." An icicle smile for my benefit. "We might even arrange a display of public sympathy at some undetermined time in the future. Maybe we introduce Onyx to the president of Costa Rica whatever the hell his name is when he's here in the fall. But we finesse the midget sister. That's not the kind of photo opportunity I'm looking for. 'President Finn and Dwarf.'" He considered the imaginary caption. "No. I guess not. I guess we just stick with no Thompson seedless at the White House for a while, right, Tuck?"

"Right, Mr. President."

"That lawyer," Fritz said, not looking at me. "Your pal. She's the wild card in this operation."

Down on the street, Onyx and Leah seemed to be arguing. Leah shouted something into his ear. Vigorously Onyx shook his head no. Suddenly Leah seized the bullhorn from him. "Are you up there, miserable *patrón* Broderick?"

"*Viva.*"

"The miserable *patrón* whose police lackeys have us arrested for saying 'dirty words' on the picket line . . ." She stretched the phrase "dirty words" into an elongated sneer.

"*Viva la causa . . .*"

". . . but who makes his women workers squat like animals in the fields because he will not supply them with field toilets . . ."

"*Nosotros venceremos . . .*"

It was then that the police moved in. Leah went limp in the streets. Onyx hesitated for a moment but then collapsed beside her. One by one the demonstrators went down, the priests and nuns among them with their arms extended, as if waiting to be crucified. The television crews recorded it all. The Roman collars on the priests. The heavy rosary bead cinctures worn by the nuns. Onyx Leon singing "Nosotros Venceremos" as he climbed into a paddy wagon. And Leah smiling. Especially Leah smiling. There was something about the way Leah smiled when she was arrested.

It was a victory smile.

"What time is it?" Fritz said.

"Two-thirty," Tuck Bradley said.

"Then the network guys still have time to make the feed to New York," Fritz said.

"Disgraceful," Tuck Bradley repeated.

"Effective," Fritz said.

Onyx Leon made the cover of *Newsweek* six weeks later.

I didn't even know I had those goddamn vineyards, my father said.

Go down there, Jack, my father said. Find out what that woman is up to.

You mean Onyx, I said.

No, I don't mean that little beaner, my father said. He doesn't have a thimbleful of brains. It's that Jew lawyer that's calling the shots. The woman.

And so I went to Hermosa.

It was the first task my father had ever asked me to perform for him. He did not think I would end up marrying Leah. Or that he would sleep with her. Or that she would abort his child.

But that was later.

BOOK FOUR

MARRIAGE & DIVORCE

I

OF COURSE I PETITIONED, under the provisions of the Freedom of Information Act, to secure a copy of Leah's FBI file after she was killed. The negotiations conducted by my attorneys to establish what might and what might not be released were long and acrimonious; the fact that I appeared more than willing to expend a sizable portion of the Broderick bankroll to get the file more or less intact gradually cracked the stone wall erected by the government lawyers until finally, nearly a year after the legal maneuvering began, boxes of papers began to arrive from Washington. So much of what had been recorded was blanked out, however, that whole sections of the remainder were almost indecipherable. And yet, even with all the deletions, there the file was, several thousand pages of transcripts and documents and wiretaps and interrogations and surveillance reports, of unsubstantiated allegations and unverified accusations, a testament to a life that at least the FBI thought was important.

I read the whole mass of material at a single sitting. There was little in it that I did not already know. There were the reports of Leah's thirty-nine arrests over the years, arrests at sit-ins and

teach-ins and marches and demonstrations, for criminal trespass
and disturbing the peace, in Oakland and San Francisco and Los
Angeles and Boston and Chicago and Detroit and New York and
New Orleans, at San Quentin and at Malmstrom Air Force Base
in Great Falls, Montana, and Nellis Air Force Base in Las Vegas,
Nevada, and at the U.S. Navy Submarine Base in Groton, Connecticut, a Baedeker of protest. There were the manifestos she
had signed and the organizations to which she belonged and the
committees on the attorney general's subversive list to which
she had paid dues and on whose behalf she often appeared as counsel. There were the names of the criminal clients she represented
and a listing of the more heinous crimes they were accused of
committing and there were the names of the dopers and the dis-
sidents she defended and the underground organizations to
which she was said to have links and for whom it was alleged that
she acted as courier and envoy. There were the restricted capitals she had visited in defiance of the warning printed in her
passport and there were photographs of her with Raúl Castro in
Ciego de Avila and with Carlotta French in Haiphong. There were
allegations of sexual indiscretions with, among others, myself, as
well as with Onyx Leon and with Mercury Baker and with Lottie
French and with a number of people whose names I did not recognize and with several others identified only as "[NAME DE-
LETED]."

There were allegations of drug abuse and allegations of treason
and allegations of communism and allegations of lesbianism.
There was a report that she had an illegal abortion in the San
Fernando Valley and a supplemental report that the alleged father of the fetus she had aborted was "[NAME DELETED]." There
was no mention, however, of the two miscarriages she had during
the four years of our marriage. The first was on a DC-8 to Boston.
She began spotting over Reno and was bleeding profusely over
Denver. Over Chicago she locked herself in the lavatory and ex-
pelled the fetus, the amniotic sac and the placenta. She spent the
night at Mass General and, over the protests of her doctors, appeared in court the next morning to plead her client not guilty on
all the charges filed against him. The second miscarriage occurred
a year later at an anti-Vietnam rally in Chicago. Her supporters

claimed that a policeman had struck her in the stomach with his nightstick, setting the miscarriage in motion, but in fact Leah had noticed the signs in the car on the way to the demonstration and was in the emergency room at Cook County Hospital when the riot on the picket line actually erupted. The story about the policeman and his nightstick passed into radical lore, and if Leah never affirmed it, neither did she ever deny it. It was after this second miscarriage that she had a complete workup of gynecological tests, the results indicating that she had what the medical team called "an incompetent cervix" which would preclude her from holding a fetus beyond the second trimester without corrective, and highly speculative, surgery. Her cervix, I would often tell her later, was the only thing about her that was incompetent.

Over time, the reports in the FBI file became more fervid. There was an allegation that she had smuggled heroin into San Quentin and automatic weapons into Soledad. There was an allegation that she had fornicated on an American flag at the 1968 Democratic National Convention in Chicago. There was a photograph of her bare-breasted at what was alleged to be an SDS convention and another photograph of her at what was claimed by "[NAME DELETED]" to be a Weathermen hideout in a deconsecrated Catholic church in Ashtabula, Ohio, a photograph in which she was wearing a T-shirt on which was printed the slogan, CUNNILINGUS IS CUNNING.

On close scrutiny, the woman in the T-shirt turned out to be Harriet Hecht while the photograph of Leah bare-breasted was taken not at an SDS convention but by me at the cottage I had rented for two weeks at Stinson Beach that winter before we were divorced. The descriptions of Leah were no more reassuring. "Sources describe Kaye as being of medium height and fair complexion . . ." "Source said Kaye is short and dark in the manner of a Lebanese or a member of the Jewish persuasion . . ." "She is said to have long straight black hair . . ." "Kaye has tight curly hair sometimes tinted blond . . ." "Subject Kaye is approximately 40 years of age . . ." "Kaye, who is 30 . . ." "[NAME DELETED] indicates Kaye has a mannish appearance . . ." "Kaye is described as delicate . . ." "She wears modish clothes not in keeping with her pro-Communist life-style . . ." "Kaye is known to favor 'hippie' dress in keeping with her counterculture life-style . . ."

Occasionally I would find references to myself in the file: "SUBJECT KAYE was present when elements of the DEA abetted by local narcotics authorities raided the premises she occupied with a man alleged to be her husband, one JOHN BRODERICK aka 'JACK' BRODERICK, on suspicion of possession of controlled substances. Please note that SUBJECT KAYE does not use the same surname of alleged husband, JOHN BRODERICK, nor does she wear a wedding ring. Both KAYE and BRODERICK were taken into custody." The entry failed to mention that no controlled substances were discovered on the premises occupied by SUBJECT KAYE and her alleged husband, JOHN BRODERICK aka "JACK" BRODERICK, and that all charges against them were dismissed.

That was the year we were living in the big old house on San Luis Road in the hills above Berkeley, with a view across the Bay into San Francisco, and on a clear day all the way out to the Golden Gate. I had bought a run-down building in downtown Oakland which I had tried to give Leah as an office for The Justice Department, but she insisted on paying a rent commensurate with all the other rents in the neighborhood, thus allowing her to maintain the stance that she accepted nothing from the Brodericks while at the same time keeping me firmly planted in the landlord class. We had a cook and we had a gardener and Ramona Leon slept in one spare bedroom and in the others I could usually find a parolee or a black nationalist out on bail or an unfrocked radical priest on his way to Vera Cruz and from there to the hills of Cristo Rey, that Vatican of liberation theology. Mercury Baker stayed there for three weeks when he was released from Folsom, his uniform those prison denims with the white P stenciled on the shirt and on the legs. It was a uniform that made the neighbors nervous, former freedom marchers and peace activists though they all were, and he was escorted by a three-hundred-pound black bodyguard he called The Shadow, who made me nervous. As Leah was usually in court or off on some barricade, I was the beneficiary of Mercury's constant stream of jailhouse wisdom, I suppose because I was a writer, in his mind one of those sedentary honkies he had been hustling since he learned to talk.

"A criminal is merely a man of extremes," Mercury Baker said one afternoon as we were sitting on the redwood deck overlooking the rose arbor where the Japanese gardener was pruning the hybrid teas. The sentiment sounded familiar and then I realized why: it came from a meditation on the criminal mind in that week's *Time* magazine. Mercury seemed to have read it as well, and been impressed. He was tipped back in a chair, feet perched on the railing, master of all he surveyed, for all the world acting as if he were granting me an audience. I felt like a supplicant, as he intended me to feel, a provider of the Royal Crown Cola stocked in the refrigerator, which only The Shadow drank, bottle after bottle, drained at a gulp.

"Right on, motherfucker," The Shadow said. Arms folded, hair shaved to the skull, he stood behind Mercury's chair, glowering at me, as if daring me to disagree. He was dressed in a black T-shirt and black spandex slacks and as usual he seldom opened his mouth except to down a Royal Crown or to punctuate with an approving obscenity whatever Mercury happened to be saying.

"A man who robs a 7-Eleven instead of the dignity of a fellow human being," Mercury said. I was suddenly reminded of Germany Baker on Death Row: *A pig gets himself offed, it some kind of big damn deal.* Educated by the *Time* essay, Mercury Baker was smoother than his brother.

"Or Lucky Discount," The Shadow said. "Stay away from the fucking Thrifty. That Thrifty's got heavy security." The Shadow had served a penance imposed by the state of California in the same cell block with Mercury Baker at Folsom. He had also done time in Illinois with Germany Baker. "Fucking electric eyes."

Mercury Baker picked at a huge white tooth with the sulfur end of a kitchen match. "A man who uses a blade or a piece rather than a threatening personality."

"You got to watch out for that kind of fucker," The Shadow said, nodding in agreement. He took a bottle of Royal Crown from the Scotch plaid cooler at his feet, flicked off the cap and let the full eight ounces drain down his throat without a single con-

traction of his Adam's apple. "I know this dude," he said, still
nodding. "He go to see his lady. He was carrying this shotgun.
It go off, that fucker." He did not explain why the dude was
carrying a shotgun or what happened to his lady when the
shotgun went off. I think he had forgotten the point he was trying
to make. If indeed there was a point. "The fuckers will do
that."

Mercury Baker smiled at The Shadow. He seemed to appreciate the parable of the shotgun, as if the interruption explicated his
text. He picked up his own sermon, his actor's voice ingratiating
and sinuously ominous. "A man who kills in fact rather than with
hassling and bad-mouthing."

The Shadow belched, a liquid rumble. "That's the worst fucking kind of all, that kind."

On the lawn, the gardener held up the underside of a leaf.
"Aphids," he shouted up at me. I nodded. "I spray?" he asked. I
nodded again. I wondered if he would agree that murder was no
more pernicious than hassling or bad-mouthing, the moral equivalent of aphids. And wondered how he would look with a two-
inch stub of a Dixon Ticonderoga number three stuck in his
mouth if he happened to disagree.

"The laws I break are on the books at least," Mercury Baker
said.

"Fuck, yes," The Shadow said.

Mercury Baker's smile was like poisoned honey. "I may be low,
but I am not ignoble."

I repeated Mercury's free translation of the *Time* essay to Leah
later that evening. She was propped up in bed, reading a brief on
Onyx Leon's latest misadventure with the law. He had been arrested in Boston on charges of inciting a riot at the headquarters
of a supermarket chain which continued to sell the grapes his
farm workers and their supporters were trying to boycott. A policeman was hospitalized as were two picketers, one of whom was
on a life-support system. Leah was leaving for Boston the next
morning to take over Onyx's defense. I would have to say her interest in my report was limited, but she turned down a corner of
the brief to mark her place and listened without an untoward display of impatience. When I finished, she reopened the brief and

smoothed out the turned-down corner. "So what's your complaint?"

Even in bed her conversational style was that of the cross-examiner.

"No complaint," I said carefully. "Call it an oral report on an afternoon's seminar on criminal philosophy conducted by Professor Baker at 5551 San Luis Road, Berkeley, California. The adult education department."

Leah looked at me for a moment and then returned to her brief.

I was irritated by her apparent indifference. It was as if she were already in Boston. "Four units," I said. "Resolved: A criminal is merely a man of extremes. Discuss."

"Look," she said. She closed the brief. Then she set the alarm. Then she placed them both on the night table. The deliberate delay was her way of ensuring my undivided attention. I had seen her use the same tactic in the courtroom. "It's useful."

"What's useful?"

"What he said."

"Useful." I drew the word out. "As an idea."

She ignored the sarcasm. "Yes."

I was hardly surprised. In the arena where she performed, words were as important as deeds. I accepted the premise, however equivocally. "For the record, he gives me the creeps."

"He gives a lot of people the creeps. That's also useful."

"And that three-hundred-pound gorilla. I suppose he's useful, too."

"Very."

"Because he attracts attention, I suppose."

"That would tend to make him useful, yes."

"Just tell me one thing. What does a murderer need a bodyguard for?"

She did not seem unduly perturbed by my calling Mercury Baker a murderer. The nature of her world was that murder was often a word with useful connotations, a word that carried its own implicit message that he who was identified as a murderer was a force to be reckoned with. "That's a useful question." She yawned. "And anyway he's not a murderer. He was acquitted of murder." She switched off the light. "Not guilty. Let's fuck. I'm

off early in the morning." There was not a beat between the discussion of murder and the sexual invitation. It was a perfect example of Leah's utilitarian approach. "I hate fucking pickups in
strange hotel rooms."

It was on the plane to Boston the next morning that Leah had
her first miscarriage.

As I read the FBI report, I tried to remember what it was like
being married to Leah. Of course I remember the drug busts and
the constant surveillance and I remember the vaginal strip
searches when she came through customs or when she visited her
more notorious clients in jail. I remember that she took taxis
whenever possible because she feared the authorities might plant
illicit substances in her car and I remember that she always carried rolls of coins in her purse, ten or twenty dollars' worth, conducting most important business from pay telephones on the not
unwarranted suspicion that her telephones were tapped. I remember how avidly she would read me her Berkeley class notes
from the *California Monthly:* " 'Lee Dutton,' " she would read,
" 'is now the manager of the Berkeley branch of the Western
Bank and Trust and indulges his love of rock music by encourag-
ing musicians and music groups to do their banking with
WBT.' " I remember how that made her laugh until the tears
came, great choking explosions of laughter, and I remember that
then we made love.

In fact I remember fucking Leah most of all. In a way fucking
her was a learning experience. Bed was where she held forth on
genocide and Yanqui imperialism and racism and political prisoners and Amerika with a *k*, each topic an aphrodisiac in itself.
There was seldom any postcoital *tristesse*. She would lie in bed
after fucking—she insisted on calling it fucking, "lovemaking"
was suburban bullshit, "balling" was liberal bullshit—blowing
smoke rings one after the other, her free hand on my spent cock,
and she would talk about the conditions in the farm labor camps,
if that was her concern of the moment, about how one-third of
the Chicanos in the United States lived below the poverty line,
how their birth rate was twice the national average as was the
mortality rate for Chicano infants less than a year old, how their

unemployment rate was twice that of Anglos, how they averaged only eight years of schooling, how almost eighty percent of them worked at unskilled or semiskilled jobs, facts, facts and more facts, inundating me with facts until she fell asleep or it was time to fuck again.

None of this was in the FBI report.

II

I ASKED LEAH TO MARRY ME in Lottie French's bathroom. In the crapper, she would often say later. I don't think she meant it as a metaphor for the marriage that followed. I can still remember the smallest details. I was sitting on the bidet. Leah was putting on lipstick, squinting at herself in the makeup mirror over the vanity table. Light bulbs framed the mirror and the table was covered with boxes of Kleenex and jars of cleansing creams. There were three telephones in the bathroom, each with ten buttons and an intercom. One telephone was on the double sink, one on a wicker stand next to the bidet, the third on a brass swivel next to the toilet. There was an automatic Rolodex card file on the swivel and a duplicate on the sink. The bathtub was freestanding in the center of the room, with brass legs and antique gold fixtures; the same gold fixtures adorned the shower and the two sinks. Next to the toilet was an enameled red bamboo magazine rack filled with copies of *Rolling Stone* and *Hard Times* and *The Village Voice*. Adjacent to the bathroom itself was a fully equipped exercise room with a whirlpool bath and a ballet bar and a massage table and weights and pulleys. On the far wall there was a life-sized poster of Lottie in tights, leg warmers and headband, her face contorted and bathed in sweat, pulling on the rowing machine in the corner.

Leah considered my question, all the while blotting her lipstick with a piece of Kleenex. Then she swung around and looked at me on the bidet. "You're sitting on that wrong."

Through the open window I could hear the rock-and-roll band playing on the tennis court outside. "That's not what I would call an answer."

Leah ignored my response. "You're supposed to face the wall when you sit on a bidet." She took the Rolodex from the sink, put it in her lap and began riffling through it. "That way the water hits you right where it should. In your sweet spot, as one of my hooker clients used to call it. It's perfectly designed. Like the Eames Chair. Or the 1955 T-bird."

Someone began banging on the bathroom door. "I don't suppose I'll ever have any use for it." I silently cursed my pomposity. The banging continued. Then I heard Alex Fahr's voice. It always had the same effect on me as fingernails scraping down a slate blackboard. "Who's in there? Come on, for Christ's sake, someone must be in there, you can't stay in there all day." Leah put a finger to her lips. Neither of us spoke. Alex pounded on the door again. Then I heard a woman's voice: "Alex, maybe someone OD'd in there." The banging stopped suddenly and after some urgent whispering, I heard Alex again: "I think we should get out of here." The woman said, "What about Pluto?" Her name was Boston Bailey and she was Pluto Fahr's consort. When we met two hours earlier she said that Pluto gave very good head for such an old man. Alex said, "He's asleep." Boston Bailey said, "We can't just leave him here." Alex said, "You want to carry him?" Boston Bailey said, "I just think . . ." Alex said, "Stop thinking, it's not your long suit, he's senile, if someone OD'd in the can, they'll know he didn't have anything to do with it." After a moment, I heard the bedroom door close. Then there was silence.

Leah smiled. At Alex's expense or mine I was not sure. She seemed intent on not answering my question. Which in point of fact had not been a question at all. I think maybe we should get married, I had said. Sitting on the bidet. A proposal barnacled with qualifiers. *Think. Maybe. Should.* The whole scene was an invitation for rejection.

I cleared my throat. "Well . . ."

Leah studied the Rolodex. I looked out the window. There must have been three hundred people milling around Lottie's black tile swimming pool. Par for the course when the guest list was a hundred. I don't want a ratfuck, Lottie had said. Which of course was exactly what the invitation had invited:

COME JOIN
CARLOTTA FRENCH, PLUTO FAHR AND OTHERS
AT 9292 BEL AIR ROAD FOR A CELEBRITY AUCTION
TO BENEFIT ONYX LEON AND HIS VALIANT
CENTRAL VALLEY AGRICULTURAL WORKERS UNION
MUSIC   WINE   BUFFET   DRESS—FUNKY
RSVP—BILL CALLAHAN & ASSOCIATES PUBLIC RELATIONS
PRESS CONTACT—PAUL JULIAN

The sweet heavy smell of marijuana drifted up from the pool to the bathroom window on the second floor. In the crowd below I finally caught a glimpse of Onyx. He was in a wheelchair because the herniated disk in his back had flared up again. Only a few of the guests seemed to recognize him and I knew that many others thought the Mexican farm laborers he had brought with him were Lottie's household help got up in work clothes in honor of the occasion. At Onyx's side stood his tiny sister Ramona, looking bewildered, as always in a Peter Pan collar and a plain black dress fitted loosely so as to partially disguise the hump on her back. I saw Bobby Gabel offer her a hit off his joint. Ramona shook her head wildly. I thought for a moment she would climb into the wheelchair with Onyx.

"Anabel Rutland," Leah said suddenly. She took a pen and an address book from her oversized leather bag and copied a telephone number down from the Rolodex. "Anabel Rutland," she repeated, slowly and with apparent satisfaction.

"What about her?"

"I can hit her up for money."

I took a deep breath. Leah always was guided by an exact system of priorities. The possibility of a pledge from Anabel Rutland took precedence over the proposal I had tendered. Especially with all the escape hatches I had provided along with it. I knew she would call Anabel Rutland. She would begin by asking for ten thousand dollars. Ten thousand was always her starter figure with the rich. Within the realm of possibility, she would say. Best not to sound too greedy. She had adopted me as her guide in these matters. What's real money to the rich? she would ask. Usually in bed. A dollar ninety-eight, I would say. Talk of money always made me uncomfortable.

Leah concentrated on the Rolodex as if she had discovered a map of Treasure Island. She scribbled down names and addresses and telephone numbers. I looked out the window again. Another band was taking over on the tennis court. On the other side of the pool I spotted Leah's mother. She was sticking toothpicks into the canapés. Beatrice Maye was catering the party. Maye not Kaye. Her second husband was a man named Loring Maye. Who had succeeded Leah's father, Millard Kaye. Both were long since dead and buried. Neither loss had seemed to burden Bea with undue regret. Her maiden name was Faye. Which actually made her Beatrice Faye Kaye Maye. I would wager it was a combination of surnames that was not much discussed around the water cooler at The Justice Department. Bea was Leah's special cross. She was a party consultant in Beverly Hills. Her specialty was theme bar mitzvahs. A fact I had to worm out of Leah. With a quid pro quo. I told her what real money was and she told me about her mother. Leah tended to play down the Beverly Hills connection. Her mother still lived in Encino. In the same house where Leah had grown up. On a cul-de-sac called Wellesley Place. We had spent the night before at the house on Wellesley Place. All the cul-de-sacs in the development were named after eastern colleges and each one had a different kind of theme house. The houses on Yale Place were mock Georgian, those on Dartmouth Place mock Palladian. The house where Leah grew up was mock Tudor. She was tempted to regard my liking of Beatrice Maye as a hostile act. She was also furious with her mother for the way she had arranged to cater the party at Lottie's. What Bea had done was call Lottie's

public relations team and identify herself as the mother of Onyx
Leon's counsel. She offered to donate the food and her services if
she could cater the event. A pro bono cateress, I had told Leah.
She was not amused. Bea had also provided a reference. Buddy
Seville. Who was represented by the same public relations firm.
The Vegas headliner and telethon host. A man with his own golf
tournament and his own disease. Amyotrophic lateral sclerosis.
The H.O.P.E. Foundation was Buddy Seville's. For twenty-four
hours every Fourth of July the H.O.P.E. telethon helped raise
money for what Buddy Seville called "my gang." Bea said she
catered all of Buddy Seville's affairs. Both the private affairs and
the affairs for Buddy's gang. Her offer was accepted. A fait ac-
compli by the time Leah found out about it. Too late to hire another caterer. Bea was oblivious to her daughter's displeasure.
She thought the party at Lottie's should have a Mexican motif.
Miniature flautas and kosher tacos. The toothpicks would be
topped with red, white and green paper Mexican flags.

"Leah . . ."

Leah looked up. "Yes," she said.

"Yes what?"

"Yes, I think we should get married."

Bea saw me standing in the window. She waved one of her
toothpick Mexican flags. I had not mentioned to Leah that Bea
expected the fundraiser to generate a great deal of party business.
Doing it free was a good investment. Pluto Fahr was always giving parties, she had told me. Carlotta French had a number of
elegant dinner parties. And Martin Magnin. She would love to
cater one of Martin Magnin's premieres. I wondered if Leah
would let her cater our wedding. "I didn't expect it."

"Expect what?"

"Expect you to say yes."

"Nobody ever asked before."

"Nobody ever asked you to marry him?"

"Nobody ever asked me to marry him in the bathroom before."

She opened her leather bag and dumped the Rolodex in it.

"Leah, that's stealing."

"No, it's a gold mine." She looked surprised. "Where else am I
supposed to get Marlon Brando's telephone number? Big-deal lib-

eral. Let's see if he puts his money where his mouth is." She was belligerent in that way she always got when someone—especially if I were that someone—appeared to question her reasoning. She pointed to the other Rolodex. "It's not as if it's the only one she has." I knew my charge had disconcerted her. "And there's another one in the bedroom. I noticed it when we came in here."

"It still doesn't belong to you."

Leah zipped her bag shut. "Then I'll give it back." Her voice was clipped. "As soon as Ramona types out all the numbers. Does that satisfy you?"

I did not answer.

"And I'll tell Lottie I took it." This decision seemed to restore her equilibrium. "She won't be the first guilty liberal I've pushed around." She looked in the direction of the exercise room. "Just the first one with a rowing machine." Then she turned toward me. "What I don't need is a conscience."

Nor was it a role for which I felt suited.

She unlocked the bathroom door but did not open it. Instead she turned and leaned against it, contemplating me. "You're going to be a real pain in the ass to be married to."

The celebrity auction was Alex Fahr's idea. He was opposed to the idea of a fundraiser. Fundraiser qua fundraiser was the way he had put it at the strategy session at The Justice Department two months before. Onyx was not asked up from Hermosa for the meeting. Nor any of the Mexican leadership of the Central Valley Agricultural Workers Union. CVAWU. We can speak more frankly among ourselves, Alex had said. Onyx might cloud the issue. Muddy the waters. So to speak.

Cut the bullshit, Leah had said. You just don't think Mexicans can count.

I just don't think that Onyx is as familiar as he might be with cash flow, Alex said stiffly. You've got to realize the dynamics of the situation.

The dynamics of the situation are that we're broke, Leah said. CVAWU doesn't have a pot to piss in. We're looking at a thirteen-thousand-dollar-plus American Express bill we can't pay. We can't charge, then this strike is in the toilet.

My point exactly, Alex said. That's why this auction I'm proposing will put him in a more viable situation. Liquidity's what
we're looking for.

What's the matter with a simple fundraiser? Leah said.

With a fundraiser qua fundraiser, nothing, Alex said. As long
as you're Bobby Kennedy.

That sell-out artist, Harriet Hecht said.

With Onyx there's a small matter of who we can get, Alex said.

He was on the cover of *Newsweek*, Phyllis Emmett said. She
was at the meeting to take notes and pour coffee.

A fundraiser means putting a price on the invitation, Alex said,
ignoring Phyllis Emmett. A hundred dollars a ticket. A thousand
dollars a table. Onyx doesn't have that kind of pulling power.

Fucking liberals, Harriet Hecht said.

That's why the way to go is wine, cheese and celebrities, Alex
said. Pluto's a big draw. So is Carlotta French. I know someone
named Bobby Gabel who's really tuned in.

He produced *Fidel, Fidel,* Phyllis Emmett said. I made a novena for Che after I saw it.

Jesus Fucking Christ, Harriet Hecht said.

He can produce a lot of heavy hitters, Alex said.

What can we auction off? Leah asked.

A blowjob from Carlotta French, Harriet Hecht had said.

Leah and I got lost driving from her mother's house in Encino
to Lottie's in Bel Air. The night spent under Bea's roof had put a
cramp in Leah's disposition that was not improved by my leaving
the invitation in Encino. We drove into Bel Air through the West
Gate, up past haciendas and pastel Mediterranean palazzi. The
streets climbing into the hills were eerily empty. There were no
cars and no parking boys to indicate a party in progress. Leah was
fuming. At Bea as much as at me for not remembering the address. At dinner the night before Bea had said wasn't it interesting that Carlotta French lived in a house that once belonged to
Zsa Zsa Gabor. It was the kind of information that Bea had at her
fingertips and as always it threw Leah into an incendiary silence.
She did not speak during the latkes and apple sauce Bea had specially prepared ("It's her favorite, Jack, did my little girl tell you

that?"). If Bea noticed Leah's silence, she never let on. She chat-
ted with me about the wonderful job Buddy Seville was doing
with amyotrophic lateral sclerosis, he had raised ten million for
his gang at last year's H.O.P.E. telethon, perhaps he could host
a telethon for Mr. Leon, if Mr. Leon played golf he'd be a real
addition at The Buddy Seville Open in Las Vegas, Buddy's
been married seven times, is that more or less than Zsa Zsa,
Leah?

Leah sulked.

"Zsa Zsa," I said suddenly.

"Not you, too?" Leah said irritably.

I jerked the car around and backtracked down the hill, searching for the old woman I had suddenly remembered seeing only a
few moments before. I found her parked on the same side street
just off Sunset Boulevard. She was wearing a white straw hat
with sunglasses cut into the visor and she sat in a camp chair beside a battered Chevrolet. The red and white sign propped
against her car said, MOVIE STAR MAPS—FIND THE HOMES OF
YOUR FAVORITE STARS—ERNEST BORGNINE, BARBARA RUSH,
OTHERS. The map cost five dollars. Carlotta French was not
listed, but as I suspected her house was: 9292 Bel Air Road: "Former Mansion of Zsa Zsa Gabor."

For the first time that day Leah's irritation showed signs of
abating.

I wouldn't say she laughed.

Just smiled.

A parking boy took the car at the house. The *paparazzi* were
out in force. Sightseers and autograph hounds pressed close and
then abandoned us as not worth their while. We walked through
the polished oaken gate, past a sign that said, ATTACK DOGS ON
DUTY. At the front door, a young woman in a miniskirt checked
our names off the guest list, all the time moving to the beat of the
rock-and-roll music filtering through the open French doors leading to the tennis court. We were immediately engulfed by the
crowd. A moment later Leah was swept away. It was several moments before I spotted her with Alex Fahr. Alex was introducing
Leah to his father. Pluto Fahr was unmistakable. His face simply
stopped beneath his lower lip. It was as if his chin had not been

attached. His walleye seemed focused on the enormous breasts of
the blond woman against whom he was leaning for support.

"This is Pluto," Leah said when I finally made my way to her
side. "And Miss Bailey."

"Everyone calls me Boston," Miss Bailey said. "Say hi to Jack,
Pluto."

Pluto Fahr dropped his face between Boston Bailey's breasts.
"This is Hortense, this is Lavinia."

"Isn't he a scream?" Boston Bailey said. "He's always giving
my tits names. Marigold's my favorite . . ."

"I was just telling Pluto how much Onyx appreciates his help,"
Leah said.

"Onyx is the Mexican in the wheelchair," Boston Bailey
shouted into Pluto Fahr's ear. "The one with the sister that's the
hunchback."

A flicker of life appeared in Pluto Fahr's eyes. "Notre Dame."

"The Hunchback of Notre Dame," Boston Bailey interpreted.
"He's not as senile as people think." She removed Pluto Fahr's
white sailor hat and kissed the top of his bald head. "Are you,
sugar?" She fell into baby talk. "I put you to bed later, you can
kiss Marigold nighty-night-night."

Leah seemed struck dumb. From the front door, a voice
boomed, "Pluto." The owner of the voice elbowed past Leah and
me. He was wearing a blue sweat suit opened to reveal a miniature gold mezuzah on his chest. Pluto Fahr disappeared into his
arms.

"Buddy," Boston Bailey said. She introduced Leah and me to
Buddy Seville.

"One of the all-time greats," Buddy Seville said. "Put 'em up,
Pluto." He bobbed and weaved like a fighter and then pinched
Pluto Fahr on the cheek. Once again Pluto disappeared into Bos-
ton Bailey's bosom. "You taking good care of him, hon?" Buddy
Seville asked her.

Boston Bailey assumed the voice of a floor nurse. "He gives
very good head for such an old man."

"Isn't that swell?" Buddy Seville said. His eyes seemed to fill
with tears. "One of the greats," he repeated. "I used to be his
opening act. El Rancho Vegas. I was Buddy Singapore then." He

lowered his voice. "That was before his trouble. With the committee and all."

"I thought you were Sandy Cairo then," Boston Bailey said.

"How'd you know I was Sandy Cairo?" Buddy Seville said. "I can't even remember when I was Sandy Cairo."

"You told me," Boston Bailey said, lifting Pluto Fahr from between her breasts. She was enjoying the repartee hugely. Leah listened in silence. It was the first time I had ever seen her speechless. "When we were married."

"I was married to you?" Buddy Seville seemed genuinely surprised. He began snapping his fingers. "Wait a minute. Wait a minute. I remember the boobs. It's the name I'm having a little trouble with. Give me a little help, hon." A triumphant snap. "Miami."

"Boston," Boston Bailey said. "You were always naming yourself after cities. That's how I got the idea."

"Is that a fact?" Buddy Seville said. "Miami. How are you, Miami?"

"Boston," Leah interjected.

Buddy Seville paid Leah no attention. "You were my second wife, right?" he asked Boston Bailey.

"Fourth," Boston Bailey said.

"The Fontainebleau's in Miami," Pluto Fahr said suddenly.

"Is he sharp as a tack or is he sharp as a tack?" Buddy Seville said to Leah and me. He leaned close to Pluto. "Manny Federico was the headwaiter in the big room at the 'Blue, remember Manny, Pluto?"

"In Miami," Pluto Fahr said.

"You didn't give him a big tip, he'd have the waiters drop a tray in the middle of your act."

"Miami," Pluto Fahr said. He was starting to nod off again.

"He's in the joint now, Manny," Boston Bailey said.

"You know Manny?" Buddy Seville said. "I didn't know you know Manny."

"He introduced me to you, Buddy," Boston Bailey said reproachfully.

"What a swell thing for him to do," Buddy Seville said. "What's he in for, Manny?"

"Pimping."

"Is that a fact?" Buddy Seville gave Manny Federico's pimping conviction a moment of vigorous nodding, then grasped Pluto Fahr once more and tried to shake him awake. "What's this shindig for, Pluto? Indians? Or sickle-cell anemia?"

"Mexicans," Boston Bailey said.

"Mexicans." Buddy Seville began snapping his fingers again. I could almost hear the joke computer in his brain begin to whir. "Hey." He seemed to have the one he was looking for. "Why did God give Mexicans noses, Pluto?"

Leah said, "Why?"

"So they'd have something to pick in the off-season," Buddy Seville said. He paused, as if waiting for the applause in the big room at the 'Blue to subside, and then said, "I love Mexicans, they're beautiful people."

"Oh, Buddy, you're a riot," Boston Bailey said. She bent and shouted into Pluto Fahr's ear, "Buddy says it's so they can pick their noses in the off-season."

Leah started to say something, thought better of it, turned and walked away.

"Beautiful people," Buddy Seville repeated. If he had noticed Leah's departure, he gave no indication. "The president of Mexico's a very good personal friend of mine. Felipe somebody."

I drifted into the living room with the crowd. The walls were all white. Pieces of pre-Columbian sculpture filled the black lacquer bookcases. On an adjoining wall a Stella hung next to a Diebenkorn *Ocean Park*. The room was bisected by a marble reflecting pool. A number of half-eaten flautas were floating on its surface. Light as a feather was Bea's claim for her flautas. At least light enough to float, I thought. Which was not exactly the point of a flauta. On the far side of the pool I saw Phyllis Emmett, her face buried in a plate of hors d'oeuvres, hovering behind Carlotta French, who I knew she dearly wanted to meet. She's my favorite star, Phyllis Emmett had told me, she's so committed. Lottie paid her no attention. She looked distracted. She picked soggy flautas from the reflecting pool but had no place to drop them. Instinctively Phyllis Emmett offered her own plate. Lottie seemed to think she was one of the catering staff. She dropped more flautas onto the plate and then as peremptory as a mother superior she pointed Phyllis Emmett in the direction of the kitchen. I had to smile at Phyllis Emmett's sweet innocence. She held the plate as if it were Veronica's veil. An offering from Carlotta French herself. Who had deigned to speak to a mere postulant.

I searched the room for Leah. No luck. Someone bumped into me and spilled a glass of white wine all over my gabardine suit. "Sorry, man."

"That's okay, man," I said without conviction. I was sopping wet.

"Cool?" He was wearing a T-shirt that said, 10K RUN FOR PEACE.

"No, cold," I said, shaking the wine from my hand and trying to hide my irritation.

The man in the T-shirt stared at my suit. For a moment I thought he was going to offer to pay for the dry cleaning. "You the heat or something, man?"

I looked around and realized I was wearing the only suit in the room. Everyone else was expensively casual. Suede, buckskin, silk shirts, tinted glasses. No wonder he thought I was a cop. "No, I'm not the heat or something."

"Yeah, well," he said enigmatically. He returned to his conversation as if I were not there. His companion said, "I hear Lottie used the Yugoslavian army as extras on the picture."

"She fucked it," the man in the 10K RUN FOR PEACE T-shirt said. He positioned himself casually in such a way as to exclude me from what he was saying. The second man listened intently for a moment, then sneaked a quick look at me and said, "You're kidding, the fuzz?"

I moved slowly toward the French doors leading outside to the terrace. Rock music blared up from the tennis court. The living room was packed. People kept looking to see who had arrived. Kisses were blown and waves exchanged. I detoured into a conversation that did not stop when I barged in uninvited.

"You like the sound?"

"I like it," I said before I realized the question was not directed at me. The two men talking did not waste a glance on my interruption. They were too busy playing imaginary guitars to the music outside.

"I got the boys booked into Prague this summer. On the European tour. A gig in Budapest, too."

"It's cool?"

"You want to know how cool it is? They know how to say split the publishing in Czech. That's how cool it is."

"That's cool."

"You can say what you want about communism, but those boys know how to structure a deal."

"They're very creative dealwise in those places."

For a moment the crowd thinned. I turned away and saw Carlotta French on her hands and knees, a roll of paper towels beside her. Someone had stepped in the reflecting pool and tracked water across the rug. She rubbed at the stain but only succeeded in making it larger. I helped her up. We had been introduced but I thought she would only remember that I was someone who was somehow connected with all the people who were messing up her house. Her face was a study in perplexity. Then I saw why. Buddy Seville was descending on her. He planted kisses on both cheeks.

"This is Mr. Broderick," Lottie said. She patted her cheeks distractedly with the paper towels, as if to wipe off Buddy Seville's two kisses.

"Jackie, right?" Buddy Seville said.

"Close enough," I said.

"I never forget a face," Buddy Seville said. "Swell place you got here," he said to Lottie. He glanced behind a brocade drape and ran his fingers up and down the window molding. "Debugged?"

Carlotta French stared at him.

"A joint like this, you should get it swept every couple of weeks," Buddy Seville said. "I saw a couple of guys outside, I was coming in. Federal Strike Force. Taking pictures . . ."

Lottie suddenly looked ill. "Of whom?"

"You. Pluto. That Mex . . ."

I knew she had not counted on the Federal Strike Force. Not at a celebrity auction.

"Those babies hang around, you got to get the place swept,"
Buddy Seville said. "My joint in Vegas, it's swept every other
week. The place in the Springs, the joint in town here, the same
thing. You got a guy?"

Lottie fiddled with the roll of paper towels and shook her head.

"I know a guy," Buddy Seville said. "You know Jilly Frascati?"

Lottie nodded vaguely. Jilly Frascati was the aged former head
of one of the five New York families. He had retired to Las Vegas
after his release from the federal penitentiary in Atlanta in hopes
of dying in his own bed. "I know who he is."

"This guy sweeps Jilly's. You couldn't get a better reference
than that."

Lottie seemed stricken. Bad enough the Federal Strike Force
was outside the gate and strangers were dropping flautas in her
reflecting pool. She had not also expected to get a reference from
Jilly Frascati via Buddy Seville. Over her shoulder I saw someone
waving at me from the terrace. It was Bea. She seemed to have
cornered a thickset man with great half-moons of sweat under the
arms of his brown silk shirt. I eased myself past Lottie and Buddy
Seville, who was writing, on a damp paper towel, the telephone
number of the man who swept Jilly Frascati's.

"This is Mr. Magnin," Bea said when I got outside.

"Call me Marty." Marty Magnin grabbed my hand in almost
palpable relief and in a square dance move tried to slip by me and
away from Bea.

She blocked his exit. "I was just telling Marty about my specialty."

"Theme bar mitzvahs," Marty Magnin said carefully. "You
ought to get her to tell you about it."

Bea already had.

" 'Mr. Wonderful' is one of our biggest themes," Bea said. "Of
the traditional variety. Top hat, white gloves."

"That's very traditional," Marty Magnin said.

"You know the Sterlings?" Bea said. "He's Carlotta French's
accountant."

Marty Magnin stared blankly at her. "Larry," he said after a
moment. "Sure I know him. Larry Sterling." He seemed trying

to convince himself. "Sterling, Kolb and Finger." Now he
seemed to be on surer ground than he was on "Mr. Wonderful,"
however traditional. "They're very good business managers, one
of the best firms in town."

"I did their son's," Bea said. "Rancho Sheldon."

"Rancho what?" Marty Magnin said. His eyes were darting
from Bea to me. He had not expected a discourse on theme bar
mitzvahs at a celebrity auction for Mexican farm workers. He had
not even expected to meet any Mexicans. A cruise around the
yard, a little business with a couple of agents and a tax deductible
check to show his heart was in the right place—that was what was
on the agenda. Not Beatrice Faye Kaye Maye.

"Rancho Sheldon," Bea repeated. "That was the theme. The
invitations were miniature Stetsons. You know, like the cowboys
wear."

"What a . . ." Marty Magnin stumbled. Language seemed to
have deserted him. "What a . . ." He tried a third time. "What a
cute idea."

"We had a branding iron for table selection."

Marty Magnin looked at me accusingly. He wanted to blame
someone for being trapped with Bea and I was as good a candidate as any. "You heard about this?"

"Not this particular wrinkle."

"We branded the table on your hand. So you'd know where
you were sitting. Of course it all washed off. The napkins were
bandannas that were actually Wash 'n Dries."

"I missed that party," Marty Magnin said.

"We had the Bunkhouse table and we had the Corral table and
the Roundup table. The Chuckwagon was where we served the
food and there were these little PortiSans we decorated like out-
houses . . ."

"I'm sorry I wasn't there," Marty Magnin said. "I must've been
in London. I know him a long time, Larry." He sought a way out
of the conversation. "I use Gurnick and Gurnick . . ."

"Nanette Gurnick." Bea clapped her hands. "What a small
world. I did her bat . . ."

Marty Magnin looked miserable.

"A 'No, No, Nanette' theme. She's so pretty, Nanette. You
must've been there."

"I was in New York. At the Sherry. I sent her a check, I think . . ."

"She came in riding a white circus horse. You know what I did?"

Marty Magnin shook his head.

"I auditioned horses until I was absolutely sure I had the right one."

"You take care of all the details," Marty Magnin said.

"Right down to the pooper scooper," Bea said. "In case Nanette's horse had an accident."

"No shit," Marty Magnin said.

Onyx Leon said, "The average farm worker in Hermosa has seven children. The average farm worker in Hermosa lives in a house which he rents for fifty-five dollars a month . . ."

His amplified voice carried into Lottie French's library. I sat on an oatmeal tweed couch and watched a thin sharp girl named Quentin rolling joints. I had never seen anyone, not even Wendy Chan, roll joints so fast. There were already a dozen lined up on Lottie's beveled glass desk.

"That is gross," Quentin said.

"What's gross?" Bobby Gabel said. He untangled his angular frame from the chair where he had been sprawled, took a joint from the desk and lit it. He held it out to me. I shook my head.

"Living in a place that costs fifty-five dollars a month," Quentin said. She opened another packet of ZigZag papers and continued her manufacture. "You can't even get a place in the Valley for that."

Bobby Gabel looked at me and shrugged. "She's sixteen, man. What're you going to do?"

Onyx Leon said, "The average farm worker in Hermosa sleeps three and four to a room. He makes payments on his car if he has one. He makes payments on his refrigerator if he has one . . ."

I walked to the French doors and looked down on the tennis court. Onyx was sitting up with difficulty in his wheelchair. The hand that held the microphone shook, making his voice first too loud and then difficult to hear. Six or seven farm workers, unmistakable with their swarthy faces and dirty jeans and heavy wool checked shirts, clustered around the wheelchair, hanging on his every word. Some of the guests listened, most carried on with their conversations. I heard a piercing laugh, and then another.

Onyx Leon said, "Two-thirds of the families have no private flush toilets, less than one-third have community flush toilets . . ."

"Gross," Quentin said.

Bobby Gabel came close to my ear. "This is not the way to go, man."

"What's not the way to go?"

"Auctioning off tickets to Buddy Seville's opening in Vegas," Bobby Gabel said. He had a way of moving his head slowly whenever he spoke, to and fro, as if searching for the secret camera that might be recording his movements. "That kind of shit."

I did not disagree but I was not about to admit it to Bobby Gabel. "It's a start."

Onyx Leon said, "We work only eight months a year, they pay us only a dollar and ten cents an hour and they ask us, the *patróns*, why we risk a strike. They do not understand, the *patróns*, we are not that much worse off on strike than we are when we are working in their fields. In fact, we are better off because now we have our *dignidad* . . ."

"*Viva la huelga*," the farm workers gathered around Onyx chanted in unison.

"*Viva la huelga.*" The exuberant squeal was familiar. "*Viva la huelga.*" I tried to identify the voice. "*Viva la huelga.*" Then I saw Boston Bailey. She was standing next to Alex Fahr. Her arms were raised in exhortation. She seemed transported by the moment. La Pasionaria with breasts the size of watermelons. Alex did not take his eyes off them. "*Viva la huelga.*"

Buddy Seville was not to be outdone. "If the chick is for it, I can get behind it, too." He grabbed the microphone away from Onyx. "Let's hear it for the Mexican. *Viva* the Mexican."

Beside me, Bobby Gabel surveyed the scene. I had never seen anyone who could use languor to such studied effect. His voice was conspiratorial. "I know on good authority where there's heavy bread that can be made available."

I found myself falling into his speech rhythm. "Heavy bread for Onyx?"

He nodded.

"Where?"

"Ninety miles off the coast of Florida." I noticed his lips hardly moved when he talked. I wondered if it were a conscious effort to thwart possible lip-readers.

"Cuba?"

"Shhhhh," Bobby Gabel hissed. I felt as if I had compromised security.

On the tennis court, Buddy Seville would not relinquish the microphone to Onyx. "Listen, why did God give noses to Mexican people . . ."

"Who's this good authority you mentioned?" I realized with a start that I was whispering myself.

"The best." His eyes swept the room, empty except for Quentin, who was still rolling joints with metronomic efficiency at the desk. Then he leaned close and breathed into my ear, "Fidel."

"Fidel told you."

"He told a friend of mine. The friend got word to me. I don't want to go into how."

I think I said, "I dig," but I hope not. I hope it is only an aberrant memory. Over the years, Bobby always had a friend and the friend was always a friend of Fidel's. Or Ho's. Or Yasser's. Once Bobby told me he had talked to Carlos on the telephone. In Paris. I was staying at the Ritz, man. I get off on the contradictions. I pick up the telephone and this dude says, *Je m'appelle Carlos.* We were going to meet. In the Buttes-Chaumont. You ever been there? What a field of fire, man. No wonder he picked it. He didn't show. Bad vibes. A tap on my phone at the Ritz maybe. He trusts his instincts, Carlos. That's why he's lasted so long. I came through JFK on the way home. I got strip-searched. Up the ass even. It was like getting fist-fucked. I couldn't piss for a week.

"No fingerprints on the bread, man," Bobby Gabel said out of the corner of his mouth.

Buddy Seville had started to sing. "South of the border, down Mexico way . . ."

"Rancho fucking Sheldon," Marty Magnin said to me at one point later in the afternoon. "Theme bar mitzvahs. Who was that cunt anyway?"

"My mother," Leah said.

Marty Magnin was not even momentarily nonplussed. "Tell her she's got a great gimmick there."

I hear Bobby Gabel. "Names are such bullshit." He was discoursing on Malcolm X. "Malcolm had the right idea. I even thought of changing my name to Bobby G at one time . . ."

"I didn't know that," Quentin said. "Gee."

"Now I know why you didn't," Leah said.

Bobby Gabel acknowledged the remark with an ironic nod. A languid smile moved in sections across his face. "I know this chick, she named her kid Twenty-six Julio," he said. "I mean, that is something. That is a fuck-you name." He repeated it slowly, for effect, in case anyone failed to make the connection. "Twenty-six Julio."

"I bet she named it after Julio Lombard," Quentin said.

Leah considered Quentin for a moment. "Who is Julio Lombard?"

"Julio Lombard," Quentin said deliberately, not trying to mask her disdain for anyone who would ask such a question, "is the president of Mandala Records."

"I didn't know you knew Julio," Bobby Gabel said. Surprise did not come naturally to him.

"I don't actually know him, Bobby," Quentin said. "Actually I only met him today. But I've been with eight of his artists." She began to count them off. "Lee Dallas, Robbie Keegan . . ."

Lottie French took Leah away. A guest had a thousand-dollar-check for Onyx.

". . . Erik Sorkin, Jay Roberts," Quentin continued.

Her countdown was interrupted by the appearance of Ramona Leon at my side, tugging at my sleeve. "Hello, Jack," she said in that vowel-swallowing quick way that accented her otherwise perfect English. "Have you seen Leah?"

"Isn't she cute?" Quentin said. She got down on her haunches as if she were talking to a puppy. "I never knew a midget before. You're so cute." She began to chuck Ramona playfully under the chin. "Listen. I forgot to take my pill this morning. You wouldn't happen to have an extra Enovid, would you?"

Ramona clung to my sleeve.

"How many miles to Babylon, man?" Bobby Gabel said. He was perched on the side of Lottie French's desk, sucking on a water pipe. "Three score miles and ten . . ."

"Is Babylon in France or England?" Quentin said.

"Out of fucking sight," Bobby Gabel said.

I remember Jimmy Dana. "Hollywood," he said, "is where the shitheels come for the finals."

He was wearing a blue blazer and light gray slacks and a pink button-down shirt open at the neck. I think now the way he was dressed was the reason I was drawn to him that day. In that setting we both looked like creatures from another more conventional planet.

It occurs to me now that I met all three of them for the first time that afternoon on Bel Air Road. Marty Magnin, Bobby Gabel and Jimmy Dana.

And that Bobby and Marty and I were all at Jimmy Dana's funeral.

And that Jimmy's funeral was the same day Bro and Leah were killed.

The time bombs of memory.

Jimmy Dana said, "I think there's a great screenplay in Onyx, Marty."

"Who's Onyx?" Marty Magnin said.

"He's the reason we're here," I said.

"Oh, that Onyx," Marty Magnin said. He shook his head. "I don't think so. The elements don't mesh."

"Why not?" Jimmy Dana said.

Marty Magnin pointed toward a group of farm workers huddled at the edge of the tennis court. I had the sense there was a moat around them. No one approached. They were like an unpopular exhibit at a zoo.

"They've all got gold teeth, these Mexicans," Marty Magnin said. "I don't see thirty million worldwide for a bunch of fat people with gold choppers." He held up his hands. "Mind you, it's a good cause. I'm going to step up to the table. I just got to talk to my accountant first."

"Gurnick and Gurnick," I said.

"How'd you know that?" Marty Magnin said.

Jimmy Dana tried again. "It's a revolutionary movement, Marty. No one's ever organized the farm workers before."

"You say revolution, then maybe I'll go for a draft," Marty Magnin said. He patted a sweating brow with the sleeve of a silk shirt. "What's a revolution without a little tits and ass, right?"

"Right," I said.

"I see a bridge, I see the bridge blowing up, I see someone getting a little Latin pussy up on the hill when the bridge goes . . ."

"It's not that kind of revolution, Marty," Jimmy Dana said.

"Broad strokes for now," Marty Magnin said, brushing aside the objection. I could see how much he was taken by his own conception. "I don't want to get bogged down in details, that's what I hire a writer for . . ."

"It's a question of . . ." Jimmy Dana faltered.

"Taste," I suggested.

"Taste, what do you mean, taste?" Marty Magnin said. "I got perfect taste. You ever seen a single pussy hair in a picture of mine? Tits and ass, but never bush."

I wanted to tell Leah. It was a definition of taste I thought she might appreciate. Our life together was pitted with such misconceptions. I always had what she construed as a fatal tolerance for the frivolous. Then I heard the mournful strains of a guitar, all but drowned out by the rock music that had started again on the tennis court. I knew instantly who was playing. Aurelio Lira, one of the farm workers who had accompanied Onyx. I pushed through the crowd into the living room and finally saw Leah. She was staring across the room at Aurelio Lira. He stood in front of the Stella, a slender youth with delicate, almost effeminate good looks, plucking at the strings of his guitar and singing along softly, oblivious to the people around him:

> "Yo te suplico que vuelvas a querer
> A otro tirano que se burle de tu amor
> Dejalo triste y apasionado . . ."

I managed to catch Leah's eye. It was the same song Aurelio was playing that day weeks before when she and I went to bed with each other for the first time. Went to bed with. How Leah would disapprove of that construction. Fucked. I think at that moment there at Lottie's I decided to ask her to marry me. I started toward her and without looking stumbled into the reflecting pool. Water squished in my shoe, my trouser leg clung to my skin. Immediately Lottie was at my side with her roll of paper towels. Her patience had passed the snapping point.

"For God's sake, don't drip on the carpet," Lottie said.

"You asshole," Leah said pleasantly.

"I've got to talk to you," I said.

"It's a Persian fucking rug," Lottie said.

"Lottie, we need a Xerox machine," Leah said.

"I can't give a Xerox machine," Lottie said.

"Sell the rug," Leah said. "Onyx needs money."

"I'll go half," Lottie said. "Get Bobby to pick up the other half."

"Bobby's already picking up the American Express bill," Leah said. "That's twenty grand." I noticed she had upped the figure. "A Xerox machine is only four thousand."

"Jesus Christ," Lottie French said.

"That means yes," Leah said.

"That means get your boyfriend off the rug," Lottie French said.

"Well, what's on your mind," Leah said to me.

"First I want to dry off," I said.

We made it to the front hall. I tried the door of the bathroom. Quentin was inside with the man wearing the 10K RUN FOR PEACE T-shirt. She was cutting a line of coke. "This is Julio," she said. "Julio Lombard." And identifying me: "He's the one that's the friend of the midget." She inhaled the coke through a rolled-up bill, then passed it to Julio Lombard. I noticed that the bill was a hundred. "She's so cute, that midget," Quentin said.

Julio Lombard declined the cocaine.

"Now you're going to find out if I really am the heat," I said, closing the bathroom door.

"What was that all about?" Leah said.

"Local joke," I said.

The next bathroom was locked. We went upstairs. A bedroom door was also locked, and a second. There was raucous laughter

behind the second door. I knocked but no one answered. Empty
wine bottles littered the corridor and the table tops were scarred
with cigarette burns. I tried a third door. This one opened. The
room was in total darkness. The curtains were drawn, the air
conditioning icy. A crack of light under a far door. The bathroom. I took Leah by the hand. We bumped into a chair as we
made our way across the room. I saw a white sailor hat fall on the
floor. Pluto Fahr was sound asleep in the chair, his head lolling
against his chest.

He did not move.

For a moment I thought he was dead.

Then one eye opened. "The Fontainebleau's in Miami," he
said.

The eye closed again. Now I heard sounds from across the
enormous room. Heavy breathing, low moans. I tried to acclimate
myself to the dark. I finally made out the bed. And saw a pair of
generous white thighs pinned upright by a pair of heaving shoulders. The long legs attached to the thighs pointed straight up toward the ceiling. I recognized the gold sandals the woman on the
bed had not bothered to remove. "Oh, Alex," Boston Bailey said
to Pluto Fahr's son.

We made it to the bathroom. I locked the door behind us. A
comment seemed in order. Some sense of spurious outrage for the
record. "Jesus Christ," hissed through clenched teeth was the
best I could come up with.

"You don't have to whisper," Leah said equably. "It's only
Alex. And that number with the silicone tits. And the silicone
ass." She seemed totally indifferent. "I bet she's a silicone fuck,
too."

I don't know why I persisted. It certainly was without a great
deal of conviction. Perhaps I was having second thoughts about
my proposal. Perhaps I was stalling. "It's a fucking zoo."

"So what? It's useful."

How often she used that word. The most important one in the
pragmatist's dictionary. "Useful," I said, drawing it out. Sarcasm
was the rampart I so often retreated behind when I knew Leah
was right, however uncomfortable she made me.

"What's wrong with useful?" She began examining her face in

the vanity mirror. "Onyx's credit card bill's been taken care of and we're going to get a Xerox machine. That's nearly twenty grand right there. I'll watch Alex fuck to get that. And listen to that boob from Vegas. His money's good." A remark she immediately amended. Leah would not get too far out on any limb with Buddy Seville. "I think." She opened jars of cold cream and tested an eyebrow pencil against the back of her hand. "You know your trouble?"

I waited for her to tell me.

"Your sensibility's too refined." She stood up. For a moment I thought she was going to pee. Leah never regarded a leak as any reason to interrupt her tactical planning to improve the world. I wonder now what would have happened if she had. It occurs to me as I contemplate that moment how badly matched we really were. She believed in social engineering while I was really only interested in social nuance. Whether, for example, the direction of a life could be changed if someone took a piss. Perhaps with that sensibility she thought too refined I might have postponed my proposal had she hiked her skirt and peed. Perhaps another opportunity might not have arisen. Perhaps then she would be alive today. And Bro, too. But she didn't. She smoothed the wrinkles from her skirt and sat down again. "Now what is it you wanted to talk to me about?"

I sat on the bidet. "I think maybe we should get married."

III

EARLIER.

Hermosa.

Formerly Yerba Hermosa.

Beautiful grass.

Grass so high, when the range was open, it could be plaited over a rider's saddle. Then drought. Followed by vineyards, irrigation and civilization. VETS. LO DOWN. TERMS. FHA AVAILABLE. The grass went, and when it did, so also went the Yerba in Yerba Hermosa. The grape growers campaigned for a new name. Uva Hermosa. Beautiful grape. Uva Hermosa did not catch on.

Which left Hermosa.

As in beautiful.

Beauty in the eye of the beholder. Twenty-eight churches, four elementary schools, one high school, a general hospital with forty beds, a twice weekly newspaper, four banks, eight doctors, three dentists, three optometrists and two chiropractors. Rotary, Elks, the Slav Hall. Eleven bars, Mulligan's Restaurant, Pakula's Furniture, a Foster Freeze, a Burger King and a Waffle Iron. The Moonbeam Motel. No bookstore. Two movie theaters, the marquee on the more run-down advertising PELÍCULA—DOMINGO Y

LUNES. And out by the freeway that bisected the town, the Anglos on one side, the Mexicans on the other, two road signs embedded in the shoulder at the exits at either end of the city limits, one for cars driving north, one for cars driving south: TIRED? HUNGRY? CAR TROUBLE? NEED GAS? STOP IN HERMOSA.

"Whatever happened to that fellow, Jack?"

"What fellow's that, Burl?"

"That fellow Bro was talking about at the Grove. The colored fellow. You know the one I mean."

"He was executed."

"Just like Bro said he was going to be. That's wonderful. At least somebody's doing some goddamn thing right for a change. You never know these days. Wouldn't've surprised me if someone brought the son of a bitch up to the Grove as a guest."

"It's a changing world, Burl."

"And not for the goddamn best."

"I'm still telling that joke you told." We were sitting in the bar of the Slav Hall. The linoleum was worn through to the wood, the air conditioner wheezing at supercool. When we had come inside a moment earlier, the temperature on the digital thermometer on the Bank of America branch across the street was registering 113 degrees. Behind the bar there was a neon sign for Olympia beer, with the slogan, "It's the Water," blinking on and off. "At the Grove. When we were all there. You, me, Bro . . ."

"You hear the best goddamn stories at the Grove, Jack. That's what makes it worth going up there every summer. Which one was it anyway?"

"The one that goes, 'What's six miles long and travels four miles an hour?' "

"A Mexican funeral with one set of jumper cables," Burl Grgich answered without hesitation. "You remember that one, do you? That's some compliment, you being a writer. It's a hell of a story." He was built like a wine cask. His biceps were so thick that they had forced the notches on the sleeves of his white short-sleeve shirt. He owned nearly thirty thousand acres of farmland both in Hermosa and up and down the central valley. His father was ninety-three and still going strong, the first grower of Yugo-

slavian descent elected to the Bohemian Club, nominator of his
own son, who was the second. "God, I love the Grove."

"One set of jumper cables," I repeated appreciatively. Burl
Grgich had spent the afternoon driving me around his vineyards
in his pickup. There was a pump shotgun in the rifle rack in the
truck's rear window. We had sampled every variety of grape he
grew. Cardinals, Thompsons, Ribiers, Red Malagas, Emperors,
Almerias, Calmerias and Muscats, some tart and not ready for
picking. And with every bunch a short course both in the care
and feeding of grapes and in the economic chaos facing the
grower if Onyx Leon succeeded in organizing the pickers. I
learned it took five years to bring a vine into full production. I
learned that the productive life of a quality vine ranged from
twenty-five to thirty years. I learned about taxes and depreciation
and the capital investment in trucks and tractors and sheds and
sprinklers and box-making machinery and refrigeration systems.
He was a Yugoslavian and proud of it. A farmer and proud of
that, too. And in the marrow of his bones he believed that the
Mexicans picking his grapes took equal pride in his pride, and in
his entitlement as well. I listened and nodded and shook my head
and said, "Is that right?" and "I didn't know that" and "I'll be
goddamned," all of which only made Burl Grgich even more
forthcoming, and now I was repaying his openness by playing
him like a fish on a line. "See what those dumb jugheads down
there have to say," had been my father's last instruction before I
left for Hermosa. And to Hugh Broderick's son they had much to
say. All I had to do was listen sympathetically. The reporter's
deception. Give a little, get a lot. Speak the language. "You wonder how they think those damn things up," I said.

"You know who told it to me? Raúl Espinosa." Burl Grgich
eyed me peculiarly, as if suddenly realizing that under the circumstances a Mexican joke was perhaps not in order. "The labor
contractor."

"He must be a goddamn card."

"He is," Burl Grgich said with almost visible relief. "That's
why I love Mexicans. They tell great jokes on themselves."

"I knew a couple in the Marines like that," I lied. My service in
the Marine Corps was always good protective coloration in such

situations. Semper Fi. Nothing more trustworthy than a former gyrene. Especially in the bar at the Slav Hall. Watering hole of the Hermosa power elite. Dances twice a year, a growers' lunch on the second and fourth Tuesday of every month, membership limited to Slavs and those married to Slavs. Above the Oly sign on the bar was a gallery of small tinted photographs. Past presidents of the Slav Club. Planinc. Dragan. Srebic. Vukovich. Dizdarevich. Fira. Grgich, father and son. I had already been to the chamber of commerce. Of the thirty-eight ranches in Hermosa, twenty-nine were operated by Yugoslavians. There were sixty-one Dizdareviches in the telephone book, twenty-three Firas, fourteen Grgiches. Dumb jugheads. My father's verdict. "What does a fellow do for a drink around here?"

"What'll it be, Jack?"

"Dos Equis." The wrong brand to order, considering the prevailing paranoia on this side of the freeway. I felt like a secret agent who had lapsed for a single phrase into his native idiom in a hostile foreign land. By such transgressions is the infiltrator exposed. But I was a Broderick, and conditional absolution was granted.

"A Mexican beer," Burl Grgich said with heavy and trusting jocularity. "Anything for a laugh. Just like your dad." An evaluation of my father that made my head spin. "Whose side you on, anyway?" There was appreciative laughter at the bar, where my identity appeared to be known. Several men in open-neck short-sleeve shirts seemed to be waiting for a summons from Burl Grgich. It occurred to me that in Hermosa his holdings gave him the stature of a Hugh Broderick. "Give the man an Oly."

The bartender poured the beer. Ice crystals formed on the side of the glass. Time to bring up Onyx, I thought. Whom Burl Grgich had referred to throughout the long hot afternoon's reconnaissance of his vineyards as "this Onyx Leon." An effective and thoroughly punctilious construction. As dismissive as his repeated references to "this so-called strike." The code was there for me to use. I would be suspect if I didn't. "Tell me about this Onyx Leon."

"He's no more Mexican than your dad is, Jack. Him or his midget sister. They're from Cristo Rey." The significance of the revelation escaped me. "People from Mexico think people from Cristo Rey are nothing but niggers."

Vigorous nodding from the eavesdroppers at the bar. The formalities of the code still demanded my observance. "I suppose everybody's got to have a nigger, Burl."

"Goddamn right," Burl Grgich said, pumping a finger into my chest as if I had broken new theological ground. "You know the trouble with this so-called goddamn strike? Outsiders."

"I guess I never thought of it that way."

"Like that bird from Cristo Rey and his midget sister." I had noticed before on the Anglo side of Hermosa that Ramona Leon was never mentioned by name. It was as if her infirmity had taken on some satanic dimension and her very name had become a totem of darkness. "Can you imagine those two, trying to pass themselves off as Mexican?"

"That's really something."

"I knew you'd feel that way, Jack. It's about time someone told our side of the story. You get these so-called reporters up from Los Angeles. A bunch of goddamn fairy Trotskyites. Long-haired kooks. You tell them, some goddamn union moves in and takes over the food industry, there's no goddamn way this country can survive if that happens, they don't want to listen. They just want to know why I don't hand out bedding in my labor camps. No blankets, no pillows. They steal them, is why."

"I'll be goddamned."

"I'd be broke, all those goddamn blankets."

"I never thought of it that way."

"Bruno. Harry. Mike." Burl Grgich beckoned to the men at the bar. "Get over here." I was introduced to a Dizdarevich, a Mamula, a Pavlovic. "This is Hugh Broderick's boy." An introduction I had grown used to. I wondered about him. He was nearly my father's age and still introduced at the Grove as Milovan Grgich's youngster. "He's going to tell our side of the story for a goddamn change."

I chose my words carefully. "As you know, my father's getting hit just like you are . . ."

The floodgates opened.

"That thing at your sister's funeral . . ."

"That's what kind of animals these people are . . ."

"Outsiders . . ."

"Agitators . . ."

"That goddamn Jew lawyer . . ."

"One thing I know for a goddamn fact, and that's that my pickers don't want no goddamn union . . ."

"They've got a real fine relationship with us . . ."

"Really personal . . ."

"A union would destroy it . . ."

"What strike . . ."

"My people are working . . ."

"The true farm workers are in the fields working . . ."

"They can make a dollar seventy-eight an hour, piecework . . ."

"Happiest bunch of people you ever saw . . ."

"Typical Mexicans . . ."

"Happy-go-lucky . . ."

"They don't have a union, but they're in a top bargaining position . . ."

"Some only want to work for two weeks, some want to work two months . . ."

"That's the way these people are . . ."

"If my workers were unionized, they'd have shackles around their necks . . ."

"It's that goddamn midget . . ."

"Trotskyites . . ."

"That damn Jew . . ."

"This working one day and taking off two, that's the nature of these people . . ."

"A lot of my best friends are Mexicans . . ."

"Don't tell me about nonviolence . . ."

"I know for a fact, they bought four thousand marbles, they fire them at the workers in the field with slingshots . . ."

"In the fields, that's where your true Mexican is . . ."

"Milo Caratan, ask him about goddamn nonviolence. All his packing boxes were burned . . ."

"His people cried when that happened. All they wanted to do was work . . ."

"When my people are unhappy, they come to see me . . ."

"This isn't a strike, it's a revolution . . ."

"All those so-called Catholic priests . . ."

"I think they're Episcopalians in disguise . . ."

"They turn their collars around and pretend they are priests . . ."

"Goddamn outside agitators . . ."

"I own a ranch, not a voting booth. We can't have a ballot every morning, the Xs go to work, the Ys stay home . . ."

"This used to be a wonderful country . . ."

"Fulgencio asked me to be his son's godfather . . ."

"Where these people going to make more than a dollar seventy-eight an hour, answer me that . . ."

"You know what this Onyx Leon is trying to do? Replace my power structure with his . . ."

I took it all down. I said, "Let me get that straight" and "I want to make sure I have this right." Outside the novels of Mary McCarthy, I had never heard the name of Leon Trotsky invoked so often. I bought a round of drinks and when my turn came again, another. On his fourth boilermaker, Bruno Dizdarevich pulled a dog-eared printed announcement from his back pocket and smoothed it on the table in front of me. The mimeographed flyer was smeared with ink. NOW YOUR TOWN CAN HAVE A PROFESSIONAL RIOT, it said. No more "amateur" demonstrations. NAME YOUR CAUSE. WE WILL DEMONSTRATE. Riot kits. Press "service." We specialize in hand-picked hoodlums who can't speak English. All have passed the go-limp test.

Approval was unanimous. Bruno Dizdarevich beamed.

"That's the funniest goddamn thing I ever saw, Bruno . . ."

"I'd like to order up a thousand of those, Bruno . . ."

"Send them to every member of the legislature . . ."

"That bunch of clowns . . ."

"Send it to that Jew lawyer . . ."

"She can use it as toilet paper . . ."

"Send it to his midget sister . . ."

"What do you think of that, Jack?"

"Isn't that the funniest goddamn thing you ever saw, Jack?"

"I'll be goddamned," I said.

. . .

I was staying at the Moonbeam Motel. Burl Grgich dropped me off in his pickup.

"Aren't you married to Bruno Dizdarevich's sister?"

"Luka Dizdarevich. Bruno's cousin. I'm married to Luka's sister."

I noticed he did not mention his wife's name. She was Bruno's cousin. Luka's sister. Identity enough for a woman. Who was supposed to remain at home and docile. No wonder he could not comprehend Leah Kaye. "It's Sophie, isn't it, your wife?"

"Silvia."

"Of course. Luka Dizdarevich. I suppose he's a farmer, too." I realized I was being patronizing. Like all you Yugoslavians was what I meant. If Burl Grgich decoded the message, he took no offense. To him it was only a fact.

"In Tulare," he said.

"Grapes?" It was a tic, this quest for meaningless information.

"Alfalfa."

"Really."

"I don't have a goddamn thing in common with him," Burl Grgich suddenly volunteered. It was as if the battering ram of my hearty interest had finally at the end of a long day caused an indiscretion. "Not a goddamn thing."

"Why's that?"

"He's in alfalfa, I'm in grapes." He made it sound as if it were the most natural reason in the world for two people not to get along. "I got nothing to say to the son of a bitch."

I nodded profoundly, as if I understood. He nodded back, as if he thought I did.

We shook hands and I got out of the pickup. I waited until he pulled out of the parking lot and then walked slowly and deliberately toward the ice and vending machines in the small service alley between the two buildings of the motel. In the darkness where I could not be seen and where I had a clear view of the lot and the surrounding streets, I drank a can of Coke and waited for ten minutes. When I was sure that no one was watching, I got in my car and headed west across the freeway, all the while checking my rearview mirror to see if I were being followed. A week in Hermosa and I was acting like a spy, trusting no one and equally sure I was not trusted in turn. Capitalist cocksucker was Harriet Hecht's verdict, and it seemed the prevailing opinion among the Anglo volunteers at the farm workers' headquarters on the west side of town. Only Leah seemed willing to give me the benefit of the doubt and I thought I knew the reason why: if I were a spy, she thought I could be turned and run by her.

In the moonlight, the west side of Hermosa looked not that much different than the more affluent east. But after a week my eyes had adjusted to the fact that the freeway was a social as well as a geographical line of demarcation. It was not just that the skins of the people on the west side were darker. The bungalows were shabbier, the cars older. Occasionally a drainage ditch was exposed and there were more potholes in the street. Just west of the Southern Pacific tracks was a strip of lo-ball and draw poker parlors. Octavio's Four Deuces. The Tampico Flush. Club Mazatlán. My first night in town I had felt some misplaced reporter's obligation to sample opinion on the west side. My Spanish, although confined to the present tense, was serviceable, and in the Tampico Flush I had asked an old migrant field hand in a sweat-stained straw field hat what he thought of the situation in Hermosa. Without hesitation, he had replied, "This used to be a good town before." A number of draft beers later he explained he meant before the construction of the freeway had leveled the red-light district. The strike, in his opinion, was only a further and somewhat anticlimactic step in the decline of Hermosa.

I had told the story to Burl Grgich.

A way to establish my bona fides.

In the event that being Hugh Broderick's son and heir to his Hermosa acres was not enough.

I had not told the story to Leah.

I turned down the street just past Club Mazatlán, making sure one last time that I was still not being followed. Onyx Leon's headquarters was a faded, shell-pink bungalow where the pavement ended and a dirt road continued. One window was boarded up. Blown out by a shotgun blast from an unidentified passing car the second night of the strike. Ramona Leon had been alone in the house. The shotgun pellets had blasted the plaster two inches above her head. She was alive by virtue of being a midget. Onyx

Leon's midget sister. They shot it out themselves, Burl Grgich had told me. It was a way to get sympathy, he had insisted. The cinder-block walls of the bungalow were peppered with buck-shot. Another attempt at sympathy, according to Burl Grgich.

Who had said the real Mexicans were in the fields working.

There was a light on in the bungalow. And pinned to the front door a paper reproduction of the CVAWU's flag—a red field with the single word HUELGA.

A goddamn Trotsky flag, Burl Grgich had said. The American flag isn't good enough for them.

A dog began to howl. Immediately my car was surrounded by shadowy figures who seemed to have materialized from nowhere. Two of them were carrying baseball bats, which they kept tap-ping against the windshield, rat-a-tat-a-tat-tat, as if it were a drum. I cut the engine and kept both hands in sight until the front door of the house opened a crack and Ramona Leon peeked out. "He's okay, he's okay," she shouted as she ran toward the car on her tiny legs, and when I unlocked my door, she said reproach-fully, "You should always call first, Jack."

"Sorry, Ramona."

Leah did not even look up from the work she was doing when we came into the house. It was as if she were oblivious to the commotion of my arrival. A reception I was not unfamiliar with. One accorded to a capitalist cocksucker. The interior of the bun-galow was a dusty chaotic shambles of plywood partitions and battered desks. On the floor next to the mimeograph machine, Aurelio Lira sat picking at his guitar, murmuring as if to himself, "... *A otro tirano que se burle de tu amor.*" His faded blue work shirt was unbuttoned to the waist, revealing a smooth, thin, brown hairless chest. A pair of black rosary beads hung from his neck. Ramona handed me a cup of coffee. Aurelio Lira refused one, shaking his head, not interrupting his lament: "... *Dejalo triste y apasionado.*" I took a chair and put my feet up on a desk. On every available inch of wall space there was a profusion of area maps, survey photographs, telephone numbers and picket instructions. Strewn around the office were tattered copies of the Sears, Roebuck catalog and, for reasons I did not understand, old issues of *Coed* magazine. In that office earlier in the week, I had happened upon a hefty Mexican woman with most of her teeth missing, her head buried in a *Coed* article called, "How to Act on a Double Date." "What is tipping?" she had asked, and then reading laboriously, "Bring your coat to the table. Tipping is expensive."

Another story I told Burl Grgich.

Although I did not tell him the reason the fat woman was in the CVAWU office was to give an affidavit swearing that one of his field foremen was charging pickers twenty-five cents for every cup of water they drank.

Nor did I tell him the affidavit stated that the cup was an empty beer can.

An empty Oly can.

And that sixty-seven of his pickers had to drink from that same empty Oly can.

Or that his foreman had made $34.75 selling water in just a single day.

Leah had given me a copy of the affidavit. Something else I neglected to tell Burl Grgich.

Leah who had finally decided to acknowledge my presence in the office. "I bet you liked the son of a bitch."

"I've known him for a long time."

"I bet you have." She propped her feet up on the desk next to where Aurelio Lira was sitting on the floor. He busied himself with the strings of his guitar. I had the sense that it was an act of will for him not to look up her skirt. "So what do you have to say?"

"About what?"

She gestured impatiently in the general direction of the east side of Hermosa. "About what's going on over there?"

"Nothing."

"Nothing, or nothing you're going to tell?"

I shrugged.

Aurelio Lira struck up another chorus, louder this time, his ear almost touching the guitar.

"Aurelio, for Christ's sake, shut up," Leah said. He looked stung, then stared angrily at me, as if I were responsible for the reprimand. I returned the stare. I had heard the rumor that he

had replaced Alex Fahr in Leah's affections. At least when Alex
was not in Hermosa. Which was most of the time. He was always
on the road. Raising money. Promoting support from other
unions. Burl Grgich had heard the stories about Aurelio Lira, too.
She's doing it with a Mexican, he had told me that afternoon. The
one with the guitar that looks like a fairy. They're so goddamn
immoral, those goddamn people. "Ramona," Leah said, "is that
truck from Los Angeles unloaded yet?"

"Not quite, Leah."

"Aurelio, go help unload that truck."

Aurelio Lira slung the guitar on his back sulkily and with great
deliberation tucked his shirt into his jeans, as if he were waiting
for the order to be rescinded. When it was not, he stopped at the
back door and ran a comb through his hair. A mating call that had
no effect whatsoever on Leah. As opposed to Ramona. Who
looked as though she would have liked to bronze the comb.

"Move it or lose it, Aurelio," Leah said sharply.

He slammed the door behind him. For the first time I realized
that Onyx was not in the office. Which was not all that surprising.
It was no secret at strike headquarters that he did not like the way
Leah ordered him around. Ordered him around in front of Ramona, ordered him around in front of the strikers, worst of all
ordered him around in front of the Anglo volunteers. He complained to Leah that they smoked dope and were promiscuous
and that a number of male volunteers wore flowers braided in
their pigtails. He was particularly offended by Harriet Hecht and
the latest instruction on her T-shirt: TRY BI.

"Where's Onyx?"

"In San Francisco," Ramona Leon blurted out. "With Alex,
Jack."

Sweet Ramona. For a moment I thought Leah was going to
flash at her. It was apparent she had not wanted me to know that
Onyx and Alex were in San Francisco. She took a deep breath
and then a second and finally she said, "They're talking to Harry
Bridges."

"Why?"

"Trying to get a commitment from the longshoremen not to
load Hermosa grapes."

"Will he play?"

"It looks that way."

"That's news."

"It's also a goddamn secret," she said, her anger suddenly no longer in check. "A secret I don't want you to repeat to your pals over there on the east side."

She had a talent for being offensive, but I let it go. Outside, Aurelio Lira had begun to play his guitar again, serenading those he was supposed to be helping unload the truck full of food and provisions for the strikers. "*Yo te supplico que vuelvas a querer . . .*"

Leah listened, and then said irritably, "Where's that truck from, anyway?"

Ramona shuffled the papers of the manifest. "Saint Margaret Mary Alaocque's parish in Long Beach." Her smile offered a blessing to the parishioners at Saint Margaret Mary Alaocque's. "Canned food. Carnation powdered milk. Spaghetti-Os." Ramona looked up from the manifest. Her brow was furrowed. "Spaghetti-Os are not part of the normal diet for Mexican people, Leah."

Leah bit off her answer. "Then starve."

"I'm sorry, Leah, that's not what I meant," Ramona answered in some confusion. "We should be very grateful." She returned to the papers on her clipboard, reading so rapidly the words stumbled over one another. "Two cases of Dole's fruit salad, four cases of Sugar Pops, a case of capers . . ." Again she questioned Leah. "What are capers, Leah?"

"Jesus Christ."

"A case of sardines . . ."

"Jesus H. Christ."

"A case of Angostura bitters . . ."

"Jesus fucking Christ," Leah said.

"Maybe we can trade it," Ramona said hopefully.

"To whom?" Leah said. "The bakeries here won't even give us their day-old bread." She directed her bitterness toward me. "That's the doing of that son of a bitch Grgich. He told the bakeries, they give us day-old bread, they're through, finished, no one will do business with them. Day-old bread. For strikers. Who don't have enough to eat." She flicked her forefinger at me, as if it

were a bullwhip. "Who will drink the goddamn Angostura bitters. Because it's better than starving."

I listened. There was no comment that would suffice.

"He also told the doctors—all eight in town—he told the doctors not to treat any strikers as patients." The words came in
short gulps of breath. "It's very neat the way they do it. No violation of the Hippocratic oath. Nothing like that. Nurse comes
out. Nurse says doctor's not taking any new patients. Nurse says
doctor already has more patients than doctor can handle." Her
hand grasped the platen handle of the typewriter on the desk in
front of her so tightly that her knuckles turned white. "Fuck doctor." She spat the words out. It was as close as I had ever seen her
come to losing control. After a moment, she regained her compo-
sure. "Ramona, what are the food requirements for next week?"

"Just a minute, Leah." Ramona scurried to another desk and
grabbed a manila folder, which she opened and began to read.
"Two hundred pounds of tortilla flour, one hundred pounds of
dry red beans, one hundred pounds of pinto beans, two hundred
pounds of potatoes, fifty pounds of coffee, fifty cases of canned
fruits and vegetables and enough powdered milk or canned milk
for four hundred fifty children."

Leah did not take her eyes off me throughout Ramona's recital.
Aurelio Lira was still playing outside. Finally Leah said, "And
that son of a bitch . . ."

"What son of a bitch?"

"Your pal . . ."

"What pal?"

"Your pal from Bohemian Grove. That pal. That son of a bitch.
Grgich. He says no one is out on strike. He says the real Mexicans
are in the fields working. He says if they wanted a union they
wouldn't be working. What do you say about that?"

Ramona Leon positioned herself between us, like a referee in a
prizefight.

"I'd say he doesn't get along with his brother-in-law."

An answer she wasn't expecting. An answer that just for a second made her hesitate. "Why?"

"He's in grapes. His brother-in-law in Tulare's in alfalfa."

She let her hand rest on Ramona Leon's shoulder. "So what?"

"So if he doesn't think he's got anything in common with his brother-in-law, who's a farmer, then he sure as hell has even less in common with Onyx." I paused. "Let alone you."

I saw Aurelio Lira peeking through the window. He did not miss a beat. ". . . *Dejalo triste y apasionado.*"

Ramona Leon wiggled her fingers at him. Leah did not remove her gaze from me. "You think I needed you to tell me that?"

I wanted to say, I think you need someone to tell you this is going to be rougher than you think, but discretion ruled. I knew Leah well enough by now to know how she would have calibrated her answer.

Don't patronize me, you son of a bitch.

Something on that order.

Aurelio played.

I said, "Good night, Leah."

Ramona said, "Good night, Jack."

"Good night, Ramona," I said.

IV

I SLEPT WITH LEAH for the first time two weeks later. In our joint recollections, the event was of more significance to me than it was to her. What I remember first is the heat. And the way the beads of sweat glistened on Leah's upper lip when she slept afterward. I remember the dark brown freckle on the pale pink aureole of her left breast and I remember that her toenails were painted a deep burgundy and that the polish had neither cracked nor peeled. I remember that I went down on her and she went down on me and that I explored her with my big toe. I remember the sheets were gray with grime and crusted with the effluvia of other matings of other people. There was a large hole in the cheap cheesecloth curtains in the window and I remember I could see the foothills of the Sierra through that window. The cottage belonged to Harriet Hecht. She had rented it so that the volunteers could smoke dope far from the disapproving gaze of Onyx and talk revolution and fantasize (Leah would tell me later) about the number of Molotov cocktails it would take to set fire to Burl Grgich's sheds or whether it would be a more meaningful statement to blow up the Slav Hall. I remember that Harriet Hecht's diaphragm, in a blue plastic case monogrammed H.H. and well-dusted with cornstarch, was in the same drawer in the bedside table as a paperback copy of Frantz Fanon's *The Wretched of the Earth*. And I remember most of all that Leah, in the heat of passion, was pricked in the ass by a pin lost in the folds of the sheets, a pin—one of many made up by Harriet Hecht—that said, PROMISCUITY IS REVOLUTIONARY.

Leah chose not to remember that.

She remembered instead a day full of the kind of activities attendant to protest that had a higher priority than one of the two or three thousand couplings of an active sex life.

She remembered it as the day Phyllis Emmett was arrested on the picket line the strikers had set up outside Bruno Dizdarevich's No. 2 Ranch.

She remembered that Harvey Fletter was the sheriff of Hermosa County.

Remembered that Harvey Fletter himself, and not one of his deputies, had arrested Phyllis Emmett.

Exactly the way she had planned it.

She remembered that Hugo Dizdarevich, Bruno's oldest son, had buzzed the picket line in his father's Cessna Commander, buzzed so low that the picketers went flying like tenpins, so low the Cessna clipped a wire from a utility pole when it climbed and banked to come around again.

Leah remembered that the identification number stenciled on the wings of the Cessna Commander was OH-21C.

Remembered because Harvey Fletter said he hadn't seen any damn identification number on any damn wings.

Remembered because Harvey Fletter said it was no big damn deal.

Nothing to get your balls in an uproar about. If you had balls. Which you don't. So you can't. If you get my damn gist.

So don't you go making any big damn fuss now, Harvey Fletter had added.

That was when Harriet Hecht threw a brick at Harvey Fletter.

Which led to her arrest.

And a night in the Hermosa County lockup.

Leah had not planned on that.

But it did mean that the cottage in the foothills of the Sierra was vacant that night.

Leah had the extra key.

She just did not remember that the day Phyllis Emmett was arrested was also the day we first fucked.

Are you sure?

Absolutely.

I would have thought Oakland. My place.

Wrong.

Not your place on Green Street?

You never liked to spend the night at my apartment on Green Street. You said the water was too hard, you couldn't wash your hair. Believe me. It was that cottage that Harriet Hecht rented. In Three Rivers. And it was the same day Phyllis Emmett got busted.

That dumb bastard.

What dumb bastard?

Harvey Fletter.

"That dumb bastard will walk right into this one," Leah said in Onyx's office the morning that Phyllis Emmett was arrested. Outside it was still dark. The first tendrils of dawn were just snaking across the horizon. Leah had been in the office since before three. There were dark circles under her eyes. The powdered cream in her coffee had congealed and the whole mess was leaking through the soggy Styrofoam cup onto her khaki skirt. She paid no attention. She was also wearing a navy blue polo shirt and around her shoulders a green cardigan buttoned at the neck to ward off the night chill the sun would soon burn off. There was no more coffee. Someone had left the hot plate on all night and it had burned a hole in the bottom of the pot. Ramona Leon said it was her fault, she should have remembered to unplug the hot plate, she did it every night, she didn't know why she forgot last night, maybe because she was so nervous about what was going to happen this morning, that had to be it. No one paid any attention to her, not even Onyx, but Ramona kept right on talking. She said the 7-Eleven did not open until eight o'clock. She said when the 7-Eleven opened she would go buy a new coffeepot. She said she would pay for it herself. Aurelio could go with her. She said the 7-Eleven was on the east side and she did not like going to the east side alone. She said that was why she wanted Aurelio to go with her. She said she would also buy a new can of coffee. She said the Yuban was too bitter, maybe she would switch to Maxwell House. Or Chase & Sanborn. She said she would get a jar of instant, too. For Onyx. Onyx preferred instant. She said Onyx also preferred Sweet 'n Low. She said sugar was bad for Onyx's back.

"You can count on it," Leah said.

Onyx did not seem convinced.

He was slumped in his wheelchair, his right leg propped on the stool Ramona had provided for him. The herniated disk in his back was acting up again. A long time later Leah would tell me that Onyx always took to his wheelchair when he didn't want to do something. It was a way to elicit sympathy and support, she said. It makes him feel like Franklin D. Roosevelt. Judging people harshly came as naturally to her as breathing. "I do not understand why we are doing this thing, Leah," Onyx said.

"Because it's a test case, Onyx," Alex Fahr answered, enunciating with the kind of precision one lavishes on slow learners. I would not have been surprised if Alex had a supply of cookies in the jacket pocket of his tan poplin suit and intended to give one to Onyx once the lesson was mastered, with a bonus cookie to Ramona as well. He sneaked a glance at me. I knew he still could not understand why Leah permitted me to be there. I wasn't really sure about that myself. Perhaps she thought I had a certain value as a reliable witness. More likely she was simply indifferent to my presence. In any event, she never felt the slightest need to explain her actions to Alex whatever the circumstance. An attitude she would subsequently take with me. Alex looked at me again, as if trying to will me to disappear, and then in that elocution teacher's voice said, "The sheriff has an injunction against our people shouting 'Huelga' on the picket line . . ."

"That pig cocksucker can't do that," Harriet Hecht said, looking belligerently around the office as if daring anyone to contradict her. She was still aggrieved that Leah had selected Phyllis Emmett rather than her to be arrested that morning. "Not even in fucking Hermosa County."

Onyx flinched.

"Onyx, you want the decaffeinated, don't you?" Ramona asked.

Onyx ignored her.

"We just want to see how far this gets in court," Alex said.

Leah watched. I knew her mind was made up. She was going ahead, Onyx or no Onyx. Onyx's permission was only window dressing. She knew he would give in, he always did, but for the moment she would play no further part in coaxing him.

"Because it's unconstitutional," Alex said.

"Don't bet on it with this fascist fucking court," Harriet Hecht snarled. For a change there was no writing across the front of her white T-shirt. A new restriction imposed by Leah in an attempt to mollify Onyx. The kind of revolutionary cant and sexual theology that could be reduced to a T-shirt billboard seemed to upset him as much if not more than the refusal of the growers to even acknowledge the existence of the strike. Harriet Hecht had complied grudgingly with Leah's order. Although not, I noticed, to the point of wearing a bra beneath her T-shirt.

"Aurelio, I think we should get him the Maxwell House," Ramona said. Aurelio Lira, his guitar strapped across his back, seemed mortified at the way he had been preempted by Ramona. He tried to move away from her, but she clung to his heels, reciting her itinerary and shopping plans at the 7-Eleven.

"But I think I should be the one who is arrested," Onyx said. He tried to pull himself up in the wheelchair as if to assume command stature. "I am the leader of the union."

Leah caught Alex Fahr's eye.

"You're too valuable right here, Onyx," Alex said smoothly. "We need you to talk to the media when the pigs move in."

"Then it should be a Mexican who is arrested," Onyx persisted. "A farm worker. Who is out on strike. Because he believes in his union. This is our strike. I do not understand."

"What don't you understand?" Alex Fahr was becoming peremptory.

"Why the fat girl is the one who will be arrested."

I looked around quickly for Phyllis Emmett. She had not yet arrived. I knew she went to Mass every morning at six-thirty. A secret she shared only with me. Because I had the good fortune to be Father Augustine's brother. She told the other volunteers she was jogging. She would have been consumed with embarrassment to hear herself described as "the fat girl." And then because of her essential sweetness she would have said, Onyx is right, I am a little overweight, no, don't mince words, *fat*. I'll have to say a novena for Onyx, she would have said, he'll think he hurt my feelings.

Onyx said, "Why not Ramona?"

Harriet Hecht stage-whispered, "Is he fucking kidding?"

Ramona seemed not to hear that her brother was proposing her for arrest. "Aurelio, maybe we should make a list so we don't forget anything."

Onyx reconsidered Ramona. "Or Altagracia Guerrero?"

"The reason, Onyx . . ."

"Mariano Figueroa. Cecilio Nava. Pascual Soto. Pascual speaks very good English . . ."

"You don't understand, Onyx," Alex Fahr said. "The reason is . . ."

"Pascual was born in Hermosa . . ."

Leah checked her watch. It was now light outside. I could see she was beginning to lose her patience. For the first time she seemed to notice the coffee stain spreading over her skirt. Irritably she flicked at the spot with her fingernail. Then she cleared her throat and when Alex looked over she tapped the face of the watch.

Alex nodded. "The reason . . ."

"His wife speaks English, too. Jalisca. Although not so good as Pascual. But she is very pretty, Jalisca. She has had four children, but she is not fat like the fat girl. She only looks like she had two . . ."

Alex tried again. "What I'm trying to say, Onyx . . ."

"And she's very polite . . ."

"The reason . . ."

"Everyone likes Jalisca . . ."

That was enough for Leah. "Let's get to the point," she said sharply. "The reason is she used to be a nun. She still looks like a nun . . ."

Alex nodded theatrically in my direction, but Leah did not take her eyes off Onyx.

"She'll look like a nun when she's arrested, she'll look like a nun in court, she'll look like a nun on television." She paused. Everyone in the room was looking at her. Moistening a forefinger, she rubbed deliberately at the spot on her skirt. The moment was hers. When she finished, she looked up, as if surprised that all activity had stopped while she concentrated on her dry cleaning. "That's the battlefield, Onyx." She waited for the words to sink in. "A former nun gets more airtime than Jalisca Soto."

Onyx started to speak, then sank back into the wheelchair.

Alex Fahr said, "What Leah means, Onyx . . ."

"Leah doesn't need a translator," she said pointedly.

Alex flushed.

"You understand, Onyx?"

"I understand, Leah. It's just . . ."

"She used to be a nun and she's not a Mexican."

She was twenty-seven that summer, almost twenty-eight, seven years out of Berkeley, where she had been on the rush committee at Delta Phi Epsilon, the second-best Jewish sorority (the best was Alpha Epsilon Phi, but A E Phi had not invited her back the second night, she once told me with that unequivocating candor that always made me vaguely uncomfortable, which of course was the reason for the candor in the first place, uneasiness being something she might exploit if it were to her advantage to do so), four years out of Boalt Hall, where she had not made the law review. She was a virgin when she arrived at Berkeley, losing her virginity during halftime of a basketball game between Cal and Oregon. She remembered it was halftime because she was listening to the game, in which she had no interest, on the radio in Lee Dutton's apartment on Ridge Road. Lee Dutton—the same Lee Dutton who would become the rock-and-roll-loving manager of the Berkeley branch of the Western Bank and Trust—put his hand on her breast the moment the first half ended and they undressed and consummated the act on the Murphy bed in his apartment in plenty of time for them both to shower and enjoy the second half in its entirety. She remembered the final score was Golden Bears 65, Ducks 62.

In short, an entirely conventional background. She resigned from D Phi E on a matter of principle at the end of her junior year when a movie producer's daughter from Holmby Hills was

blackballed for wearing pink rather than white gloves to a rushing
tea, but not even in the broadest sense of the term could this be
described as a political statement. In fact it was only an excuse to
move out of the Delta Phi Epsilon house, she told me after we
were married. She had come to despise the restrictions of sorority
life, especially the chatty homilies of the housemother who called
sanitary napkins "sannies" and asked regularly if the curse were
perhaps a little late this month. She wanted no more of mixers
and date nights and open houses and faculty desserts and wished
instead to move into the off-campus apartment of the latest of Lee
Dutton's successors. I should also add that the movie producer's
daughter became in time an assemblywoman in the California
legislature who in her fundraising appeals constantly assailed
Leah as a "butch handmaiden of international terrorism." It is a
testament of sorts to Leah's success that the use of her name became a standard feature of this kind of literature, a name guaranteed to loosen the purse strings of the paranoid and the niggardly.

During law school she spent a summer in Mississippi with
SNCC. She was an early member of SDS. She fasted for civil
rights and picketed for civil liberties and marched for nuclear disarmament. She ran a mimeograph machine. She stamped letters
and compiled mailing lists. In a generation awakening to the possibilities of political action, there was nothing extraordinary in
this curriculum vitae. Nothing to indicate her instinctive familiarity with the techniques of protest or the habit of command she
assumed so naturally it might have been passed to her by the law
of primogeniture. I think no one was more aware than Leah herself that her past offered so few clues to her present. Years after
we divorced, she let Bro persuade her, against her better judgment, to give a statement to the oral history project at Fritz Finn's
presidential library at Princeton, a statement meant to define and
elaborate upon her years in the trenches of protest. (It is incum-
bent upon me to note here that Bro, to Fritz's extreme irritation,
successfully sidestepped every request to be interviewed for the
project. His taped observations on the Finn years are stored with
the rest of his papers and memorabilia in The Augustine Broderick Collection at Harvard.) When I discovered Leah's tape
after she died, Fritz ordered that I be given a copy, and some-

times I play it now just to hear the sound of her voice. I quote it in full:

"My name is Leah Kaye. My mother's maiden name was Beatrice Faye. My father was Millard Kaye, my stepfather Loring Maye. My mother caters theme bar mitzvahs. I am a lawyer. I have no great revolutionary ideas."

That was it.
Nothing else.
—30—
A self-portrait by a butch handmaiden of international terrorism.

She was not given to introspection. What she knew how to do, she did.

She knew when she arrived in Hermosa that she would need two-way radios and borrowed them from SNCC. She put some radios in the cars she dispatched before dawn to discover what fields would be worked that day. She knew the signs were packing boxes stacked by the side of a road or a foreman's pickup parked down a lane. She kept a roving picket caravan on the road ready to be radio-dispatched whenever the scout cars reported a work crew picking in a vineyard. She knew how the various growers reacted to the pickets. She knew that Bruno Dizdarevich or one of his sons flew over Hermosa in his Cessna Commander and she knew he moved his crews when he spotted a picket caravan heading toward his fields. She knew that Jack Pavlovic had his foremen play their car radios at top volume so his pickers could not hear the voices on the picket line. She knew that Burl Grgich drove spraying machines down the edge of his property line, shooting insecticides and fertilizer at the pickets.

Her mother catered theme bar mitzvahs, but this is what Leah knew.

"Leah, if anyone has a knife or a gun or anything sharp, they must leave it behind."

"You heard Onyx." She inspected the picketers herself. She took a Swiss army knife from Mariano Figueroa. A bicycle chain

from David Andujar. A jagged shard of pocket mirror from Altagracia Guerrero.

"Leah, what if the sheriff does not arrest the fat girl?"

"He will."

She had already called Harvey Fletter to make sure. In the office, I had only heard her side of the conversation. The next
morning, coiled around each other in Harriet Hecht's spare room,
she told me what Harvey Fletter had said. This was my introduction to the often disconcerting fact that for Leah bed was just
another forum. Under the circumstances, my reconstruction
might be uncertain in some of the nuances, although it is generally accurate.

"This is Leah Kaye, Sheriff."

"You're going to have to give me a little help now, missy."

*He thought he'd get to me, calling me "missy," the dumb red-
neck.* "I'm the counsel for the agricultural workers union."

"So you're the one."

"I'm the one what, Sheriff?"

"The little lady's been causing all the fuss. You and those
long-haired friends of yours. This used to be a good town before
you and your crowd showed up."

He thought I was going to argue with him. "Sheriff, I've been
informed you have an injunction against the strikers . . ."

"What strikers you talking about, missy?"

"The strikers you're going to arrest this morning, Sheriff."

"Ain't no strikers in Hermosa, missy. Those so-called strikers
you're talking about, they're nothing but a bunch of rabble-
rousers. I don't like to stand downwind of that bunch. The
smell's too rank."

He really did think I was going to get mad. "I think the injunction says the pickets can't say 'Huelga' on the picket line,
Sheriff."

"You going to make my job easy for me, missy?"

Here's where I goofed. "It's going to be a hot day, Sheriff. I
don't want you to get too much sun." *It was a mistake saying
that. Off the point. Like I was only having a friendly conversation with him. All it did was give him an opening.*

"I grew up in this sun, missy. Don't bother me. You and those outsiders of yours don't like it, nobody will miss you, you decide to leave."

I had to get it back on track. Who cares about the sun anyway? "We're going to be at the Dizdarevich Ranch No. Two today, Sheriff. Corner of Avenue Ninety-nine and H Lane."

"You going to be there, missy?"

"I'll be there, Sheriff."

"You won't be yelling 'Huelga,' though, will you? Your kind always lets someone else do that, don't you? You'll let someone else spend that night in jail you should be spending there."

You have to hand it to him, he was still trying to get under my skin. "No one's going to spend a night in your jail, Sheriff. We have something in this country called a writ of habeas corpus. You may have heard of it." *I wasn't counting on Harriet throwing that brick. Throw a brick at a cop and you're going to do a touch, writ or no writ. Anyway I shouldn't have been snotty with him. It's always a mistake to get snotty with a cop.*

"You got a little friend, I hear."

"Dizdarevich Ranch No. Two, Sheriff."

"That little Mexican boy. What's his name now?"

"Avenue Ninety-nine and H Lane, Sheriff."

"Aurelio, isn't it?"

That fuck.

Leah's version of pillow talk.

All things considered, I was not as interested in Harvey Fletter as she. Aurelio Lira was more on my mind. It was Leah's idea that I accompany her and Aurelio to Harriet Hecht's. Aurelio was not consulted. I could not say he was enthusiastic about my tagging along. Leah insisted that I drive the van she lived in that summer. She ate and slept in the van. Entertained Alex Fahr in the van. Aurelio as well. He did not have a license and she felt too pumped up to drive. By her definition the day had been a considerable success. Phyllis Emmett had performed with a special flair at the corner of Avenue 99 and H Lane. "Huelga," she had shouted in her tiny voice over the bullhorn. "Huelga, huelga." And then for emphasis, her confidence rising, she had begun reading Jack London's "Definition of a Strikebreaker." An imaginative touch of her own: "After God had finished the rattlesnake, the toad and the viper, He had some awful substance left with which He made a strikebreaker." It was then that Harvey Fletter took out his handcuffs. Phyllis continued from memory as she was led away to a police car: "A strikebreaker is a two-legged animal with a cork-screw soul, a waterlogged brain and a combination backbone made of jelly and glue . . ." Good television. Made even better when the Cessna Commander sent the CBS camera team flying. A nice piece of film for Cronkite.

Leah said.

It was cool at the cottage in Three Rivers. Somewhere higher in the Sierra I could hear owls hoot and the baying of what Aurelio said was a wolf. Leah said she would fix dinner. Dinner was a can of Campbell's vegetable soup split among the three of us and the remains of the package of doughnuts Aurelio had bought that morning on his trip to the 7-Eleven with Ramona. I rinsed the dishes. Aurelio played his guitar. Leah called Walter Reuther in Detroit, person to person and collect, and enlisted his support for Onyx and the farm workers. I finally went to bed in the spare room. Aurelio kept playing. And then he stopped. After a while, through the thin walls separating the two bedrooms, I heard her say no, not there, here. She was incapable of not giving orders. I tried not to listen. I found *The Wretched of the Earth* next to Harriet Hecht's diaphragm. I read.

I fell asleep thinking of Phyllis Emmett.

I awoke before dawn. Leah was at the door. Her hair was wet from the shower and wrapped in a towel. She closed the door behind her. I could see through her thin cotton nightgown. She unwrapped the towel and dried her hair.

I looked.

"You wouldn't happen to have David Rockefeller's home number handy, would you?"

I shook my head. And kept on looking.

"If you want to look, look," she said finally. "If you want to get it on, let's get it on. I've got a lot to do today."

Somewhere in the house I could hear Aurelio playing again. *Yo te suplico que vuelvas a querer.* It was the only song I ever remember him playing. *Dejalo triste y apasionado.*

Oh, let his passion in sadness linger.

In sadness linger.

"Why now?" I said when Harvey Fletter was no longer on her mind.

"Because it was going to happen sooner or later."

How she hated to waste time.

Dejalo triste y apasionado.

"What about him?"

"He'll get over it."

I never did.

BOOK FIVE
GRUNTS

UNITED STATES MARINE CORPS

TO: CG, 3d Marine Division

FROM: CO, 3/9

SUBJECT: Combat Operations After Action Report

DATE: 25 March 1969

280910HJ Company I (YD 158146) was fired upon by 4 NVA using S/A in shelter. Returned S/A fire and killed 2 NVA. While sweeping through a fortified position, encountered a platoon size NVA force in bunkers and hooches. Fired S/A and arty, then regrouped and was reinforced by the CP group and one platoon. Held up attack and hit enemy with air strikes. Results: one friendly KIA and 9 WIAs and 3 NVA KIAs. Further search of air strike area uncovered three shelters 8' x 12' x 20', 3 bunkers, 2 SKS rifles, 2 AK47 rifles, 1 RPD LMG with three drums of ammo plus assorted 782 gear. Also picked up were assorted medical supplies and documents. 281000HJ Company M (YD 192158) found ten bunkers 9' x 5' x 5', 3 bunkers 6' x 5' x 8' and seven burning shelters. There was a large assortment of cooking and household items, 18 machetes, 2 rice grinders, 10 dead pigs and 12 live ones, 15 chickens, 50 lbs of meat, corn, vegetables and rice mixed. Killed livestock and destroyed structures. 281015HJ Company L (YD 187124) found sleeping area large enough for 25–30 people. Also found one individual crawling through bushes and apprehended same. He claims to be a civilian but is wearing a military uniform. Person is crippled and is about 30 years of age. 281130 HJ Company I (YD 158157) under heavy S/A fire from 2 NVA squads. Returned S/A fire, reinforced by CO CP and one platoon; mortar and arty missions in progress. 281500HJ Company N (YD 193155), while searching a bunkered area, observed 2 NVA running and killed both. In their possession were 25 lbs rice, 1 rain suit, 3 ponchos, assorted tobacco and cigars. Both soldiers were well-groomed in khaki shirts and shorts. 281630HJ Company L (YD 190124) found 3 bunkers and 2 shelters, 3 SKS rifles with bayonets, assorted clothing, cooking utensils, 30 lbs rice and some medical gear.

I

a/931.5-0/2: JB [*Aftermath*]—*Edited Extracts from Interview with John Broderick, Oral History Project, The Frederick Griswold Finn Presidential Library, Princeton University, Princeton, N.J.* [N.B. THIS TRANSCRIPT AND ANY OF THE MATERIALS FROM WHICH IT IS DRAWN INCLUDING NOTES AND THE MASTER TAPES AND THEIR DUPLICATES AS WELL AS THE UNEDITED TRANSCRIPTS CANNOT BE RELEASED WITHOUT THE WRITTEN PERMISSION OF JOHN BRODERICK AND AFTER HIS DEATH WITHOUT THE WRITTEN CONCURRENCE OF HIS HEIRS AND THE ATTORNEYS FOR HIS ESTATE OR IN THE ABSENCE OF HEIRS BY THE ATTORNEYS FOR THE ESTATE ACTING FOR THE ESTATE.]

Why did I go to Vietnam? Oh, Christ, I don't know. I suppose the best answer is that it was the place to go between marriages. Although I didn't know then that I was between marriages. I mean, I hadn't even met Anabel yet. Which is not to say I had never heard of Anabel. She was married to a jockey, for Christ's sake. I hate to sound like my father, but when a woman as rich as Anabel Rutland marries someone who doesn't reach up to her tits, well, it's the kind of thing you read about in the newspapers.

HEIRESS WEDS WEE WINNER. WEDDING BELLS FOR JOCKEY AND HIS FILLY. Anyway. What was the question? I don't think it had anything to do with Anabel. Anabel is another chapter. A short chapter, as long as we're into short. And not for Fritz's library.

Fuck Fritz.

Oooops. Mustn't be beastly about Fritz. Not in his own library. Fancy that. The Frederick Griswold Finn Presidential Library. A hallowed hall of academe. You know how many separate documents and pieces of paper there are in this joint having to do with the Finn presidency? Seven million, two hundred thirty-four thousand, five hundred and ninety-seven. Every one annotated. I got that from Fritz himself. Last year at his sixtieth birthday party. At Averell and Pamela's in Washington. "I thought I was a pretty good president," he told me. "But if you think I'm going to read seven million, two hundred thirty-four thousand, five hundred ninety-seven pieces of paper just to see how good I was, well, then, Sugar Ray Robinson will be secretary of state before that happens." He said that. He really did. Former president Frederick Griswold ("Fritz") Finn. Of course he was a little pissed that night. As I am now. You know, he's the only president since Truman not to write his memoirs. Except for poor Jack, of course. "Poor Jack" is what Fritz always calls him. "I write my memoirs," he says that night at the Harrimans, "then I've got to read those seven million pieces of paper, and on the whole I think I'd rather be a colored congressman from Detroit."

Fritz said that. But I bet he doesn't say it on any piece of tape you've got here at the Frederick Griswold Finn Presidential Library. Fritz is indiscreet, but only when it suits his purposes. And never when the eye of history is focused on him. Anyway, I'm indiscreet enough for the both of us. *In vino veritas.* What I don't understand is why the fuck he wants me on tape. Maybe because I'm deniable. Perhaps even unstable. I mean, what else can you say about someone with the Broderick name marrying a woman like Leah Kaye?

That was a line we heard a lot after we were married. Never directly, of course. It was just hanging there in the air, like pollen. With all it implied. Jew. Communist. Traitor. Terrorist.

No one ever called her a dinner dawdler.

Bea told me that after we were married.

"I always made Leah finish her plate when she was a little girl. Or she didn't get dessert. She was such a terrible dinner dawdler. And let me tell you another trick, Jack, in case you and Leah ever have children and get a thumb-sucker. Mittens will put a stop to that. Woolen mittens are the best. They taste bad. Cotton mittens have a tendency to taste good."

I bet when the historians come to The Finn Library they won't expect to learn that cotton mittens have a tendency to taste good.

Bea unhinged my father. The only person I ever met who could. "Hello, Hugo," she would say whenever she saw him. She was under this delusion that he liked to be called Hugo. He fled from her presence. I wonder if that's why I liked her so much.

For Bea, every cloud had a silver lining. I remember her telling me Leah had scoliosis as a teenager. "It was a blessing in disguise, Jack. She had the worst posture you ever saw. Look at her now. Stand up, Leah, show Jack your posture. She never would've had a posture like that if she hadn't had to wear that brace. Very good for the posture and very good for the bosoms. That's the bright side of scoliosis."

That's something else the historians won't expect to find out here. The bright side of scoliosis.

Anyway.

We were talking about Vietnam, weren't we? Which really doesn't have anything to do with Fritz. Any more than Leah's thumb-sucking does. Oh. I see. We're interested in "The Finn Years." Prelude to Aftermath. I get it. I guess I'm a footnote to the Finn years. His sister-in-law's brother. His girlfriend's brother. My brother's brother. A keen observer of the Finn mise-en-scène, as the frog cinéastes would say. I sometimes wonder what would have happened if Fritz had served a third term and had to deal with Vietnam. I suppose he would've fucked it up the same way everyone else did. My father always said Vietnam was an accident waiting to happen. The situation, not the place. An accident of history.

So why was I there?

I guess for the same reason people slow down and look at a traffic accident. The gawk effect. That's what the traffic engineers

call it. You slow down and gawk at the tangled iron. See if you
can spot any dead bodies. It's like you get points for every stiff
you see lying by the side of the road. Meantime the traffic is
backing up behind you. That's the gawk effect.

I wanted to gawk at an accident of history.

It wasn't just the gawk effect, of course. Let's face it, there was
the Leah factor. Going off to war isn't such a bad way to get over
a busted marriage. In the vulgar lobe of your brain, there's an
I'll-show-you aspect to it. You say to yourself, "Think how she'll
feel if I get a tiny piece of shrapnel in my brain pan and come
home in a bag." Nothing disfiguring, of course. Just a little chunk
of RPG shrapnel no bigger than a pencil point. Big D. Instant
zero. Canceled like a bad debt. Oh, beat the drum slowly and play
the fife lowly.

It brings tears to my eyes.

It wouldn't have played worth a shit with Leah, that tune.

I remember once in Hermosa. Her van was firebombed. It was
right after we began seeing a lot of each other. You notice how
delicately I put it. A lot more delicately than she would, you can
bet your sweet ass. There had already been one incident with the
van. Someone had spray-painted the words JEW BITCH on it. You
know what she did? Nothing. Just kept on driving it around Hermosa with the words JEW BITCH still on the side door, like it was
the name of a laundry or something. Onyx wanted to scrub it off.
She wouldn't let him. She didn't scare. That was the message she
wanted out. Well, someone must've heard it. Because four or five
nights later, maybe a week, the van was firebombed. And totaled.
She couldn't have been happier. "They're worried," she said to
me. She meant Burl Grgich and the other growers. "They never
did this when they weren't worried." She always looked at things
that same way. With the relentless logic of the demonologist.
Well, I wasn't that fucking happy about it. We had slept in the
van only the night before. She never did like staying with me at
the Moonbeam. That's the motel where I had a room. It was too
plastic for her, the bed had a foam rubber mattress, that sort of
crap. But that night it was too hot to stay in the van and so pissing
and moaning she finally agreed to sleep at the Moonbeam. On the
floor. Onyx called at three in the morning. "If you see Leah, Jack,

tell her the van was firebombed." As if he didn't know she was
staying there. Naturally Burl Grgich said Leah did it herself. The
old Reichstag fire theory. "We could've been in it," I said when
we finally went out there to take a look. "We weren't," she said.

Bottom line. Always the bottom line with her. That's what I
mean when I say Leah wouldn't have been all that choked up if I
had tapped out in Vietnam. She expected casualties in the war
against what she called, at teach-ins and sit-ins, "the oppressor
classes." And in this instance, the bottom line was that as a member of the oppressor class myself I would have been a more desir-
able casualty than most. She would've found some useful point to
make about that. The oppressor class devouring its young is what
immediately springs to mind. Never mind any residual sense of
loss she might have felt. Personal feelings were bourgeois bullshit.

That's the way she thought.

Take it or leave it.

I don't want to talk anymore.

No, I will not explain why.

I don't give a fuck about Fritz. Or his library. And I definitely
don't give a fuck about the Finn years. . . .

END TAPE

I asked to have my tape returned from the Finn Library after
Leah was killed. I assume the request went directly to Fritz and
he was only too happy to oblige. I don't imagine revisionism was
what he had in mind when he gave his benediction to the oral
history project and saw to it that the best and the brightest of the
Finn years were invited to contribute. Needless to say, possible
quislings were ruthlessly screened and the former opponents
from the Congress and the country at large so graciously philosophical in the reminiscences of their opposition that the impression tendered was of a new and previously undiscovered age of
Pericles in the mid-twentieth century. As far as Fritz was concerned, I was a malcontent, a family burden given to drink and
controlled substances and idle behavior. While an implicit purpose of an oral history might be the settling of old scores, I am

reasonably certain he never intended that any scores be settled against him, or that I be an accredited scorekeeper.

Of course the reason I cut the tape short had nothing whatsoever to do with Fritz, as difficult as he would find that to believe. The actual reason I stopped so belligerently was that I have never been able to talk about Leah to anyone, with the possible exception of Bro, and even with him the rare confidences exchanged were so elliptical as practically to require a decoder. Even as pissed as I was, I was not so pissed that I was prepared to deliver myself about Leah to the dogged young graduate student T.A. who was my assigned interrogator that afternoon at Princeton (and whose questions were excised from the transcript so as to give the appearance of a seamless reflection). As it was, I had already chattered on like a magpie, in part because of the third (or was it the fourth) Bloody Mary at lunch, in part because I was beguiled when my debriefer volunteered that he himself was preparing a Ph.D. thesis on one of the more recondite accomplishments of the Finn years—the regeneration of spiritual values as manifested by the presence of Dom Augustine Broderick, O.S.B., as the shadow theologian of Fritz's administration. Benevolent amusement replaced common sense and so with the tape running I meandered full tilt past scoliosis and dinner dawdling and idle behavior in the Moonbeam Motel as if they had anything to do with "The Finn Years—Aftermath." Fortunately sobriety and concomitant discretion returned in time to cut me off when I veered back toward Hermosa and that first summer with Leah. Had I continued, I fear I might have found myself talking about my father, and he was another subject I preferred not to share with the historians.

Not in that context.

Considering what happened after I went to Vietnam. Where I suspect I would not have gone if my father had not dispatched me to Hermosa in the first place.

I have become a believer in cause and effect.

So allow me this detour. It will take me to Saigon presently.

If you want a more direct route, take Cathay Pacific.

"You have five minutes."

So began my father with his usual charm and his usual forthrightness when I was ordered to report on what was happening in Hermosa. That summons offers a clue to his style. "Mr. Broderick expects you for lunch Friday the 31st at 1:15 in his suite at the Carlyle. Please be prompt." That was it. Nothing more. The message had the unmistakable officiousness that my father's secretaries always assumed as if it were a fringe benefit of the job. His indifference to any of the logistical disruptions that his more peremptory demands might create was an attitude they seemed to appropriate automatically. The Carlyle was in New York, the message left on the answering machine at my apartment in San Francisco, and I did not call in from Hermosa to pick it up until the afternoon before the scheduled lunch. The problem was mine to solve. Either I canceled or I took the red-eye out of Los Angeles.

I took the red-eye.

My father was not partial to the extraneous, a trait he shared with Leah, and by the time my plane landed at JFK I had made a mental list of things I would not tell him. Scoliosis no. Nor any mention of Leah's dinner dawdling. Nor would I tell him of my last encounter with Burl Grgich. In my father's private rating system, Burl Grgich would forever be a jughead and jugheads did not matter.

Burl Grgich was for my own memory bank. The meeting took place at the prescription counter at the Rexall on Hermosa's east side.

"You miserable fifth columnist son of a bitch." Burl Grgich's tone was so eminently reasonable that I did not realize at first he was talking to me. He did not meet my eye and when I finally looked over he seemed in fact to be addressing the rows of antacids and decongestants on the shelf next to him. "You ever dare come to the Grove again, you son of a bitch, I'll let everyone up there know you're nothing but a goddamn wetback in disguise."

I was buying condoms at the Rexall, thus compromising any reply I might have made. My purchase rested on the prescription counter while the pharmacist counted my change. A dozen prophylactics in a box that was a triumph of the package designer's art. RAMESES—FOR COUPLES WHO CARE, the tasteful yellow lettering announced. "Individually Foil-Wrapped. Lubricated Ends.

Designer Colors." Plus a four-color wraparound photograph of a young couple who cared, running through a meadow hand in hand. I tried to pretend the package was not mine.

"I'd buy a rubber, too, I was going to stick my thing in that Jew bitch." Burl Grgich still did not take his eyes from the bottles of Maalox and Formula 44. "Considering all that wetback stuff that's been getting into her lately."

As Leah would have considered any defense of her honor in the Rexall deranged, I simply picked up my purchase and departed without comment. In the interest of narrative detail, however, if at the expense of gallantry, I should point out that I bought the condoms for Phyllis Emmett and not for myself. Her vow of chastity was another casualty of the war against the oppressor classes. There was a seminarian from the Jesuit community at Los Gatos arrested with her at the junction of Avenue 99 and H Lane, and in the Hermosa County cooler their eyes locked. Once they were released, the demands of the flesh presented problems that neither of those two virgins had anticipated in the convent or the seminary, and it was thus with some inarticulate embarrassment that they entrusted to me the logistics of birth control, a man whose putative experience in these matters was somehow sanctified in their minds by the fact that my brother was a priest. Which explains how I happened to run into Burl Grgich at the Rexall prescription counter. This was another Hermosa story I would neglect to tell my father. He detested local color.

There was also no need to tell him about Bro. Bro's appearance on the local scene was as usual documented in the newspapers and newsmagazines and on television. Bro in Roman collar and shirtsleeves arriving in Hermosa at the wheel of a semi, leading a fifty-vehicle caravan loaded with food and supplies for the strikers. Bringing with him as well, from the papal nuncio and the six American cardinals, blessings for Onyx, who had embarked on a penitential fast to reinforce his allegiance to nonviolence. Reinforcement had seemed in order after a small cadre of strikers and volunteers had responded to the firebombing of Leah's van with some night riding of their own, slashing tires and roughing up scabs and burning packing crates. Leah maintained so discreet a silence about the night riding that Onyx did not tell her about his

fast until its sixth day because he was afraid she might try talking
him out of it. In fact her only regret was in not dreaming up the
idea herself. She was immediately alert to its potential for exploi-
tation and from the moment Onyx told her she choreographed its
every move.

At Leah's orders, tents were pitched so that the faithful maintaining a vigil for Onyx could be protected from the blistering
sun. At Leah's orders, first aid stations were set up for the old
Mexican women who crawled on their knees from La Purísima,
the Catholic church on Hermosa's west side, to the pallet set up
outside union headquarters where Onyx lay for the duration of
the fast, taking only an occasional swallow of water or juice. It
was Leah who negotiated with Bro to arrive with a truck from
each of the fifty states and it was Bro who persuaded the *Life*
photographer to accompany him in the cab of the eighteen-
wheeler. I never did ask Bro where he had learned to drive a semi
with its thirty-four forward gears; I was afraid he might tell me
Jimmy Hoffa had taught him. But there he was, detouring to
Hermosa while on his way to Medellín and a conference on liberation theology, celebrating on the twenty-third day of the fast, in
fluent Spanish, an outdoor Mass for Onyx. The moment was
captured in the pages of *Life*. A bleed color spread of Bro kneel-
ing in the dust at the edge of a grapefield, cradling Onyx against
his white vestments as he gave him communion. I remember the
Life photographer asking me if I could get Bro to "repeat the action" with the communion wafer, asking also if the Mass might be
restaged in an orange grove, because oranges would give his pictures more of what he called "chromatic pow."

"You have five minutes."

Not enough time to explain chromatic pow to my father in his
suite at the Carlyle. I wondered how to begin. "The growers," I
said tentatively, "have put on a lousy performance."

There was no response. I did not have Leah's gift for brutal di-
rectness. Or his.

"They're sullen and stolid. If you don't like what they're
doing, they call you a communist."

He looked out the window, his back to me. It was as if he knew
I was avoiding the point. I thought of Bro's wire. It had come
from Sapporo, the next stop on his itinerary after Medellín.

DOMINUS VOBISCUM was all it had said. The Lord be with you. The wire had made Leah laugh. I wished the Lord were more on my case than he seemed to be at that moment.

"They're so goddamn paternalistic. All this crap they pass out about, 'We know our workers and they're happy.' It doesn't ring true and they know it doesn't ring true. These guys simply cannot understand why the pickers want to be responsible for their own condition."

I felt like a train that had been rerouted onto the wrong track. There was no way to get off. I kept on talking.

"Listen, the picker is the low man on the economic totem pole. It doesn't matter how much you pay him an hour. He only works four months of the year. People live by the year, not by the hour." At last I seemed to get his attention. He knows rhetoric is not my style, I thought. He wants to know what I'm getting at. "That's what the growers cannot understand. The pickers are just miserable sons of bitches with no control over their own destiny. Most of them don't speak English and they've never known anything better than breaking their hump in some vineyard somewhere. That's why the growers can get away with this paternalistic shit. They'll tell you until they're blue in the face they can't put toilets in the fields because toilets cost too much. Just one field crapper's the difference between breaking even and going broke. They really believe it."

I glanced at my watch. Leah would just be landing in Detroit. Where she had gone to pick up a check for Onyx from the UAW. The fruits of that telephone call to Walter Reuther the first night we slept together. I did not seem to have anything else to say. And had used only two of the five allocated minutes. My father stared at me expressionlessly. In that split second, I suddenly realized that his contempt for the rest of the world was predicated on a lifetime of trusting no one but himself. Finally he said, "I should've known that sheeny lawyer would sell you a bill of goods."

It was a response that at least allowed me to get to the point. "We were married the day before yesterday."

By a judge in Bakersfield. With a bailiff and a court stenographer in attendance.

Dominus vobiscum.

His expression did not change. "Maybe you're not as dumb as I thought."

The remark of a pig heavyweight. That was what Leah called him the night they finally met at the house on Washington Street. By way of a wedding present he had recognized Onyx and his union. A business deal, he claimed. He owed a favor to George Meany. Or perhaps he only wanted George Meany in his debt. I never could read his tally sheet of favors granted and favors owed.

"I always wanted to meet a pig heavyweight," Leah said.

"And I always wanted my son to marry a smart Jew lawyer," my father said.

How do you do?

So pleased to meet you.

My father said, "You weren't up against much. Birdbrains and peaheads with big shoulders. That bunch of jugheads down there, they've all got twenty-seven letters in their names and an IQ to match. They think they're fighting your beaner pal with the midget sister, but they're fighting time and they don't know it, and there's not a tougher customer around."

My father said, "You wouldn't have pushed me around like I was some dumb jughead. I would've had your union election ten minutes after you showed up in town. Brought in those clowns from the NLRB to supervise and make sure everything was on the up and up. Made sure all the beaners voted. And you know what would've happened. You would've lost. You and that little greaseball and the dwarf. Nobody had ever heard of him and that would've been the end of him and good riddance."

My father said, "You really wanted to win quick, you should've gone to Hoffa. He wants to stay out of the can, Jimmy. A tough little number. 'I got a lot of vices, Hugh,' he told me once, 'but being wrong ain't one of them.' You go to Hoffa, you say, 'Listen, everyone thinks you're nothing but a goddamn hoodlum. You need to pretty yourself up. The way to do it is help the poor migrant Mexican. You give the beaners a hand, people won't call you Hoodlum Hoffa anymore, you'll be Huelga Hoffa.' You did that, those jugheads wouldn't've known what hit them. Jimmy would've sent his goons down there and the only sound you would've heard was the sound of jug bones breaking."

My father said, "You're like all the other sheeny revolutionaries, you don't want a union, you want a movement. You're too
stuck up for something like the building trades and a living wage.
Well, I've got a little secret for you. Try selling that to your
beaners. All those greasers really want is a seat on the gravy train,
and that's the card you should've played."

My father said, "You don't even know what's going to hit you
when this is all over. They're going to shake your hand, pat you
on the back and say, '*Hasta luego.*' Which is beaner for 'Get lost,
we don't need you anymore.' Then the smoothies will take over.
The ones with the blazers and the blow-dried hair and the air
travel cards. The ones that know how to cut a deal with George
Meany down at Bal Harbour. They'll trot your greaser out once a
year for some union dog-and-pony show, then put him back in
his box until they need him again. He's already last year's news
and you don't know it."

My father said, "The trouble with people like you, sister, is
you've got something against winning. You're only interested in
making a point, like all the other bleeding heart meatballs."

My father said, "You know, I was wrong about you. I thought
you were smart."

If I recall only his side of the conversation, it was because of
the deep impression he made on Leah. Although she would never
admit it, I suspect that in some private recess of her mind she
found a certain merit in at least some of what he said. He was not
her usual adversary, a storm trooper of the status quo or an assistant district attorney with political ambitions. My father had the
supreme confidence of a man who had said no to the four presidents who had asked him to be secretary of the treasury, the sense
of place that came from Dick Daley seeking his political counsel
and Charles de Gaulle his advice on restructuring the franc.
("That lunkhead with the big nose" was the way he invariably
referred to the occupant of the Elysée Palace.) He observed toward Leah the same amenities he observed toward any head of
state. There was no attempt to outflank her. He attacked and kept
on attacking, a field marshal of the oppressor class, search and destroy. It was a tactic she herself often used, and I think each recognized in the other a fellow player, a mirror image, she as

indifferent as he to the casualties inflicted. I also think that what
was to happen began to happen that night on Washington Street.

Bro was also a factor in my going to Vietnam. Writers need a
war, he said. It's the ultimate boom-boom. Better even than fucking. Professionally speaking, of course.

It's interesting about Bro. After Fritz left office, I thought he
had no place to go except back to the monastery. Or to the missions. Perhaps to a discreet martyrdom somewhere. Dom Augustine among the lepers, fingers dropping off one by one, like parts
from a cheap Christmas toy. Of course that was not Bro's way.
He always landed on his feet. Where he landed, with the blessing
of the Benedictines, was The Finn Foundation. Founded by Fritz
after his two terms in the White House with five million dollars
of Finn money and ninety-five million of my father's, the second
sum receiving a good deal less publicity than the first. Fritz was
the chairman, which meant that he got dressed up in white tie a
lot (he is the only man I know not a symphony conductor who
looks good in white tie) and Bro a special consultant, a sinecure
that allowed him to spend a large portion of his time traipsing
around the world to various countries whose gross national product was less than the funding of The Finn Foundation. The Finn
Foundation was concerned with famine and soil erosion and
boundary disputes in the Third World and new democratic constitutions in former dictatorships and racism and crime and justice and all those important words that foundations are
tax-exempted to try and solve; the donors and their heirs are honored and the IRS is stiffed. Dickie Finn controlled the foundation's purse strings. Except for the fact that Dickie was a horse's
ass, not even my father could complain about his stewardship.
"Dickie," Fritz Finn once said, "is only the second guy around
who could multiply loaves and fishes."

The Finn Foundation transformed Bro into a kind of professional troubleshooter in a Roman collar. All that expertise he was
supposed to have picked up in Washington was enormously reassuring to whichever administration was running things in Washington after Fritz left office. Whenever a new crowd took over,
there were people actually assigned to "get Bro Broderick on

board." He had those cuff links. The ones he always wore. And was wearing the day he died, on the sidewalk outside Glide Memorial. They were gold from Buccellati and engraved with the presidential seal. A gift from Fritz on the occasion of his farewell address. And an implicit reminder of a life dedicated less to God than to the nation's service. So there Bro was. In place. A member of the establishment who had set up a flourishing shop as a kind of Hessian devil's advocate. More Hessian than devil's advocate, in my opinion. But then I could never resist giving Bro a shot.

Usually a cheap shot.

I took for granted the sanctifying grace of his presence when Leah and I split up. He saw me through what the more raffish newspapers called a "splituation." By proxy I was news. BRODERICK HEIR AND RADICAL LAWYER IN APARTSVILLE. BRO'S BRO AND BRIDE PFFFFT.

Actually the divorce was simplicity itself. Leah of course did not want a settlement. She flew down to Juárez one morning and was back in San Francisco in time for dinner. With me, as a matter of fact. She gave me a copy of the papers, she tucked away a plate of spaghetti carbonara, we fucked in my apartment on Green Street and she was asleep in her own place in Oakland not long after midnight. The next morning she flew to Birmingham for a civil rights march. All the old gang was there. Onyx and Mercury and Harriet Hecht, even Lottie French. An hour and a half after she landed she was arrested. Disturbing the peace, trespass, marching without a parade permit, all the usual charges. It was the twenty-eighth time she had been busted. She kept count. With that passion she had for order. There were times I wanted to ask her if she knew how many times we had fucked, but I never did. I was afraid she would tell me.

So there she was in the slammer again. No big deal. But this time they decided to give her a full vaginal strip search. When the policewoman stuck her finger up there—rubber gloves, K-Y jelly, the works—Leah began to moan, Oh, God, you must love your job, Jesus, that's good, it's never been like this. You can imagine what happened next. The policewoman hit her with a pair of handcuffs and broke her nose. By the time Leah was able to call me after she was sprung, she had already announced her intention

to file a ten-million-dollar civil suit against the Birmingham Police Department. Which in due course she did. Needless to say,
the Birmingham Police Department in its turn said officers had
found an unspecified amount of marijuana "secreted in" Leah's
person. "In" her person, not "on," the official statement quoted in
the newspapers said, in case anyone missed the point of where it
was supposed to have been secreted. "I'm okay," Leah said from
Birmingham. "What about the dope?" I said. "Jack," she said, "if
I'm carrying, do you think I'm going to put it up my cunt? You
have any idea what grass would do to a yeast infection?" I was
sure she had already researched how the chemical components of
marijuana and Flagyl and a yeast infection would interreact and
was fully prepared to spell it out in court. Before she hung up, she
said, "I miss you."

That was the first forty-eight hours after the divorce.

It was also a fair approximation of the four years we were married.

In case you might wonder why we got divorced. Or why we
got married in the first place.

The occasional adultery never figured.

The Birmingham Police Department eventually settled Leah's
suit for $77,500. The terms of the settlement were supposed to be
secret. That provision of the agreement cut no ice with Leah.
Asking her to keep quiet about sticking it to the city of Birmingham to the tune of seventy-seven grand was like asking the sun
not to rise. She announced the terms at a press conference. The
settlement was immediately revoked and Leah hit with a contempt citation. BFD. She always said that. Big fucking deal. Her
response was to hold a second press conference. Where she said
she could not be held in contempt because the city of Birmingham and the officers of its courts were beneath contempt.

I read about the controversy in *Time*. I cut the story out and
carried it in my wallet. In case I forgot what Leah was like. And
the way she seemed to affect people. The last paragraph of that
Time story was a case in point: "As for Radical Gadfly Kaye (former daughter-in-law of billionaire Lone Raider Hugh Broderick and sister-in-law of Insider Cleric Augustine 'Bro' Broderick), she now faces disbarment proceedings in three states.

Next stop on her left-wing hegira: Hanoi. She travels there soon as guest of Ho's minions, along with new best friend and constant traveling companion, Actress-Thinker Carlotta French. Ho Chi Hum."

I picked up that copy of *Time* at the daily five o'clock press briefing at the Rex in Saigon. The five o'clock follies. Where the light at the end of the tunnel was always lit. Jive at five, film at eleven. Actually I got to like the follies and would make a point of dropping by the Rex whenever I was in Saigon. I even developed an ear for the language the MACV PIOs spoke. It was possible to chart the conduct of the war by the levels of their obfuscation. "Collateral damage" or "circular error probability" generally meant that a civilian target or a hospital in Hanoi got hit by mistake. "P-4" was my particular favorite. I heard it first from a Defense Department analyst who had flown out from Washington to reassure the locals on how well the war was really going. He had only been in-country twelve hours, long enough however to have had one of the tailors on Tu Do run up a poplin CBS jacket for him, a great white hunter number full of buckles and epaulets and pockets that had pockets of their own. His field was strategic bombing. The objectives of strategic bombing, he said, were the four Ps. P-1, P-2, P-3, P-4. Ports. Petroleum. Power. Population. In order of priority. In this conflict. That was the way he talked, hands buried deep in the side pockets of his new safari jacket to lend the casual touch. P-4 was population. P-4 was never targeted. Repeat "never." Unless, however, it became necessary to "deprive the enemy of a population resource." I was trying to get used to the idea of thinking of people as P-4 when I picked up that copy of *Time* after the briefing at the Rex and read about Leah and Lottie.

GRUNTS, Tape 47, B-side. Unedited Extracts from Interviews with Sp4 Richard Kane, 322 Avn Co, 55th Avn Bn ("Neither Fear Nor Favor"). Venue: Bien Hoa. Interviewer: John Broderick. Date: April 25, 1969.

K: I tell you about the lezzie?

B: If I have it on the other tape, it doesn't matter, tell me again.

K: She had a real shape on her, nice set of jugs, you know what I mean?

B: Yeah.

K: The chicks these days, they wear some new kind of brassiere, you can see their whatchamacallits right through the shirt even.

B: Their nipples.

K: Yeah. You know what that comes from?

B: What what comes from?

K: Calling their things "whatchamacallits."

B: The nipples, you mean.

K: Yeah. You say that word down to Holy Sepulchre, you see what happens to you. A whack in the mouth for talking dirty.

B: That's funny.

K: Maybe you think a whack in the mouth is funny. Those fucking nuns can really hit. Whack. I was in basic at Fort Ord there, it was Thanksgiving, I was going through the chow line, they were having turkey, you know, and the mess sergeant, he says to me, "You want a breast or a leg, soldier." I nearly creamed in my fatigues. You don't say that word at Holy Sep. In that parish, you say "white meat." Not that other word. I say that other word at home, my old lady would start blessing herself, making the sign of the cross, you know what I mean? Like I committed some kind of mortal sin for talking dirty.

B: So you get to 'Nam and you start talking about lezzies.

K: Oh, yeah, I nearly forgot about her. You know, I still say "white meat" when I have chicken or something.

B: Really? What do you say when you talk about a robin red breast? Robin red white meat?

K: Jesus. I never thought of that. I guess I'd just say "robin," I was talking to my old lady, "you know with the kind of red front . . ."

B: (*Laughter.*) Let's get back to the lesbian.

K: The what?

B: The lezzie.

K: Oh, yeah. She was a stew on the plane I was coming out in from Travis.

B: How'd you know she was a lez?

K: Jeez, that's what I'm coming to, okay?

B: Okay. Sorry.

K: We take off from Travis, seven o'clock in the morning, a big fucking 707, Braniff. They must make a mint on those charters, Braniff. Twinks out, short-timers home. Stiffs, too. Anyway. I'm sitting next to this fucking master sergeant, a fat guy, you know, he's going to take over a PX in Da Nang, you know, those were his orders. He's wearing Class A's, the only fucking guy on the plane, none of the officers are wearing Class A's even, we're all in fatigues, except, you know, this guy. And he's giving me all this shit, you know, he'd rather be out in the field with the men, but you're in the army, you learn to follow orders, the army wants him to run a PX, then he's going to run the best fucking PX in 'Nam, that kind of shit. Maybe next tour he'll get the opportunity to be out with the men. Fuck him, you know what I mean? He's got this briefcase with him, never lets the fucker off his lap. The stew tells him he's got to stash it under the seat during takeoff and he says to her no way, like he's carrying the secret plans for the invasion of North Vietnam or something in there. You know what he's got in there, it turns out?

B: What?

K: Eight rolls of toilet paper.

B: (*Laughter.*) He was prepared.

K: Yeah, well, fucking lot of good it did him. We come down the coast, you know, from Yokota in Japan, and we get over Bien Hoa and the pilot starts circling. I look out the window, you know, to see what's happening, you know, and down below I see this hooch and someone's spray-painted on top of the hooch, FUCK YOU. I think maybe the bastard knows something I'm going to have to learn awful fucking fast. Then the pilot comes on the intercom and says when he rolls to a stop he wants everyone out of that plane fast, leave everything on board, you'll get it later, just hit the ground and head for a slit trench, the VC are dropping mortars on the perimeter. I wonder why the fuck he doesn't turn around and the stew, the one turns out to be a lez, she says the radar's down at Ton Son Nhut, Da Nang's socked in and so's Cam Ranh Bay, so it's either Bien Hoa or the South China Sea.

B: Welcome to Vietnam.

K: That's just what I was thinking. Anyway the plane comes

to a stop and everyone's yelling and pushing, you know, trying to get the fuck out of there. There's this big colored guy, a corporal in camouflage fatigues and boots all spit-shined to shit, he starts climbing over the seats and this runty little Jap major, he tries to slow him down, and the colored guy gives him an elbow right in the mush, really cold-cocked the bastard. I finally get through the door and down the slide and I hear this noise, *ka-wump, ka-wump*, I didn't know what the fuck it was at first.

B: Mortars.

K: I figured that out myself. So I take off and roll into this slit trench and I'm trying to catch my breath when I see the stew trying to make it across the tarmac. She's got this blue Braniff uniform on, with the blue hat, you know, the one that looks like a little box . . .

B: Pillbox.

K: What?

B: Pillbox. That's what they call those hats. Pillbox hats.

K: Yeah, well, she's wearing one, and the wings over her left titty, and she's hobbling, her skirt's too tight and she's lost a heel. A minute later she lands right on top of me in the slit trench. Her skirt's all up around her waist there and I can see her pussy underneath her panty hose and her whatcha-macallits poking against her brassiere, like it's making her hot, a mortar attack. So I put my hand on it, what the fuck, I thought I was going to die, this was the way it was, no way I was going to last a year. And she says, "You want to cop a feel, soldier, okay, but I like girls." That's how I knew she was a lez.

B: It wasn't your lucky day.

K: Luckier than that fucking master sergeant. He gets it. In his Class A uniform. A piece of shrapnel. That briefcase of his, it cracked open, and there's these eight rolls of toilet paper all round him, that's how I know what he had in there, the briefcase. (*Laughter.*) You're out here long enough, even Big D has its humorous side after a while.

B: Big D?

K: You know, cooling it. Checking out. Crispy critter time. That's generally what happens, you go down in a slick. Deep fried. Crispy critter.

B: Burning to death.

K: Jeez, have it your own way, you know what I mean?

B: Sorry. I'm just trying to get it straight. So it's on the tape. They're a bitch to transcribe sometimes, these tapes.

K: Yeah. Okay, okay.

B: Anything else?

K: About what?

B: The humorous side. Big D.

K: Yeah, well, I remember this other guy, the sergeant in charge of the POL bladder over to the Fifty-fifth, a lifer, a colored guy. You know, a real pain in the ass, this guy, he's only been in-country a month maybe, he knows all the answers. He gets his flight time in on the beer runs over to Ton Son Nhut, you know the kind I mean?

B: Uh-huh.

K: Well, he gets his in the last place he expects to get it, I bet. On the crapper. Bad enough he gets offed taking a shit, but he was pounding his hound in there on the crapper, is what he was doing, this jungle bunny. Whacking away at that thing, it looked like a fucking clarinet that Benny what's his name plays . . .

B: Goodman.

K: Who?

B: Benny Goodman. The guy who plays the clarinet.

K: Yeah. He had the shits.

B: The sergeant.

K: I don't mean Benny what's his name, man. The lifer. I been telling him ever since he gets here, this coon, you want to stop the shits, you eat the peanut butter in the C rations, forget the grape juice, it's the grape juice that makes you crap. The fucker always gets it wrong. It's why he's a lifer, this colored guy, you know what I mean? He throws away the peanut butter and drinks the grape juice every time. It's really not like taking a shit, it's more like pissing out your asshole. You ever get the shits here in 'Nam?

B: Everybody gets the shits in 'Nam.

K: Even Westmoreland and them?

B: He doesn't shit ever.

K: Jeez, I got to remember that, that's rich.

B: What about the sergeant?

K: Oh, yeah. Like I say, he's sitting on the crapper letting go and beating his meat at the same time and this incoming round lands right outside the latrine, he never knew what fucking hit him, you know, that nigger.

B: Like the master sergeant.

K: What master sergeant?

B: The one with eight rolls of crap paper.

K: Yeah, that was mortars, too.

B: Yeah.

K: Let me tell you something . . .

B: Sure.

K: The thing with mortars is, you walk rounds in until you get the range, then once you get the range, you fire for effect. But this here was the first round. No warning. I mean, not even a nigger's so dumb he takes off for the crapper during a mortar attack.

B: Maybe it was a lucky shot.

K: And maybe it wasn't.

B: How do you mean?

K: All I know is this. You got to watch the dinks, and I mean the friendly dinks, friendly, my ass, when they're digging a position for you.

B: How so?

K: They work like bastards, you know what I mean? All smiles. "Hey, Joe, you want a Coke, you want to boom-boom with my sister?" Fuck 'em, they're all VC as far as I'm concerned, you get right down to it.

B: That's one way of looking at it.

K: Listen, it's the only way. I was in Vinh Long in January, TDY, we were clearing an area for a maintenance depot, and we caught this one guy putting in trimmed poles, every one of the fuckers was trimmed, and they were pointing directly at the perimeter defenses.

B: No shit?

K: No shit. The little fucker denies it, of course. You can line up our machine-gun positions on those trimmed poles he was putting in, but still he denies it. The lieutenant says make him talk, I don't care how, I didn't see you do it, I'm going to go take a leak, just do it. So we get a rope, me and another guy from the two-fourteenth, and we put one end around this slope's neck and throw the other end over a four-by-four rough terrain crane. You know, lift the crane up a little bit and make the fucker talk.

B: Did he?

K: Not exactly. The thing is, the crane operator, he was new on the job, OJT in fact, and he jerks the controls a little bit. Sayonara, you know what I mean?

B: Yeah.

K: All I'm saying is the same thing could've happened here. That latrine's not thirty yards from the bladder and the bladder holds twenty-five thousand gallons of aviation fuel. It figures.

B: I guess.

K: So there's this sergeant, he's got his pants down around his ankles and his joint in his fist. Both fists. It happened so fast he never even let go his cock, they tell me, the guys in graves registration. I never knew you could jack off with two hands. You ever jack off with two hands?

B: No . . .

Leah saved all the letters I wrote her from Vietnam. After she died, I found them in that Bekins warehouse in Oakland where she stored everything pertaining to her life in even the most peripheral way.

May 25
Bien Hoa

. . . I started teaching a remedial English course for college credit at nights here on the base. Rem. Eng. Comp. II it's called (Rem. Eng. Comp. I appears to have gone AWOL). English Made Easier. 101 Ways to Improve Your Vocabulary. Essentials of Composition. Helpful Hints Toward More Powerful Reading. The more powerful reading I have in mind is *All Quiet on the Western Front.* I thought it would be a statement, but none of the brass here on the base seems to have heard of it. The way I keep ahead of my students is that I have the answer books and the Cliff Notes (which are full of insightful remarks on the order of, "the general mood of a work is referred to as the 'atmosphere' "). Actually I rather like teaching. Those who can, do, those who can't, teach. You always said I was one of those careful people who put a new roll of toilet paper on the back of the crapper before the old one on the roller was used up. It's the carefulness of the pedant. If you ever doubted I was

a pedant, here's a lesson I devised for Rem. Eng. Comp. II. Q:
Why is English spelling so difficult? A: Because in English
there is no single letter to represent a single sound. Q: Can you
spell "fish"? A. G-H-O-T-I. EXPLAIN: "Gh" represents the
"f" sound in "cough," "o" the "i" sound in "women" and "ti"
the "sh" sound in "nation." I feel like Mr. Chips. Out of fucking sight, my students say. You have to consider my students.
One of them told me he considered "asshole" the most perfect
word in the English language. Because you call someone an
asshole and there's no doubt what you mean. There's a certain
flash of gutter wisdom in that remark. Don't ask me why they
take the course. I don't even know why I'm teaching it. I think
I just got bored and I'm not ready to go home yet. Wherever
that is. One thing that might turn out to be interesting. I've
started to tape some of my students. Their adventures. Maybe
I'll try doing something with it someday. Although who'll
want to read about a bunch of grunts I don't know. The only
ground rule is that I promised never to identify them. It's like
confession. Confession is Catholic psychoanalysis, I used to tell
you, and it's free. These are guys who go to war like they'd go
to the Chrysler plant back in the world. Out in the morning,
back (?) at night. I suspect and fervently hope that a large part
of what they tell me is horseshit, but I can't be sure. Maybe
they're giving old Chips the straight scam after all. One of the
guys I've been talking to is from San Francisco, a mick from
the Mission, from Holy Sepulchre parish, he calls it Holy Sep,
of course, I bet he never even went across the line into Saint
Jude's (always called with true Mission wit Saint Jew's) until
he was on his way to Fort Ord. Resentful and suspicious.
Imagine my father if the Brodericks had stayed in the Mission
and didn't get rich and you'd just about have it. You see why
I'm interested . . .

GRUNTS, *Tape 51, A-side. Sp4 Richard Kane (Cont'd—2d
Session—See Tape 47, B-side), Bien Hoa, May 26, 1969.*

B: How do you mean, you're superstitious.
K: Like with my fatigues. I always wear clothes that used to
   belong to some dead guy. The way I figure, the clothes can't
   get it twice is why.
B: That's a good enough reason, I suppose.

K: You bet your ass, it is. You know what winning this war means to me? It's got nothing to do with Charlie. Fuck Charlie, as far as I'm concerned. Winning the war means getting Richie out of here alive.

B: When's your DEROS?

K: Fuck DEROS. DEROS is just another shit date. You want to know why?

B: Sure.

K: Awhile ago, January, maybe after Christmas, I fly into Fire Base Emil. Emil. It should've been Fire Base Emily, I hear, after some general's girlfriend, a Red Cross chick he was balling, but the guy cutting the orders fucked up, you know, and spelled it "Emil." That's 'Nam in a nutshell, the whole operation, you want my opinion.

B: Yeah.

K: So we're going into Emil, bringing in mail, the LZ's cool, there's another slick with us, it's going to pick up some guys from the one-oh-worst, short-timers, going home, DEROS already stamped on their orders. The slick picks up these guys, they're waving like bastards, you know, to the guys on the ground, giving them the finger because they're going home and the other guys are staying, when all of a sudden, I don't know why, the slick loses its rotor and goes in. Hits the ground and blows up. Charlie didn't get it, it's there one minute, a second later it's just a ball of fucking flame. Somebody fucked up, you know what I mean? Somebody didn't check the Jesus nut or something, the whole thing flies apart. Those guys, the short-timers, they went home all right, except they went home in a bag. That's why DEROS doesn't mean a shit. What means a shit is putting your feet on the ground at Travis. That's why I always wear some stiff's fatigues, I get a chance. They're, you know, unspooked, you know what I mean?

B: Lightning doesn't strike twice.

K: Yeah, that's the expression I was trying to think of. I wanted no part of that shit, though, the first time I saw it. I was just a twink. A real FNG. Fucking new guy.

B: Yeah.

K: It was at Di An, when I was processing. There's this big pile of clothes and shit outside the GR Point. Boots, fatigues, helmets. Off the bodies of these guys they're ship-

ping back home after they get them all stitched back together. Just between you and me, sometimes they don't
stitch them up all that good either. My first crew chief,
Honeycut his name was, Honey we called him, they sent
him back to CONUS with two left arms. One of them belonged to a colored guy. His old lady sees the box, he gets
back to Philadelphia, and she insists on opening it up.
Wants to make sure it's old Honey, I guess. She must've
shit when she sees one nigger arm.

B: I bet she did.

K: It was at Belleau Wood it happened. I hear that was some
kind of big victory in World War Two or something.

B: World War One.

K: I always failed history. The dates. Who the fuck cares?

B: Uh-huh.

K: It's funny, you know. You ever notice these big operations,
a lot of them have code names from the wars we won. Belleau Wood. Utah Beach. You want my opinion, Pearl Harbor is what they should call this caper.

B: I like that. Pearl Harbor. Listen. Tell me about Honeycut.

K: You mean, like how he got it?

B: Yeah.

K: Shit. All we were doing was dropping off some body bags.
A platoon from the First Cav had taken a lot of casualties,
but the LZ was cool now, we hear from the Cav on the
ground. A milk run. That's all this is supposed to be. We go
in, we dump the bags, we laager until they fill the bags and
when they fill the bags we go back, load them on board and
bring them back to Camp Evans. Simple. We go in just before dusk. Just in case, we give the tree line a good going
over with the M-60s, Honey and me. Just in case, you know,
like I said. Then we come around again and drop the bags.
The skids don't even touch the ground. I'm throwing the
bags out when all of a sudden we get hit by a rocket from
that same fucking tree line. I don't know if I jumped or was
blown out, I just know I'm heading for a hole when the
chopper spins in. Both the pilots are cooked and when I
looked up, there's Honey sitting on the ground, one arm
gone and with the other he's holding onto his balls with all
his might. You squeeze your nuts, it's not supposed to hurt
so much, the pain, you know, they tell me. By the time the

dust-off gets in, Honey's in shock and all he can say is don't forget my arm. Find his fucking arm, I say. They find an arm, all right. The wrong one.

B: Oh, shit.

K: What's the matter?

B: I thought I pressed the stop button by mistake. I got it now.

K: It's okay.

B: I think so. I hate these things. Let's see. By this time you were already wearing clothes that belonged to dead guys.

K: Oh, yeah. I forgot. It was at Di An. I go through the replacement company there and they give me a new pair of boots, 8½C, I wear a 9½D, too bad, that's all they had. So fuck it, I go back to the GR Point. All these guys are going through the clothes like it was the annual rummage sale at Saint Jew's or something. And the first thing, right off, I find a pair of boots that fit, 9½D, brand-fucking new. Shem. That was the guy's name they belonged to, the boots. Shem. It was written in each boot. Along with his serial number. In Magic Marker. He must've been a neat bastard. And a twink, too, the boots were so new. Shem. What kind of name's that anyway? Jewboy?

B: Maybe.

K: Then what the fuck's he doing here, a Jewboy? I thought they all got deferments, the Jewboys and the college boys. They think I'm some kind of fucking criminal, those guys, because I'm here and they're not. I should've gone to college is what I should've done. I could've gone to USF. But I hate those fucking Jesuits. You know what I want to know?

B: What?

K: Since when does going to college or being a Jewboy make you 4F, like you lost a leg or something, you know what I mean?

B: Yeah.

K: Those rich bastards. You don't see any of them out here either.

B: Right. Listen. Uh. You get anything else besides the boots at Di An, the GR Point there?

K: Not there. Later I picked up a flak jacket off the pile at Lai Khe. Belonged to a brown bar. Pugh, I think his name was. Harold Pugh. I sit on the fucker. The family jewels never have enough protection, you're riding in the door of a Huey.

I even wear a cup like the linemen on the Forty-niners wear, Charley Kruger and them. It's just a little extra protection, like the brown bar's flak jacket. Jeez, I remember one time last month, we were picking up some wounded, you know, at Duc Hoa. We were heading back over the trees, it's like a green blur down below, and this little Arvn grunt, it was Arvn wounded we were picking up, I tell you that?

B: No.

K: Well, it was Arvn, and this little Arvn guy, he looks down and he sees his pecker's been shot off. You know what he does?

B: What?

K: He rolls himself out the door. I mean, he doesn't say a word to anyone, you know, just out the door. I guess he thinks life without a pecker's not worth much. Unless he was trying to fly, that little gook.

B: And he couldn't.

K: No fucking way.

B: You tired?

K: Why should I be tired?

B: We're almost at the end of the tape.

K: So let's finish it up.

B: Okay.

K: Where was I? Okay. I got the boots from the Jewboy Shem and the flak jacket from the brown bar. The fatigues I got at Long Binh. Conran, the name tag said. He must've got it from a sniper. There was a neat hole right through the chest. It was a bitch getting the bloodstains out, though. What I liked about the fatigues was he had this motto or something sewn on the back of the jacket, Conran. "Fighters by Day, Lovers by Night, Drunkards by Choice." I liked that.

B: That's nice.

K: Yeah. My helmet comes from another guy in the company. Melcher. There's a crease along the top, like someone tried to open it with a can opener. It was all jagged, you know what I mean?

B: Yeah.

K: You got enough left on that tape?

B: I think so, yeah.

K: Well, what happened, you know, is somebody fucked up.

B: How?

K: I think it was because he leaked his brains all over the inside of the helmet, Melcher, so the guys at the GR Point didn't clean it out real good. There was some caked blood and dried skin inside. And this letter in the sweatband someone forgets to take out. A Dear John from his girlfriend. Patti.

B: That's the girlfriend?

K: Yeah. It's all about how she's going to marry his friend Candy that goes to Penn State grad school. What's grad school?

B: Where you go after college.

K: So you can stay out of 'Nam?

B: I suppose that enters into it.

K: I thought so. He was fucking her brains out, Candy. That's what Patti writes Melcher in the letter. She missed it so bad. She missed Melcher going down on her, eating her pussy. That's what she says. In the letter. I read it. With his thumb up her ass. You get letters like that?

B: Not lately.

K: I get a letter like that, someone's going to get a rap in the mouth, you know what I mean?

B: Uh-huh.

K: That's why she ties up with Candy, Patti says. Her missing it so bad, you know. That's the reason. One thing Candy won't do, though. Go down on her. It smells like fish.

B: Candy said that?

K: No. I say that.

B: Oh.

K: And that's what she really missed. She writes this.

B: That's what you said.

K: In a fucking Dear John. Like when he came back, Melcher, he could drop by the house and get himself a faceful when Candy's off at graduate school there.

B: What'd you do with the letter?

K: Put it in an envelope and sent it back to her, Patti. There was all this dried blood on it, you know what I mean?

B: Uh-huh.

K: Even a little chunk of his hair, Melcher. Maybe some of that brain goo from inside the helmet, too. I don't check it that close. I guess the reason he was carrying it in the sweatband there was so he wouldn't forget.

B: I guess.

K: Maybe he was trying to figure out how to answer her. I took care of that for him.

B: You did?

K: Yeah. I tell her when I come home, I'm going to drop by, I'm ever in the Penn State area. I tell her, you know, I'm going to eat her out, then I'm going to waste her. Like she's some kind of fucking mama-san, you know what I mean? And waste that fucking Candy, too, he gets home from grad school.

B: You wrote that to her?

K: Yeah. I wrote that to . . .

END TAPE

In time I was to learn a great deal about Richie Kane that I did not commit to tape. His father died when he was nine. There were ten children. Richie was the oldest. His father was a painter for the California Department of Transportation and he painted the spans on the Bay Bridge five days a week, fifty weeks a year, year in and year out, finishing one side of the bridge and beginning the other, San Francisco to Oakland, Oakland to San Francisco. One day he fell from the bridge and was killed. Because he was not wearing his safety belt, a violation of Caltrans safety regulations, the department's insurers tried to withhold his life insurance and death benefits on the grounds of negligence. This action left his widow destitute, with ten children under the age of nine (there were two sets of twins) living in a three-bedroom, one-bathroom house in the Mission that she would be forced to vacate because she could no longer afford the rent. Her story was made for the San Francisco newspapers, including my father's. According to the clips, they jointly sponsored a public subscription to ease the burden on the Kane family, a campaign that netted $2,491.48. The donations from local business and service organizations included a year's supply of toilet paper, a thousand bags of potato chips, free diaper service for one year, two hundred hours of dance lessons for any member of the Kane family at the Arthur Murray Dance Studios, a Sunday brunch for four at the Starlite Roof of the Sir Francis Drake Hotel, a year's supply of Wheaties, the Breakfast of Champions, a free membership in the

Planned Parenthood League, and Thanksgiving and Christmas turkeys with dressing and trimmings from The Broderick Holiday Turkey Fund, the charity for the underprivileged established in the will of Gertrude Mary Mahoney Broderick.

"Some rich bitch" was the way Richie described the Kane family's holiday benefactress when he was at Bien Hoa.

He never made the connection.

Nor did I help him.

He attended Holy Sepulchre junior high school, where he was an altar boy so proficient that he was twice selected to serve as an acolyte at the archbishop's annual Christmas midnight Mass. In 1964, he graduated from Saint Benedict Joseph Labre high school, which was also in the Mission. In both junior and senior high, he was an average B and C student who occasionally failed deportment because of a sullen and unpredictable temper compounded by a tendency to answer back his teachers in class. His play at third base for the Saint Benedict Joseph Labre baseball team attracted enough attention for him to be scouted by the Philadelphia Phillies. The scouting report, however, said that he had limited range in the field, inadequate long-ball power and an attitude problem. The scout graded him a marginal prospect with only Class AA potential and recommended that the Phillies not sign him to a professional contract. The attitude problem mentioned by the scout stemmed from an incident during a CYO league game between Saint Benedict Joseph Labre and Saint Jude's. Twice he missed a bunt sign and failed to sacrifice a runner to second base. When he was reprimanded by his coach, the altercation escalated into a fistfight. The fight led both to his dismissal from the team and the withdrawal of a baseball scholarship he had been offered by the University of San Francisco. After graduation from Saint Benedict Joseph Labre, he applied for both the police and the firemen's academies, but there was a municipal hiring freeze in effect and he was forced to seek employment elsewhere. When he was finally drafted in 1967, he was working as an apprentice crane operator for a construction company in Daly City.

Most of this information was printed in the newspapers after he was arrested.

What I remembered most vividly about him was not printed in the papers.

For example.

On the second picture I wrote for Marty Magnin, the costume designer had a single card credit. "Gowns by Mr. Joel." There's nothing I can do about it, Marty told me. The fageleh's got it in his contract. Like much of what Marty Magnin said, the statement was not entirely true. Mr. Joel was in fact Marty's second cousin, Joel Winkler. I was still new enough in Hollywood to think Joel's opinion was of value and so I asked him how he visualized the picture that would be made from my screenplay. He did not hesitate a second. "Dove gray and pale peach," he said. For all intents and purposes, I bailed out of the picture at that moment. Which is perhaps why, when "Gowns by Mr. Joel" flashed on the screen in San Jose; I suddenly found myself thinking again of Richie Kane.

"Gowns by Mr. Joel."

That was the connection.

Boots by Shem.

Fatigues by Conran.

Helmet by Melcher.

Flak Jacket by Brown Bar, Lai Khe.

The names and the bits of uniform all came back as if I were reading the designer captions from a page in the Men's Fashion Supplement in *The New York Times Magazine*. Came back to me at the Cineplex 4 in the Hamilton Heights shopping mall nine minutes from the San Jose airport and the Warner Brothers G-3 that would fly us all back to the safety of Los Angeles as soon as the preview cards were counted.

The picture sneaking at the Cineplex 4 was every bit as dove gray and pale peach as Joel Winkler had promised. Rather than watch, I burrowed deep in my seat as if I were under artillery attack in a bunker in Kontum and pretended not to be a member of the official Warner Brothers party. Instead I concentrated on Richie Kane. I remembered Honey's arm. Remembered Foxtrot One and Grunt Six.

Remembered what he said smelled like fish.

The film I wrote was called *Penelope Chadwick* at the sneak in

San Jose, a not much more inspired *Lovers by Night* when it went into general release a few months later and died a blessedly quick death. The new title was of course contributed by Richie Kane. Taken from the gold embroidering curlicued around the smoldering purple dragon sewn on the back of the fatigue jacket he had plucked from the KIA clothes pile at Long Binh.

Fighter by day.

Lover by night.

Drunkard by choice.

I do not think that any man has ever been so poorly defined.

II

_____

IN ALL, I WAS IN VIETNAM for more than two years. The first
year I chugged all over the country, usually with the Marines, the
peacetime shavetail experiencing in a limited way (because I
could always leave) the narcosis of combat. As it happened, a
number of platoon leaders and junior company commanders with
whom I had served at Lejeune and Twenty-nine Palms were now
majors and light colonels commanding battalions or on regimen-
tal staff and their inbred suspicion of any reporter gave way, however reluctantly, to the brotherhood of the corps. It was like PLC
at Quantico all over again. I flew missions in H-34s off the _Iwo
Jima_ and once, as a rite of passage, in the backseat of an F-4 off
the _Enterprise._ The pilot indulged in some airborne acrobatics to
see if he could make me sick and he succeeded so well that I threw
up in my oxygen mask and nearly drowned in my own vomit.

After Bro died, I read the pieces I filed from Vietnam again.
They were with his papers at Harvard. Each article and scrap of
newsprint had been dated and pasted, in the order of publication,
in a scrapbook. The cover label was written in Bro's unmistakable
calligrapher's hand: "Jack in VN, '67–'69." As he had never mentioned reading anything I had written in Vietnam, the keeping of

the scrapbook moved me in a way the pieces did not. They seemed the product of a different incarnation. Dak To, An Khe, Pleiku, Tai Ninh, the A Shau Valley. Operation Daniel Boone, Operation Port Royal. Fire Base Georgia, Fire Base Portia, Fire Base Julia. At the Widener that day, the datelines and the campaigns and the names and the faces all blurred into one. They do still.

Some things, however, I do remember.

I remember the foreign legionnaire haircuts favored by the marine officers and the perverse pride they seemed to take in the fact that week after week the marine casualty rate was proportionately higher than the army's. I remember the acetate overlays on their command maps and the grease pencil arrows creating a pincer, whap, we've got the fuckers, you grab them by the balls and their hearts and minds will follow.

I remember the quiet of the French military cemetery in Saigon.

I remember just before going to Khe Sanh memorizing, in some dim attempt at historical analogy, the names of the nine French strong points at Dien Bien Phu—Gabrielle, Béatrice, Anne-Marie, Huguette, Claudine, Françoise, Dominique, Eliane and Isabelle—and I remember the day after I arrived in Khe Sanh hunkering down during a rocket attack, paralyzed with fear, trying to keep myself calm by thinking of the women I had fucked who had the same names as Dien Bien Phu's strong points. No Anne-Marie but an Ann and a Mary. No Eliane but an Elaine. Frances and Gaby. I tried to conjure up a Huguette, her breasts and thighs and pubic hair, her opulent ass, and then the A-4s came in with napalm and the attack lifted.

I remember that same trip to Khe Sanh seeing Mercury Baker's poster for the first time. The head shop best-seller back home. It was pinned up in a hooch just off the airstrip. Mercury in his P-printed prison denims, a pair of hand grenades hanging casually from his belt. I remember I did not tell the black marines in the hooch that the poster was my ex-wife's idea, something she arranged during the period before I finally threw Mercury out of our house on San Luis Road in Berkeley. The grenades were actually dummies from the property department at Paramount

where Lottie French was making a picture that spring. It was
Leah who dragooned Lottie into getting the prop grenades, Leah
who browbeat Lottie into paying for the photo session, Leah who
persuaded Mercury to keep wearing the prison denims as his own
demonic personal signature. Leah who left the house on San Luis
Road herself within a month after the departure of Mercury
Baker and The Shadow. I did not mention that to the black marines in the hooch at Khe Sanh either.

I remember hating tree lines. I remember the way napalm can-
isters seemed to tumble in dreamy slow motion from beneath
F-100s clipping along at Mach 1 just above the deck. I remember
the racket of a Spooky's miniguns killing bushes at 6,000 rounds a
minute. I remember a C-130 dropping a 15,000-pound B-82 bomb
in the middle of the jungle at Con Thien, *tha-wump*, trees flying
in every direction, and when the dust settled, there it was, an instant chopper LZ. I remember the decals on the turret of a tank in
the 2/3 marines, little people, painted yellow, in sandals and
cone-shaped hats, each one neatly x-ed out. I remember a crew
chief in a dust-off from Duc Pho who always carried a box of
Saran Wrap with him, it's the best way to stop the bleeding in a
chest wound, he said, one of those motherfuckers that sucks like a
pump, *whiiih, whiiih*, like you're pulling on some prime red.
Slap the Saran Wrap on, that caps it, I'd like to give a testimonial
to those boys from Dow, napalm and Saran Wrap, good old
American know-how.

I remember there were thirty-three indigenous snakes in Vietnam, thirty-one of them poisonous. I remember leeches so gorged
with blood they seemed the size of golf balls and I remember the
constant smell of shit, shit burning off in waste-disposal oil
drums, shit smeared on VC punji sticks, dysentery shit crusting
the hairs of your ass.

I remember the siege heat.

And the way the cold bruising monsoon rain pounded against
your body until you began to flinch.

I remember a young marine in Hue during Tet lying in the
back of an APC getting ready to die. He could not have been
more than nineteen and he had a gaping hole in his chest. He
opened his eyes and there staring him in the face was an Auricon

16-mm sound camera in the hands of an NBC cameraman, who had decided to film the moment. The boy tried to smile for the camera. One of the other marines told the cameraman to back off. Bullshit, the cameraman said. Cowboy style. Bullll-shiiiit. The marine whipped the barrel of his M-16 around, knocking the Auricon from the cameraman's hands, and then blew it apart with an entire clip. That was a great shot, the cameraman said. What the fuck is the matter with you anyway? When I looked over at the boy on the back of the APC, he had died, the hi-mom television smile plastered to his face.

I remember a psy-ops movie at the replacement processing center at Bien Hoa, LBJ welcoming the twinks to Vietnam, and I remember being tipped that a short-timer communications specialist had rigged the film with a laugh track, *This is freedom's battleground*, ha, ha, *the communists are not like us*, ho, ho, *they have no feelings*, har, har, *no respect for human life*, ho, har, ha, *no respect for private property*, hee, hee, ha, ha, and by this time the twinks were rolling in the aisles. The sound was cut, the lights went up, the MPs were called, but the Spec 5 who had laid in the track was already halfway across the Pacific on his way to Travis and a discharge. A VC infiltrator by any other name, the MP company commander said, just color him yellow and call him Charlie Cong.

I remember a PX officer in Cam Ranh Bay who offered me a deal on a warehouse full of Sansui amps and I remember a real-estate officer who leased in-country R&R hotels and as a lucrative sideline recruited the Saigon bar girls who serviced them. I remember standing on the roof at the Caravelle in the long rose-colored dusk, vodka gimlet in hand, listening to the nightly artillery barrage on the outskirts of Saigon and debating whether to have dinner at Broddàrd's or to join up with the spooks at the Eskimo in Cholon.

I remember a spook at the Eskimo whispering to me about a secret new sensor shaped like a dog turd that could be dropped from the air into the jungle to monitor NVA troop movements down the Ho Chi Minh Trail.

I remember asking the spook next time I saw him how the turd-shaped sensor was working and he said the bugs weren't ironed out yet, it was back to the drawing board, the new deal was a chemical compound that could turn the trail into a quagmire of grease, a regular shoot, *whoosh*, the little fuckers would slide all the way down from the DMZ into the South China Sea.

I remember the spook choked to death at a pizzeria on Tu Do when no one knew how to administer the Heimlich hold.

I remember how frigid the air conditioning was in the various military and government offices in Saigon.

I remember a secretary from the Phoenix Program telling me on the roof of the Caravelle that she was a Pi Phi from the University of Arizona. I remember feeding her a steak and five Rob Roys at Broddard's and I remember fucking her at the apartment I kept on Tu Xuong Street mainly so I could get laid occasionally without having a chambermaid reporting the indiscretion to the GVN security agencies who checked up on reporters. I remember how the secretary from the Phoenix Program sang off-key in the shower afterward, "Oh, he stood in the steeple and pissed on the people, but the people couldn't piss on him." It was an old Air Cav song, she said, she loved the Cav, those boys really knew how to party.

I remember the secretary from the Phoenix Program gave me a persistent case of the crabs.

I remember I gave the crabs to Wendy Chan.

"I just want to know one thing, Jack. Who'd you get it from?"
"From the Air Cav, I think."
"What's that supposed to mean?"
"It means there's a Goldwater girl I know, she's very tight with the Air Cav."

Wendy Chan scratched her bush vigorously. She was in Saigon on a press junket that she seemed to regard as little more than a valuable entry on a future résumé. With the crabs she had picked up from me only the Vietnamese equivalent of Montezuma's revenge. She was standing naked in the window of the apartment on Tu Xuong Street, kneading a pea-sized pellet of hash into a pipe she had paid too much for at an Indian souvenir shop on Nguyen Hue. The pipe was cheaply carved and adorned with gilt lettering that said, "Yea, verily, I pass through the Valley of Death unafraid, for I am the meanest motherfucker in the valley." Wendy had thought the pipe a necessary addition for her collection of head shop paraphernalia. She sucked through the stem, checking the draw. "I just want to make sure you didn't get it off some gook."

I reflected on assimilation and its discontents but said nothing. Too weighty a subject for Wendy Chan. And "tedious" the way she would see it anyway. "Tedious" was her standard response to any hint of introspection. She had graduated to the CBS affiliate in Los Angeles since I had last seen her. Reporter, weekend anchor and hostess of a Sunday afternoon talk show. She had just returned from a week in the delta, a junket laid on by the MACV public affairs office for local television personalities the Defense Department had specially flown out from the states. Talk show hosts from "Good Morning, Grand Rapids" and "A.M. Little Rock" and "Thursday in Trenton." Wendy's Sunday show was called "2 for L.A." MACV had billed the junket "Operation Big Picture" and pulled out all the stops. Each junketer received brand-new fatigues and combat boots. Troops were produced for interviews from the viewing areas reached by all the individual shows. There were special briefings from corps commanders and MACV brass. Dinner with the American ambassador. A visit to a base camp. Lunch in what a JUSPAO press release called "a typical chow line," where the visitors were fed frozen shrimp, chicken-fried steak and cherry cobbler. A ride in a Huey making a Coke and ice-cream run. A cruise on the Mekong in a navy PBR and the chance to fire the boat's twin fifties into the jungle across the river. Pictures and brochures of favorite R&R sites. "Bangkok—Pearl of the Orient." "Hong Kong—Asia's Banker." "Taiwan—Freedom's Isle." War in a week, with PX privileges and an accompanying press kit.

"Actually she was a Pi Phi," I said. As a reality fix I added, "In the Phoenix Program."

"Really," Wendy said. "You should get some Kwell. K-W-E-L-L. That'll always get rid of crabs. You can get a tube at the embassy commissary, I bet. You don't need a prescription. You just rub it in." She started to sing, a Mary Martin *South Pacific* imitation. " 'I'm going to wash those crabs right out of my hair, I'm going to wash those crabs right out of my hair, and send them on their way. . . .' "

I obliged Wendy with a smile. The crabs she had picked up from me her first night in Saigon seemed a musical comedy commonplace in her life, Kwell a kind of pubic aspirin.

"Give some to your friend from Phoenix."

"The Phoenix Program."

"What's the . . ." She paused to light the hash pipe with a Zippo inscribed with the insignia of the Fourth Division. Another souvenir of her stay in Vietnam. "What's the Phoenix Program anyway?"

Of course the Phoenix Program had not been included on her itinerary. Talk about the Phoenix Program might have encouraged the kind of negative press coverage that Operation Big Picture was designed to counteract.

"Basically it's a program where the CIA tries to reeducate Vietnamese who are suspected of being politically unreliable."

"Nothing wrong with that." She took a long hit, then two shorter ones and passed the pipe to me. "How?"

"Ordinarily with a bullet behind the ear." With a rush of hashish paranoia, I wondered suddenly if the apartment had been bugged. As the hotel rooms of reporters at the Caravelle and the Continental were supposed to be bugged. "If you can believe what you hear," I added casually for the benefit of any listening devices that might have been in place. "I don't really."

"Out of sight," Wendy Chan said.

She never bothered herself with the morality of short-term solutions. *Out of sight.* I would have liked to have heard Leah's take on that response to the Phoenix Program.

"I suppose it is at that."

"You ever go to the embassy?" The Phoenix Program apparently had nothing to offer that might make the grade on "2 for L.A."

"Sometimes." To buy J&B at the commissary. And the small cans of Planters cocktail peanuts. And toilet paper. Four-roll packages of ScotTissue. "Cottony Soft," the cellophane wrapper said. The local toilet paper had the quality of an emery board.

These were tales from the combat zone I had neglected to tell Wendy Chan.

"It's weird. They run mirrors under all the cars that enter the compound."

"To see if there's any bombs underneath."

She accepted the explanation with bland disinterest. "Like a dentist looking for cavities."

"I think that's the general idea."

In the street outside the apartment a car backfired. I started, waiting for the return fire. Car noises had a tendency to spook the trigger-happy ARVN MPs. Wendy took no notice. She was studying the printed inscription on the pipe. "Where's this Valley of Death anyway?"

"In the Twenty-third Psalm." I was becoming arch. A side effect of the Montagnard hash we were smoking. I had traded for it in the Highlands. The hashish for a Duracell pencil flashlight I had purchased at the embassy commissary. As a gesture of good faith I had also given the Montagnard headman a can of cocktail peanuts. He had thrown out the peanuts and kept the can. "Also in Tennyson."

"I thought it was in Vietnam."

There were times when I found her extreme literalness engaging. Usually when I was stoned. "Here, too."

"Out of sight," she repeated. It was as if she had won some obscure point. She took the pipe back. "At the embassy." She took a healthy hit. "There's this tech sergeant I met." And a second hit. "He's a fairy." Then a third. "In charge of the floral arrangements."

I held one eye shut with a finger in an effort to keep the room from moving and tried to think of the name of a flower. Any flower. "Delphiniums. Delphinia. Strictly speaking." I was drifting into that postcoital narcotic haze where so many of my memories of Wendy Chan seemed to take place. "I mean strictly speaking delphinia is the plural of delphinium. Not delphiniums."

"Roses," Wendy Chan said. "American Beauties." She was at the pipe again. "In the middle of all this bullshit, here's this fairy tech sergeant making sure all the cut flowers at the embassy and the residence are fresh. It's beautiful."

"Right," I said, holding the word for several redundant sylla-
bles.

Wendy Chan arranged herself between my legs. "You know
what the terrific thing is?"

"The contradictions." I beamed, pleased that my brain seemed
to be functioning at some low wattage capacity.

"Contradictions are for assholes." She ran the warm bowl of
the hash pipe across the hairs of my stomach. "What's terrific is
he's from Arcadia."

"Out of sight." I wondered if there were any Montagnards in
mythic Arcadia. With mythic hashish. That could be traded for
cottony soft four-roll packages of ScotTissue.

"Next to Pasadena," Wendy Chan said.

"Oh. That Arcadia."

She drew deep on the pipe and then brought the smoke back
up from her esophagus and exhaled it along the ridge of my abdomen. "Which makes him perfect for the show."

Two for L.A., I think I said. El Lay, *olé.* When are you coming
home, I think she said.

Or perhaps she said when are you coming.

Or did you come.

Or can't you come.

III

THERE WAS A FOOD FIGHT at the next table. Three civilian construction workers wearing mesh baseball caps with Brown & Root construction company patches were catapulting Boston cream pie off their spoons. Their targets were the open mouths of the two giggling Vietnamese bar girls sitting with them. The girls wore matching turquoise nylon bowling shirts with the Brown & Root logo on the back. Each had her name stitched in red thread across the pocket over the left breast. One was JoAnn, the other Vikki. Both wore purple eye shadow and brown lipstick. Cream and chocolate stained their blouses. One of the civilians had a purple birthmark that seemed to cleave his face into two more or less equal parts and a tattoo of a naked woman with an exaggerated pubic triangle on his left arm. The woman in the tattoo was identified as DOREEN—BARTLESVILLE, OKLA. The civilian with the tattoo took aim with his spoon, holding it back with his forefinger, sighted and fired. The shot ricocheted off Vikki's chin and onto her chest. She chirped with laughter, scrunching up her nose, then with her finger removed the gooey blob from her shirt. For a moment she cleaned her chin with her tongue, then stuck the cream-covered finger into her mouth, rotating it slowly as if she were fellating it. JoAnn giggled behind her hand while the three Brown & Root workers clapped and whistled their approval.

"What?" I had been watching the scene and not paying any attention to Richie Kane.

"You ever take the pledge, I said," Richie Kane repeated impatiently.

"The pledge?" I watched Vikki run her tongue across the length of her finger.

"Not to drink until you're twenty-one. You're Catholic, right?" He pronounced it "Cat-lick."

"My brother's a priest." An ambiguous answer that did not address the question but which seemed to satisfy him.

"I knew you were Catholic."

"Really?" I had to lean across the table to make myself heard. We were sitting in the Charles E. ("Commando") Kelly EM Club at Bien Hoa. Onstage a five-piece all girl USO band was playing "Mrs. Robinson" as if they were racing each other to the finish. The band was called The Barry Sisters Plus Two.

"Everyone from San Francisco's Catholic," Richie Kane said. "That I know anyways."

I nodded and looked over at the next table. JoAnn had taken a direct hit in the mouth. Boston cream pie dribbled down her face.

"I ever tell you about Lomasney?"

"Who?"

"Monsignor Lomasney. The pastor at Holy Sep."

I shook my head. The construction worker with the purple birthmark placed his tattoo against Vikki's lips and asked her to go down on Doreen from Bartlesville, Okla. Vikki smirked suggestively and then French-kissed the tattoo. The construction worker flexed the muscle in his arm as she did, making the tattooed pudendum jump up and down.

"He don't have no asshole," Richie Kane said, as if to identify Monsignor Lomasney more clearly to me. "Shits in a bag. It's tied to his side is the way I hear it. Cancer. I wish it'd kill the pious fuck, you know what I mean?"

I nodded absently as if I did know what he meant. Resentments seemed to stick to Richie Kane as flies did to a roll of flypaper.

"His brother's a big deal in the Department of Sanitation there. Ants Lomasney. You know him?"

Again I shook my head.

"Shit, you don't know anybody, do you?"

"Not at Holy Sep," I replied carefully.

"They're always taking the nuns at Holy Sep out to Candlestick, the monsignor and Ants. Like it's some kind of big fucking deal. Like they don't get the tickets for free or something. That mother superior there, Mother Immaculata, she thinks she's such a fucking howl with her imitations. She's always doing that colored guy that was on the TV with Jack Benny, what the fuck's his name . . ."

"Rochester," I said.

"Who the fuck cares?" Richie said. "I got better things to do than watch some dinge on the TV." He threw his head back and emptied half a bottle of Carling's. He was wearing the fatigue jacket that still carried Conran's name tag. Fighter by day, lover by night, drunkard by choice. "She'd rap you across the knuckles with a ruler, Immaculata, you didn't take the pledge. Every year the same thing. I'd say I wasn't going to take no pledge, so she beat me across the knuckles until I bled. Then she beat me for bleeding." Richie belched. "Finally one year I says to her, 'Mother Immaculata, there's one thing you never read in the paper.' 'What's that?' she says. 'Nun Dies,' I say. 'You know why?' 'Why?' she says. 'Because nobody gives a shit,' I say. Whack. Right across the fucking knuckles."

"I can see why," I said. The Barry Sisters Plus Two segued into "Strawberry Fields Forever." The redhead on bass ran her tongue over her lips and smiled at me, but I resisted the temptation and did not smile back. The Kwell that Wendy had recommended was fighting a losing battle. The body count was high but there seemed to be no light at the end of the tunnel.

"So she sends me down to the principal's office, to Lomasney," Richie Kane said. "The monsignor, not Ants." He snapped his fingers for another Carling's. "That means the rubber hose. He's a regular Willey McCovey with that rubber hose in his mitts, Lomasney. A home run every time he belts you across the ass.

You'd think with that bag of shit hanging from his side it'd fuck up his swing, but it never did."

He seemed lost for a moment in his past. Against my better judgment I framed a smile for the redheaded bass player. I wondered if she were a Barry sister or one of the Plus Two. Perhaps the crabs would lie doggo. Perhaps the Kwell's search and destroy war of attrition was paying dividends after all. If not she would be at her next gig at Cam Ranh Bay before she noticed.

Richie Kane interrupted my reverie. "So did you take the pledge or what?"

"I just moved my lips."

"I should've done that. The fucking nuns, they'd listen to you at Holy Sep. 'Richard Kane, I don't hear you.' Well, clean the fucking wax out of your ears, Sister, is what I should've said." He paused while a Vietnamese waitress cleared away the empty bottles before slapping down another round of Carling's. "You take the Legion of Decency pledge?"

I paid for the beer. "I just moved my lips there, too."

"It was a mortal sin you saw a condemned movie. *Baby Doll.* That was condemned. You see that one?"

"Sure."

"Then you committed a mortal sin, you saw *Baby Doll.* You couldn't even get out of hell with a plenary indulgence, you know that?"

I suspected that if I went to hell it would be for other reasons than seeing *Baby Doll.* Right at that moment the redheaded bass player seemed a more likely candidate for speeding me on my way to perdition.

"I liked the ones 'objectionable in part,' " Richie Kane said. "You remember *Pinky?* I saw it on TV once. That was one. Jeanne Crain played a nigger trying to pass. That was why it was objectionable in part, I bet." He nodded in the direction of five black enlisted men sitting at an adjacent table. "Fucking niggers all want to be white, that's their problem. Martin Luther Kinkyhead and all of them." Without a pause, he added, "She's Catholic, I bet you didn't know that."

I was slow making the transition from Martin Luther King. "Who?"

"Jeanne Crain."

"Oh." I watched him across the table. With his thumb he was picking the label off his bottle of Carling's. He had been to Bu Dop that day. To pick up two VC prisoners for interrogation. Neither would talk. Finally the ARVN intelligence officer along on the flight had thrown one of the two out of the chopper. The prisoner had clung to Richie's leg as he tried to crawl back inside the Huey. It was him or me, Richie had said on my tape. Then he had kicked the prisoner loose. And watched him fall six hundred feet into the jungle below. The remaining prisoner had defecated in his pants. And talked. You better fucking believe he talked, Richie had said on the tape. I wondered suddenly if the experience in the chopper had triggered the memories of Monsignor Lomasney and Mother Immaculata, wondered how Holy Sep had prepared him for Bu Dop.

"So's Irene Dunne. The fucking nuns at Holy Sep, they know all the Catholics in Hollywood. Loretta Young. Frank Fay. Except he was divorced, he went to hell unless he made a perfect act of contrition before he died. Spencer Tracy. Bing Crosby. Gary Cooper was a convert, I bet you didn't know that. You remember Don Defore? He was their favorite. And Macdonald Carey. A Catholic name, but you never know. A lot of them are Jews, change to Catholic names. Don Defore, though, he's the real thing. A daily communicant, Mother Immaculata says. He always makes the nine first Fridays. You ever make the nine first Fridays?"

Before I could answer, a misfired dollop of Boston cream pie splattered off the table onto Richie Kane's fatigue jacket. He shot out of his chair, his knee catching the edge of the table and knocking over a bottle of Carling's. The beer ran across the flat surface and spilled into my lap.

"What the fuck . . ." Richie Kane said.

In an instant, the construction worker with the purple birthmark was at his side. "Hey, listen, man, I'm sorry, we were just having a little fun, let me buy you a beer."

Richie looked at the cream congealing on his shirt and repeated, "What the fuck . . ."

"Hey, Vikki," the construction worker said, "you do laundry?"

Vikki giggled.

"They're very good at laundry, these people," the construction worker said. He peered at Richie's name tag. "You're Conran?"

"Richie."

"I'm Blue, Richie. Blue Forbis. From Bartlesville, Oklahoma." He flashed the tattoo on his arm at Richie. "You ever in Bartlesville, Richie, introduce yourself to my friend Doreen here. She'll do you as good as Vikki does laundry." Blue Forbis put two fingers in his mouth and let loose a piercing whistle that for an instant drowned out The Barry Sisters Plus Two. "Hey, Vik, a little help, we got to clean off my friend Conran, right, Rich?"

Vikki passed a copy of *Stars & Stripes* to Forbis. He took the newspaper and tried to wipe the cream from Richie's fatigues. He succeeded only in spreading the stain.

"Jesus, man, I'm sorry," Blue Forbis said. He dropped the paper on the table. I took the copy of *Stars & Stripes* and used it to absorb the beer that had puddled in my lap. "I'll tell you what. You want Vikki, she's yours. That ought to square things. She sucks you off, it's like she's priming a pump, right, Vik?"

Vikki pursed her lips and shook her finger at Forbis. A round of beers arrived. Forbis laid a ten on the tray and told the waitress to keep the change. "How about you, man?" he asked me. "You okay?"

"Just a little damp," I said.

"Jesus, man, I'm sorry about that. You want JoAnn over there? She can fix you up."

"I'll stick to the Carling's."

"You don't know what you're missing, man."

"Give me a rain check."

"You're beautiful, man." Blue Forbis grasped me in his ham-sized arms and bestowed a wet kiss on my cheek, then gave the same bear hug to Richie. "The beer's on me. Your money's no good here."

Richie mumbled his thanks.

"What a great fucking country this is," Blue Forbis shouted over the music. It was the first encomium I had ever heard about Vietnam. "Five hundred a week and all the pussy you'd ever want."

"That's an angle I hadn't thought of," I said.

"They're going to be building fucking airfields here till the year two thousand, the way I see it."

"Probably."

"No taxes and fuck yourself dry."

"Right."

"You're beautiful." Another kiss and Blue Forbis took a seat back at his own table. Vikki sat on one knee, JoAnn on the other. On the bandstand, The Barry Sisters Plus Two spun into "Spinning Wheel." I hummed along. *Ride a painted pony, let the spinning wheel spin.* Then I felt a surge of activity below my navel. The torrent of beer that had spilled in my lap seemed to have flushed the crabs from their hooches. Which took care of any lingering idea I might have entertained about the redheaded bass player. The spinning wheel had spun. And was not stopping here. She would depart for Cam Ranh Bay unencumbered with my parasites. With no guerrilla force of *Phthirus pubis* at large in the foothills of Venus. I took the soggy copy of *Stars & Stripes* and once more tried to mop my lap dry. Perhaps Carling's would prove more toxic than Kwell.

"They got it taped, those guys from Brown and Root," Richie Kane said over the noise. "I finish my tour here, that's what I want to do. Construction . . ."

"Right." But I was only half listening. The sudden constricting chill I felt had nothing to do with the spilled Carling's. What had vacuumed my breath away was a beer-soaked photograph on the front page of the *Stars & Stripes* in my lap. Lottie French with a North Vietnamese official. She was wearing the flight helmet of an American pilot and sighting through the scope of an anti-aircraft weapons system outside Hanoi.

"I got my union card," Richie Kane said. "Heavy equipment operator . . ."

"Right," I repeated distractedly. The second photograph was of Leah. She was standing beside the burned-out shell of an F-100. Presumably the one flown by the pilot whose helmet Lottie was wearing. I thought thank Christ it was Lottie rather than Leah who had been photographed in the flight helmet. Not that Leah would not have tried it on. I knew her too well to think that.

"I know how to operate most of the equipment they use out here," Richie Kane said. "Sheepsfoot roller, rock crusher, rough terrain crane . . ."

"Really." I spread the squishy copy of *Stars & Stripes* on the table so I could read it more easily. The story accompanying the photographs said that Leah and Lottie had each been given a ring forged from the metal of the F-100 and engraved with the date it had been shot down by the SAM unit in the photograph. The brief speech Lottie had made at the presentation was quoted in part: "We are here to bear witness against the imperial American killing machine and to show our solidarity with our brothers and sisters who are its victims." Lottie's line, but Leah's rhetoric. Or to be precise, mine. I had written the sentence to punch up a speech Leah had given outside the Dow Chemical office in Santa Monica three years earlier. On my part the gesture was an attempt to slap a Band-Aid on our already hemorrhaging marriage. The sentence worked better than the Band-Aid. I suppose it was a compliment of sorts that she was still using the material.

"What're you reading?" Richie Kane said. "The Giants lose again or something?" He took the paper and read the story quickly. I watched as The Barry Sisters Plus Two wound up their set, more or less together. "Cunts," Richie said when he finished. And then a second time: "Cunts."

I did not mention that I knew Leah.

Was once married to Leah.

Loved Leah.

IV

Vientiane, May 25

Dear Jack,

As always, in a hurry. We flew to Orly, then had to rush to catch a UTA or TAT flight (I can't remember which, you know how I'm always going to United when I've booked Amerikan), anyway the French subsidiary that goes to the Pacific. It was a stretch DC-8 with only four or five people on board, along with Lottie and me. I think one of the five was CIA. At least he looked the part, trench coat, flattop haircut, cuffs on his pants, a copy of the *Reader's Digest,* the flight was all tourist, but he sat in the same section with Lottie and me, all the way to Phnom Penh. We stopped in Athens for a couple of hours, where we were accosted by a hireling from the Amerikan embassy, who said if we persisted in going to Hanoi without official sanction we would have to surrender our passports when we got back to New York. (Strike "hireling." I never talked that way to you when we were married. I think it's because of Lottie. She uses words like "lackey" a lot. To me!!) Anyway, we had a pleasant chat. I asked him if he saw any basic difference between the government's attitude toward

Hanoi and its attitude toward a basic Amerikan ghetto, in Detroit, say, or Watts. He was one of those earnest numbers, nice
teeth, nice smile, nice level gaze, always ready to acknowledge
my point except "you really don't have anything new or original to offer." I bet he was on the debating team at Yale. "Realistically speaking." I think he began every sentence that way.
Realistically speaking, I said, Amerika's racist domestic policies are conceived by the same militaristic mindset that's turning Hanoi into one big bomb crater. You really don't have
anything new or original to offer, he said. A condemned ghetto,
I said. Things are not that black and white, he said. A gook
South Bronx, I said, a playground for your war games. I think
we'll just have to agree to disagree, he said. He was so goddamn
reasonable, Jack, a true dead soul. Answer me this, I said. Isn't
Hanoi just another ghetto to you respectable murderers in
Washington? Isn't what the B-52s are doing just a new kind of
urban development? I think we'll just have to agree to disagree,
he said again. Then they announced the plane was leaving and
he said this has been a truly invigorating discussion, Mrs. Broderick (get that, Mrs. Broderick!), I just wish you weren't
blind to certain facts. Like what? I said. Like the role of North
Vietnam in subverting a duly elected government, he said.
That's when Lottie said fuck you, lackey. I think we'll just
have to agree to disagree, he said.

Athens to Colombo, a long hop over the Arabian desert. The
main thing I remember is waking up and looking down to see
the desert all lit up from the fires of the oil wells. (Or some
kind of fire. Now that I think of it there aren't any fires in oil
wells.) And Lottie. After fuck you, lackey, she got all worried
about losing her passport. She has a picture shooting in Tuscany in September, she's having trouble with the IRS, she
needs the bread, she's always wanted to work with Antonioni,
the whole picture depends on her, it's a real change of pace
part, Michelangelo won't be able to get financing without her,
it's him she's thinking about and the little people, the grips and
the gaffers (I don't know what grips and gaffers do, but I don't
think they're "little"). All in all by the time we landed in
Phnom Penh I was beginning to think she was the most tedious
cunt I've ever met. Listen, Lottie, I said, cool it, if they didn't
take Ramsey Clark's passport and Susan Sontag's, they're not
going to take yours, tell the little people not to worry. I think

she wanted to jump ship, she thought I was going to say go home, Lottie. She dialed the wrong number if she thought that.

When we finally got to Phnom Penh (after a couple of hours in Colombo), Lottie wanted to visit Angkor Wat, etc., for a day or two, so I went with her, although what I really wanted to do was crash. She kept on saying it was beautiful, what a great location, she'd have to tell Michelangelo, maybe they could shoot in Angkor rather than Tuscany, she was always looking at it through her hands, you know, like a movie director. I thought it was okay (Angkor Wat, I mean, not Lottie's act). Actually I thought it was overrated bullshit, a bunch of ruined temples, yawn, yawn. The ruins I want to see are the hospitals the B-52s have leveled in Hanoi. I just want to get there.

The flight from Phnom Penh to Vientiane was something, a Royal Air Lao DC-3, seats on one side of the aisle, cargo on the other, including chickens and a pig that had slipped its tether. It was walking up and down the aisle and it really stank. Lottie was filing her nails with an emery board when the pig stuck its snout in her lap. She took one look, leaned over and threw up—all over me. The movie star puke looked so good the pig began licking it off my skirt, right in the crotch, which is where Lottie had unloaded.

I'm tired all of a sudden. Listen, happy birthday, I almost forgot. There's a lot I have to tell you, I don't want to, but you're going to hear about it sooner or later, I'd rather you heard it from me, but I don't know how, which is why I've been chattering about Lottie, I just don't know how. I hate to leave it like that, but I always was a pain in the ass, remember? I'll get around to it, Jack, but not tonight.

xoxo

Leah

Vientiane May 27
(same letter, call it Part II)

J——

Wouldn't you know it, we didn't get off this morning like we were supposed to. The thing is, the ICC (that's for Interna-

tional Control Commission) plane leaves for Hanoi only six
times a month, every Friday and every other Tuesday, along a
prearranged corridor and at prearranged times, and as long as
the plane sticks to the schedule no one shoots it down in the
corridor. Well, today another plane on the runway ahead of us
blew a tire and it took so long to haul it away that the Indians
who run the ICC canceled this flight, which means we're stuck
in Vientiane for another week.

I will try to be positive about Vientiane, and even Lottie.
Best foot forward. The Pathet Lao seems to want Laos badly so
it can't be all bad. Picturesque is the word I would use if I were
choosing my words carefully. The streets are unpaved and
there are only a few dessiccated (desiccated? dessicated? fuck
it, it's one of them) trees. It's hot and the only color is the saf-
fron on the robes the Buddhist monks wear. We're staying at a
place called the Constellation. The best hotel in Vientiane.
There's no hot water, the telephones don't work (a hardship
for Lottie as she wants to call her agents at the William Morris
office) and the entire ground floor is an open-air bar with
nothing but flies and a couple of whores who drink beer all day
and play pinochle with the two wire service reporters assigned
here. The reporters are delighted to see us, we're a big story
(or Lottie is) and they ask us questions about our loyalty to the
US of A and aren't we giving aid and comfort to the enemy and
when we get to Hanoi will we ask Ho Chi Minh to stop the war
like we're always asking Amerika to. Yesterday's lies for tomorrow's newspapers. Across the street from the hotel (it's the
main drag and all rutted) there's a tailor shop with a sign in
English, "Jack of One Trade." You see what I mean about picturesque.

Last night we went to a nightclub, a twenty-minute trishaw
ride from the Constellation. The nightclubs have names like
the Blue Angel and El Morocco and they're part-time whore-
houses when something heats up and there's a lot of Amerikan
reporters around. They're just shacks on stilts. We started off
at the Copa. A girl read my fortune and said my second marriage would be the happy one. (I thought it was funny, but I
don't know if you will, but I can't scratch it out because then
you'd wonder what I had second thoughts about and scratched
out.) Then to El Morocco but we didn't go in because Lottie
thought the stilts holding the shack up didn't look safe. Finally

to the Blue Angel. There was a girl there named Janis (all the
girls are called Linda or Stacy or Debbi, names they'd picked
up from Amerikan boyfriends, I guess), but Janis was after
Joplin, she had a 45-single of "Me and Bobby McGee" she had
memorized, it was the only English she knew. She sang it and
when she came to "Freedom's just another word for nothing
left to lose," I started to cry, me, the tough Jew commie lawyer.
Anyway, leave it to Lottie to spoil the moment. It wouldn't do
but she had to climb up onstage and sing "Help Me Make It
Through the Night."

Oh, Jack—

xoxo

L

Vientiane June 2

(still the same letter, it'll all go out together in one envelope, I
hope it gets lost, but it won't, no such luck)

Well, I guess I can't avoid it any longer. I know you know
something's wrong. Chatty Cathy's not my style, you must've
figured that out already. I don't want you to hear it from anyone else, not even Bro, although he's not exactly in the parish
priest business, I don't think this is a sick call he'd be thrilled to
make. He knows by the way. About Hugh. And me. There it
is. I finally got it out.

What do I say? It was just one of those things? It wasn't. I
was lonely? I wasn't. I just wanted to get fucked? There are
less complicated ways to get fucked. I was interested. No more,
no less. If it happened, I was going to let it happen, if it didn't,
no harm done. Of course it happened. Because Hugh is who he
is and I am who I am. Never apologize, never explain. Except
that's what I'm trying to do, isn't it? I just don't know how to
get from there to here.

Let me take a deep breath.

I had asked him for money.

Because the INS was trying to deport Onyx again. Those
cases are long and expensive and Onyx isn't exactly a big draw
at the radical box office anymore. Yesterday's news, last year's
saint, we gave at the office. Which is why I hit Hugh. He

doesn't exactly follow fashion. It was pure brass on my part. The kind of thing he'd expect from Jack's Jew wife. Jack's Jew ex-wife. He said how much. I said ten thousand. He gave me five hundred. It was more than I expected. I told him it was tax deductible. He just laughed. He said he didn't need that beaner and his midget sister as tax deductions. You know the way he talks. Remember that night we had dinner with him on Washington Street, it was the first time we met. I called him a pig heavyweight and he said I thought you were a smart Jew, sister, but you're just like all the other meatballs, you've got something against winning, you're only interested in making a point. Nobody had ever called me a smart Jew before, not to my face at least. I never did know how to handle him. And I didn't this time. It was at Lottie's, of all places, "former mansion of Zsa Zsa Gabor," remember, that was how it was listed on the movie star map you had to buy so we could find it the first time we went there, that fundraiser for Onyx when I tried to steal the Rolodex and we decided to get married in the bathroom and how could I bring that up now? She was on location in Chicago and she let me stay in the house, I just had to pay the gardener (typical Lottie). The reason I was in L.A. was I was trying to keep Eugene from being sent back to Folsom, the D.A. was claiming violation of the terms of his probation because of those fucking dummy hand grenades on the poster, just basic pig harassment, and Hugh just happened to be in town on business, so I hit him for Onyx's defense while I was at it, oh, shit, you don't want to know the details, I won't give them to you, it happened, that's how it started, what more

The letter ended there. There was a brief postscript added the next day.

p.s. June 3—I've said all I'm going to say about that. The ICC flight leaves in 45 min., so I'll mail this now. There'll be a representative of the Pathet Lao on board, he's allowed to remain in Vientiane as a result of a pig concession in the pig Geneva agreement of 1964. He looks like an old man, but in fact he's only 39, a freedom fighter since he was 11, absolutely convinced of the rightness of his own cause and its ultimate triumph over Amerika's fascist stooges, prepared for any sacrifice, even his own death, and if final victory only comes after he's killed, it's a price he's willing to pay, he's that dedicated to the people's struggle. You listen to him and you know all the rest is bourgeois bullshit.

L

BOOK SIX

AFTER ANABEL

I

A WORD HERE about my marriage to Anabel Rutland. A word is all that it deserves. The marriage is no more important to this narrative than it was to Anabel, or to me. Anabel was a marriage addict, which of course meant that she was a divorce addict as well. I had nothing else to do.

The first time I saw Anabel she was fucking. It occurs to me now that I had seen or heard both the women I ultimately married fornicating with other men before they became involved with me. I note this only as a concidence. Anabel's consort on this occasion was Jimmy Dana, who, in the years since we first met at the fundraiser for Onyx Leon in Bel Air, had become both a reluctant collaborator (I rewrote many of his screenplays and he fewer of mine) as well as the closest approximation of a friend that I had. Jimmy and his wife Callie had a house in East Hampton that summer before their divorce. I had just quit, or been fired off, a picture I was rewriting in France for Marty Magnin. Whether my departure was voluntary or involuntary depended on which set of lawyers was doing the talking. I steadfastly contended that I had been fired, because if I had quit I would have been in breach of contract and it was a matter of principle with

me not to lose my profit participation; Marty's lawyers claimed
that I had left of my own accord because of "artistic differences,"
which in their interpretation would have meant that I forfeited
my points in the interest of maintaining my integrity, integrity
maintenance being a common bargaining chip in Hollywood
contract negotiations, a chip never granted voluntarily to the
party who might have integrity he would be willing to negotiate.
The director of the picture in question was one of those who
wore wire-rimmed aviator glasses and many gold chains hanging
from his neck and desert boots and a safari jacket and a viewfinder which he never took off, even at meals or, according to the
script girl, in bed. He had not liked my rewrite. When I asked
why, he said he was missing the essence. I asked him to define essence and he said, "The aroma off the roast, you know what I
mean, man?" I told him where he could stuff the essence, the
aroma and the roast and booked a flight back to New York. Before
I left Paris, I called Jimmy in East Hampton and he insisted that I
drive out to Long Island for the weekend as soon as I landed.

I took the Concorde, and with the six-hour time difference between New York and Paris, touched down at Kennedy at 9 A.M.,
two hours earlier than my scheduled departure time from Charles
de Gaulle, the beauty of the Conc, as Marty Magnin calls it. By
nine-thirty I had cleared customs and before noon the limousine I
had hired deposited me at Jimmy and Callie Dana's house on Lily
Pond Lane. There was no one about. The house was a rambling
weathered clapboard cottage surrounded by a wide veranda
which was cluttered with all the paraphernalia of a beach
house—swimming trunks and jockstraps and bikinis and bath
towels drying on the sun-dappled railing, a Scrabble set on which
someone had spelled out the word "clitoris," baseball mitts, bad-
minton rackets, several battered shuttlecocks, empty beer cans,
dirty coffee cups, old copies of *Time* and *Newsweek*, two half-
eaten doughnuts and a box of See's chocolates with the bottoms
of all the soft-centered pieces crushed in. I put my bag down,
picked up that morning's *New York Times* and settled in a
wicker chair to await Jimmy and Callie's return. In a moment I
was asleep.

I awoke to the sound of voices inside the house and with that terrible taste you have in your mouth when you wake up after dozing on a plane. My watch said seven o'clock, but of course that was Paris time. I hadn't reset it when I landed. One o'clock then. I hadn't even been asleep an hour. I listened to the voices coming through the open window. There was a bedroom on the other side of the window. I remembered that from my reconnaissance of the veranda. Jesus, I heard a voice say. Jimmy's voice. Christ, he said. Oh, God. It's like a telephone pole, isn't it? Tell me it's like a telephone pole. Yours is like a peach, Jimmy said. An Elberta peach. It's like fucking a peach melba. And then the woman's voice. Not so fast, I heard her say. Not so goddamn fast. The voice did not belong to Callie Dana.

I did not move. Obviously Jimmy and whoever was with him had not seen me when they came into the house. They must have come in through the kitchen door. And by the sound of things been in a hurry. My suitcase was by the front door. I opened my eyes a crack. I could see through the thin white organdy curtains into the room. Over the vanity table there was a large three-way mirror. In the mirror I could make out the bodies on the bed. I did not think they could see my reflection in the same mirror, but I could not be sure. I feigned sleep, eyes opened just enough to see what was going on in case they spotted me.

They lay back. Now I suddenly recognized the woman's spoiled pouty face in the mirror and the mane of blond hair on the pillow. Her picture was always in the newspaper. Anabel Rutland at Santa Anita. Anabel Rutland marries Kenny Carpenter, the jockey. Anabel Rutland at Vail. Anabel Rutland marries Billy Killian, the skier. Anabel Rutland on Maui. In Cancun. At the Golden Door. At Wimbledon. Anabel Rutland marries Johnny Baxter, the tennis player.

"You're sure Johnny's not coming back?"

"And miss a day at the Maidstone? You know Johnny."

"As well as I want to know him. I'm not sure I want to meet him at the other end of a gun."

I do not think Jimmy Dana would dispute me if I said his only genuine talent was a considerable gift for adultery. He had spent a large part of his adult life sleeping with other men's wives and his constant fear was of being shot in flagrante delicto by an outraged cuckolded husband. That's how I'm going to go, Jack, he would say, mark my words, it's in the cards. It's not the dying I mind so much, it's just that it's such an undignified way to check out.

"He's happy at the Maidstone," I heard Anabel Rutland say. "He can win some money playing tennis, but not so much that anyone can really accuse him of being a hustler, and then he'll get someone to buy him lunch. It makes him feel important again. That's what he always says. 'Important again.' As if he was important before I married him. He never got beyond the quarter finals in any major. And he'll probably find someone lonely. He's very good at that. He can tell her how terrible it is being married to a woman like me. Rich and selfish. That's what Johnny always says I am. He's never happier than when he's feeling sorry for himself. It's a sure way into someone's bed. I bet he's doing it right now."

"The bastard."

I could hear them laugh. I have always hated the dreary diction of adultery, the endless speculation, both angry and remorseful, about the deceived spouses and the degree of the spouse's culpability in the mate's infidelity. I thought it was only the element of danger, the chance and consequences of getting caught, that made adultery in any way appealing.

"Maybe with Callie."

"Too neat," I heard Jimmy say quickly. A residual loyalty to his wife. Callie Dana was not the kind of woman to repay her husband's adultery with a touch of her own. To do that would only undermine that air of superiority she had always so carefully nurtured, that attitude whose only purpose, I had often thought, was to make anyone who came in contact with her slightly uncomfortable. Callie was usually called strong, strong being an adjective people use to describe someone, generally a woman, they should admire and do not actually like. It was an appraisal I shared. I wondered where she was. Probably antiquing, I thought. The search for an authentic spinet was a preoccupation of strong admirable women. I was wrong. "Anyway she's in the Lionels."

"Where?"

"There's East Hampton and there's Southampton. And then there's the Lionel Hamptons. That's where the blacks live." I heard Anabel laugh. Even in bed Jimmy assumed the bright patter of the professional dinner guest. "An errand of mercy. The maid's grandson. He went skydiving. The parachute didn't open. Callie's over there with the maid. She baked a ham."

"Johnny doesn't even know the name of our servants."

"My point. So he's not with Callie."

"Where are you going?"

"To take a shower." And wash away his sins. Jimmy was one of the few people I knew, and certainly the only one in Hollywood, who actually believed in the idea of sin, and I suspected that his slighting reference to Callie made him consider the commandment he had just broken. After a moment I could hear water splashing in the shower and then Jimmy singing lustily:

> *"And was Jerusalem builded here*
> *Among those dark Satanic mills?*
> *Bring me my bow of burning gold,*
> *Bring me my arrows of desire . . ."*

William Blake. "Jerusalem." It was too perfect.

I watched Anabel stretch up the covers and smooth the bed. She pulled on a pair of bikini bottoms and for a moment stood in front of the mirror checking the flatness of her stomach and then her breasts for imperfections. With the hard edges of her palms she massaged the ridges of her thighs and then began tweezing away hairs that peeked beneath her bikini. When she was finished, she sat on the stool and pulled her hair up into a French twist, holding it with one hand and with the other inserting a tortoiseshell comb to keep the twist in place. To examine the effect, she adjusted the farthest panel of the mirror. Two things happened then. I felt the first pang of desire and Anabel caught my reflection in the panel. She did not start nor did she look around, out toward the veranda where I was stretched out in the wicker chaise pretending to be asleep.

Jimmy came back into the room, toweling himself off vigorously.

"Tell me about your friend," Anabel said. I could see her close the two outer panels of the vanity mirror so that Jimmy could not spot my reflection.

"Jack? I've known him since the year one. Since the summer of the grape strike anyway. Nineteen sixty something. When was that anyway?"

"I'm sure I wouldn't know."

"Of course not. The voice of reaction." I opened my eyes a centimeter. Jimmy's hands were trying to memorize the geography of Anabel's breasts. "I thought only liberals had tits as nice as this."

She took a can of Johnson's baby powder from the table and sprinkled some on her hand. Then she began to pat the powder between his legs. "Where did you meet him?"

"Lottie French's. At a fundraiser. For Onyx what's his name. Buddy Seville was there. Paul and Artie. Warren. Pluto Fahr. Christ, he wet his pants, Pluto. All over a damask chair. I thought Lottie would have a heart attack. Oh, that's nice, Anabel."

I closed my eyes again. I did not think I could manage it through another coupling.

"And you've been friends ever since?"

"Do we have to talk about Jack? At this very moment?"

"Why not?"

"God, you turn it on and off like a faucet. All right, then. Not exactly friends. Jack's gift for friendship isn't very highly developed."

"Associates?"

"More than that."

"Acquaintances."

"Somewhere between acquaintance and friend. He's fun, Jack. Charming. A lot of the time he's even nice. He's just not very giving. He's one of those damn watchers."

I knew Anabel was goading him for my benefit, sure that I was awake and listening. As I would soon learn from experience, she was a collector of indiscretions. A scavenger. Especially in the calm of postcoital languor before guards were posted and defenses fortified. I heard a drawer bang and opened my eyes a crack. Jimmy was slipping into a pair of navy blue Jockey briefs.

He hefted his basket a second longer than he needed, then held the elastic waistband open and doused himself liberally with the Johnson's.

"But you work with him a lot."

"Since his first picture. *The Invaders*. I had a solo credit on that until he came along. He'd just written that book of his. *Grunts*. Actually he hadn't written it at all. He'd only compiled it. From a bunch of interviews. A cut-and-paste job was all it was. Marty brought him in for a polish."

"And he rewrote it."

"Bullshit. He didn't write two lines of dialogue in the whole picture. But when it went to arbitration, the damn guild gave him a credit."

Actually I had not written even a single line of dialogue on *The Invaders*. That was not what Marty Magnin had hired me to do. He had read the studio coverage of *Grunts* as well as the front-page notice in *The New York Times Book Review* ("... searing ... gives food for thought ..."), although not, it soon became apparent when he called from Paris, the book itself. "It's a searing book, kid," he said long distance from the Plaza-Athénée. "Gave me a lot of food for thought." Right there I knew I was going to like Marty Magnin. "There's no picture in it, but maybe you can help me out anyway." He had made a war movie—what may have been Green Berets in what appeared to be an unnamed Asian country besieged by what seemed to be a Slavic invader— that he was unable to cut together and he wanted me, with the benefit of my Vietnam experience, to write a voice-over that he thought might possibly splice together the loose ends in Jimmy Dana's screenplay. A week later Marty ran a rough cut of the picture for me in the screening room of his house in Beverly Hills. "What do you think?" he said when the lights came up. I had been trying to frame an answer to that question for most of the preceding two hours. "You might call it an allegory," I said carefully. "I don't need you to tell me it's a piece of shit," he said. "I figured that out all by myself." I said, "Maybe it can be saved." He said, "Maybe another lifeboat could've saved the *Titanic*, too." I said, "It has a universal theme." He said, "Just what I need. A hit at Bloomingdale's." In any event, I wrote the voice-

over for Marty Magnin and *The Invaders* went, in his words,
"straight to cult." Its only profit was to me. I had a new career as
a screenwriter.

Jimmy tried on a pale pink guayabera and modeled it for Anabel. "What do you think?"

I heard her mumble something.

"Actually Jack's never really understood film at all," Jimmy
said. I stifled a laugh. "Film" is another of those words that can
reduce me to convulsions. The kind of people who say "film" also
call reviewers they have never met by their first names, "Pau-
line," say, or "Andy," and can recite every line of Merle Oberon's
dialogue in *Wuthering Heights* and know that I made two point
six million from my seven-and-a-half net points on Marty Magnin's remake of *Mildred Pierce* and that the definition of my net
was in a most favored nation position with Lottie French's and
assume the reason I had the most favored nation clause in my
contract was because I was fucking Lottie, which I wasn't; it was
Bobby Gabel that semester. Jimmy invariably said "film," most
effectively in meetings, often with the adjective "major" attached,
as in, "What we all want here is a major film." In fact, Jimmy's
major strength as a screenwriter was a well-deserved reputation
for being what in Hollywood is called "a good meeting." It compensated for his tin ear. The good meeting has a meteorologist's
sense of which way the wind is blowing. He is an interpreter of
silences and a reader of eyebrow movements, a master of options,
tactical advances and strategic withdrawals, with a fund of gossip
available to cover that awkward moment when he must deposit
blame for an unfortunate idea on someone else's doorstep. In
Jimmy's case, the doorstep of choice was often mine. "I mean, he
has no grasp of the ecology of the medium."

It seemed the most venial of all the sins of which I had ever
been accused. Carefully I tried to shift my position to ease the
cramp in my hip and the stiffness in my neck. The wicker
creaked. I froze, but Jimmy had disappeared into the closet. Anabel, however, stared through the gauzy curtains toward the chaise
where I lay. She walked toward the window, rubbing suntan lo-
tion on her face, then sat on the sill. She never looked directly
across the veranda toward the chaise, but continued oiling her

breasts and stomach and legs, talking back into the room. "Has he ever written another book?"

Jimmy emerged from the closet, carrying two pairs of espadrilles. "Are you kidding?"

He had the professional screenwriter's disdain for the writer of books. He anticipated condescension and fired first. In fact I had written another book. Of a sort. I ghosted Lottie French's autobiography. The most crucial part of the arrangement as far as I was concerned was to keep my contribution quiet, and I was more or less successful. No money changed hands—always an appealing feature to Lottie—but in return she did agree to do *Mildred Pierce*, which I suspect she planned to do anyway. The job took only two weeks and I declined not only credit but any mention in the acknowledgments. Her publisher wanted to call the book *French Kisses* and the jacket to have a blowup of those famous and generous French lips on which much of upper-echelon Hollywood and the radical left, male and female, foreign and domestic, had sat. Lottie, however, insisted on something more tasteful and settled on *Carlotta French's Me, Myself and I,* the possessory credit being part of the title, and one that did not actually leave much room for "As Told To," had I so desired it. What I got from the book was exactly what I wanted, Lottie's recollections of herself and Leah in Hanoi, the tapes of which I still have. It goes without saying that these recollections never made it into the manuscript for *Carlotta French's Me, Myself and I,* beyond a few general thoughts on peace through understanding, the community of nations and how men of all colors, races and creeds should reason together and beat their swords into plowshares. That was the section of *Carlotta French's Me, Myself and I* that took most of the two weeks to write.

"His wife balled his father." Anabel stood in profile by the window a few feet from me, arms folded, her thumbs flicking back and forth over her nipples.

"No, she didn't." Good loyal Jimmy. He always liked Leah. Who thought he was ridiculous. Of course he was. That was not the point. The point was that he was never really mean-spirited. Jimmy liked me, too. Except in pillow talk.

"That's what Edgar Hoover told my grandfather."

"I mean she wasn't his wife then."

"That's splitting hairs."

"I didn't say she was a nun, Anabel. I only said she and Jack weren't still married . . ." His voice trailed off, then he added fastidiously, ". . . when that happened. They were already divorced."

"She had an abortion."

Jimmy was snappish. "I bet your grandfather had to pull out J. Edgar's fingernails to get him to tell that."

"In Encino."

I could never escape Leah for long. I wondered if she had any secrets that were not in the custodial care of the government. She and I had a fight the night before I left for Paris and the rewrite Marty Magnin had prevailed upon me to undertake, with the director who never removed his viewfinder. About Mercury Baker. He was in trouble again. He either had or had not killed a black prostitute in south central Los Angeles. He either had or had not thrown her off the roof of a four-story building on Avalon Boulevard. His alibi was The Shadow. The Shadow said he was driving Mercury Baker to Bobby Gabel's at the time the murder was supposed to have occurred. In Bobby Gabel's silver Benz, The Shadow said. Then the three of them went to a party at Hef's. Bobby Gabel said the Merc was blissed out the whole night. Not the way you'd be if you just tossed a chick off a roof, Bobby Gabel told reporters. Bobby Gabel said the police were hassling the Merc. Because the Merc had a series in development with NBC. Bobby Gabel said that with charges outstanding the series with the peacock was in the toilet. Hef said he would hold a fundraiser for the Merc at the Mansion. Hef said he had a definite commitment from Harry Reems to attend. Bobby Gabel and Lottie French stood Mercury Baker's $250,000 bail. The evening newscasts reported that Lottie French had arrived at the bond hearing in a sable coat and Armani slacks. After bail was arranged, Bobby Gabel lent Mercury Baker the apartment in the Hollywood Hills he kept for his girlfriend of the moment. The girlfriend of the moment moved into Lottie French's pool house, then into Lottie French's bedroom. Mercury Baker telephoned a radio call-in host and said that a criminal was only a man of ex-

tremes who robbed a 7-Eleven rather than the dignity of his fel-
lowman. I heard the show on my car radio and that night I asked
Leah if she remembered the afternoon I had spent with Mercury
at the house on San Luis Road in Berkeley. She said she did not. I
did not remind her that it was the day before her first miscarriage.
I said how coincidental it was that so many people happened to
meet violent ends whenever Mercury Baker was in the neighborhood. Leah said my reservations about him and his revolutionary
role constituted an endorsement of racism. I said she failed to understand her client's predisposition to aberrant social behavior.
She said she was not surprised that I used the word "client," with
its pig implication of superior and inferior roles. I said I thought
the murder of a prostitute was definitely an inferior act. She said
Eugene Baker was her brother. I said if that were the case then
her brother had a fool for an attorney, or "sister," if that were
what she preferred being called. She said she hoped my plane
would crash. It was the kind of ugly argument we never had
when we were married. The day after I checked into my hotel
in the Place des Vosges I received a cable that said, GLAD
AIR FRANCE 316 ARRIVED SAFELY. The wire was not signed.
A few weeks later I read a small item in the *International
Herald Tribune* that said the Los Angeles district attorney
had dropped all charges against Mercury Baker for insufficient
evidence.

"That's ancient history, Anabel," Jimmy said. He had settled
on beige espadrilles and was hauling on a pair of white sailcloth
slacks.

Anabel did not answer for a moment. Finally she said, less to
Jimmy than to my inert form on the veranda, "I wonder what it
was like being married to a woman like that."

"Ask him at dinner tonight. That's one way sure to get the attention of the whole table. You'll have to explain who she is to
Johnny, though. Johnny doesn't pick up on anyone who isn't
seeded. 'You see, Johnny,' you say, 'Leah's at least a quarter-
finalist among all those people the FBI's keeping an eye on for
us.' " I was surprised at the sharpness in Jimmy's voice. He was
more irritated with Anabel for her remarks about Leah than I had
thought. Johnny Baxter was only a handy surrogate target. "Put

it that way and he might understand. If you speak slowly
enough."

Anabel made no effort to come to Johnny Baxter's defense. She
turned at the window and looked deliberately out toward the
hideaway where I lay, every muscle screaming from having been
locked in the same position for so long. It was as if she were trying to will me into acknowledging my awareness of her presence.
Nothing overt. Just some small private gesture between us that
she would not share with Jimmy. A slight body movement would
more than suffice. The cock of an eyebrow. The wiggling of a finger. A resigned and imperceptible smile signifying surrender. I
remained still. Eyes flickering, I watched her as best I could
through the cobweb of wicker. Slowly she knotted the strings of
her bikini top around her neck and her back. Then she fitted the
twin pieces of cloth over her breasts and said, "Actually I'm not
all that interested in her."

"You rich people are all alike," I heard Jimmy say. Suddenly
he appeared beside her at the window. I thought the jig was up.
But he was not interested in anything on the veranda. He put his
arms through hers and concentrated on helping her adjust her bikini cups. "Short attention span. Jack's the same way."

"He's not rich," Anabel said. She extricated herself from his
grasp and pulled the organdy curtains together. I was to be her
secret only. "His father's rich." She moved away from the window. Jimmy followed. "And his father's not as rich as my grandfather was."

"At that level who cares? What's a hundred million or so matter one way or the other?"

"It matters."

I saw her open the bedroom door and she and Jimmy disappear
into the hall. I scrambled to my feet.

"Is anyone home? Jimmy? Callie?"

"Jack."

"There wasn't anyone here. I went for a walk on the beach."

"Callie's out shopping for dinner. This is Anabel Baxter."

"Rutland."

"Jack Broderick."

"Jimmy's told me so much about you."

II

_____

What's a hundred million or so matter one way or the other?
It matters.

There in a nutshell was the dynamic of our marriage. A grudge
fuck a day or so after we met segued into a grudge marriage during the abbreviated course of which neither of us ever mentioned
the incident at the house on Lily Pond Lane. DOMINUS VOBI-
SCUM, Bro wired again, this time from Lourenço Marques. It
seemed his standard comment on the women I married, the difference being that where Leah had thought it funny, Anabel did
not. My father received Anabel once at the house on Washington
Street, with a display of courtesy I found far more intimidating
than his usual bad manners, which at least were genuine, and
thereafter managed to schedule himself so that he was never in
San Francisco when we were there, or in New York or Los Angeles or any other port of call where we might possibly meet.
Jimmy and Callie divorced, Jimmy married Frankie Pierson, he
and I cuckolded each other without much enthusiasm and Anabel
and I finally separated. To itemize the charges, counts and specifications attendant to our divorce would be superfluous. The
marriage is worth remembering only for Leah's wedding present,

347

a needlepoint pillow which had actually been worked, in red and black yarn to Leah's precise specifications, by her mother. Bea, in fact, had discovered in custom needlepoint a flourishing sideline to her theme catering business. Her silent partner in this venture was Marty Magnin, who was now able to complement the gift of a dirty cake with a pornographic pillow. All of this was part of the shared history from which Anabel was excluded, as she was also excluded from the particular resonance of the quotation on the pillow Leah had sent: A CRIMINAL IS MERELY A MAN OF EX-TREMES—EUGENE BAKER.

Anabel did not think that was funny either.

I did not explain. I was not prepared to conduct a seminar on my life with Leah, and the priority she allocated to "funny," nor do I think Anabel was interested enough to attend.

The pillow was relegated to the office I rented in the old movie studio on La Cienega that Bobby Gabel had bought to house his production company. It decorated the leather psychiatrist's couch where I would occasionally entertain Frankie Pierson, sometimes on those afternoons when I was reasonably certain that Anabel was entertaining Jimmy Dana. I went to the office early every morning, usually before Anabel was up, if she were in town, which became increasingly infrequent as the overseeing of her interests in Rutland Enterprises claimed more and more of her time. I did not begrudge these claims, in fact welcomed her absences the more frequent they became. Although I was always in demand, I had time to spare, in part because I had no hobbies other than the odd joyless adultery, in larger measure because I wrote quickly, the legacy of my newspaperman's training. A ten-week assignment I could often finish in two, a three-week rewrite I might knock off over an arduous long weekend.

Out of sheer inertia, I spent much of that spare time with Bobby Gabel. He was still in his Mercury Baker phase.

"You know what the Merc needs?" he said one afternoon.

I shook my head.

"Visibility."

I nodded sagely, even though my considered opinion was that Mercury Baker had more visibility than he could reasonably handle. We were sitting in Bobby's office. It was so large that it easily accommodated a player piano, a Steinway grand, a Ping-Pong table, a custom-designed pinball machine called TARGET PPS, PPS standing for Pig Power Structure, and an old fashioned Wurlitzer jukebox filled with revolutionary songs from around the world of insurrection. On an elevated pedestal next to the Louis XV table that served as Bobby's desk was a dictionary stand lit by a pinpoint ceiling spot. Open on the stand, like a missal on an altar laid for Mass, was Bobby's FBI file, bound by Bottega Veneta in black leather with gold lettering that said,

THE UNITED $TATE$ OF AMERIKA

V.

ROBERT POLI GABEL

"The Merc could be the schwartze Fidel if he's handled right," Bobby said.

My eyes fixed on the far wall and the photo blowup of Bobby surveying the landing beach at Bahía de Cochinos, a bandolier and a Kalashnikov strapped to his Abercrombie & Fitch camouflage fatigues.

"Is he still using your apartment in the Hills?" I said.

"You know the Merc," Bobby said quickly. His face disappeared behind a cloud of marijuana smoke. "He'd rather be on the bricks."

I selected another nod from the library of nods I used to converse with Bobby Gabel.

"It's like Folsom up there," Bobby added after a moment.

I contemplated the maximum-security-prison potential of a three-bedroom, fifteen-hundred-dollar-a-month apartment in the Hollywood Hills. "I can get behind that."

"The only reason he's still there is because he needs to see some people."

"What people?"

As always he gave the impression that he was a case officer running a network of moles. "People who've got reasons they don't want to be seen on the bricks."

"Who?" I persisted.

He offered me a hit. I shook my head. He took a long drag. I

had the sense that I did not have all the clearances he required
and that he needed to weigh the risks before he answered. "I put
him together with some people in the television department in
the William Morris office."

I thought William Morris agents were definitely people who
would not want to be seen on the bricks. Especially with Mercury
Baker. "I thought NBC passed."

"We've come up with a new concept."

"Really."

"A spin-off from his book."

Leah had never mentioned a book. And she usually kept me
apprised of all Mercury Baker's ventures and adventures. My disapproval was a kind of sustenance for her. "What book?"

"It's called *Letters to Germany*."

"His brother?"

Bobby unscrewed the speaker on his telephone and examined
the inside as if he were looking for a tap. "The one you saw iced
at Q."

"He never wrote any letters to Germany. They never laid eyes
on each other."

"These are the letters he wanted to write."

"And now he's written them." It was neither a statement nor a
question, but a hesitation in between.

"Not exactly." Bobby Gabel stood up and began idly leafing
through his FBI file. The pinpoint ceiling spot gave him a halo
effect. "He knows what he wants to say."

Suddenly I could see where this was heading. "Except he needs
someone to say it for him."

Bobby smiled. "You'd be perfect. You know him. He trusts
you. You know the way he thinks."

There were two things about which I was certain. Mercury
Baker trusted no one. And I had no idea how he thought. Nor did
I wish to know. "I think I'll pass."

"You did it for Lottie. It's the same thing."

I deserved that. "Once is enough."

"The Merc'll be disappointed."

I shrugged.

"You were the first name he ran past the people from the Morris office. They were delighted."

"I'm honored. It's still Pasadena."

Bobby waited, as if hoping I would change my mind. After a
moment he strolled to the Wurlitzer and selected a record. The
turntable began to spin and the scratchy music of a children's
jingle filled the office:

> *"Somos Fidelistas,*
> *Marxistas, Leninistas,*
> *Y mañana seremos*
> *Tremendas Comunistas."*

I could hear cheering and shouting in the background.

"Oriente," Bobby said softly. Then he mouthed the words,
"Fidel's birthplace." It was as if he were passing information unknown to any of the world's security agencies. I watched as he
patted his hands on the jukebox to the rhythm of the jingle. "I recorded it there last July twenty-sixth. The quality's shit, but you
get the idea."

I think the idea was that I join the revolution and ghost *Letters
to Germany*. A kind of cultural reindoctrination that would ab-
solve my ghosting *Carlotta French's Me, Myself and I*. I had to
admire Bobby's ingenuity. On the record, the children of Oriente
segued into another chant:

> *"Pim-Pan-Pum*
> *Mao Tse-tung."*

"Cute," Bobby said. He switched off the jukebox and returned
to the FBI file on the elevated stand. He seemed refreshed by the
interlude. The movement was better off without my counterrevo-
lutionary tendencies. He was all business. "We'll go right into
screenplay for the MOW once the book's done."

I did not ask who would do it. Getting the book written seemed
to have diminished in importance. "You're going to finance this
yourself?"

"That's the only way we can get the investment tax credit. The
ITC's what it's all about in television."

"You said 'we.' "

"The Merc and me. Partners."

"Equal?"

"More or less," Bobby said smoothly. "After costs are re-couped."

I was willing to bet the Broderick fortune that Bobby would let the William Morris people take the cost recoupment meetings with Mercury Baker when and if that time ever came. I decided to play the scene out. "I suppose the MOW will be the pilot for the series."

"The series will need a broader approach, of course."

"Of course."

"The Merc'll be in the joint in the MOW. We see him on the street in the series."

"More story potential."

"That's the way we see it."

"The slammer is limited."

"As a story venue," Bobby agreed.

I wondered how far I could go. "How about black ex-con gets elected mayor of small southern town?"

Bobby shook his head dismissively. "Liberal bullshit." He concentrated on his FBI file. I waited. Then he looked up and tapped the page he was reading. "You know, these people are real amateurs. They say here I was in Caracas the eighth of August, 1972."

"Where were you?"

A small satisfied smile. "Not in Caracas."

The air of unearned mystery clung to him like an inexpensive cologne. I pushed on. "How about black ex-con becomes private eye?"

I could see the flicker of interest. I added another element. "His parole officer's his sidekick."

Bobby's lips barely moved. "Nice."

"I don't mean some old guy."

He nodded in agreement. "We don't want Uncle Remus."

"Exactly."

"A schwartze Walter Brennan."

"Wouldn't work."

"We're agreed on that, then."

"Absolutely."

He stared at me across the dictionary stand. "Who?"

"The Shadow."

"As the sidekick?"

"The parole officer."

"It has possibilities."

"Of course The Shadow's not into love like the Merc is." I tried not to laugh.

"We could make a virtue out of that."

"He's not exactly into hate either."

"No reason to make a meal out of that."

"You mean hate?"

Bobby nodded.

"Then we're in sync," I said. "The Shadow's not into love like the Merc, but he's not into hate either."

"Something in between."

"That's fantastic." I knew I had gone too far, but it was too late to retreat. Bobby was captivated and the further I advanced toward the absurd the more captivated he became. A moment passed. We stared at each other. Bobby rolled a piece of Kleenex into a spitball. I straightened a paper clip and then tried to bend it back into shape again.

"He's a former defensive tackle for the Green Bay Packers," I said.

"Which one?"

"The sidekick."

"The parole officer."

"The Shadow," I said.

"That would explain his size."

"Right."

"Good. He weighs four hundred pounds."

"He's got a knee injury."

"I'm not into knees." Bobby walked to the bookcase and tried on the faded fatigue cap he always said Fidel had given him at Playa Girón. Not just any fatigue cap. Fidel's own, Bobby said. A claim I tended to doubt. It was so small it sat on the top of his head, like a beanie.

"That's why he had to retire. His knee blew out."

"So?"

"So it's given him all this rage."

"And he can't handle it."

"Right."

"Why?"

I scratched my head with the paper clip. "Because he was twenty-four years old and making seventy-five grand a year playing DT for the Pack, maybe even the Pro Bowl, the cover of *Sports Illustrated*, then he's clipped, it's over, he's in the toilet."

"The Merc was in the slammer. That's what I call the crapper."

I snapped a finger. "That's it, that's the switch."

"What?"

"It's the Merc who keeps the parole officer cool."

"Nice."

"And it's the parole officer who wants to lean on everyone."

"The Shadow."

"Right."

"And the Merc keeps him in line."

"The ex-con."

"Role reversal," Bobby said. He removed the fatigue cap and placed it back in the bookcase under a Lucite square.

"That's what I was thinking."

"We can play with that."

"You've got the room."

"Illusion versus reality."

"In that neighborhood."

Bobby sat down, putting first one Bally boot up on the Louis XV table, then the other. "They're not queer for each other?"

"No."

"Okay."

"That was when they were in the slam," I said after a moment.

"The Merc?"

"And The Shadow."

"You heard about that then?"

I nodded.

"From Leah?"

"He lived with us for a while in Berkeley when he got out of Folsom."

"The Merc."

"The Shadow, too."

"I knew that."

"I read his probation report."

"I never read pig shit," Bobby said.

I pointed to the pedestal and his FBI file. "You were just reading that."

"For the laughs."

"He was a snitch inside."

"The pigs say."

I nodded.

"Everyone's a snitch inside," Bobby volunteered finally.

"He didn't get a pencil stuck in his mouth, though."

"Who'd try?"

A reasonable question. "Pimped, too. All the new little boys who came in. Tried them out first, then peddled them."

"Just trying to make a buck. It's called free enterprise."

"Muscle. Smack. Speed. Ice man."

Bobby buffed each Bally boot in turn with the sleeve of his black silk shirt. "Sometimes I think the Merc could run Metro."

"He couldn't run it worse than it's being run now."

"Right." He examined a blemish on his left boot. "Are you married to the Green Bay Packers?"

I shook my head.

"I was thinking the Detroit Lions."

It took me a minute to figure out why. "Motown."

"Diana Ross under the opening credits."

I nodded appreciatively.

"One thing to keep in mind," Bobby said.

"What?"

"The Merc is the star. Not The Shadow."

"Easy."

"How?"

"Blow The Shadow away in the fourth episode. That way Mercury can become the parole officer."

"Interesting," Bobby said. "Let me run it past the Merc."

"And the William Morris people."

"Not necessary. I just need them to rough out the parameters of the deal."

"No creative input."

"That's not their franchise."

"Of course."

"On the whole I like it."

I doubted that Leah would. Bobby seemed to read my mind. "You still see Leah?"

"We talk."

Neither of us spoke for a moment. As if to himself, Bobby chanted, *"Pim-Pan-Pum."* Then he said, "I saw Lottie when she got back from Cannes." Lottie French had been a judge at the film festival. "You hear how she arrived?" I shook my head. "She shows up at the Hotel du Cap with a secretary, those two faggots she always travels with, the makeup man and the hairdresser, Ike and Mike, her brat and the brat's au pair girl, the one that used to be the dealer, what's her name, Quentin."

I suddenly remembered Quentin. Quentin, who had asked Ramona Leon for a birth control pill the day at Lottie's house in Bel Air when Leah and I decided to get married. Bobby seemed to have forgotten that Quentin was with him that afternoon.

"Anyway," he said, "she tries to stick the festival with the tab for the whole bunch."

"Typical." Lottie's reverence for the value of a dollar was legend. I wondered if she had called the festival officials "lackeys" when they tried to bill her.

"I also hear," Bobby said, "she was making it with some Bulgarian director the whole time she was there."

"What's his name?"

"Sonja something." He had the manner of a secret policeman offering a nugget from an illegal wiretap. "Sonja Velcheva."

Sonja, I thought. Sonja from Sofia at the Hotel du Cap.

"Is Leah still tight with Lottie?" Bobby said. "As tight as she used to be?"

With Bobby there was no such thing as an innocent question. I could make the connection. Lottie and Sonja at the Hotel du Cap, Leah and Lottie in the Marco Polo Suite at the Peninsula on their way back from Hanoi. The story was rarely out of currency.

I framed my answer carefully. "Leah never really was a member of the collective."

Bobby leaned back and put his hands behind his neck. "I've been giving Leah a lot of thought."

"Oh."

"Vis-à-vis this project."

I was fairly sure I knew what was coming.

"I don't think she's exactly right for it. She's not really an entertainment lawyer after all."

He might have been talking about firing an agent.

"The Merc and I were thinking more along the lines of Ornstein and Shay. Tax specialists," he added unnecessarily. "Estate planning. Top litigators. On the civil side, of course."

"Of course."

"The Merc's into ITCs. I think Leah would be the first to say that's not her area of expertise."

"Probably."

That night I called Leah in Oakland. I had not spoken to her in six months. I had the feeling she thought my life was beside the point. Not that she had ever said anything. If pressed, she would have said she had more important things to consider than whatever life I chose to lead.

Ramona said Leah was in Cristo Rey until the end of the month. She had left the day before.

"She usually tells you, doesn't she, Jack, when she goes away?"

"Usually." Not usually. Always.

"She's been very busy, Jack," Ramona said. "It must have slipped her mind."

I asked why she was in Cristo Rey.

"You remember Sister Phyllis, don't you, Jack?"

I did not remember at first.

"The fat girl, Jack. With the glasses."

"Phyllis Emmett." For whom I had bought a package of rubbers in Hermosa that summer so many years earlier.

"She's working down there. In a *comunidad de base*."

I ran through my rusty Spanish. "A base community?"

"You know, Jack, the option of the poor."

Then I recognized the phrases. Bro had used them during his flirtation with liberation theology. Base community. The option

of the poor. From there only a hop, skip and jump to the legitimate right of insurrectional violence. Just the drug for Leah when
the Merc was into investment tax credits and Lottie was eating a
Bulgarian director at the Hotel du Cap. Whatever else Leah was,
she was the keeper of the flame, the defender of the faith.

"Phyllis is in Cristo Rey," I said slowly, "and Leah went down
there to see her."

"Oh, no, Jack, that's not why she went down there."

As always, it was maddening trying to elicit information from
Ramona. "Then why did she go down there, Ramona?"

"It's a terrible place down there, Jack." She offered it as a reason, and then I recalled that she and Onyx had both been born in
Cristo Rey. "*La violencia.*"

"And that's why Leah went down."

"With Freedom Watch." The human rights organization
whose lawyer she had become the year before.

"And she's going to see Phyllis."

"That's right, Jack. When she's there."

"Where is she?"

"At a people's church in Chalatenango, Jack. Working against
the international imperialism of money."

Ramona had certainly picked up all the phrases. "I meant
Leah."

She gave me the telephone number of a hotel in Cristo Rey.
"You want to speak to Harriet, Jack?"

I told Ramona I definitely did not wish to speak to Harriet
Hecht.

The international operator said all circuits to Cristo Rey were
busy.

III

A series of conversations with Leah between 1970 and 1979 as remembered by the narrator and edited by him into a single monologue subject to the imperfections of memory:

"You know what I was voted in my senior class poll at William Howard Taft, that fat fascist, high school in the Valley? 'Most Likely to Become a Math Teacher.' I finished second to Rachel Hyams in 'Neatest Handwriting.' Kennedy Hirsch was 'Most Likely to Succeed.' That's what I thought of when Lottie and I got to Hong Kong after we left Hanoi. The Morris office had booked her into something called the Marco Polo Suite at the Peninsula, very BFD, it's where Steve McQueen stayed when he made *The Sand Pebbles*, Lottie said, and when we checked in, there were these two Chinese room boys who came with the suite, Wang and Wellington. I called them Petty and Larceny, which Lottie didn't think was very funny. She kept on telling them she had just seen their brothers in Hanoi, and of course they didn't know what the fuck she was talking about. They just kept saying, 'Yes, missy,' 'No, missy,' with their hands out, every 'Yes, missy,' was ten dollars Hong Kong. And when I looked out the window at the harbor, all I could think of was Kennedy Hirsch, Miss Most Likely to Succeed, Taft High. I'd been to Hanoi and she hadn't and I was as much a Valley girl as she was for thinking that. Bea did her daughter's bat last year, she's Kennedy Chasalow now and she's had a mastectomy, so I guess we each have our own ideas on what life is all about. The bat was such a success that Kennedy Chasalow with her one tit asked Mother to do a fundraiser for Operation Bus Stop, that's the organization that's been set up to stop busing in the Valley.

"Mother did it.

"There was a POW I met at one of the camps outside Hanoi. His name was Hirsch, too. I guess he's the reason I thought so much about Kennedy. A navy pilot. The war crimes commissioner who always traveled with us, a tiny Vietnamese with a wispy white beard, he said the prisoner had been a POW for just a few days. I asked him what carrier he was off and he said his name was Ellison Hirsch and he was a lieutenant commander and his serial number was such and such and so and so. 'Don't you realize you've been trained to be a professional killer?' Lottie said. Then she asked the war crimes commissioner if we could take him to Kham Tiem Street. We'd been there after the raid the day before. Lottie said she wanted to show him what the B-52s had done. It was like those pictures on the news after an earthquake. A whole street of mud and brick houses just leveled. There was so much rubble that people were carrying their bicycles on their heads, there was just no way to ride through it. It seemed like everyone was wearing a white mourning band. That's what you wear wrapped around your head if you've lost someone close. I could see this crane trying to lift the concrete slab off the top of a bomb shelter, it had taken a direct hit. It finally got the slab off, but everyone inside was dead, fifteen, sixteen people. You could tell the women who had family inside because they wrapped veils around their faces before they began to cry, they don't like anyone to see them cry. But the war crimes commissioner said no, we couldn't take him to Kham Tiem Street, it would interrupt the cleanup, and then he recited the figures of the dead and the wounded, forty-seven dead and seventy-one wounded on just that one block. Before they took this flier back to his compound, I asked him if he were related to the Hirsch family in Sherman Oaks and he said he had an Uncle Myron Hirsch in Denver, that was as far west as his branch of the Hirsch family had ever got.

"There are a couple of things I'll never forget. The little concussion pop in your inner ear when a bomb goes off. And the claustrophobia in the shelters. I hated it so much that finally, when the sirens went off, I just stayed put at the Hoa Binh, that's the hotel where they put us up. I'd take the mattress off my bed and wedge it against the window and I'd put a pillow over my head. I was terrified, but less so than I was in the shelters, where I wanted to scream every minute. I still have trouble in elevators. That's why I use the fire stairs wherever I can, not to keep in shape, which is what I tell people. Lottie loved the shelters, of course. She seemed to think they were some kind of people's theater. She talked about the communion, the rapport with the people, you know, in that way actors do when they say they can feel the love pouring across the footlights, Johnny, or Merv, or whatever the fuck talk show they're on. She even accused me of putting my own safety ahead of the revolution by staying in the hotel. As if the Hoa Binh was safer than a shelter. Fuck off, Lottie, I said. I hated that Mother Courage routine.

"I know what people say. That Lottie and I got it on in the Marco Polo Suite. I think it was Wang and Wellington who put that out. Every reporter in Hong Kong used them. I'm surprised they never got a byline. All those show business liberals, that's the only thing they really wanted to know about the trip, did Lottie and I go down on each other. The fact of the matter is, we didn't, Wang and his buddy Wellington notwithstanding. Lottie saw *Dr. Zhivago* twice, she was checking out the cameraman or the art director or somebody for that picture she was going to make in Tuscany with Michelangelo what's his name, and I got three silk blouses made at Ascot Chang's that I wanted for the San Diego Six trial that was scheduled for a suppression hearing right after I got back. That's all that happened in Hong Kong. Anyway, the thing with Lottie happened in Tacoma at the Fort Lewis sit-in, it was right after the scrape, you know the one I mean, and that was it, over and out, we were barely civil to each other that whole trip to Hanoi. I wouldn't have gone if I hadn't made a commitment to the Committee for Solidarity with the American People, it was bourgeois bullshit not to go.

"I won't talk about the scrape, Jack. That episode is over."

"Bourgeois bullshit," Leah said in 1970, 1973, 1974, 1977 and 1979.

IV

THE DIVORCE FROM ANABEL RUTLAND was perhaps the only thing I ever did that pleased my father unequivocally. He took me to lunch at the Pacific Union Club shortly after the decree nisi was issued and for once he did not talk about Bro. He was in what for Hugh Broderick might be called an expansive mood.

"You're well rid of that one, Jack. I warned you about that Rutland bunch, and don't you say I didn't. The old man was always just one step ahead of the sheriff. Or would have been if the sheriff hadn't been in his pocket like a pet rat. He should've been in the hoosegow, that's where, making pig bristles into paintbrushes at fifteen cents an hour, and it would've been the only honest work he ever did, and that's a fact."

"What was it between you two?" I did not expect an answer and of course did not get one, but that I had asked the question without his boiling over semaphored some small truce.

"He used to sit there in that big ranch house outside Rutland-ville, in his cowboy suit, looking like he was Wild Bill Hickok, the Indian scout, when the only horse he ever saw until he was thirty-seven years of age was pulling the garbage wagon he was driving in Providence, Rhode Island, and that's the truth, that's where home, home on the range really was. 'Oh, give me a home, where the buffalo roam,' " my father sang in the sedate dining room of the Pacific Union Club, impervious to the stares of the other men having lunch, singing because he was Hugh Broderick and he knew he could get away with it. "And that was his next stop, Jack, Buffalo, New York . . ."

I was meant to enjoy his revisionist history of old Marshall Rutland's westward odyssey, and I did, in no small measure because it was so unusual not to be the object of his disdain. My father relied on caricature, and as always the caricature was informed with at least a scintilla of truth. In his telling, Marshall Rutland came slowly across those great blank plains just before the turn of the century, settling finally, after a series of reverses, in Riverside County, that whole southern rim then as now a nirvana for the larcenous. He bought land cheap, my father said, and sold it dear, sticking oranges onto the branches of Joshua trees to entice the rubes from Iowa and Indiana. The rubes were enticed and thus Marshall Rutland made his stake, in the process beginning his transformation from garbageman into a land baron Johnny Ringo, with 129,000 acres of Riverside and San Bernardino counties to back up the authorized version of his life.

The rendition made me smile, for the Brodericks' way west from the peat marshes of Sligo had been no more heroic than the Rutlands' from Providence. But as I listened to my father ridicule the ranch in Rutlandville that duplicated the Alamo, I suddenly realized why he so detested Marshall Rutland, even into the grave. It had nothing to do with a joint business venture gone sour. There were many of those in my father's career, and whenever one happened his reaction was always the same—don't look back, don't get mad, get even, if only to make a point. No, that was not it. What seemed to my father pointless about Marshall Rutland was the creation of a specious past. My father only cared about legends made in the present, and by children and grandchildren. That was where I had failed him and I knew then that I had been the real subject of this monologue all along. I was his Anabel.

"I think I've been a disappointment to you." I was as surprised to hear myself speak as he was to be interrupted.

"In what way?" I was gratified that he did not deny it.

"Look, for once, just once, let's be honest with each other. . . ." It was the reflex rhetoric of psychoanalysis, a religion I had abandoned as I had Catholicism, and I knew even before the words were out of my mouth that it was the wrong note to take.

"I don't need you to tell me to be honest, bucko. I don't need that at all. I've always been as honest with you as I have with The Justice Department and the Internal Revenue Service."

I was to him as the attorney general and the tax collector. I could not help but laugh, even though I knew the response it would bring. It was batten down the hatches, I was in for it.

"Have a good laugh," he said. "You're good at that. You and all those smart Hollywood Jewboys you hang around with. I know that crowd. They're all five feet tall and wear their hair in a jungle bunny frizz, and they got the Star of David on a gold chain around the neck, and they march, they never miss a march, that bunch, Selma, they're there, Attica, count on it, with an air travel card and a return ticket. Sammy Davis," he said suddenly, "I bet you know him . . ."

He did not wait for an answer.

"That wife of yours. She's worth that whole pack of tap dancers."

"I thought you didn't like Anabel." But of course I knew he was talking about Leah and not Anabel and I also knew with a chill certainty that what we had never mentioned, never even intimated, would not and could not now remain unmentionable.

"You know the one I mean. The Queen of the Jews. She gets the stigmata every time a darkie goes to the penitentiary, that one, which means she does an awful lot of bleeding. And she's got a mitt like a snow shovel when it comes to scooping up the dough, but none of it ever sticks, it all gets to where it's supposed to go, even the small change, that's one thing you can say about her."

"I suppose you had her checked out."

"Don't you think I didn't. And clean as a whistle, too. Not like those other jokers you know, taking their cut off the top when they rent Yankee Stadium so they can have a rock-and-roll benefit for dinge deadbeats."

Then I said it.

"Did you have her checked out before you fucked her or after?"

And so at last it was on the table, but for all the effect the question had I might just as well have asked him if it were Tuesday or Wednesday.

"You're a cream puff if you think you can put me away with that one. I've had experts work me over, professional hard cases with subpoenas and polyester suits, they thought they were going to get nominated for president by kicking me in the teeth, and look how far those bozos got, and they're tougher than you are. All it proves is that she's a blabbermouth, not that I mind that, and that you're not even as smart as I gave you credit for, and that I do mind, because I don't like sizing up people wrong."

He wiped his lips with a napkin, never taking his eyes off me. "And to answer your question while I'm at it, yes, you are a disappointment to me. You're satisfied being just what you are, and what you are is a rich man's son, and that lets you go play Solly the Stooge to that bunch down there in Hollywood. They keep you around like you're a cocker spaniel, and they throw you a can of Alpo every now and then because they think maybe you're hooked into me. And don't tell me how well you're doing. I know exactly how well you're doing, how much you make, you don't need the money I settled on you, but I don't hear you give any of it to the Maryknolls either. You laugh a lot about it, like you laugh a lot about me, and if that's what you want, that's okay, too, a lot of people made that mistake. And no, that's not the reason I . . ." He wavered for an instant, trying to find the appropriate verb, then settled for a prepositional detour. ". . . that's not the reason about me and your wife, even though she wasn't your wife then, she'd dumped you just like everyone's always dumped you. You probably think I owe you an explanation about that, but you think wrong, you're not going to get one."

I think he expected me to get up and leave at that moment, or to make a scene, both being plot devices I had used in similar situations in bad screenplays, the confrontation scene being more obligatory in movies than it is in life. Instead I ordered coffee and a cigar and a pony of 1879 Napoleon brandy, a gesture which of course was another movie cliché, the freighted scene with no dialogue. My father was equal to the tension. He did not seem to care one way or the other if I left or if I stayed. The situation, such as it was, was saved by an interruption. Several men who seemed to know my father ventured tentatively up to our table, like butlers asking for the afternoon off. My father introduced me, displaying not the slightest enthusiasm for their unsolicited company, and these intruders, immediately and uncomfortably aware of his lack of interest, talked for a few moments with obsequious bravado about the 49ers and how the homos were ruining San Francisco and what a chump the president was until at last they were driven away by Hugh Broderick's obvious indifference to their ideas on any subject.

"Good," my father said when the men departed, and rose to leave. "Have another brandy if you want." He motioned to a waiter and pointed to my glass. "Stay as long as you wish."

"No," I said. "I'll leave with you."

We emerged together from the Pacific Union Club into the cool San Francisco midafternoon. The sun had already fallen behind the spires of Grace Cathedral. As we waited in silence for his car and driver, I gradually became aware of a disturbance down the street in front of the Fairmont Hotel. A sound truck was stalled and tying up traffic on Mason Street. One of its tires had gone flat. The driver of the panel truck was arguing with a policeman, who had driven up in a three-wheel motorcycle. Cars blew their horns, the cop his whistle. Over all the noise, from inside the truck, a recorded voice blared from the loudspeakers. "Voters, this is Richie Kane. We cannot let San Francisco be taken over by hippies, yippies and social deviates. Vote for a better city. Vote for Richie Kane for county supervisor. Remember Rich is better. . . ." That was the entire message. A few seconds pause and then the recording was repeated. "Voters, this is Richie Kane . . ."

There was a poster-size blowup of Richie Kane on the side of the truck. He was heavier than I had remembered him and he had shaved the mustache he had worn in Vietnam. Across the top of the poster, in bright red letters, was the slogan, RICH IS BETTER.

". . . hippies, yippies and social deviates," the recorded voice intoned above the din on Mason Street. By now the stalled truck and its amplified message were attracting attention. "Social de-

viates" had only one connotation in San Francisco. Small groups
of men and women jeered at the truck, most shouting obscenities.
Then I saw a young man in tight white jeans threading his way
through the jammed traffic. He stopped in front of the truck and
from point-blank range threw what appeared to be a brick at the
windshield. The glass shattered and a moment later the driver
stumbled from the front seat, blood streaming down his face. Before the policeman could react, the young man disappeared into
the lobby of the Fairmont.

My father looked on impassively. "Rich is better," he finally
said scornfully.

Sirens screamed.

Two police cars skidded to a stop on California Street.

"I know him," I said. I got no response. "I know him from
Vietnam." I was trying to make some connection. I scavenged my
memory. "He only wore the uniforms of dead men." My father
showed no hint of interest. About the time you were fucking my
wife, I wanted to say. Which led to a scrape in Encino. According
to Mr. Hoover. "At Bien Hoa."

"Vote for Richie Kane," the recording blared.

My father stirred. "His campaign people asked me for money."

"And?"

"I don't give money to losers."

Someone inside the truck turned up the volume. "Remember
Rich is better . . ."

We parted on California Street. His chauffeur held open the
rear door of the stretch Mercedes and he got into the backseat
without saying good-bye. His face contorted into a cough as he
pressed the button that rolled up the smoked-glass window. It
was the last time I ever saw him lucid.

He had the stroke later that same evening.

V

I REMEMBER watching television.

What struck me immediately was the almost total absence of film footage about him. A tribute to a lifetime spent avoiding the press. The only clip the local channels were able to dig up was in black and white. My father, wearing a cutaway, escorting Priscilla, in her wedding dress, into Old Saint Mary's the day she married Dickie Finn. He seemed to be threatening the cameraman.

There were still photos of the six presidents he had served as special envoy, but no mention of his insistence that he be directly responsible only to the president on each mission, a guarantee he demanded in writing.

Of course there were references to his wealth.

In excess of a billion dollars.

Reported to be near a billion dollars.

Estimated at over five hundred million dollars.

Billionaire promoter, the most raffish of the local channels proclaimed.

Friend of the mighty.

Mystery philanthropist.

A cut to Fritz on the steps of UC Med Center. "There's one thing we all know about Hugh Broderick." I could hear the whir of flash cameras in the background. "He has that indomitable will to survive." Fritz raised his hand, as if to stay the applause he fully expected to hear. The politician's reflex. Out of office, he seemed to me slightly ridiculous and beside the point, as do all former presidents, even with the constant convoy of Secret Service men plugged into their beige earphones. Two pressed so close that they were in the picture with him. "The day hasn't dawned when I'd bet against Hugh Broderick." He smiled and cocked a finger as if he were prepared to work the crowd and press some flesh. Then it seemed to occur to him that something more dignified might be in order. "Our prayers are with him."

Bro's turn. Bro in black suit, black dickey, Roman collar. ". . . an intercranial thrombosis. In other words, a blood clot in an artery of the brain." He shot his cuffs and I saw the Buccellati cuff links engraved with the presidential seal. Also the Mark Cross case carrying his breviary and the stole and oils for extreme unction. I had not seen it since the day he had anointed Germany Baker at San Quentin. "The thrombosis is in the left cerebral hemisphere and I am advised by the medical staff that it is inoperable." He had the cool precision of a professional briefer. "Vital signs are stable and at the moment his life is in no imminent danger." Bro held up the Mark Cross case. "As a precautionary measure, however, I did give him the last rites and hear his confession . . ."

"Does that mean he was able to speak?"

"It means that I was satisfied in his ability to comprehend to such a degree that I felt comfortable in giving him the sacrament of absolution . . ."

Bro and Fritz waving to reporters.

"At UC Med Center, this is Ben Hayakawa returning you to the Action Central news desk . . ."

Serious reflection and heavy nodding by Roger and coanchor Heather at Action Central.

"Thanks, Ben, for that update on the condition of billionaire philanthropist Hugh Broderick, father as we all know of the late Priscilla Broderick Finn, who as Ben Hayakawa just indicated was married to the younger brother of former president Finn, that's Richard Finn of our fair city, father also of Augustine 'Bro' Broderick, who has done so much to make this world a better place to live in, a real credit to San Francisco, and of John Broderick, the Hollywood screenwriter of such hits as *Lovers by Night* and *Mildred Pierson* ..."

"I think that's *Mildred Pierce*, Rog? Wasn't Carlotta French in it? I think she got an Oscar nomination ..."

"Right you are, Heather, my mistake. Mildred Pierson was actually a lady I used to know in Phoenix when I was at KPHO there." Roger smiled roguishly at the camera. "And a dynamite lady she was." Then his serious demeanor. "Just as the whole Brodcrick family has been a dynamite force on the local landscape for so many years ..."

"You can say that again, Roger. And we shouldn't forget The Broderick Holiday Turkey Fund ..."

"My favorite story of holiday giving every year, Heather. Dressing and drumsticks. Mmmmmm. Dynamite." Roger tapped his fingers professionally on the anchor desk. "Right. What else do we have?"

"Roger, in other local news, supervisorial candidate Richie Kane today denied charges stemming from an incident Tuesday in front of the Fairmont Hotel. Local leaders of the gay community have charged that Kane slandered Bay Area gays by referring to them as 'social deviates.' In a statement released this morning at his headquarters in the Mission, Kane denied the allegations, saying that by social deviates he meant only those people who have a consistent pattern of breaking the law, saying in addition that he has always had a cordial relationship with local gays and would continue to do so after he is elected. Kane also cited those people who turned over his sound truck on Mason Street Tuesday as just the kind of lawless social deviates he was talking about ..."

"We'll keep watching this one, Heather."

"Right, Roger. Weather and sports next ..."

I remember bringing myself up to date on Richie Kane.

I had seen him only once since Vietnam, in Golden Gate Park

the spring before the Christmas bombing. I was in San Francisco doing research on a rock-and-roll picture I ended up never writing—something on the order of MOR female vocalist meets heavy metal guitar and their triumphs and tragedies—and staying at the apartment on Green Street that I still maintain, however infrequently I am there. As it happened, Bro was also in town, to give a lecture, sponsored by The Finn Foundation, on the emerging Africa, and after many telephone calls we finally arranged to have lunch at a dingy coffee shop at the edge of the Panhandle.

"Why here?" Bro said when he slipped into the booth. He was anonymous in jeans and a denim jacket and the full beard sprinkled with gray he had cultivated on his latest trip to study the reasons for the failure of democracy in newly independent Africa.

"I go into the park most afternoons. To hang out and see who's playing."

"A geriatric hippie."

"You should talk. You look like an undercover narc."

"And I thought I was blending in."

After lunch we walked in the park. The smell of marijuana hung in the cool spring air. Here and there pickup groups were setting up amplifiers and tuning their instruments. Everywhere people were passing out mimeographed pamphlets. STOP THE BOMBING. WHEN THE REVOLUTION HITS THE STREETS. On a knoll, we stopped for a moment and listened to a lecture on how to make a bomb. Gelignite. A sixty-minute timer. An alkaline battery. Lead azide.

"You make a bomb that way, you're going to come away with a stump, you're not careful." The voice came from the far edge of the crowd. "You're not boiling an egg with that timer, you know."

"Murderer," someone shouted.

"Baby killer."

The voice shouted back. "Okay, make it your way. Blow your fucking head off. Who the fuck cares?"

Then I saw him. He detached himself from the fringes of the crowd and moved briskly toward us, shouting invective back over his shoulder. He was in full dress military uniform, trousers bloused, spit-shined black boots with white laces, white piping through the left epaulet of his khaki shirt, campaign hat squared. It was only slightly less unusual to see an American uniform in Golden Gate Park than it would have been in Haiphong. Which is why I peered so closely at him as he passed. "Richie?"

He did not break stride. "Fuck you, asshole."

Then his step faltered. He stopped and looked back, trying to place the face that knew his name. "Mr. Broderick?"

I did not correct the formality. "Richie." I considered how to introduce Bro without excess elaboration. "This is Bro. Bro, this is Richie."

Richie nodded curtly. Bro seemed of absolutely no interest to him. While we at least shared Bien Hoa and Rem. Eng. Comp. II. "You see those fucking assholes back there, Mr. Broderick?"

I nodded.

"That gelignite's not the most stable fucking stuff in the world, you know what I mean?"

"I'll buy you a cup of coffee, Richie."

We returned to the same coffee shop. Richie ordered two doughnuts and a cup of coffee.

"I thought you'd be out by now," I said.

"I re-upped."

"When?"

He picked up a jelly doughnut in both hands, as if it were a sandwich, and bit into it. A dab of jelly squirted out the back and landed in his coffee cup. "Sixty-nine."

"I thought you were a short-timer when I left."

"I had almost five fucking months left." He used his spoon to rescue the jelly floating in his cup, avoiding my eye as he did. "I'd had it. I wanted out, you know what I mean?"

I explained to Bro. "If you re-upped, you could transfer out of a line unit."

Richie licked the jelly from his spoon, all the while staring suspiciously at Bro. "You ever in 'Nam?"

In fact, Bro had gone to Vietnam with three different fact-finding missions. "Passed through. Didn't stay long. Didn't want to."

I had to hand it to him. He made it sound as if he had been dealing dope. Cornering the futures market on el primo no-seed, no-stem. The implied bona fides seemed to satisfy Richie. "I'd been to Hong Kong. R&R. Five days of pussy . . ."

"Wanchai," Bro said. With the veiled implication that he might also have done a little pimping on the side. Wanchai. That district of Hong Kong where for a price everything was available. Bro always seemed to have the appropriate information and to allow the inference that not all of it had come to him under the seal of the confessional.

"Wanchai," Richie said. "I was screwed, blued and tattooed. You know it, Wanchai?"

Bro smiled.

I waited for a moment. "Then what happened?"

Richie chewed the last of his jelly doughnut before he answered. "When I get back to the three-two-two, they tell me they lost four slicks in the five days I was gone." He ran his tongue over the bits of dough that had stuck to his teeth. "A slick blows up, there's no such thing as a million-dollar fucking wound, gets you out of combat. You're barbecued is what you are, know what I mean?"

I nodded.

"And the other way . . ." His voice trailed off. "There was this guy in the battalion, Moose something, a crew chief, he gets plastered one night, decides to shoot off his toe, get himself sent home. So he slaps a clip in an M-16, pulls the trigger and it sticks, takes his fucking leg off."

The waitress poured more coffee.

"So you re-upped."

His face suddenly darkened and for a moment I thought he was going to erupt, but the fury vanished as quickly as it had come.

"The recruiting sergeant, he says to me, "Well, three more years is what you're going to have to do, soft-on, you want to chicken out?' Fuck him, that asshole. No more sitting in that fucking door, that's all I wanted." He stared at me belligerently; I had the feeling he was daring me to question his decision. "So I signed. On the dotted line."

"Where'd they send you?"

"Cam Ranh Bay."

"Doing what?"

He did not answer directly. "The army, they grab you by the shorts, they don't let go."

"How so?" I recognize now the rhythm of our tape recording sessions at Bien Hoa. It was as if we were frozen in our roles, I always the officer and he always the enlisted man, with all the residue of resentment inherent in that condition. And still I persisted, as if it were a right. "How so?"

"I was a body loader," he said finally. "That's all I did the last five months. Load stiffs onto C-130s for shipment back home. You should've seen the shit that went out in some of those bags."

"Dope?"

"Sometimes there wasn't room for the stiffs hardly."

"Better than sitting in the door, though."

Richie laughed. The same mirthless exhalation of air I remembered from Bien Hoa. I pointed to the piping on his uniform. "You in some kind of honor guard now?"

Another unpleasant laugh. "The army decided I was so good with stiffs, I should escort them around the country when I got back. Taps, rifle salute, that shit. At the funerals, I'm the one that folds the fucking flag. The way you do it, only the blue shows. And a couple of stars."

"You had one today?"

"At the Presidio. The mother, I give her the flag, she says, 'Don't drop it now.' Fuck you, lady, I wanted to say."

After the funeral he walked up to the park.

Where he was called a baby killer.

And met Bro.

"It was instructive," Bro said sometime later that afternoon, but of course it wasn't. He began his lecture that evening at the Herbst with an anecdote about a midget emir, traveling incognito, who had taken him to a eunuch's brothel in Gondar. There was a peripheral dissertation on how the penis and testicles were removed from the candidate eunuch, slash, cut, one stroke of the blade, and sidebars on where his urine was stored and how it was evacuated until his wounds were healed and his urethra functioning via some new orifice. This was the world in which Bro was most comfortable, and it was a world which had no room for Richie Kane.

"We'll stay in touch," I had said to Richie that same afternoon, but needless to say I never did. Now I cannot remember exactly when I began to notice, over the course of my regular visits home to San Francisco, his name appearing with a certain frequency in the local newspapers. It just seemed to happen. His power base was the teachers' union, in which he had risen to the vice presidency of his local. I found it odd, from my perspective as professor emeritus of Rem. Eng. Comp. II, to think of Richie as a teacher, but in fact he was only a teacher of shop, and a teacher of shop only because he was unable to find a job as a heavy equipment operator in the construction slump after his discharge from the army. "Pro San Francisco" was his cause, "Those Who Care" his constituency, a code easily broken, as of course it was meant to be, and with time I became aware that "Viet Vet" had gradually been transmuted into "Viet Hero." I would linger over his name when I came upon it and wonder if I should get in touch, as I had promised, but then would pass on to stories about the San Francisco Cotillion or the opening of the opera, events available to me but which, for Richie Kane, might just as well have taken place on Mars. At one point, in the days immediately after my father's stroke, when I was waiting for Bro and Fritz to arrive and the doctors to complete their workup, I was unable to sleep one night and watched a documentary, "Spotlight after Midnight: The Metro Candidates at Home," and there was Richie, diving into the portable blue plastic swimming pool in the backyard of his house in the Mission flats. He was fleshy, with pimples on his back, his stomach sagging over the elastic band on his red, white and blue track trunks, and he splashed water on Rick and Kerry and on little Eileen, the youngest, who clung to the neck of his wife, Megan. Megan Kane was wearing a T-shirt over her high-waisted two-piece bathing suit, and the T-shirt said, RICH IS BETTER.

As did the billboard I could see from Highway 101 when I drove Bro to the airport.

"Remember him?"

"No."

"He was a body loader."

"I don't remember."

"The professional mourner."

"Sorry." Bro seemed preoccupied. He stared out the car window, then after a moment looked back at me. "You've hardly mentioned Hugh all the time I was here."

"Fritz wouldn't let me get a word in edgewise."

"Fritz left two days ago."

I concentrated on changing lanes. "We had a fight."

"When?"

"That day. At lunch."

"About what?"

"Leah."

"Oh, shit." He closed his eyes and pinched the bridge of his nose with thumb and forefinger. Then: "About that?"

"That" unspecified. The "that" he and I had discussed over the years only in the most elliptical way. "About that."

"Look. Whatever was said, it had nothing whatsoever to do with that embolism."

"Thank you, Doctor."

"His health's been dicey for the last couple of years, you know that." In fact I had not known that. A comment on my relationship with my father. "There's no cause and no effect, understand?"

"Who're you trying to convince, Padre? Me? Or yourself?"

He did not reply immediately. "Have you heard from Leah?"

"No."

"I'm surprised."

"Why?"

"She's fond of Hugh."

"Obviously."

"Oh, shit," Bro repeated.

I touched his arm. "I'm sorry, Bro. Bad joke. She's in Cristo Rey again. With Freedom Watch. That's why I haven't heard from her. She calls in every week or so. Ramona said she'll let her know next time."

"I thought she was just there."

"Two months ago. This is the third time this year."

Bro scratched his brow pensively. "I'm supposed to go down there in March."

"Why?"

"For the election. The president's asked me to be an observer." He hesitated. "And vice chairman of the delegation, but I turned that down. Not enough time." Listening to Bro was like trying to translate smoke signals, and I don't really think he expected me to believe him. I would have wagered that he had positioned himself to be named chairman and when that was not in the cards had let it be known he would only agree to be a foot soldier, with its potential for free-lance indiscretion, and not a rubber-stamp vice chairman. Bro was nothing if not a player, and he played whether the game was worth it or not. "I imagine I'll run into Leah. The way that goon squad runs things down there, I don't guess this election'll be anything she'll want to miss."

I had to smile. "Somehow, Bro, I don't think you and Leah are going to be observing the same election."

The thought seemed to amuse him. "Here's something else, and I don't think I want you to tell her."

"Scout's honor."

"Well, I don't know if you keep up on these things, but the Miss Global Village Contest is being held right around the same time as the election."

"So?"

"In Cristo Rey," he said. A bemused smile creased his features. "I was asked to be a judge."

I started to laugh.

"I actually got off on the invitation for five or ten minutes. I had the sense that God, via one of his more louche messengers, was trying to tell me something. I thought I could probably fold both gigs into one, they're not that much different after all, election observer and beauty contest judge. A way to establish my secular credentials. Which perhaps, in some eyes, don't need all that much more establishing. And so to keep on the good side of the Church, I thought I'd take cash for the extra plane fare and turn it over to the local Catholic charities." In the eerie yellow light of the overhead freeway lamps, his face was reflected for an instant in the windshield, and in the split second of that harsh glare I suddenly realized how much he had aged. "I like the sound of it. 'Padre Augustino vota para . . . Señorita Chile, treinta y seis . . .' " His hands molded a female form. " '. . . veinte y cuatro, treinta y seis . . .' "

As it happened, Bro did meet Leah in Cristo Rey.

As it happened, I was there too.

As it happened, Miss Global Village never did get to a vote. Nor did Cristo Rey.

Film at eleven.

VI

FINALLY MY FATHER CAME HOME from UC Med Center, in an ambulance, back into the house on Washington Street under the protective custody of a platoon of Dickie Finn's medical mercenaries. There was no real reason for me to remain in San Francisco—Marty Magnin was on my case about a script I had failed to deliver for the very good reason that I had written not even a single page and Dickie was made distinctly nervous by my continued presence, as if he thought I might use the power of the Broderick blood to preempt the authority he had taken upon himself—but I found it difficult to leave, feeling myself responsible in at least some small way for the infarction that had brought my father's life effectively to an end. I wonder now if it were this sense of remorse, which Bro had tried so unsuccessfully to assuage, that drew me toward Richie Kane. "A mick from the Mission" was the way I had described him in that letter to Leah I had written from Bien Hoa in the spring of 1969. "Imagine my father if the Brodericks didn't get rich and you'd just about have it." The words are branded on my memory now, but in fact I had forgotten the letter until I discovered it in Leah's Bekins locker after she and Bro were killed. What made me that prescient? Why else would I have courted Richie Kane?

These are the questions that haunt my dreams.

The facts remain.

From which conclusions may be drawn.

Fact: In the weeks my father was in the hospital, the only story I could concentrate on in the newspapers was Richie's election campaign.

Every day I would turn first to the local election coverage on the split page, searching for any item about him. The polls showed him a solid second among the five candidates running in supervisorial District 23. Neither of the local papers supported him. Both, in their editorials, alluded to the incident in front of the Fairmont and Richie's subsequent failure to explain to their satisfaction what he had meant by the term "social deviate." The newspaper criticism only served to make Richie more rigid. "We know who is anti-San Francisco" became the increasingly unrepentant theme of his campaign, repeated over and over on television and on the radio and in the papers, and when reporters pressed him to elaborate, Richie would only reply, "We know who our enemies are." As the race wound into its final week, his headquarters confidently predicted that voters were hearing his message and promised a last-minute blitz of advertising spots targeted at "Those Who Care."

Fact: It was in this atmosphere that I finally decided, the night before I returned to Los Angeles, to attend a rally for Richie in the heart of the heart of District 23, the school auditorium at Holy Sepulchre junior high.

I find myself wondering now if I would have gone had I not wanted, in that spirit of reckoning with which I was afflicted during those weeks, to see once more the house where my father was born, the house, with all its echoes of inchoate immigrant striving, he had effectively banished from his psychic biography. It had been years since I had actually driven through the Mission— I saw it, if at all, only from the freeway on my way to and from the airport—and so I set out early, wandering slowly through neighborhoods of neat frame houses, each identical to its next-door neighbor, the most prominent architectural feature on every one the two-car garage that stuck out in front like a square tumor. Then I turned into Geneva and down the block, on the corner, there it was, the house, still standing, in need of paint. The neighborhood had decayed from lace curtain respectability into commercial seediness since I was last there—I saw a Laundromat, a shoe repair, a candy and stationery store, a small grocery—and the ground floor of the house where my father had lived until he was six years old had been turned into a bar. The green-lettered sign on the window said, IRELAND's 32. I was not so deracinated that I failed to recognize the allusion. Ireland's 32. A united Ireland of the twenty-six counties in the Republic and the six in the North. It was not every saloon whose name made a political statement. I could almost hear my father's bitter laugh of derision.

I wonder what he would have made of the rally.

It was everything he professed to despise.

"Who are we?" I remember Richie Kane shouting into the microphone. He was sweating profusely under the lights on the auditorium stage.

"Those who care," came the chant back from the audience. I had not realized how thoroughly rehearsed his campaign appearances had become. The school hall was so crowded I had to stand in the back. In the lapel of my jacket I wore the RICH IS BETTER button I had bought for a dollar in the parking lot outside, and which I planned to give to Marty Magnin once I got back to Los Angeles. Red letters on a white background, like the banner strung from one side of the Holy Sepulchre stage to the other.

"What do we know?" Richie demanded hoarsely.

Another chant. "We know who is anti-San Francisco."

"What else do we know?"

"We know who our enemies are."

"Hey," Richie said, "I love you people, you know that?" He took a handkerchief from his pocket and mopped the sweat from his face. Over the podium, an American flag hung from the ceiling. Behind Richie, a half-dozen people sat uncomfortably in straight-backed school chairs. The only one I recognized, from the documentary I had seen on television, was Megan Kane. "You want to meet Megan?"

A cheer rose from the audience. Megan Kane stood and smiled uncertainly.

"My wife Megan," Richie said. The demands of the campaign

had made his voice thin and raspy. "Megan Danaher that was, from over to Saint Jude's there." Applause. "She's got a teaching credential." More applause. "But the only teaching she's doing now is teaching our kids, Rick and Kerry and little Eileen, the values that I want to see come back to our city, the values I want to see our city stand for when I'm elected next Tuesday . . ." The crowd whistled and stamped its feet. No one seemed to mind that Richie had not spelled out exactly what those values were, but the evidence was that his audience shared them. "My wife, Megan, ladies and gentlemen . . ."

From my place in the back, I concentrated on Megan Kane as she waved and sat down. She moved her head slowly from left to right, then back again, as if it were on a swivel, a smile pasted to her face, her eyes blinking constantly. This was clearly how she had been advised to act in public, but she seemed to have heeded the instruction so closely that it only lent her an eerie and unearthly air.

"Listen." Richie held up his hands for silence. "Hey, listen. Pipe down, will you? And listen." The noise began to subside. "Listen, it's really swell to be back here at Holy Sep, where I spent some of the happiest years of my life." He held up his hand again, like a lounge act comic, to quiet the whistles and applause. "The people I met here, they were real people, swell people. I remember Mother Immaculata, what a swell disciplinarian she was, God rest her soul, you ever told Mother Immaculata you were a social deviate, you'd get the ruler across your knuckles so hard, she'd break your hand . . ."

Richie let the cheering play itself out.

"And Monsignor Lomasney, the pastor . . ."

More clapping.

". . . him with his rubber hose, he swung that thing like he was Willie McCovey there, give him that rubber hose and he'd know how to take care of those social deviates my opponents spend more time worrying about than they worry about the decent people in this district . . ."

I watched Megan Kane. The smile had not left her face. Nor had her head stopped swiveling. She had pale red hair and skin so fair she looked as if she would burn if a light bulb were turned on.

I wondered if she maintained the smile when Richie was on top of her.

"Stand up, Monsignor, take a bow . . ."

On the stage, two chairs down from Megan Kane, an elderly monsignor with frayed red piping on his cassock stood and acknowledged the applause. A RICH IS BETTER button pinned the cassock together where several buttons appeared to be missing. I could not remember why his name was so familiar at first, then I had it. The legendary Lomasney. Who had a colostomy. Whose equally legendary brother Ants had been in the Department of Sanitation.

"Listen, Monsignor, when I was over in Vietnam there . . ."

The cheers drowned him out. It was the first time I had ever heard the war given an ovation.

Richie motioned for quiet.

". . . there was this chaplain at Bien Hoa, that's where I was stationed, the three-two-two aviation company . . ."

Whistles.

". . . he was exactly the sort of chaplain you'd've been, Monsignor, you were there, I swear to God . . ."

Megan Kane nodded vigorously. I suddenly thought of fish. Why? Ah. Yes. Fish was what Richie had said it smelled like. "It." The sweet spot.

". . . he drove around in this jeep and the jeep, it was called 'The God Squad,' that was its name, with God as my judge . . ."

He waited for the laughter to die down.

". . . and so one day I say to the chaplain, I think his name was Father Degnan, he was from Pittsburgh, Father Red Degnan, and I say to him, 'Listen, Padre Red, there's something I want to know,' and he says to me, Father Red does, 'What is it you want to know, my son?' And I say to him, I say, 'The Ten Commandments say thou shalt not kill, Padre, and I don't know what you're doing in 'Nam, Padre, but that's what I'm doing in 'Nam, you know what I mean?' "

Once more he milked the laughter.

"And he says to me, Father Red, he says . . ." Richie stopped and turned toward Monsignor Lomasney. "Excuse me, Monsignor, there's a bad word here, you might want to plug your ears, you know what I mean . . ."

Monsignor Lomasney smiled benignly and shook his head.

"So. Anyways. The padre, he says, 'It's God's work, my son.' And I say, 'How do you figure that, Padre?' And he says, Father Red, he says, 'The faster you kill the little commie bastards, my son, the faster their souls will get to heaven . . .' "

The auditorium erupted with applause. On the stage, Monsignor Lomasney slapped his knee in glee and Megan Kane kept turning her head from side to side, as if in rhythm with some secret rhapsody.

Richie beamed.

I could not take my eyes off him. He had acquired a certain rough polish since that day I had last seen him in Golden Gate Park, but I suspected the polish did not go very deep. Then there was that story about the chaplain. Of course I had heard it before. It was from *Grunts*. Only it had not been told me by Richie. And was to another point. The story actually came from a marine I had taped in Da Nang. The marine said he had tried to frag the chaplain's hooch. Because, he said, the chaplain was such an asshole. The grenade turned out to be a dud. Two days after the taping, the marine was killed at Tri Ton. Richie's version, however, answered one question. I had wondered if he had read *Grunts*. He had.

He began speaking again.

The campaign pitch.

My attention strayed.

". . . six years in the service of my country . . ."

No mention of the reason he had re-upped.

". . . this country I love . . ."

Not that there was anything wrong with reenlisting to get out of combat.

". . . proud that I was able to serve . . ."

It was just not something to put in a résumé.

". . . Bien Hoa . . ."

It was as if he were running for the presidency of the VFW.

". . . Cam Ranh Bay . . ."

Which to the best of my knowledge was not in District 23.

". . . people like you . . ."

He was back in CONUS.

". . . frustrated people . . ."

In the city and county of San Francisco.

". . . angry people . . ."

In LZ Holy Sep.

". . . social deviates . . ."

Finally the VC.

". . . a blight on our city . . ."

Standing in the steeple.

". . . a cancer . . ."

And pissing on the people.

". . . unleash the furies . . ."

Activate the Phoenix Program.

". . . eradicate the malignancy . . ."

Search and destroy.

"Who are we?"

"Those who care."

"What do we know?"

"We know who our enemies are."

I waited in the corridor outside the auditorium after the rally, beside a bulletin board carrying the announcement from the principal's office that Guido Macanudo, the human fly who had climbed the exterior of the Transamerica Building, and Richard Kane, the supervisorial candidate for District 23, had each been elected to the Holy Sepulchre Junior High School Hall of Fame. I heard no one in the audience streaming out of the hall complain that Richie had not addressed ways to broaden the tax base or encourage development or any other issue that may have seemed to be a legitimate concern to the voters of District 23. Those who cared did not appear to care much about such matters.

"Hey, Mr. Broderick."

"I didn't think you'd recognize me, Richie."

"From Bien Hoa, are you kidding? This is Megan, my wife. Mr. Broderick."

"How do you do."

"Megan's got a teaching credential."

"So I heard."

"You were there?"

"Of course."

"Well, what'd you think, Mr. Broderick."

"It was very vigorously stated, Richie."

"You hear that, Megan?"

Megan Kane smiled.

"I tell Megan all the time about the swell times we had in 'Nam."

"Really."

"Like that time you were reading that poem by that guy with the girl's name."

"Joyce Kilmer," Megan Kane said. " 'Trees.' "

"And I said, 'What kind of guy has a girl's name,' remember?"

I did not remember, but I nodded yes. We were ringed by a crowd of Richie's supporters.

"And Mickie Mahoney, remember him? Service Company, fifty-fifth?"

"Of course." Meaning no.

"Mickie says, 'What's wrong with Joyce? There's a Mexican guy in Service Company, his name's Jesus.' Christ, we roared, remember?"

There was a ripple of laughter from the people surrounding us.

"I liked the story about the chaplain, Richie."

His eyes darted away from mine. "Let's go into the principal's office, Mr. Broderick, okay? Megan needs to sit down." He whispered, "I think she's got a biscuit in the oven, you know what I mean?"

I looked at Megan Kane. "Congratulations."

She seemed to smile not in acknowledgment, but because her smile was permanent-pressed. We went into the principal's office. There was no window and the furniture was sturdily uncomfortable.

Richie avoided looking at me directly. "We need your help, Mr. Broderick."

"What do you mean, Richie?"

"We want to do these advertising spots over the weekend?"

"I heard that."

"It'll do it, Mr. Broderick."

"It might."

"We need money."

I cleared my throat.

"It's only ten thousand dollars, that's all I'm asking for."

"That's a lot of money, Richie."

"It's fucking pocket money for someone like you is what it is." At last a Richie Kane I recognized. He had obviously done a little homework on who I was. Or more likely on who my father was. "Small change, you know what I mean?"

"I'm not a registered voter in this district, Richie." Not the response my father would have made. *I don't give money to losers.* That was it. That was what he had said about Richie outside the Pacific Union Club. And I am sure he had stated it in exactly those terms to whoever it was who had asked him for a contribution. I began to understand his penchant for being unequivocal. Right or wrong, it saved time.

"What kind of fucking excuse is that?"

I moved toward the door. "It was nice to meet you, Mrs. Kane."

Megan Kane nodded. And of course kept smiling, first at me, then at Richie.

"You and those fucking turkeys," Richie said bitterly.

I did not understand what he meant for a moment.

"Those big-deal fucking Broderick turkeys you're always giving out. So you give one to my old lady when my old man kicks off, that does it? That's it?"

Of course.

I had forgotten.

My mother's holiday turkey fund.

"Some rich bitch" was the way Richie had described her at Bien Hoa when he did not know her connection to me.

Life seemed somehow simpler before he put two and two together.

"You know what you can do with those fucking turkeys, Mr. Fucking Broderick?"

I did not wait to find out.

The day after the election, I called Dickie Finn in San Francisco. He said doctors were encouraged by the texture of my father's stools. I asked him who had won in District 23. Someone named Crean, he said.

Richie Kane had finished second.

He had called for a recount.

There had been no last weekend media blitz.

A week later I went to a party at Lottie French's. I spent the night in Lottie's pool house with Quentin. When I woke in the morning, she was doing a line of coke. She cut a line for me and then went outside for a swim. I turned on the "Today" show. There was film footage of a grave in Chalatenango Province in Cristo Rey. The victim was identified as Phyllis Emmett, a former Roman Catholic Sister of Mercy, thirty-seven years old. Her face had been shot away. Her identity was finally established by a name tag in her undergarments.

I thought I saw Leah in the background wearing a safari jacket, but then the segment switched to Washington and an analysis of the murder by NBC's State Department correspondent. The correspondent said that the State Department through its ambassador, E. Tuckerman Bradley, had asked the government of Cristo Rey to pursue the killers of the American churchwoman with all the means at its disposal.

BOOK SEVEN

CHRIST THE KING

AREA HANDBOOK FOR CRISTO REY
PREPARED BY THE AMERICAN UNIVERSITY
WASHINGTON, D.C. 20016
FOR THE UNITED STATES DEPARTMENT OF STATE

I. COUNTRY SUMMARY.

1. COUNTRY. Official name is La Republica de Cristo Rey (in English "Christ the King") C.A. An independent nation since 1838.

2. GOVERNMENT. A constitutional republic headed by a five-member DIRECTORATE popularly called "El Cinco" (in English "The Five") after the five military officers constituting the Directorate's membership.

3. CONSTITUTION. The current constitution was written in 1980 and passed, with additional amendments mandating martial law, by the Directorate in 1981. The constitution of 1981 superseded the constitution of 1978, which in turn superseded the constitution of 1972. Since declaring its independence from Spain in 1838, Cristo Rey has had seven constitutional conventions and nineteen constitutions, three of which were never implemented. The longest continuing constitution was the constitution of 1939, which remained in effect until 1951 under the martial law government of General Enrique Ponce Moreno (1904–1951).

4. JUSTICE. Basic legal origins from Chilean code of 1850, influenced by Hispanic practice and Napoleonic Code. The Supreme Court was asked to resign by the Directorate in 1980 and habeas corpus was suspended shortly thereafter.

5. SIZE. Approximately 8,260 square miles, or the approximate size of Massachusetts or Kern County, California.

6. CLIMATE. Hot and humid along Pacific Coast, hot and humid in interior.

7. LANGUAGES. Spanish is the official language.

8. RELIGION. Roman Catholic 96 percent, others 4 percent.

9. EDUCATION. Literacy rate 46 percent. The National University of Cristo Rey and the Cristo Rey Catholic University were closed by the Directorate in 1980.

10. EXPORTS. Miscellaneous handicrafts.

11. HEALTH. Death rate 11.2 per 1,000 inhabitants in 1974 (last available figures). Infant mortality is highest in Latin America. Prevalent diseases include gastrointestinal infections and respiratory ailments. In 1974, murder was the second leading cause of death, ahead of both cancer and cardiovascular incidents.

12. FOLKLORE. General Enrique Ponce Moreno (1904–1951), who was assassinated in the Colonels' Coup of 1951, was buried with full military honors by the Colonels' Junta that succeeded his government. General Ponce Moreno lay in state for nine days in an open coffin in the Plaza del Libertador in Cristo Rey, the capital city of Cristo Rey, C.A., until the casket was ordered closed as a health hazard by the Ministry of Public Safety. On his dress uniform, while lying in state, he wore decorations and orders from 55 nations, including the Victoria Cross from Great Britain, the Croix de Guerre from France and the Congressional Medal of Honor from the United States. These last three medals were removed after the ambassadors from the United Kingdom, France and the United States protested officially to the Cristo Rey Ministry of External Affairs that the governments they represented had never awarded the decorations in question to General Ponce Moreno.

13. U.S. INVESTMENT POTENTIAL. Ideal for motion picture locations.

I

"I SEE A COMEDY," Marty Magnin had said. Four words that effectively served as my passport to Cristo Rey.

Buddy Seville was to star in the comedy Marty Magnin saw.

"I don't do comedy, Marty," I said.

"So what?" Marty Magnin said. "You're a good constructionist, the best in the business." We were sitting in the living room of Marty's beach house in Trancas. Or to be more exact, the beach house Marty leased in Trancas for whoever it was he happened to be keeping at the moment, a perfectly safe arrangement as his third wife got seasick just looking at the ocean. "You give me a construction, I'll hire someone else to dialogue in the jokes."

"I don't like Buddy Seville, Marty. Nothing personal. I just don't think he's funny."

"You didn't see him at the Mercury Baker roast?"

I shook my head.

"He's the new roastmaster general, Buddy," Marty said. "He gives the Grambling College football cheer, you know the place I mean, the schwartze college?" Marty assumed the pose of a cheerleader and began waving imaginary pom-poms. " 'Watermelon, watermelon, Cadillac car. We ain't as stupid as you think we is.' Is that funny?"

"A riot."

"Broke the Merc up."

"I bet."

"My idea is we do the H.O.P.E. telethon."

"As the narrative line?"

"Right."

"And you hang everything else off it."

"Right."

I admit now the concept had a certain meretricious appeal. I also confess that I seldom failed to watch, every Fourth of July, at least some portion of Buddy Seville's annual twenty-four-hour televised extravaganza to raise money for the H.O.P.E. Foundation. There was something mesmerizing about Buddy Seville in one of his fifty-seven tuxedos, voice going hoarse as the hours went by, face beaded with sweat, shirt open, singing his heart out to those horribly crippled victims of amyotrophic lateral sclerosis who he insisted on calling "my gang." As in, "Let's get it up for my gang," whenever the telethon tote board recorded new telephone pledges from the viewing audience responding to the crawl of area codes and numbers that ran across the bottom of the TV screen throughout the whole twenty-four hours. " 'Smile,' " Buddy Seville would sing at the beginning and at the end of the telethon, moving among the wheelchairs of those of his gang lucky enough to sit onstage in the H.O.P.E. grandstand, " 'smile though your heart is aching . . .' "

"Every time you cut away from the show," I said, "you should see it playing someplace on a TV set."

"That's just what I was thinking," Marty Magnin said.

"If you see a hooker balling a trick, she's watching the telethon over the john's shoulder."

"My idea exactly."

"No exteriors. Every scene's played inside the hotel where the telethon's taking place."

"I thought the same thing."

"You set a scene in a men's room . . ."

" . . . then the dinge handing out the towels has a little black-and-white set turned to Buddy."

"It might work," I said.

"I got the story all worked out already," Marty said. "I don't know what I need you for."

We flew to Las Vegas the next night to pitch the idea to Buddy Seville. His rambling one-story ranch house fronted on the golf course where The Buddy Seville Open kicked off the winter tour every January. There was a party in progress. It seemed to have been going on for three days. Buddy Seville was nowhere in sight. Marty asked a redhead in a miniskirt if she knew where Buddy was. The redhead said he was grabbing a piece of ass. Marty disappeared to look for him. The only person I recognized in the crowd was an elderly black in a dinner jacket. Willie Wylie, the former heavyweight champion, now a greeter at the Mojave Hotel on the Strip, where the H.O.P.E. telethon was broadcast every year, and a permanent member of the Buddy Seville entourage. He was scarcely more than fifty, but he looked old and sick, his wet brown eyes glazed and unfocused.

"How you doing, champ?"

"Can't complain."

There were four twenty-five-inch TV sets in the living room, each attached to a separate VCR, and on each set a videotape of some segment of the last H.O.P.E. telethon was playing. Buddy Seville tap dancing with the Hutchinson Brothers on one screen, Buddy Seville doing shtick with Danny Lomax on a second, Buddy Seville timing a wheelchair race on the third, Buddy Seville singing a duet with Diana Caro on the fourth. I looked around the room. I had spent a large part of a working lifetime with professional narcissists, but I had never known anyone who had so many photographs of himself as Buddy Seville. They covered every flat surface. Buddy with his various wives, with other celebrities, with politicians and businessmen and his gang. Buddy in a tuxedo, in golf clothes, warm-up suits, sweaters, vests, business suits, sports jackets, Nehru suits, Mao jackets, swimming trunks, pajamas, bathrobe. The biggest was hanging over the fireplace, a huge photo mural of Buddy and Danny Lomax and Fritz Finn, all three in dinner jackets (Fritz was the only one not wearing an After Six shawl collar), with Buddy and Danny Lomax each wearing a large gold medallion at the end of a white sash. I worked my way through the crowd and peered at the

bronze plate under the picture: FORMER PRESIDENT FREDERICK
G. FINN PRESENTS THE BOYS CLUB OF AMERICA "BIG BROTHER
AWARD" TO SUPERSTAR ENTERTAINERS DANNY LOMAX AND
BUDDY SEVILLE. Poor Fritz, I thought. It was tougher being a for-
mer president than I thought.

"You still waiting for Buddy?" It was the redhead in the miniskirt.

I nodded.

"He won't be long. He always was a premature ejaculator."

"I didn't know that."

"No reason you would, cowboy. Unless that's the way you
swing."

It seemed safer to nod.

"What's your name?"

"Jack."

"Cute name. Four letters. J-A-C-K. Like in jack-off. What're
you doing here, Jack?"

"Working."

"Hey. So am I. Hold my drink." I took her drink. She began
to rummage through her bag. "Let's see. One Binaca, a tube of
K-Y, three condoms, a vibrator, two French ticklers, they are so
cute . . ."

The catalog seemed to require at least some comment. "The
tools of your trade."

"You got it. This party's a gold mine. You interested?"

"I'll pass."

Willie Wylie tapped me on the shoulder. "You Jack?"

"Like in jack-off," the redhead said.

"Buddy wants to see you," Willie Wylie said.

"How you doing, Willie?" the redhead said.

"Can't complain."

"You busy later?"

I followed Willie Wylie back toward Buddy Seville's bedroom.

"Jackie," Buddy said. I almost looked around to see if I had
been followed into the room by another Vegas comic, Jackie and
Joey being the favored names of big-room headliners.

"Hello, Buddy."

He was sitting up in bed, smoking a cigarette, running a cordless electric razor over his face. A girl was lying next to him, her

head under a pillow, pretending to be asleep. The three television sets in the room were playing still three more tapes of the H.O.P.E. telethon. Marty Magnin was sitting on a chaise. He looked glum. I wondered if he had been in the room long enough to vouch whether or not Buddy Seville was a premature ejaculator.

"You know Willie Wylie?"

"We met coming in."

"A great champion, a credit to the fight game, a credit to this great country of ours . . ."

For a moment I thought I might be hallucinating. I had heard this intro before. Then I remembered. In the living room not five minutes earlier. Looking at one of the videotapes. It was the way Buddy Seville had introduced Willie Wylie during the last telethon.

". . . a credit to his race, Willie Wylie, you've laid a rose on the grave of Abraham Lincoln."

"Can't complain," Willie Wylie had said on videotape.

Buddy Seville threw back the covers and got out of bed. He was naked. The girl did not move. Buddy began to do minor limbering-up calisthenics. He could almost touch toes.

"Hey, champ, some Fresca." Buddy clapped his hands. "Chop, chop. White man's time." Clasping his hands behind his neck, he wobbled into a deep knee bend. Willie Wylie did not move. Buddy staggered to his feet. "Just kidding, champ." He began flashing his nose with his thumb, like a punch-drunk prizefighter. "You laid a rose on the grave of Abraham Lincoln, right?" Now he was shadowboxing, bobbing and weaving. Willie Wylie looked resigned, then struck a fighting pose of his own, going into a shell as if to slip punches. I had the sense it was a routine he and Buddy had performed many times before. "Wish old Honest Abe could've seen your left hand, champ." Buddy snapped his fingers. "Fresca. Cold."

Marty Magnin stirred. "Buddy thinks your idea's a piece of shit."

I did not fail to notice it was now my idea.

"No offense, Jackie."

"None taken, Buddy."

He slipped into a purple terry-cloth robe with his name spelled in white letters on the back. The robe had a white hood, which he pulled over his head. For one antic second, I thought he looked like the middleweight champion of the Benedictine order. "It's just that I got to play it safe with my gang."

"I can get behind that, Buddy."

"You know what I always say, Jackie."

"What's that, Buddy?"

"Where there's H.O.P.E., there's life."

The telethon's slogan for the twenty-three years of its existence. I remembered another. "Without giving . . ."

Buddy picked up the refrain. ". . . life ain't worth living." Willie Wylie handed him a can of Fresca. "I got to worry about my corporate sponsors, you know what I mean? I can't have anything reflect on my gang."

"I told him we'd do it in exquisite taste," Marty Magnin said.

At that moment the bathroom door opened. A second girl emerged. She was also naked. "Buddy, where the fuck are my clothes?"

Buddy looked at the girl as if trying to place her face, then turned to Willie Wylie. "Hey, listen, champ, go get the chick some clothes." He peeled bills from a money clip and stuffed them into the breast pocket of Willie Wylie's dinner jacket. "A pair of shoes. A nice blouse. You want a skirt, hon, or a pair of slacks?"

"I want the shit I came here with."

"Look under the bed, champ."

Willie Wylie got down on his hands and knees. From beneath the bed he began pulling odd garments. It was as if an entire women's dormitory had left its wardrobe there. The girl in the bed removed the pillow from over her head. "That red shirt is mine."

I saw more movement in the bed. Then a third girl struggled up from beneath the covers. This one was black. She wiped the sleep from her eyes, took in the room, then winked at Marty Magnin. "Hi, Mr. Magnin."

Marty tried to look innocent. "Who?"

Buddy Seville surveyed each of the three girls, then turned to me. "I thought there was only two, Jackie, honest."

"Two more and you'd have a basketball team, Buddy."

He squeezed his head between his hands. "Christ, I'm hanging over."

Willie Wylie began apportioning the clothes among the three girls.

"Listen, I got to take a shower," Buddy Seville said. "Get a vitamin B shot. We'll schmooze later." He headed for the bathroom. "Pick yourself out a chick. There's plenty to go around. I'm running a tab."

Marty and I rejoined the crowd in the living room.

"I never laid eyes on that schwartze, I swear to God," Marty said.

"She must've seen your picture in *Variety*," I said.

"That must be it."

The party had grown both in size and volume. In the hotels along the Strip, the late shows had broken and several entertainers from the main showrooms had dropped by. Tapes of the telethon were still playing on all the TV sets. I sat on a couch and watched the announcer on the screen nearest me say, "And here he is again, ladies and gentlemen, the star of this telethon, without him there's no H.O.P.E., Mr. Heart himself, Mr. Total Talent, let's hear it once more for Buddy Seville . . ."

Diana Caro flopped down next to me. We had never met but she seemed to know who I was and assumed without question that I knew who she was, a Vegas landmark, twenty-one years at the top of the bill, the golden pipes of Miss Diana Caro, ladies and gentlemen.

"He going to be in your picture?"

"It seems to be on the back burner."

She stared at the television set. "He's going to do his mud and the stars routine now."

On-screen Buddy Seville was staring directly at the camera. "You know something? I love you all . . ."

"His sincere look," Diana Caro said. "He's going to undo his tie now."

". . . you know that," Buddy Seville said, untying his black bow tie. "But I got to be . . ."

" '. . . serious for a minute,' " Diana Caro said, mouthing the words along with him.

"I get criticism," Buddy Seville said. His face filled the television screen. "Seriously, ladies and gentlemen. Hard to believe, but true. A lot of people . . ."

" '. . . don't want to believe all the love that's up on this stage,' " Diana Caro mimicked in perfect lip sync.

"They're cynical . . ." Buddy Seville's forehead was beaded with sweat. "But one thing Buddy Seville will never be . . ."

" '. . . and that's cynical . . .' "

". . . no matter what you do in this world . . ."

" '. . . no matter how much love you've got to give . . .' " It was like listening to a simultaneous translation.

". . . there's always somebody out there to carp . . ."

" '. . . somebody who wants to find fault . . .' "

". . . somebody who's looking for the mud . . ."

" '. . . when you're looking for the stars.' " Diana Caro patted her breasts as if to make sure they were still there. They seemed to be erupting from her gold lamé dress. "The man's a genius. It's his IRS speech. He gives it every year. Nobody ever twigs."

There was a flurry of activity at the entrance to the living room. Buddy Seville made his way through the crowd, shaking hands, pinching one cheek, patting another. His vitamin B shot appeared to have taken. Like the bathrobe he wore earlier, his silver jumpsuit had his name printed on the back. It was as if he thought someone might not know who he was.

"Diana."

"Buddy."

He balanced a breast in each hand, as if he were weighing fruit. "The golden pipes of Miss Diana Caro, ladies and gentlemen."

"The bags under your eyes, Buddy. They got muscles. I bet you've got them working out at Nautilus."

"I love this chick, Jackie. We ought to get married, Diana."

"We were married, Buddy."

"I remember now. After what's her name."

"That's the one."

"And before the blonde."

"Right."

He leaned close to Diana Caro and peered at her face. "You look like a Chink, for Christ's sake." He patted his jowls. "You had a tuck?"

"The guy in Florida did it," Diana Caro said. "Dr. Kepesh."

"I know that name."

"He did you."

"Is that right? I thought the guy in Palm Springs did me."

I tried to imagine under what circumstances I might agree to a face-lift. And if I would ever forget who did it. Perhaps he had it done between the dinner show and the late show. And put it on tape. Something for his gang to groove on.

"Buddy." A passing guest slapped Buddy Seville on the back. "It's Leo." The redhead in the miniskirt was attached to Leo's arm. She framed a kiss and blew it in my direction. "Leo Shimkus."

"Is that a fact?" It was obvious that Buddy Seville did not have a clue who Leo Shimkus was. "How are you, pal? I don't see you around much lately."

"I had a coronary bypass, Buddy."

"What a swell thing to have, pal." He pinched Leo Shimkus on both cheeks, then turned back to Diana Caro. Leo and the redhead drifted away. "What's a coronary bypass, Diana?"

"That's one you missed, Buddy."

"I thought I'd hit all the diets." He grabbed my arm. "Jackie."

"Buddy."

"We should schmooze."

As if on cue, Marty Magnin appeared at my elbow. "Schmooze away, Buddy."

"I want to do your picture."

"We'll do it in exquisite taste, Buddy." Marty still seemed to think this was a selling argument.

"You understand why I don't want to do anything with my gang."

"You don't want, we'll never show a wheelchair," Marty said. "Just those beautiful faces."

"I got a problem with that."

Before Marty could speak again, I said, "I've already eighty-sixed that idea, Buddy." I could feel Marty's finger jabbing into my kidneys, trying to get me to shut up. "We'll just have to come up with another showcase."

"For my talents," Buddy Seville said.

"Maybe he can have a coronary bypass," Diana Caro said.

"I hate hospital pictures," Marty said.

On one of the TV screens, Willie Wylie and Buddy Seville were shadowboxing. Willie Wylie stopped to watch the scene. His face was blank. Then he balled his left hand into a fist and for one split second I thought he was going to drop the TV set. Someone said, "How are you, champ?" Willie Wylie said, "Can't complain."

Buddy Seville snapped his fingers. "I got it."

Willie Wylie turned to see if he were being summoned. The rest of us waited.

"I got this gig coming up," Buddy Seville said. "A beauty contest. Down in Mexico, I think. Maybe it's Peru. Anyway. Someplace south of San Diego. The Miss Global Village Contest. I'm a judge."

"I love it already," Marty Magnin said.

"Cristo Rey," I said.

"Who's he?" Buddy Seville said. "I know him, Diana?"

"It's a place, Buddy," Diana Caro said. "South of San Diego."

"We build it around the beauty contest," Marty Magnin said. "You getting this down, Jack?"

"Got it, Marty."

"We'll all go down," Buddy Seville said. "We'll have a ball." He punched me in the arm. "And do a little balling, you know what I mean?"

"I see a major comedy," Marty Magnin said.

He was wrong.

II

TO: Amparts

FROM: PAO, U.S. Embassy, Cristo Rey, Cristo Rey, C.A.

SUBJECT: Chronology of Events Related to Cristo Rey Political Situation

CLEARANCE: Unclassified

DISTRIBUTION: Amparts, CODELS, OFDELS

5/10/79—In its official statement, the U.S. observer team monitoring the Cristo Rey election praises election as "fair and free, one of the most massive expressions of popular will ever seen in the region. The tremendous turnout of over one million people," the statement continues, "underscores the commitment of the people of Cristo Rey to the new democratic government of President Oscar Umberto Morales."

5/12/79—President Oscar Umberto Morales is deposed in a coup d'etat led by Colonel Arnoldo Jaime Gutiérrez and Colonel Adolfo Arnulfo Ehrlich, who will exercise power until a civilian-military junta is formed.

5/13/79—Former president Oscar Umberto Morales flies to

Guatemala, accompanied by his vice president, foreign minister and other cabinet ministers.

5/21/79—Former president Oscar Umberto Morales is assassinated in Guatemala City while taking a bath. Also
killed in the tub was Sta. Teri Carter of Miami Lakes,
Florida.

7/14/79—Eleven people are killed in growing warfare between
extreme left-wing and right-wing elements.

8/10/79—Roman Catholic Archbishop Raúl Esteban Castillo
warns in a radio broadcast that the political situation
is "explosive," criticizing what he calls "right-wing
death squads."

8/21/79—After a two-day visit to Cristo Rey, Senator Domingo
Coolidge (R., N.M.) says that Roman Catholic Archbishop Raúl Esteban Castillo, primate of Cristo Rey,
should not "mix religion and politics" and goes on to
say that "adherence to the Ten Commandments
should be his [Archbishop Esteban's] main concern."

8/26/79—In an apparent rebuff to Senator Domingo Coolidge
(R., N.M.), Roman Catholic Archbishop Raúl Esteban Castillo noted in his weekly radio address that
one of the Ten Commandments was, "Thou shalt not
kill." The archbishop never referred to Senator Coolidge by name.

10/1/79—Some 300 leftists storm U.S. embassy in Cristo Rey,
but are repelled by tear gas.

12/6/79—The economy of Cristo Rey continues to suffer from
the flight of hundreds of wealthy Cristo Reyenos,
mainly to Florida.

12/9/79—35 *campesinos* and their families are found dead in
the two ranches and the slaughterhouse they had
taken over in San Miguel. The *campesinos* had demanded wage increases and economic and social
changes. The National Police denies responsibility in
the death of the 35.

1/11/80—Roman Catholic Archbishop Raúl Esteban Castillo
presides at a month's mind requiem Mass for the 35
campesinos and their families killed in San Miguel. In

his homily, Archbishop Esteban demanded "an end to terrorism, violence and anarchy."

1/12/80—Colonel Adolfo Arnulfo Ehrlich announces that the 1981 Miss Global Village Contest finals will be held in Cristo Rey. Colonel Ehrlich goes on to thank the Miss Global Village executive committee for its vote of confidence.

1/30/80—Colonel Adolfo Arnulfo Ehrlich dies in a plane crash while on an inspection tour of Chalatenango Province.

1/31/80—Colonel Arnoldo Jaime Gutiérrez becomes president of the junta.

3/12/80—President Arnoldo Jaime Gutiérrez denies a report in *The New York Times* that military cadres loyal to him had placed a bomb in the plane carrying Colonel Adolfo Arnulfo Ehrlich on his fatal flight to Chalatenango Province in January.

3/30/80—Roman Catholic Archbishop Raúl Esteban Castillo is assassinated by unidentified gunmen during his weekly radio broadcast. Ironically the topic of Archbishop Esteban's last weekly homily was "The Reign of Terror in Cristo Rey."

3/31/80—Senator Domingo Coolidge (R., N.M.) mourns the death of "my very warm personal friend, Raúl Esteban."

4/1/80—Leftists announce strike to protest Archbishop Esteban's death.

4/10/80—Thirty-one are killed and more than 200 injured when explosions and gunfire set off a stampede during funeral for Archbishop Esteban. The National Police denies firing the first shots into the crowd of mourners.

5/15/80—Opposition Leader Mario Escobar is assassinated.

5/29/80—Social Democrat Leader Virgilio Acosta Davis is assassinated.

6/12/80—President Arnoldo Jaime Gutiérrez denies report on "NBC Nightly News" that he is implicated in assassination of Opposition Leader Mario Escobar.

6/15/80—Leftist-oriented Cristo Rey Human Rights Commission estimates that over 2,000 persons died as a result of political violence in Cristo Rey between January 1 and May 31, 1980.

6/17/80—Department of State assails report by Cristo Rey Human Rights Commission as "propagandistic disinformation ... unfounded, unsubstantiated and rife with error."

6/19/80—In his weekly White House radio talk, President Dale Corcoran says most Cristo Rey political killings are performed by "leftists and Marxists in military uniforms stolen from government supply depots."

6/20/80—U.S. Ambassador Thurloe deV. Weede blames "right-wing extremists" for financing "hit squads."

6/22/80—Ambassador Weede escapes from residence unharmed after two-day siege by right-wing sympathizers shouting, "Get out of Cristo Rey, communist. Go to Cuba. Leave us in peace."

7/4/80—Department of State announces replacement of Thurloe deV. Weede as U.S. Ambassador to Cristo Rey.

7/6/80—Career diplomat E. Tuckerman Bradley is named new U.S. Ambassador to Cristo Rey. Promises to "accentuate the positive."

7/22/80—Ambassador Bradley presents credentials, says "freedom is the ultimate human right."

7/25/80—Speaking to Cristo Rey Chamber of Commerce, Ambassador Bradley calls political killings "potentially destructive potholes along the highway to democracy."

8/15/80—Ambassador Bradley, citing human rights improvements, asks executive committee of Miss Global Village Contest to reconsider its decision to relocate 1981 contest finals from Cristo Rey to Caracas.

8/21/80—Ambassador Bradley hails decision by Miss Global Village executive committee to keep contest finals in Cristo Rey.

8/30/80—President Arnoldo Jaime Gutiérrez denies a report in the *Washington Post* that $11 million will be diverted from the budgets of the Ministry of Health and the Ministry of Education to underwrite the Miss Global Village Contest.

9/1/80—In a letter ("Dear Kay") to Katharine Graham, chairman of the Washington Post Company, Ambassador Bradley calls the paper's report on the financing of the Miss Global Village Contest "a base canard against one of our oldest friends in this hemisphere."

9/10/80—President Arnoldo Jaime Gutiérrez announces that Cristo Rey will hold free national democratic elections in March 1981.

9/11/80—Ambassador Bradley hails decision to hold free national democratic elections.

11/9/80—The body of American churchwoman Phyllis Emmett is found in a shallow grave along the highway in Chalatenango Province. She was 37 years old and was a former Roman Catholic nun.

11/10/80—Ambassador Bradley calls murder of former nun Phyllis Emmett "regrettable," but says her death must be regarded "as a detour on Cristo Rey's highway toward democracy."

11/15/80—Left-wing American activist Leah Kaye calls Ambassador Bradley's remarks on the death of former nun Phyllis Emmett "as boorish and insensitive as U.S. policy in Cristo Rey."

11/16/80—Saying his remarks on the death of former nun Phyllis Emmett were "misinterpreted," Ambassador Bradley apologizes for "any inadvertent hurt I might have caused," but warns, "There are those who would use the murder of this exemplary young woman for their own ends."

1/5/81—Superstar entertainer/singer/comedian Buddy Seville agrees to head judges' panel at Miss Global Village Contest.

III

IN THE OFFICIAL LINGO of the U.S. embassy in Cristo Rey, I was an "ampart," a cablese truncation of the designation "American participant." The ampart was under embassy sponsorship and during the course of his visit would be exposed—as an observer, lecturer or consultant—to various aspects of the social, political, economic or cultural life of the host country.

The Miss Global Village Contest fell under the general heading of culture.

Which was how I, a screenwriter using the contest as the background for a "panoramic multimillion-dollar motion picture comedy adventure" (to quote the description in the press release prepared by Marty Magnin's public relations firm), happened to be an ampart.

Buddy Seville was also an ampart.

And Marty Magnin.

Marty's bowels were exploding. He said he was too sick to read the embassy chronology. He said he would get studio coverage on it back in L.A.

Buddy Seville said he had given his chronology to Miss Thailand.

There was also a calendar of events in the folder the embassy PAO had prepared for each Miss Global Village ampart.

E. Tuckerman Bradley would greet the contestants on opening night and crown Miss Global Village at the closing ceremonies.

E. Tuckerman Bradley would say that both the contest and the national election the following Sunday would showcase the dynamic strides made by the Republic of Cristo Rey.

A nation on the move.

Turning the corner.

Facing the future.

A pillar of stability in the region.

Sowing the seeds of democracy in a manner that would show to the rest of the free world the hypocrisy of the totalitarian satellites of the evil empire.

E. Tuckerman Bradley.

Tuck Bradley.

Fritz Finn's Princeton roommate. My sister Priscilla's last diversion.

What goes around comes around, Bro said.

It was Bro who told me what Tuck Bradley planned to say at his two appearances at the Miss Global Village Contest. Bro was an "OFDEL," all caps (as compared to an "ampart"), short for a member of an official delegation. In this case, the official delegation handpicked by the president to monitor the Cristo Rey election. Bro was the only OFDEL asked to stay at the ambassador's residence.

I was staying at the Hotel General Enrique Ponce Moreno, familiarly called "the Ponce."

Leah changed residences every night.

Leah was not an ampart.

Nor an OFDEL.

Leah was a pain in the ass.

Tuck Bradley said to Bro.

IV

"I BET YOU'RE TAKING LOMOTIL," Leah said.

As of course I was. My stomach had gone queasy the day I arrived. Pepto-Bismol had failed to do the trick. I had stayed away from the lettuce, brushed my teeth morning and evening with a fresh can of Coke, did not eat anything uncooked, only drank beer so that I would not have to put ice in my drinks and still I was losing the battle. My Lomotil prescription was my last and, at least for the moment, not very effective barricade against the *turistas*. I knew Leah was not being sympathetic. A pain in the ass was as good a description as any. But then she had been a pain in the ass the day I first met her. And through all the intervening seventeen years. It was what she was best at. An epigraph for the woman I loved, I thought suddenly. "I was told it would work better than it has."

"By your doctor."

"My doctor in Beverly Hills, Leah," I said irritably. "Internist to the stars. The mogul of the alimentary canal. If it makes you happy hearing that. And I suspect it does. So if it pleases the court, I will allow you to stipulate for the record my appetite for sybaritic prescription drugs to cement my rebellious stools."

"My, we're touchy today." She smiled when she said it. As she had always smiled when she had scored a point at someone else's expense. It was when she smiled that I noticed a slight creeping under her chin and the beginnings of what appeared to be a picket fence of vertical wrinkles on her upper lip. Almost as a reflex, I sucked in my stomach and felt for the widening tonsure on the top of my head. We are both middle-aged, I thought suddenly. I hated to think I had come all the way to Cristo Rey and poisoned my innards just to find that out.

"Can we please get off my insides and proceed to more interesting and provocative topics?"

"Like what?"

"Like why you don't sleep in the same bed two nights running."

Her voice was perfectly controlled. "Because I don't want to get murdered."

That sounds reasonable enough, I remember thinking. I confess now that I did not pay much credence to what she said at first. Leah's natural professional habitat was the jungle of the hunter and the hunted, and she had always been effortlessly fluent in its hyperbole. Which was why, instead of replying immediately, I concentrated for a moment on the surroundings. We were sitting in an outdoor coffee bar in the Plaza del Libertador. In point of fact, Cristo Rey had never had a *libertador*, but that was an irrelevancy the few available histories of the nation glided past with aplomb. Dominating the square was a statue of General Enrique Ponce Moreno on horseback. By default and pride of position, Ponce Moreno had thus become El Libertador. Actually, however, the statue was of General John J. Pershing. Black Jack himself. In the cavalry field uniform and floppy campaign hat he had worn when chasing Pancho Villa without avail through the deserts of Sonora, Chihuahua and Sinaloa. This was a fact I had picked up from Bro. And he from the deputy assistant secretary of state who manned the Cristo Rey desk. The statue had been bought for a song at an auction in San Antonio, Texas. By a representative of the Majors' Junta. In 1952, the Majors' Junta, loyal to the memory of the late general, had toppled the Colonels' Junta, which had assassinated him. The price was right and Black

Jack had a mustache, as did Ponce Moreno. There was no other resemblance, but thirty years of birdshit had obliterated that discrepancy. A parable of history in Cristo Rey. I thought better of telling it to Leah. A moment when she was contemplating the possibility of her own murder hardly seemed the most propitious for an historical drollery.

"You think what happened to Phyllis could happen to you," I said finally. "Why?"

"Because I am inconvenient. People in this country who happen to be inconvenient also happen to get murdered a lot."

She still talked about murder the way she always had, with a maddening equanimity. It was the same whether she was counsel for the accused or considered herself, as she did now, a potential victim. I cannot recall how many times over the years she had discussed with me her full expectation of being taken out by some variety of pig. Dying for something and becoming in the process a martyr was never her intention. Leah was far too practical for that. It was, however, a projection that she never failed to factor into her thinking.

"Why are you so inconvenient?"

"Because I'm here. Because this election is fraudulent."

"You mean the Miss Global Village Contest is fixed?" I said in mock horror. "Because Señorita Thailand is banging one of the judges?" I wished I could have reeled the words back before they were out of my mouth. Leah did not respond. A comment in itself. I tried again. "Look, Leah. Elections in this part of the world tend to be fraudulent. The same way construction company vice presidents in Rhode Island tend to be crooked. And shouldn't be nominated for secretary of labor."

Leah ran a forefinger around the inside rim of her coffee cup. She wiped the finger absentmindedly with a Kleenex. "I think you've been in Hollywood too long."

My father had said more or less the same thing. The day he had the stroke. The day I had asked him why he had fucked the woman sitting across from me at that very moment in the Plaza del Libertador. I looked past the statue of General Moreno, toward the central market on the other side of the square. A faded pink colonial warehouse with stall after stall of bananas and plantains. And not much else. I had already decided to play a scene there. It was a good location. With strong visuals. Good locations could take the onus off obligatory exposition. The camera would focus on the flies buzzing around the rotting fruit. Across the street there was a flea market. I saw a tracking shot. With voice-over. One of the stalls in the flea market sold a combination of firewood and armadillo skins. I was sure Buddy Seville could do some shtick with the skins. Maybe make watchbands for his gang. In any event, not my problem. "JOKES TK," I would write in the screenplay. Let the staff writers for the H.O.P.E. telethon dream up Buddy Seville gags. I was just a constructionist. The best in the business, thank you very much. Perhaps if I delivered that encomium to my father, the good news might just snap him out of his enforced vascular snooze. As if all he had ever really wanted in a son was a good constructionist.

I looked up.

A soldier was strolling through the coffee bar, checking credentials. He could not have been more than sixteen years old. A few hairs on his lip passed for a mustache. His weapon was slung upside down on his shoulder. An M-16 with a flash suppressor on the muzzle. A thick elastic band held extra ammunition clips to the side of his steel pot. Slapped on one of the ammo clips was a sticker that said, SEÑORITA PUEBLO DEL MUNDO—1981.

I gave him my passport and Leah hers.

I had the feeling he could not read. Which was better than a fifty-fifty proposition if I remembered my area handbook correctly.

He stared at the photographs in each passport, then briefly at me. I kept my hands in sight on the table. "Our neighbors to the south think a gun is something you use to get a parking space." Bro had told me that before I left. "Beware of sudden movements at roadblocks and during random security checks. Our neighbors to the south also have itchy trigger fingers."

The soldier kept staring at Leah.

It occurred to me suddenly that the safari jacket she had on was the same one she was wearing in the NBC News clip when the body of Phyllis Emmett was identified.

In some circles, that might be considered evidence of political subversion.

And cause for summary execution.

That was the way my mind was running.

The soldier picked his nose. Then he took Leah's passport and held the photograph flush against her cheek. *"Por favor"* was the only Spanish phrase that came to mind and it did not seem to fit the situation. Finally the soldier dropped the passport on the table.

He sauntered out of the coffee bar.

Leah took a deep breath.

"Jesus."

"You get used to it," she said. If you ever get out of Hollywood long enough was the implication.

I ordered another coffee. "Tell me about Phyllis Emmett."

"I didn't think you'd remember her."

That finally was too much.

"Her uncle was a cop in San Francisco." I dredged furiously into my memory. Oakland. The Justice Department. The year Leah and I met. Harriet Hecht. Fellatio Is Freedom. Dial 911—Make a Cop Come. What was the uncle's name? Memory did not fail. "Uncle Eddie Dalton. She could never think of her uncle Eddie as a pig."

Leah was silent.

"She was afraid you'd toss her out on her ear if you ever found out about him."

I had the tact not to ask if she would have. Probably. On the principle of the will of the majority. A principle Leah adhered to only on an ad hoc basis.

"It was because of Bro that she left the convent, did you know that?"

It took a long time before she finally and almost imperceptibly shook her head.

In fact, had it not been for Bro, Sister Phyllis, the bride of Christ, might still be teaching the first grade. I even remembered the school. Saint Dominick's. In Chinatown. Confucius and the Baltimore Catechism. But then the passionate retreat master had to introduce her to the new church. And look what that got her.

"She used to go to Mass every morning in Hermosa." I had not been in Hollywood so long I had forgotten that.

"You thought she was jogging," I said.

If you ever thought of her at all.

"There was a seminarian," I said.

In a state of delirious transport, caught between her ample hips, and I their latex connection.

"I think she met him in the slammer," I said.

Fuck you, Leah.

"Remember?" I said.

I watched as a bird decorated the statue of the putative General Moreno. A white dropping hung on his nose, then fell on the pommel of his saddle.

"I shouldn't have said that, Jack. I'm sorry."

A certification that we were indeed getting older. Since it was the first time I could ever recall her apologizing for anything.

"What did happen?"

Leah rubbed the cover of her passport, as if she were trying to eradicate the fingerprints of the soldier. I thought for a moment she was not going to answer. Then she looked up.

"She went for supplies. She didn't come back. The Wagoneer she was driving was found abandoned. A four-wheel drive. She was the only one in the village who knew how to drive it. It was her vehicle. That's what she called it. A vehicle. It was two days before anyone at the church knew where she was. That's when I was called. A dog apparently found the grave. And ate a couple of her fingers while he was at it. They were sticking up through the dirt. Obviously she'd been buried in a hurry. Her face was shot off. It was as if it had never been there."

She was like a GAO auditor reciting a litany of figures before a congressional hearing.

"She'd also been fucked up the ass. Whether it was before she died or after, no one is sure. Forensic pathology is not a science much favored down here. The operative rule is to get the body into the ground before the cholera epidemic breaks out."

Leah held the passport to the light, examining it for fingerprints she might have missed, then returned it to the breast pocket of her safari jacket. I waited while she fastened the button. She smoothed the flap before she continued.

"Someone said the shooter was wearing a Mickey Mouse sweatshirt. Not that the someone will ever testify to that fact in court. I wouldn't hold my breath waiting for that." She cleared her throat. "I suppose the man in the Mickey Mouse sweatshirt went home, played with the children, ate dinner, shit, fucked his wife and went to sleep."

I reached across the table and ran my finger down the side of her face.

"I'm sorry about Hugh, Jack," she said after a while.

V

I MAKE A LIVING writing love scenes.

That was a love scene I never would have attempted.

And certainly one that Marty Magnin would never have allowed on the screen in A Martin Magnin Production.

For one thing, it didn't end up in bed. At least it didn't end up in bed immediately.

Marty liked the screenplay of A Martin Magnin Production to play fast. Like this:

> LEAH
> I'm sorry about Hugh, Jack.
>
> CUT TO:
>
> INT. BEDROOM—DAY
> LEAH and JACK fucking tastefully.
>
> JACK
> Has it really been that long?
>
> CUT TO:

Real life, however, is seldom played as fast as A Martin Magnin Production.

In real life, there was no jump cut to Room 421 at the Hotel General Enrique Ponce Moreno. No curtains billowing sensuously in the breeze produced by the sound stage wind machine. No string music by Tito Escobar and Los Hermanos Delgadillo filtering up from the poolside palm terrace down below.

It took a little longer than that.

A few more pink cards.

When I write a screenplay, I use 3 x 5 index cards to rough out the story line. White cards for the first act, green cards for the second, pink for the third, all pushpinned to my bulletin board. Each card represents a single scene, each scene is reduced to a single identifying phrase. JACK AND LEAH IN PLAZA DEL LIBERTADOR would be one card. With no further elaboration of the elements.

OFDELS ARRIVAL would be another card.

BRO AT THE INFIERNO.

LUNCH AT TUCK BRADLEY'S.

MISS GLOBAL VILLAGE OPENING NIGHT CEREMONY.

These were other cards I could have written out that week in Cristo Rey.

I slept with Leah between LUNCH AT TUCK BRADLEY'S and MISS GLOBAL VILLAGE OPENING NIGHT CEREMONY.

VI

BRO AND THE REST OF THE OFDELS on the election observation team arrived Monday afternoon in a special presidential 707 with the words UNITED STATES OF AMERICA painted in blue on either side of the cabin exterior.

President Gutiérrez and Tuck Bradley greeted the observers at General Enrique Ponce Moreno Airport.

Senator Domingo Coolidge, the delegation chairman, read a statement praising the election as a new democratic beginning for one of America's oldest friends in the hemisphere.

President Gutiérrez said he would honor the will of the voters.

Bro offered a blessing to the patience and perseverance of the people of Cristo Rey.

The airport arrival ceremony was carried live on local television.

I watched in the palm terrace at the Ponce. On the barstool next to me, Buddy Seville sipped a banana daiquiri. His body glistened with Bain de Soleil. He was wearing a black bikini and a Cleveland Indians baseball cap. Pinned to the cap was the RICH IS BETTER button I had given Marty Magnin and which Marty in turn had given Buddy. Marty was still imprisoned in his suite.

Another losing day with his intestines. Miss Thailand sat on Buddy's lap. Hair curled over the top of her bikini.

"Take a swim, hon," Buddy said. "I hear the water here's nice."

Miss Thailand executed a perfect dive into the pool.

"I got to get rid of this chick," Buddy said. "She's already asking me if the crown is one size fits all."

Somewhere in the distance I could hear the sound of small-arms fire.

"What's that?" Buddy said.

"Firecrackers."

"A lot of firecrackers down here, you know that, Jackie?"

"In honor of the contest, Buddy."

I thought of Leah. She had gone back up to Chalatenango for a few days with the photographer for the Human Rights Commission. Onyx Leon was already there. He was also an unofficial election observer. Chalatenango was his birthplace. Onyx had heard reports of another mass grave. Tuck Bradley had said it was an old grave. Five years old anyway. Perhaps even ten. Long before democracy had gained the foothold it had in Cristo Rey. Leah said she wanted a complete set of photographs to make sure.

She had not told me she was going to Chalatenango.

I only learned it when I found the note she had left in my box.

Too many gringos if you come, the note had said. Don't worry.

I worried.

Because she had never told me not to worry before, no matter how volatile the situation.

The small-arms fire did not make me worry any less.

"Hey, that must be Father Augie," Buddy Seville said suddenly. I watched Bro on the TV raise his hand in blessing. "Father Augie" was what Buddy had taken to calling Bro, as if he were a show business priest, the pastor of the Las Vegas Strip.

"I know only one other Augie," Buddy Seville said. In fact he did not know Bro at all. He just seemed comforted by the idea that his writer had a brother who was Father Augie on the observation team. A notion that acted to calm the lingering unease about the noises in the street that I kept insisting were firecrackers. Father Augie would not put him in harm's way. "Augie Pellegrino. You know Augie?"

I shook my head and focused on Bro, who had finished his blessing and was shaking hands with Tuck Bradley and President Gutiérrez. He was wearing a white suit, Roman collar and black dickey. Lévi-Strauss says the tropics aren't exotic, they're only out of date, Bro had told me before I left for Cristo Rey. I had never seen him look so out of date.

"Sure, you know Augie," Buddy Seville said. "Runs Five Angels Carting Company, you know, that Carmine Ca'd'Oro used to run before he disappeared."

Thirty years of working mob rooms had given Buddy Seville as clear an understanding of one nation-state in the underworld as Leah had of another.

"Oh, that Augie," I said.

"I knew you knew Augie."

Bro called as soon as he arrived at Tuck Bradley's residence. He suggested dinner at eight. He had been told of a place called El Infierno. Not an hour off the plane and he already knew where to eat.

The piano player was a pansy. Chords with his left hand, melody with his right. He was wearing an open-necked shirt with a large medallion hanging from a gold chain around his neck. His hair was fluffed and styled and as he segued from "My Way" into "The Girl from Ipanema" he seemed to be batting his eyes in my direction. The group at the next table laughed uproariously at my discomfort and began blowing kisses back at him. I recognized the son of the minister of police. He opened his leather handbag, removed a 9mm Beretta and a package of cigarettes, put the Beretta back in the bag and lit up. It was the son of the minister of police who had palmed Miss Thailand off on Buddy Seville. Miss Thailand was obviously a woman of spirit and ambition who was going to make the most of her opportunity in the Occident.

Eight-thirty came and went.

Nine.

Still no Bro.

I had taken a taxi to the restaurant, not my rented car. A little paranoia in that decision. I could thank Leah for that. Always check your car for bombs, she had said. With that perfect equanimity she had mastered. She might have been telling me to kick the tires or that the windshield wipers needed replacing. In the parking lot at the Ponce, I could not bring myself to open the car door. If Leah had been there, I would have, but Leah was in Chalatenango, and Chalatenango was where Phyllis Emmett had her face shot off by someone wearing a Mickey Mouse sweatshirt.

I asked the doorman to order a cab.

As I waited for the cab to arrive, a reporter I knew asked if he could borrow my car as long as I was not going to use it, he had a date, he wanted to get laid, he had heard of a spot at Playa Sonsonate that was just the place for a little romance if only he could get there. Check under the hood for bombs, I said when I tossed him the keys. With the beguiling blitheness of someone down there to write a Buddy Seville comedy. Sure thing, he had said. He had waved when he drove out of the parking lot.

At least I had kept my paranoid fear to myself.

Nine-thirty.

There was an arcade across the street from the restaurant. Bumper cars, pinball machines and video games. I walked across. It was something to do while I waited. The point of the video game I played was to shoot down the enemy air force. One hundred points for a transport, four hundred for a helicopter, six hundred for a jet fighter and a thousand-point bonus jackpot for a parachuting pilot who had bailed out of his crippled aircraft.

I wondered if the bonus jackpot only showed up on the game in Cristo Rey. A special wrinkle for a country caught in a civil war.

Bro appeared at ten.

"Sorry," he said. "There was this endless goddamn reception at the Foreign Ministry and then Mingo Coolidge, that moron, insisted on an organization meeting with the observers and the staff afterward." He had abandoned his white suit and black dickey for a white guayabera and light gray slacks. I caught the scent of Arden for Men Sandalwood. "I almost didn't get out at all. Tuck insists that all the observers have bodyguards. State Department orders. Mine couldn't be more conspicuous if he wore a neon sign that spelled out COP. I left him outside. I told

him you were a marine officer and never went anywhere un-
armed." He summoned a waiter and in his perfect Spanish ordered us each a rum and soda, no ice, the soda in an unopened
bottle on the side, and a grilled sea bass, lemon, no butter. Only
then did he look slowly around the room. "I think that piano
player just winked at me."

A flourish of chords. The theme from *Rocky*.

"Actually he was winking at me. But be my guest."

"I'll pass." The waiter brought the drinks. Bro sent back the
soda. The bottle was uncapped. "I don't wish to make a fuss, but
there appear to be several guns on the table next to us."

"A Beretta 9mm and an H&K P9S 45 cal. ACP, to be exact.
The Beretta belongs to the son of the minister of police, that's the
short fat one with the mustache. He is rumored to have used it
against enemies of the West. The discussion, and my Spanish
isn't as good as yours, is over which one has more stopping
power. The H&K P9S has a polygon barrel, in case you're interested. For increased accuracy."

"You seem to be a student of local color. I can't wait to see your
movie." The waiter bought another bottle of soda. Bro opened it
himself. He poured soda for each of us. "Tell me more about native life."

"Who's Art Underwood?"

Bro looked at me quickly. "Mingo's son-in-law. Another idiot.
He works at the embassy. Second secretary of something or
other. Maybe the political officer."

I had the sense of a pro forma curriculum vitae he did not really
expect me to believe. "Leah says he's the CIA station chief."

He did not hesitate. "Tuck says Leah's a pain in the ass."

"She always has been."

"True enough. Her most redeeming feature." He stirred the
soda and the rum with his finger. "Well, in this case she's right.
Which is one reason why Tuck happens to think she's a pain in
the ass. An unpatriotic one at that. Art Underwood is definitely
of that persuasion. I should say, however, for the record, that
people in Art's line of work do tend to turn up in American em-
bassies around the world. That can hardly come as a surprise to
Leah."

"Of course not. She's rarely surprised. And hardly surprised that Tuck and Art Underwood didn't seem to give a shit who killed Phyllis Emmett."

"That poor nun."

I thought I detected the professional condescension of priest toward nun. Perhaps I was too harsh. With more satisfaction than I should have displayed, I said, "You were her retreat master once."

His face seemed to slide.

"You were wearing the red silk sling. It was after your arm got broken at Hunters Point."

He stared at me without speaking.

"The postulants thought you were the cat's ass. At least one of them did."

"Oh, shit."

I told him the whole story. Or as much of it as I knew. From novitiate to shallow red clay grave.

"That poor woman," he said when I finished. I ordered another drink. Bro looked as if he could use it. "That poor, poor woman."

This time I mixed the rum and soda in the two glasses. "Leah says that Art Underwood and Tuck don't want any fingers pointing in the direction of Arnoldo Jaime Gutiérrez." I started to say, "Whom I saw you hugging at the airport on television today," but instead I said, "The guarantor of democracy in one of our oldest friends in this hemisphere. Leah says that Tuck has already certified his election."

The second drink seemed to revive Bro. His guard went back up. "And Art Underwood says that Miss Thailand is a lock."

"Until this afternoon."

"So strange things can happen. President Gutiérrez might turn out to be the Miss Thailand of this campaign."

"Are you booking bets?"

He smiled. He was an OFDEL again. Suddenly he snapped his fingers. "Speaking of elections. Do you know a reporter in San Francisco named Skip Kenna? Works for the *Chronicle*. Covers city hall?"

I shook my head.

"He says you used to work with his father. Someone called Joe Kenna."

"Joe Kenna." I had not thought of him in years. Dying of cancer that morning in Department 34, San Francisco Superior Court when I met Leah for the first time. A name I never expected to hear in Cristo Rey. Joe Kenna. Into whose care I was given to learn how to be a reporter. Joe Kenna. Who had told me in his roundabout fashion that it was the Abruzzo brothers who had firebombed Leah's offices in Oakland. Phyllis Emmett. Joe Kenna. Names popping out of the past. "I don't think I ever knew he had a son."

"He called me. He wanted to get hold of you. I said you were down here."

At the next table, the son of the minister of police was sighting along the polygon barrel of the H&K P9S.

Eyes closed, the piano player was lost in the lush melody of "Wild Is the Wind."

"What did he want?"

"He was a great fan of *Grunts*. Knew it backward and forward, he said. Teaches it at some night school journalism course. San Francisco State, I think. Maybe UC Extension."

I hoped he only wanted me to speak to his class, but already I suspected it was more than that.

"He's a Vietnam vet, he said."

I waited.

"Anyway, there was this guy who ran for some local office in San Francisco. City Council . . ."

"Board of Supervisors."

"You know who I mean, then?"

"Richie Kane."

He sounded surprised. "That is his name."

Another name, another connection. "What about him?"

"Well, apparently when he was running for office last fall, he made certain representations about being a Vietnam veteran." For a moment anyway, Bro seemed to have lapsed into the judicious phraseology of the seasoned observer. "But it seems that most of the stories he told were cribbed from your book."

I remembered the school auditorium at Holy Sep.

The God Squad jeep.

The faster you kill the little commie bastards, the faster their souls will get to heaven.

"Anyway, this Skip Kenna character got hold of the campaign literature and speeches and matched the stories up with the book. That's why he wanted to get hold of you. He wants to check it out."

"He is in the book."

"Who?"

"Richie."

"So he claims. But he won't say which parts . . ."

It smells like fish.

I'm ever in the Penn State area.

Honey, who was buried with two left arms.

". . . and this fellow from the *Chronicle* says if he was in everything he said he was in, he must've fought the war all by himself."

Skip Kenna.

Joe Kenna's son.

I had the sense of generations chasing after each other.

This time I said it. "Oh, shit."

VII

I NEVER DID get in touch with Skip Kenna.

My reasons were properly high-minded. There were ethical considerations. I had guaranteed anonymity to everyone I had interviewed for what subsequently became *Grunts* and it would have been a breach of journalistic ethics to reveal who had contributed what. In other words, the kind of empty posturing that so often ends up causing trouble.

Not that it mattered what I did. Skip Kenna was going to do the piece with or without my imprimatur anyway.

I had just never expected the book to receive the close exegesis he gave it.

As later the San Francisco district attorney's office would also give it.

Not to mention the attorneys for the defense.

Two good reasons why, when the trial began, I left the country.

Skip Kenna sent me a tear sheet in Los Angeles after the piece came out. He was very proud of it. As I suppose he had every right to be. It was good solid city desk reporting. He was, he wrote in the note accompanying the tear sheet, a Vietnam junkie, a grunt himself, nine months in Alpha Company, 2/3 Infantry, 199th LIB until he was invalided home with a million-dollar shrapnel wound in his foot. He was also very circumspect. He only pointed out the similarities between Richie's speeches and certain entries in my book. Then compared these sections to Richie's dates with the 322d Avn Co. Certain conclusions were drawn. A door gunner at Bien Hoa, for example, could not also be a marine in Da Nang. Richie was caught. His prevarications were harmless enough. He did not award himself the valor of others. There was precious little valor in the book in any case. On the other hand, he could not specifically identify his own contribution to the book without being held in some way accountable for the actions he had either witnessed or participated in. The prisoner thrown out of the chopper on the way back from Bu Dop, the construction worker hung, however accidentally, from the 4 x 4 rough terrain crane in Vinh Long.

Richie could only deny.

And could not even stipulate what he was denying.

I wonder if that was when he began to go mad.

VIII

AFTER BRO DIED, I specifically checked in both his official and unofficial diaries at the Widener to see if he had made any mention, during his stay in Cristo Rey, of either Richie Kane or Skip Kenna. There was none, directly or indirectly. The story he had carried south had apparently made no impression on him whatsoever.

He had other things on his mind.

The official diary first:

> Up at 4:30 to the sound of small-arms fire. I hear helicopters overhead trying to locate the source of the shooting. Mass at five in Ambassador Tuck Bradley's dining room with the embassy butler serving as my acolyte. His idea of altar wine is an exquisite 1959 Echézeaux. A gift from Tuck from his own private stock in the embassy cellars. He always has been the most gracious of hosts. I offered the Mass both for him and my brother Jack, who is here working on a film project. I am sorry to say that the liturgical readings for this time of year add a certain sense of foreboding to what's happening around here. The Entrance Antiphon was from the Sixteenth Psalm: "The snares of death overtook me and the

ropes of hell tightened around me; in my distress I called upon the Lord and he heard my voice." Then the reading was from Jeremiah (11:19): "I for my part was like a trustful lamb being led to the slaughterhouse, not knowing the schemes they were plotting against me. 'Let us destroy the tree and its strength, let us cut him off from the land of the living, so that his name may be quickly forgotten.' " I can't imagine beginning the day without the sustenance and comfort of the Mass, but I don't like to linger on the thought of democracy in Cristo Rey as the thoughtful lamb being led to slaughter. I make a special silent prayer to Christ the King for the future of His namesake country.

A glass of juice and a cup of black coffee after Mass and then Senator Mingo Coolidge and I are off to the Hotel General Enrique Ponce Moreno where we're both scheduled to be on "Good Morning America" and on the "Today" show. Our vehicle was reinforced with bulletproof glass and there was armor plating on the sides. Our guards insisted that Mingo and I sit on flak jackets. We had a good laugh and a good deal of ribald humor about that.

The shows were up on the roof of the "Ponce," as the hotel is called, and both were live. The GMA and the Today people were quarreling about which show would get us first and I suggested that Mingo go on one and I go on the other and then we switch. My good friend Bryant Gumbel said I should be in the State Department. Our security people from the embassy insisted that we move away from the edge of the roof during the shooting, because there was real as opposed to television shooting going on all around us down below. I was very upbeat about the election on both shows and did not mention the reading from Jeremiah, although I believe that David Hartman is a Catholic, as he told me his children are named Sean, Brian, Bridget, and Conor.

On the way back to Tuck Bradley's residence, one of those things occurred that so often serve to remind me of the consolation one of God's servants can grant at the most unexpected moments. We passed what appeared to be a funeral party walking on the side of the road and as there seemed to be no priest present I prevailed upon our driver to stop for a moment. It so happens that when I am in a situation like the one here in Cristo Rey, I always carry the holy oils in my pocket in case I come across someone in need of the last rites. To make a long story short, this was a funeral and there was a body in the coffin the mourners were carrying, a young soldier killed in a firefight, perhaps the same action that woke me before Mass just a few hours earlier. I told the family my name was Padre Augustino and needless to say, the solace a priest can offer was most welcome. The poor boy's mother collapsed in my arms and insisted that I open the window of the coffin to see her son, windows being a feature of coffins in this part of the world. You could see where the bullet holes on his face had been patched with a kind of orange wax because the rest of his body was turning green. I recited a decade of the rosary and anointed the body, which of course was greatly appreciated. Then Senator Coolidge said perhaps we should leave, as we were adhering to a rather strict schedule, but before we did, I gave the boy's mother the silver rosary that John and Yoko Lennon had given me for my birthday two years ago and that the Holy Father had blessed on his trip to Zimbabwe, where I last saw him. I could not help but think once more of the reading from Jeremiah in this morning's Mass.

And then the unofficial diary:

Jack seems to blame me in some way for what happened to Phyllis Emmett, the little nun who was killed up in Chalengo (sp?) Province. I think it's a stretch, but I'm willing to take on any burden these days. My penance for having cheated God. That awful thought continues to bow my neck, like a heavy chain scapular.

Another thing about Jack. Leah seems to be back in his life. Or just on the verge of it. My luck.

I wonder why the piano player winked at me.

Lunch with Tuck tomorrow. I asked him to invite Jack. He couldn't very well say no, but I don't think he was too happy

about it. Leah drives him batshit. She does have that effect
on people. Tuck would like to get her thrown out of the
country, but that is hardly the face a nascent democracy can
present to the rest of the world when the "Today" show and
"Good Morning America" are broadcasting live in beautiful
downtown Cristo Rey.

I didn't tell Jack that I had lunch with Leah in San Francisco
the last time I was there. Tadich's. My treat. I wonder how
it happened that three so dissimilar men in the same family
could end up so captivated by the same woman. We must all
like abuse. She told me I was a man for whom culture shock
does not exist. And said it as if she were ordering a second
cup of coffee. I trot around the world to have my basic be-
liefs confirmed. I have a Gallup poll approach to moral
issues. I see what the consensus is and then get about a step
and a half out in front of it. She kept coming at me from
every direction, like the Chinese army, a human wave attack.
I keep wishing that Hugh had kept a diary like this. I wonder what he really thought of her.

This is a few minutes later. Tuck just asked me down for a
nightcap. That comic Jack is doing the picture for is going to
be at lunch tomorrow. And the minister of police. Art Underwood's stooge. Art says they expect a turnout of 1.275
million voters Sunday. A very nervous figure. Too exact.
The president's slate is favored. Señorita Thailand should be
so lucky.

IX

LUNCH WAS A STRUGGLE.

"Have you ever noticed how the English shake hands?" Bro said. At least he was trying to hold up his end. Mingo Coolidge kept staring at me as if I were a security risk. Art Underwood kept whispering into Tuck Bradley's ear, as if he were a lawyer advising a client who was about to take the Fifth. Ardis Bradley kept fluttering her hands and talking about the wonderful detox center she was hoping the Foster Grandparents of Cristo Rey would sponsor. The minister of police kept denying there was a need either for a detox center or for Foster Grandparents in Cristo Rey. Buddy Seville could not take his eyes off the remaining guest, Dra. Lourdes Abauza, the most prominent poet in Cristo Rey, a woman in her sixties with a mustache and a generous assortment of moles on the breasts that seemed to be cantilevered out of her parrot green silk dress. "They shake hands as if they're tipping a headwaiter."

"I have noticed that, yes." Dra. Abauza nodded vigorously. "Although I have never been to England. Which is where the English live."

"That chick's not four feet tall," Buddy Seville whispered. He was wearing another jumpsuit with his name printed on the back, this one shocking pink with blue letters, its only other ornamentation his RICH IS BETTER button.

"I'm so sorry Mr. Magnin couldn't join us," Ardis Bradley said.

"He hasn't been off the crapper since he got here," Buddy said.

Dra. Abauza plowed ahead. "I am considering a poem on how the peoples of the world greet each other."

"Some of them have to stand on a stool to shake hands," Buddy Seville said.

Bro tried to bridge the silence. "Fritz Finn once told me that every time he shook hands with Anthony Eden, he felt almost as if he had to say, 'Thank you very much indeed, sir.' "

"That Fritz," Buddy Seville said, suddenly animated. "He really loved my gang, right, Father Augie?"

Bro looked at me for help. A quarter of a century in public life and Buddy's gang had somehow escaped his attention.

"The kids on the H.O.P.E. telethon," I said.

"That is absolutely fascinating," Ardis Bradley said.

Art Underwood was still pouring information into Tuck Bradley's ear. Mingo Coolidge was trying to listen.

The minister of police eyed Buddy's RICH IS BETTER button.

"There are many poems about hope," Dra. Abauza said.

"You got to send me some, hon," Buddy Seville said. He turned back to Bro. "He says to me one night at the White House, Fritz, the president, it was a little state dinner he was having for some African cat, hey, you were there, Father Augie, what was that African dude's name, he was a real sweetheart, the schwartze, you know the one I mean, we had dinner with him at the White House. A swell guy, he had more wives than Mickey Rooney . . ."

"Kwame Mbela," Bro said. He always knew when to be a straight man.

"Whatever," Buddy Seville said. "If he was okay with President Fritz, he was okay with me. We used to schmooze a lot, him and me, at the White House, my place, his place, and he says to me that night, Fritz, he says, 'Buddy, that gang of yours is what this country is all about,' I swear to God on a stack of Bibles . . ."

"That is exactly what he said," Bro agreed.

"You remember that, Father Augie?" Buddy Seville said doubtfully.

"I was there."

"I forgot that. You heard him, right?"

"Absolutely." Bro was enjoying himself, his well-developed sense of the absurd allowing him to claim attendance at a colloquy that had never taken place. He appeared rejuvenated.

"He was there," Buddy Seville said to the minister of police.

The minister nodded. I had already seen him take down in his notebook the name on the back of Buddy's jumpsuit. I think he thought it the same as Calvin or Polo.

"I know a lot of presidents in my time," Buddy Seville continued. "We schmooze, we play golf, we eat Chinese. But that Fritz, he was something else."

"A balanced evaluation," Bro said.

"That African guy, Kwame what's-his-face . . ."

"Mbela," Bro said.

"Whatever happened to him?"

"He's in Gstaad."

"God bless him," Buddy Seville said.

Conversation waned while the soup course was cleared.

"I heard an interesting story about General Ponce Moreno," Bro said after the sole véronique was served. "Perhaps you can enlighten us, Minister."

"There are many interesting stories about El Libertador, Father," the minister of police said. His name was Carlos Bequer. Art Underwood had called him "Charlie" during the sherry and Bloody Marys before lunch. He was attired in a khaki uniform with a polished Sam Browne belt and two rows of suspicious campaign ribbons over his breast pocket. It occurred to me that the wearing of unearned medals seemed to be a habit in Cristo Rey.

Art Underwood looked quickly down the table at Bro. I think he had picked up the same nuance I had picked up, an uncharacteristic hardening of Bro's tone behind the smile on his face. I had the sense that for whatever his reasons Bro was trying to pick a fight. "Careful, Charlie," I heard Art Underwood say under his

breath to the minister of police. Across the table, Mingo Coolidge
tried to stare me down. He was nearly seventy and had affected
the shoot-first-ask-questions-afterward manner of a turn-of-the-
century New Mexico sheriff. Before lunch he had mentioned that
old Marshall Rutland had been a longtime friend and adviser and
that Anabel was a hell of a gal and that old Marshall would know
how to take care of someone like that goddamn Leah Kaye
woman. I asked if he had known that old Marshall Rutland had
begun his days on horseback as a garbageman in Providence,
Rhode Island. The question seemed to end any chance of a lasting
friendship.

"Bro majored in history at Harvard," Tuck Bradley said to the
table at large, as if that explained any interest Bro might possibly
have in El Libertador. Tuck had apparently picked up the bad vi-
bration from Bro as well. He had not aged well. Bro said he had
stage-managed coups in three of his last four postings for the
State Department and the effort seemed to have given him the
untrustful beady-eyed look of the professional conspirator. I remembered suddenly that after Priscilla died he had asked me to
locate the love letters he had written her. And that when Leah
was demonstrating outside the house on Washington Street I had
called him an asshole. Another balanced evaluation.

Ardis Bradley smiled brightly. "I didn't know you majored in
history, Bro."

"History is secular poetry," Dra. Abauza said gravely, smooth-
ing her mustache.

"Now I know who that chick looks like," Buddy Seville whispered. "Don Ameche."

"This was during the revolution of 1949," Bro said.

"In 1949, there was no revolution," the minister of police corrected. "In 1949, there was only an uprising of dissident elements
that El Libertador quickly and effectively put down."

"A communist uprising, wasn't it, Charlie?" Mingo Coolidge
said.

"Of course," Art Underwood said, smiling down at Bro.

Bro returned the smile. "You'd like this, Art. El Libertador had
this foolproof way of rooting out the *insurgentes*, the *subver-*
sivos . . ."

"Doesn't anyone around here speak English?" Buddy Seville said.

Bro was not deterred. "He'd ask his prisoners to smell his gun . . ."

"That is absolutely fascinating," Ardis Bradley said.

". . . and if they refused, he would say, 'If you don't smell my pistol, then you're a communist and afraid. He who is without sin has no fear.' "

"Show me the line," Buddy Seville said.

Every eye at the table turned toward him.

"The line where you line up to smell the gun," Buddy Seville said.

"Of course," Ardis Bradley said.

"Except when the *campesino* sniffed the barrel of the gun, then El Libertador would shoot him in the face and say, 'Bring in the next one.' "

"That's one way of handling it," Mingo Coolidge said, popping a grape from the sole véronique into his mouth.

"The old double cross," Buddy Seville said. He focused his attention on Dra. Abauza. "Hey, hon, you hear about the Polish lesbian?"

"Is this an American poem?"

"She likes men."

It was an approach that I was sure worked wonders at The Buddy Seville Open, but it seemed to leave Dra. Abauza totally bewildered.

"I want you to know that I am a friend of the truth," said the minister of police, contemplating Bro. There was a murmur of approval from both Mingo Coolidge and Art Underwood, who both acted as if the minister's statement had actually addressed some aspect of Bro's story.

"None of us doubts that at all, Charlie." Tuck Bradley cleared his throat and quickly corrected himself. "Uh, Mr. Minister." Tuck looked unhappy, with Bro and me the particular objects of his unhappiness. Ever since his affair with Priscilla, we had made him decidedly nervous, both singly and in concert. "They won't stay on the goddamn reservation, neither one of them," he had once confided to Fritz Finn, and of course Fritz had passed the

observation on to Bro, and Bro to me. I wondered idly why Tuck
had bothered to invite Bro to stay at the residence. It turned
out that Fritz was the culprit who had made the suggestion. He
knew that Tuck would not turn down a former president and
he knew that Bro would contrive to upset him in some way. I
think now that Fritz was still making Tuck pay for usurping
his position with Priscilla.

"It's a curious thing about disinformation," Art Underwood
said smoothly.

"What disinformation would that be, Art?" Bro asked.

"A story like the one you just told. It gets started and then the
dissident elements take it up and then it begins to take on a life of
its own and finally, inexorably, it becomes history. There are no
witnesses to the story and so the story can't be refuted. The communists . . ." As he said the word "communists," his head moved
slowly around the table, taking us all in, the usual suspects, no
one above suspicion. And then: ". . . are much better at that sort
of thing than we are, unfortunately." As Mingo Coolidge muttered his assent, Art Underwood moistened his lips and fastened
on Bro. "Just out of curiosity, where did you hear this story?"

"Just out of curiosity."

"Of course."

"I told him." Dra. Abauza's voice was firm. She sat straight up,
but her head still barely cleared the back of her Duncan Phyfe
chair, one of the dining-room set the Bradleys had brought with
them to Cristo Rey. "My brother was an aide to General Ponce
Moreno. He reloaded the pistols he used during these . . ." She
sought the proper word. I looked at her with new admiration.
". . . *interrogaciónes?*"

"Interrogations," I said.

"*Gracias.*" She nervously scratched one of the moles on her
breast. "He wrote this in a letter he had smuggled out to me before he was executed."

"By whom?" Ardis Bradley seemed to think she was playing
Twenty Questions.

"General Ponce Moreno."

"So," Bro said quietly, "there was a witness to history."

Art Underwood shrugged.

"Perhaps you will write an epic poem about this one day,

Señora," the minister of police said, staring across the table as if to memorize her features.

"Perhaps I will," Dra. Abauza said.

" 'Triste Cristo Rey' would be a good title," I said to no one in particular.

Silence descended over the table. Even Buddy Seville could not think of anything to say. Tuck Bradley finally elected himself to fill the breach.

"It's a sad fact, Bro, and I don't think anyone in Cristo Rey is proud of it, and I know the minister will back me up on this, right, Charlie . . ."

The minister of police nodded, even though he had not yet heard what he was supposed to agree with Tuck about.

". . . that in 1974, murder was the second leading cause of death in this country . . ."

"After gastrointestinal diseases," Bro said. "I keep hearing that. I'm sure someone said it after Phyllis Emmett was killed . . ."

"That woman was a political activist," Mingo Coolidge interrupted. "We ought to be very damn clear about that."

I started to speak, but Bro headed me off. "Perhaps you'd feel differently if she were a constituent from New Mexico, Mingo." I had to admit Bro wasn't bad. You didn't feel his venom until your muscles wouldn't react. He continued while Mingo Coolidge struggled for an answer. "Murder here is presented as if it's some kind of illegal national blood sport, like cockfighting." He mimicked the statistic. " 'It's the number two cause of death after infections of the GI tract.' Saying that only makes murder feasible. As if it's just some kind of pernicious diarrhea."

Mingo Coolidge glared at Bro.

"God cements the bowels," the minister of police said suddenly.

"Then He ought to see Marty Magnin," Buddy Seville said.

"How's that, Charlie?" Art Underwood said.

"A famous saying of El Libertador," Carlos Bequer said. " 'A constipated priest is a trustworthy priest. God cements the bowels.' "

"He's in Room 516," Buddy Seville said. "The corner suite. You follow the Kaopectate bottles."

The minister of police was on a roll. "El Libertador said it was

a greater crime to kill an ant than it was to kill a man, because a
man who dies is reincarnated while an ant dies forever."

The formulation seemed to give pause even to Mingo Coolidge.
His fork stopped halfway to his mouth as he stared down at the
minister of police.

Tuck Bradley tried to recoup. "I suppose these ideas may seem
bizarre to the North American . . ."

"Hell, no," Buddy Seville said.

". . . but actually they're in keeping with the Hispanic tradition . . ."

Tuck was saved from having to continue by a knock at the dining room door. A marine from the embassy guard detachment
stood at attention waiting to be acknowledged. He was in camouflage fatigues and web field belting. His head was shaved up the
sides to bone-white scalp. The black and olive drab name tag on
his fatigues identified him as VAN STRANDER.

"Excuse me," Tuck Bradley said, beckoning the marine into
the room.

Ardis Bradley said that the Hispanic tradition was absolutely
fascinating in its own way.

Tuck glanced quickly in my direction as the marine whispered
something in his ear. I heard him say, ". . . a woman who says her
name is Mrs. Broderick." I strained to listen. "She says her husband is having lunch here." Leah. I had left a message for her at
the Human Rights Commission telling her where I would be in
case she returned from Chalatenango. If she had called herself
Mrs. Broderick, something was surely up. Leah did not expend
energy on useless scenes unless there was full media coverage and
a point to be made. Tuck looked at me once more. I could hear
him say, "Tell her my office hours are eight to six at the embassy.
Tell her to phone and make an appointment."

I rose from my place. "Corporal."

"Sir."

The old Marine Corps training. The first thing the boot
learned when his feet hit Parris Island was the chain of command.
There may be a God in heaven but the only God the boot acknowledged if he valued his soul was his platoon leader. I had not
forgotten my platoon leader's voice. Corporal Van Strander
snapped to attention.

"At ease, Van Strander. Mrs. Broderick is outside?"

"At the front gate, sir."

"I'm Mr. Broderick. Show her in."

Van Strander tried to sneak a look at Tuck Bradley.

"On the double, Corporal," I said.

"Sir."

Van Strander started to salute, as if I were in uniform, then caught himself. He about-faced smartly and after a nod from Tuck Bradley trotted from the dining room.

"Shall we have coffee?" Ardis Bradley forced a smile. "We also have Darjeeling tea. A gift from President Gutiérrez when Tuck and I arrived. Someone had told him India was our favorite post. Before Cristo Rey, of course."

No one made a move. Art Underwood drummed his fingers on the table. Dra. Abauza after her moment of courage tried not to look at the minister of police. Mingo Coolidge stared from Bro to me and back. Behind me, I heard Buddy Seville say, "Hey, Father Augie, what the fuck is going on?"

"Wait and see, Buddy."

Presently the sound of combat boots on the hardwood floor. Then Corporal Van Strander with two marines holding their weapons at high port. Between them stood Leah. Her face was streaked with dirt and sweat had leaked through her safari jacket.

"Ambassador Bradley," I said. "Mrs. Broderick."

X

_____

AFTER THAT it was headlines.

AMERICAN LABOR LEADER
KILLED IN CRISTO REY

Onyx Leon, of course. He had found the mass grave he had gone looking for in Chalatenango Province. Then the people who were apparently responsible for the mass grave had found Onyx. It is a reasonably safe assumption they did not realize he was a prominent American labor leader when they were hacking off his head. He had the look of a Chalatenango _campesino_, which indeed was all he ever was. Had he resembled an Anglo, he might well have been spared, as the murder of an American citizen so soon after the death of Phyllis Emmett, would have been a profound embarrassment. Leah and the photographer from the Human Rights Commission had found the mass grave without much difficulty, but Onyx was harder to locate. Then one of the women in the village had identified a body from the mass grave as that of her daughter. She had hesitated at first because her daughter had not been pregnant, while the victim seemed hugely so

444

under her covering sheet in the makeshift morgue. A look under the sheet revealed that her stomach had been opened from sternum to pelvis and that what had made her seem great with child was the head of Onyx Leon.

Leah had photographs taken.

For the record.

It was the photograph of Onyx's head in its final resting place that made Ardis Bradley lose a large part of her sole véronique when Leah slapped it down on Tuck's dining room table.

"This is an outrage," Tuck had said. I am still not absolutely clear whether he thought the outrage was what had happened to Onyx or Leah's bad manners first in gate-crashing his luncheon and then her major contribution toward making Ardis sick.

"What was he doing up there anyway?" Mingo Coolidge had said.

"I believe he was born there," Bro had said.

Mingo Coolidge shut up.

Dra. Abauza crossed herself.

"There'll have to be an investigation, Charlie," Art Underwood said.

"I am a friend of the truth," the minister of police said, his apparent all-purpose answer.

"I know that guy," Buddy Seville said. "I did a benefit for him, I think."

"There is no reason, no reason at all, to implicate the government in this unspeakable tragedy," Tuck Bradley said. He seemed to be rehearsing for the press conference he knew he would have to face.

Bro and I were leading Leah out of the dining room at that point. The only thing I can remember saying was, "What in the name of Christ did Priscilla ever see in an asshole like you, Tuck?"

ENTERTAINER EXITS

BEAUTY PAGEANT

No further explanation necessary.

Buddy had plainly had enough.

He departed with Miss Sri Lanka.

I was not even aware that Miss Sri Lanka had been warming up in his bullpen.

His official reason for leaving was the grief he felt over the loss of his very warm personal friend, Onyx Leon. He announced plans to set up an Onyx Leon Scholarship at the University of Nevada, Las Vegas.

EXPLOSION MARS
BEAUTY CONTEST
OPENING CEREMONY

CRISTO REY—(AP)—A bomb exploded in the new Sala de Las Americas in this capital city tonight, throwing the opening ceremonies at the annual Miss Global Village contest into a turmoil.

According to authorities, scores were injured in the blast. The death toll stands at two, with indications it may go higher.

Shortly after the explosion, an unidentified caller telephoned a local newspaper, *El Diario de Hoy*. The caller said he was a representative for the FDLP, the umbrella organization of left-wing guerrilla groups fighting in Cristo Rey. The caller, according to the newspaper, said the FDLP claimed responsibility for the blast.

In Mexico City, Mario Lescayo, official spokesman for the FDLP, said the call was a hoax. The FDLP, Lescayo said, did not engage in "blowing up beautiful and innocent young women."

In his statement, Lescayo called Cristo Rey President Arnoldo Jaime Gutiérrez a "killer," who had ordered the murder earlier this week of American labor leader Onyx Leon.

In Cristo Rey, U.S. Ambassador E. Tuckerman Bradley, who was scheduled to officially greet the contestants at the beauty pageant, blamed the blast on "Marxists, out and out Marxists, who prefer to fight with bullets rather than ballots."

Bradley said the upcoming national election Sunday will "give the lie to these thugs."

He denied reports that the government of President Gutiérrez was preparing to impose martial law and cancel the election.

"That is pure communist disinformation," Bradley said.

Bradley talked to reporters outside the smoldering Sala de Las Americas, which had been built especially for the pageant amid protests from student groups.

The ambassador was wearing a white tuxedo jacket, which was torn and filthy with dirt and blood from his efforts in the rescue operation.

In another development, embassy spokesman Arthur Underwood said there are strong preliminary indications that the brutal assassination of Leon was carried out by communist guerrillas masquerading as "a so-called right-wing death squad."

Both Bradley and Underwood praised the investigation into the killing being conducted by Minister of Police Carlos Bequer.

Tuck was on all the network newscasts wearing his dirty white dinner jacket.

On every show, there were zoom shots to his torn and blood-stained sleeve.

The two people killed were Miss Thailand and the pansy piano player from El Infierno, who was working with the pit orchestra.

When the bomb went off, the son of the minister of police had climbed up onstage and began firing wildly with his 9mm Beretta. Half the audience seemed to be carrying handguns. Most began shooting. Miss Thailand and the pansy piano player were caught in the crossfire. I thought it a wonder they were the only two killed.

I saw the firefight on the videotape Marty Magnin had made of the opening ceremony. He of course had never made it to the Sala de Las Americas.

His bowels again.

CRISTO REY IMPOSES
MARTIAL LAW
ELECTION CANCELED

"This is only a temporary setback," Tuck Bradley said on all three network newscasts. "A detour on the highway to democracy."

LABOR LEADER, 53,
EULOGIZED

Bro said the Mass, on a hill overlooking Hermosa, on the ranch my father still owned.

Ramona clung to my leg, weeping uncontrollably.

There were flowers from Fritz and Fiona Finn, wreaths from Marty Magnin and Buddy Seville.

Nothing from Lottie French.

Leah had called Lottie and said that with Onyx gone the farm workers would need all the financial assistance they could get.

Lottie said she would have to check with her business manager. Lottie said that *Up the Lazy River* had not done the box office she had anticipated and that she was in a shortfall cash position.

Jimmy Dana sent a check for a thousand dollars.

Leah was not at the funeral. She was getting arrested in San Francisco. She had tried to get the longshoremen not to unload a shipment of bananas from Cristo Rey. The union leadership had refused her plea. So she had hired a helicopter and dropped hundreds of photographs of Onyx on the pier where the ship was being unloaded. The photograph that was taken in the makeshift morgue in Chalatenango Province.

The longshoremen walked off the job.

I paid for the chopper.

And Leah got busted.

Things hadn't changed all that much. Best when we were in bed.

The rest of the time she was still a pain in the ass.

"Who is Mel Pincus?" Callie Dana asked one afternoon the following January.

"President of the Writers Guild, why?"

"A loathsome little man who wears color-coordinated clothes."

"That's the one, why?"

"I can't handle this, Jack," Callie said, passing me the typewritten note she had extracted from Jimmy's Book of Common Prayer. The effort expended in trying not to cry seemed to have made her face contract. "You can take care of the arrangements, can't you?"

"Of course."

I walked Callie to her sensible Volvo station wagon and kissed her on both cheeks. Back inside the house, I watched a couple of surfers in black wet suits trying to catch a wave, then sat down at Jimmy's desk and spread out the note from his prayer book.

"This is what I would like for my funeral . . ."

Book Eight
UNDER THE RED
WHITE AND BLUE

I

OF COURSE THE NETWORKS interrupted regular daytime programming and trotted out their regular anchormen, Bro having been on first-name terms with every anchorman since John Cameron Swayze and Douglas Edwards. The double murder on the steps of Glide Memorial had everything a network would demand of a miniseries, with the added attraction of real people and real money and real glamour. The Broderick billions, plural now I noticed. The Finn connection. Violence in America. Vietnam. Radical politics, and the failure of same, Leah's life having been transmuted by an alchemy known only to anchormen into a failure. I was the Hollywood angle. Noted screenwriter and author. Brother of. Once married to. Twice nominated for an Academy Award. Actually only once nominated and not a winner, but like the plural Broderick billions the exaggeration was under the circumstances acceptable. There were stills of me with Lottie French and with Anabel, the Rutland billions being another developing story line, along with Anabel's taste in husbands, but not a single photograph of me with Leah.

Leah was only a chalk outline on the sidewalk outside Glide Memorial.

I tried not to look at the bloodstains within the chalk marks.

On CBS, Wendy Chan was patched in from Washington, where she had recently become moderator of "Face the Nation." She was identified as a "veteran commentator on the American scene." I wondered how she liked "veteran" as an adjective. She was also identified as "a longtime friend of the Broderick family." I remembered the droning of the police band in her apartment on Russian Hill and I remembered giving her the crabs in mine on Tu Xuong Street and I was not surprised that her account of the execution of Germany Baker at San Quentin only occasionally jibed with my memories of the same event.

She said Mercury Baker had been a witness.

He had not.

She said Bro had been beaten up by a demonstrator.

He had not.

She said Leah had rescued him.

She had not.

She said it was her understanding from an unimpeachable source that Leah was taking instructions from Bro as a preliminary step toward being received into the Catholic Church.

She said this information should lay to rest the rumors of a possible romantic entanglement between Ms. Kaye and Father Broderick.

"Back to you, Dan," Wendy Chan said.

Alex Fahr was another familiar face. Lawyer and best-selling author of *Pluto: A Son's Story*. There was no mention of Boston Bailey in *Pluto: A Son's Story*. Nor any mention of Alex's own role as an informer for the FBI. Leah told me that in bed one night after our return from Cristo Rey. "He did it so Pluto could get back on the air," she said. "The FBI said they'd clear him if Alex cooperated with them. Those old pictures of Pluto's were worth a fortune, so he did."

"When did you know?"

"I always more or less suspected."

"And you never confronted him?"

"Why? He didn't know I knew. That's one reason I kept on fucking him. So he wouldn't suspect. Alex never was very smart. And he had access to all that money. I made sure what he had to tell wasn't all that important. The money was."

I still was not convinced. It seemed realpolitik for the sake of realpolitik. "How can you be so sure?"

"Hugh told me."

My father, the red check source. Leah never mentioned him again in all the time we were together that year before she was killed.

Alex said Leah was a competent attorney. With a talent for attracting high-profile cases. And the sense to seek legal guidance from better qualified litigators than she. That he was one of those better qualified litigators he left implicit. Alex added that coincidentally he was helping Mercury Baker edit his long-awaited *Letters to Germany*.

The Merc.

The Merc was unavailable for comment. I think I might have cracked if he had been. The last time Leah had seen him he had threatened to cut her legs off with a Black & Decker chain saw. Trust Leah to remember the brand name. This was another post-coital revelation after Cristo Rey. It concerned the night Leah returned to The Justice Department late and discovered Ramona trapped between Mercury's legs. "The bitch go up on me," Leah reported him as saying, and when she called him an animal he reached for the Black & Decker he had taken to carrying in his Samsonite attaché case. The Shadow was able to calm him down and get him out of the building. It was shortly thereafter that Mercury became interested in ITCs and in Ornstein & Shay, tax specialists and estate planners.

Richie was the most familiar of the familiar faces.

He was "disgruntled," the network anchormen all said, and there in the gathering dusk of that late afternoon, lying on an overstuffed pair of Pierre Deux pillows on the terra-cotta tile floor of Marty Magnin's living room in Trancas, I wondered if any of the assassins who had blossomed on the American landscape the previous quarter of a century had escaped being described as "disgruntled."

The networks also said that Richie had "nourished a grudge."

And that he "flourished in a climate of violence."

And then there were the facts, facts passed along in up-to-the-minute bulletins.

Murder weapon facts. A Bulldog .44 Special relinquished by the alleged assassin to the arresting officers, said CBS.

A single-owner weapon purchased by mail from an advertisement in *Soldier of Fortune*, said NBC.

The executives of Laurel Arms refused to be interviewed on camera, said ABC.

On NBC, a spokesman for *Soldier of Fortune* said that the right to bear arms was guaranteed under the Constitution of the United States.

All three networks deplored the ease with which it was possible to purchase a mail-order weapon and then each proceeded to show exactly how easy it was: a potential buyer had only to write to Laurel Arms, Department 4F-DK1, 909 Charter Oak Lane, Meriden, Connecticut 06020.

The Right Reverend Monsignor Eugene Francis Lomasney was the subject of the next special bulletin.

Pastor at Holy Sepulchre Roman Catholic Church in the Mission. Where Richie had taken a cab after he had pumped three from his Bulldog .44 Special into Bro and three more into Leah. And rang the doorbell at the rectory and asked the Right Reverend Monsignor Eugene Francis Lomasney to hear his confession.

On all three networks, Monsignor Lomasney invoked the seal of the confessional. He did reveal however that he had advised the penitent—he only referred to Richie as "the penitent"—to give himself up to the proper authorities. Monsignor Lomasney said he was pleased to hear that the penitent had followed his advice, which meant that the conditional absolution he had granted him was no longer conditional.

The three network anchormen seemed baffled by the concept of conditional absolution.

That is how the afternoon went.

I watched, switching channels constantly, searching for the latest nuance, the newest wrinkle, the unconfirmed speculation, watched because the longer I watched the longer I did not have to go to San Francisco, the longer I could avoid the Minicams, the longer I could pretend that what I was seeing had no direct connection to me, in fact was just another national tragedy, as all three networks called it, one that, as long as I remained in Trancas, I could experience vicariously.

. . .

"Marty, how do you happen to have a license plate that spells out 'fornicate'?"

"Oh, you noticed that, did you?"

"So did Dan Rather."

Marty Magnin turned off the television set. "You want to play a little backgammon?"

I turned the set back on. "I want to watch TV."

Marty turned it off again. "That was a nice funeral today, wasn't it? You take away Mel Pincus, it had a lot of quiet class."

"Maybe he can do the two coming up in San Francisco, Mel, if he's free."

"You don't want to dwell on that, Jack."

"That's very good advice, Marty."

I picked up the remote control, but Marty stood squarely in front of the TV set. "I tell you about my kid's Christmas pageant?"

Marty had been telling me stories about his son ever since we arrived at the house in Trancas. Anything to keep me diverted from the seamless montage of assassination on the tube. I don't think it occurred to Marty that my interest in what I was watching might perhaps be pathological, I only think he wanted me to leave.

Marty was well into his story. ". . . so I go to the Christmas pageant at his school, my girl clears the afternoon, no calls except if it's Lew Wasserman trying to get hold of me from London. The nuns at Good Shepherd are very big with their pageants, they don't want just any call interrupting things, but I figure they know Lew's not just any telephone call. Anyway, you know the plot, Joseph, his chick . . ."

"Mary . . ."

". . . that's the one, Mary. Joseph, Mary, no room at the inn, that routine. My kid, he's the innkeeper, get it? Under the titles. Not even a box, 'Martin Magnin, Jr., as The Innkeeper.' So I sit down and smile a lot at the sisters, like the kid's mother's not my third wife, first shiksa, I mean, the first one I married, not the first one I shtupped, you know what I mean?"

I nodded.

"Well, the opening's slow. There's that star in the sky and

there's these three wise men and there's Joseph and his old lady . . ."

"Mary . . ."

". . . and Mary's getting ready to drop this kid, and they show up at this inn, her and Joe, and out comes my kid, Marty Magnin, Jr., ready with his one line, and I got to look like I'm busting my buttons, he's got so much talent. So Joe says to my kid, 'My wife Mary is with child.' You should've seen the broad playing Mary, I thought she was going to go into a tap-dance number, nine years old and she's playing it cute as a bug in a rug, that's not the way I see the part, but what the hell. And Joe says, 'Is there any room at the inn?' Here it is, the big chance for my pain-in-the-ass kid with his one line. 'No,' he says, 'there's no room at the inn.' He gets through it, I give a big wink to Sister Felicitas with the mole on her nose, and then I hear my kid say, 'But come on in and have a drink anyway. . . .' "

In the last rays of twilight I could see the waves pounding against the dunes on the beach. I got up from the floor and put my arms around Marty Magnin.

"Thanks, Marty."

I knew it was time to go to San Francisco.

II

I LEFT FROM BURBANK to avoid the press, in a Rutland Enterprises G-3 that Anabel had volunteered, piloted by Teddy Shaffer, my successor as her husband, and himself in the process of being supplanted by Timmy Tatum, the surfer.

What I remember most about the next forty-eight hours was how tangential Bro and Leah were to the minuet of mourning, little more than catalysts, actually, for a festival of grief. The arrival of Fritz, and with him that caravan that attaches itself like a caboose to the train of a former president, had transformed the house on Washington Street into a miniature Camp David. Fritz's Secret Service contingent had been doubled from seven to fourteen, both because of Bro's White House connections and because authorities still had not ruled out the possibility of a conspiracy. They clustered around Fritz, their backs always to him, eyes constantly and rhythmically on the scan, murmuring now and then into the little two-way radio disks attached discreetly to their lapel buttonholes.

It was Fritz in fact rather than I who assumed the role of host at the Washington Street wake. He accepted the position not because he wanted it or sought it but because it was just another of

the responsibilities assumed by a former president, and I was
more than happy to yield it to him. Dickie Finn stage-managed
the event as if it were a three-day state visit. The tables in the upstairs living and dining rooms were set with Meissen and gilded
Val St. Lambert crystal, pieces that had not been out of the china
and crystal cabinets for years, and everywhere there were vermeil
centerpieces filled with tulips and lilies. At the front door were
Dickie's two daughters, Daisy and Dinah, each the picture of my
sister Priscilla, and the two girls, young women now, had their father's unerring managerial instinct, knowing immediately and
without question who not to admit into the house and who to
funnel upstairs to mingle with the great and the near great and
the groupies of the great and the near great.

The mayor came, and the new cardinal and the governor and
both United States senators and congressmen and members of the
legislature and much of the membership from the Mandalay
camp at Bohemian Grove and the baggage of various Finn political campaigns and peace overtures and economic initiatives. They
offered me polished and automatic regrets, which I accepted in
the spirit with which they were given, a lingering two-handed
handshake from the more sincere, and then they would move on
to my father, sitting in his wheelchair and guarded as he was always now by Lizzie Innocent, Lizzie whom I was to bed—or
who bedded me—that very night.

On my father's face was plastered a luminous, loony smile, as if
he believed that at the stroke of midnight at this terrible fete, his
burned-out bulb of a brain would suddenly light up like a pinball
machine. His crazy grin was especially disconcerting to this
group of people, practiced as they were in the art of evasion and
rational discourse, in compromise and negotiation and deceit.
Voices soft and sepulchral were met by demented rictus slash and
unblinking pale pastel blue eyes staring up from the wheelchair.
Even the most self-assured began to stammer, left sentences
hanging, started to nod without speaking, and then suddenly
would drop my father's hand, which thudded back into his lap
like a rock dropped from a freeway overpass, and make a dash for
the bar and the Stolichnaya, the Perrier, the Montrachet, the gin,
the tonic, the Roederer Cristal. I knew of course they had not

come to see my father or me, they had come to see Fritz, or be seen by him. Those who had worked in his administration fell upon each other, like dermatologists at a medical convention, searching for the bags and wens and other ravages of time on each other's faces, looking for the skin tone that would certify they had once been young, men of promise.

There was also the obligatory call from the president.

The Secret Service detail had set up a command post in a guest suite on the third floor with a bank of telephones that included hot lines to police headquarters and to the FBI, both locally and in Washington. It was here that I took the call from the White House. First I was alerted that the president was going to call and that I should keep myself available. Then the White House operator said that the president first had to speak to the winner of The Buddy Seville Open golf tournament in Las Vegas. Then it was my turn.

"John, this is Dale Corcoran."

"How do you do, Mr. President."

"John, the American people as well as Terry and I are sharing this loss with you."

"Thank you, Mr. President." I wondered for a moment what the American people and Terry and Dale had shared with the winner of The Buddy Seville Open.

"The loss of your brother Augustine hits this country hard. No nation however bountiful can ever have enough good men and Augustine Broderick was certainly a man for all seasons."

"That's very kind of you, sir."

There was a spasm of static on the line. "Sorry?"

"I said that's very kind of you, Mr. President."

Fritz Finn slipped into the communication room and putting a finger to his lips picked up an extension.

"And how is your dear father?"

I thought of that sweet loony smile. "Better than we had any reason to expect, Mr. President."

"I am proud to call Hugh Broderick a close personal friend and that he is feeling better is at least a modicum of good news on such a tragic occasion."

I had often heard my father before his stroke on the subject of

Dale Corcoran and I thought there would now be a reason for his dreamy grin if he had heard the president's claim of close personal friendship. "Thank you, sir."

"I want you to know, John, and I want the American people to know, this administration will not tolerate this kind of mindless violence."

In the background at the other end of the line, I thought I could hear the whir and click of flash cameras and suddenly I realized that this telephone call was a photo opportunity and the real reason why Dale Corcoran had trotted out his fancy diction. "That is most reassuring, Mr. President."

"It is a stain on the national escutcheon."

I saw Fritz roll his eyes.

"It is indeed, sir."

"Well, then, John, you have my deepest sympathies, and of course Terry's."

"I can't thank you enough for calling, Mr. President."

"You are most welcome, John." At the other end of the line I could hear the voice of a presidential aide ordering the photographers to leave the Oval Office. "And now I wonder if you could tell me if former president Finn is available. We are of different parties, as you know, but he is a man whose advice I have always valued in time of turmoil."

Fritz nodded and made a circle of his thumb and forefinger. "I'll see if I can find him, sir," I said.

I put him on hold. Fritz waited for a moment and motioned for me to listen on my telephone. The Secret Service man at the switchboard looked on impassively. Then Fritz plugged into the president.

"Hello, Corky," Fritz said. I knew it was a nickname that Dale Corcoran detested and I also knew this was skirmishing on a presidential level.

"This a conspiracy, Fritz?"

"There doesn't appear to be any evidence to support that, Dale." Smooth Fritz. He would not push the nickname too hard. Only when he needed a little breathing room.

"My people say it was probably just a nut case."

"I would think so."

"But there is a communist connection, right? With that woman."

"Doubtful, Dale."

"Well, she went to Hanoi, for Christ's sake."

"With Carlotta French. You had her to dinner at the White House last year."

"Because the goddamn queen of England asked for her, that's why."

"Still . . ." Fritz let the word hang between them, the clear implication being that he would have told the queen to see Lottie French at Buckingham Palace the next time she was in the neighborhood.

"And that woman is a deviate from what I hear."

Fritz stared at me. "Again doubtful."

"What about the son? He sounded like a cool customer when he was talking to me."

"Good description."

"What the hell's a Broderick doing marrying a Hanoi deviate? Is he queer?"

Fritz smiled. "I have no empirical evidence on that score."

"I hear the old man had a whack at her once." Fritz's face was a study. "That old prick. The son said he was getting better, but my information is the old bastard doesn't have both oars in the water."

"Your information is sound, Corky."

"All right, Fritz, if I hear anything on this end I'll let you know. I don't want you getting knocked off with these missile talks coming up. I want your support."

"Thank you, Mr. President."

"I'm sorry you heard that about Leah, Jack," Fritz Finn said.

We were sitting together in my room, the room I had as a child, the room I had not spent a night in since I got my first apartment in San Francisco a quarter of a century before.

"It wasn't exactly a secret."

"But not one you wanted to share with Corky," Fritz said. "God, sometimes I think we had better presidents when they had names like Woodrow and Franklin. Did anyone ever call Wilson

'Woody'? Jesus. I suppose it's only a matter of time before we get one named 'Magic' or 'Dr. J.' "

"I suppose." There was a Secret Service man stationed just outside the door. I could hear the drone of conversation from the crowd a floor below.

"I had the FBI do a check on her."

"I thought it was probably you."

"It was just something to keep in a file."

"Just in case. Because she had a White House connection."

"Yes, goddammit. Jesus, Jack, you know the people Leah was mixed up with."

"She was a lawyer, Fritz."

"Who just happened to handle every moon shot and slam dunk around."

"Does that include my father?"

"That was after my time, Jack."

"Of course." In the ensuing silence, I took my Hotchkiss yearbook from the bookcase and looked at my entry: "Prefect. Literary editor, *The Raven*. Glee Club. Tuck Shop. Basketball manager. Conscientious yet nonchalant. Princeton is very lucky to get such a great guy." I wondered what ever happened to such a great guy. A stranger. I had no memory of the Glee Club or the Tuck Shop. I was a former prefect of conscientious nonchalance talking to a former president of the United States about my late former wife's adultery with my father, a liaison that seemed to have been of interest to five different presidents. "I suppose you know she flunked the bar exam the first time she took it."

"I'm sorry, Jack. I really am."

"It really doesn't matter much now, does it? The old man looks like Daffy Duck and Leah . . ." I thought of the chalk outline outside Glide Memorial.

"What were they doing at Glide anyway?"

I could hear Leah talking, lying in that tiny single bed with the moire headboard. As she talked, she was giving herself a breast examination. A new nightly ritual. "AA," she called her latest scheme. Anti-apartheid. AA would pressure the UC regents to divest the university's shares in companies doing business with South Africa. Bro could help. Bro knew Desmond Tutu. Bro could get Desmond Tutu to address a rally in People's Park. Let's fuck.

"Some scheme involving South Africa. There was a notice about it in the papers." That Richie must have seen.

"Which one was he . . ." Fritz could not finish the sentence.

"Was he after?"

Fritz nodded.

All of us, I wanted to say.

Richie was a human time bomb.

I fooled around with the fuse.

Imagine my father if the Brodericks didn't get rich.

"I don't know," I said.

When I came back downstairs, I saw the new cardinal whispering into my father's ear as if he were preparing him for extreme unction. He was wearing a scarlet cassock and on his lap he balanced a plate of quiche and cold shrimp. At his elbow was a glass of wine.

"The mercy of almighty God, Hugh, works in strange ways," I heard the cardinal say. He popped a shrimp into his mouth. "It is not for us sinners to question the ways of the Lord."

I could almost hear the reply I knew my father would have made. Save that snake oil for Donald Dimwit.

"It is God's way to test our faith."

I saw Lizzie's hands tighten on the handles of my father's wheelchair. I suspected her tolerance of His Eminence was even less than his would have been.

"Without these tests of faith, Hugh . . ." The cardinal pondered the end of the sentence and tried another shrimp. Suddenly his face began to turn red and his hand went to his throat. No one seemed to notice. Canapés were passed and glasses refilled. Then Lizzie pulled the cardinal up by his shoulders, kicked away his chair and grabbed him from the back around the solar plexus. Locking her fingers, she yanked him back into her crotch and then jerked her knotted hands upward. The shrimp lodged in his windpipe flew out of his mouth and landed squarely on top of my father's bald head. Feet firmly planted, Lizzie once again yanked the cardinal into her pelvis and when she did a red stream of cocktail sauce exploded from his mouth all over his scarlet cassock.

It was all over in a moment. I looked at my father with the shrimp stuck to his pate and for an instant I thought his grin even more luminescent, as if one cell in the appropriate lobe had reactivated for a microsecond. Then the look, existing probably only in my imagination, vanished.

"The Lord will bless you, my child," the cardinal said to Lizzie, "for saving a life even as unworthy as mine." His face was flushed and his cassock wrinkled and unbuttoned and soiled with phlegm and shrimp sauce. He held out his ring, but Lizzie did not kneel and kiss it. After a moment, the cardinal in rumpled disarray was swallowed up in the swirl of celebrating mourners who passed the word that His Eminence might have croaked if old Hugh's nurse, the one over there with the pretty ass, hadn't saved the old goat's bacon with a Heimlich hold.

"Pious bastard," Lizzie said. She picked the shrimp from my father's head and then not knowing where to drop it, she stuck it into the pocket of her green silk blouse. Immediately a grease stain began to spread. It was a gesture so spontaneous that at that moment I realized how much I wanted her. She seemed to translate my thoughts.

"Later," she said quietly. "When everyone's left."

III

I SLEPT THAT NIGHT in my father's house, in my room. Lizzie was gone long before I awoke. There was no sign of her presence. No lipstick smear on the pillow, no mascara smudge, no curly pubic hair in the sheets. At breakfast she fed my father oatmeal. Always the adjutant, Dickie ran through the plans for Bro's funeral the next morning at Old Saint Mary's. Departure from Washington Street with motorcycle escort at ten-forty. The Mass was scheduled for eleven. The cardinal would officiate. Fritz would deliver the eulogy. One of his speechwriters would draft it. He'd like to speak to you, Jack, Dickie said. For the brotherly touches.

Fritz wondered if my father should attend.

Dickie thought not.

Lizzie wondered why not. Quietly, firmly, all the while spooning the cereal into my father's mouth, not allowing a single drop to dribble.

Dickie was startled by her intrusion. Lizzie said my father could sit in his wheelchair, in the aisle by the first pew. Dickie wondered who would take care of him. Lizzie said she would. It was obvious Dickie did not want her sitting with the family. I sided with Lizzie. Dickie argued. Hugh is incontinent, he said.

I exploded.

This is the funeral of my father's son, my brother, it is my family, you silly son of a bitch.

I was surprised by my own vehemence.

I think Jack is right, Fritz said. Ending the impasse by presidential fiat. I suspect that Fritz knew Lizzie and I had slept together the night before. It was the sort of thing he intuited. I also suspect he knew Lizzie was not the reason why I had insisted that my father attend the funeral. I simply was not going to let Dickie make that decision, as if it were a management prerogative. It was after all a Broderick who had been killed. The Finns were supporting players, a subtlety to which Fritz was attuned, if not Dickie.

"When are you going to Oakland?" Fritz asked later in the morning when, for a moment before the day's crowd of celebrity mourners descended on us, he caught me alone at the same window where we had watched Leah and Onyx demonstrating against him and my father so many years before. I had the sense that Fritz was seeking me out, I think because he felt extraneous and he knew I wanted nothing from him.

"In a bit." I was trying to avoid it.

"I'll go with you, if you wish."

However tentative the offer, he was sincere and I was touched, because sincerity did not come easy to him. "Somehow I think you'd be a distraction."

"Somehow I think I would, too." He smiled. "It's no picnic being a former president, Jack. Something like being an extra spare tire. When they need someone to go to a state funeral that's not important enough for the president to go to, and too important for the vice president, they trot out former president Finn, stick him on Air Force One, he knows where the booze is hidden and the extra toilet paper is kept, and fly him over to see some prick I never liked much anyway get planted. Between state funerals, I'm at liberty. Between engagements, like an actor. What the hell am I supposed to do? Go play in some pro-am? How many times can you play golf with Bob Hope and Arnie Palmer? 'How's your slice, Mr. President?' " He was silent for a moment. "I hate golf."

I saw the future. Like Fritz I was condemned to be a survivor.
"Watch it when you go over there," he said after a moment.
"Why?"

"Because every law enforcement agency in the country's going
to be there taking pictures. You'd think it was a Mafia funeral. A
whole new collection of updated photographs for the files. Of all
the old crazies. Except the men've got bald spots now and they
see a proctologist and a nutritionist, and the women, their tits are
bouncing off their knees, if they've still got both of them, and everyone'll be wearing hundred-dollar Nikes and two-hundred-
dollar jogging suits and they'll be rapping about how great it was
at Selma and comparing their times at the Honolulu Marathon
last year."

The other condemned survivors. So that is what Richie Kane
had accomplished, I thought. A last surveillance of Leah. "You're
sure?"

"Of course I'm sure. It's one of the perks of being a former
president. They keep you plugged in."

Fritz was on the money.

The photographers were on the roofs of the buildings adjacent
to and across the street from The Justice Department and inside I
was the only man wearing a suit. As I had been at Lottie French's
fundraiser for Onyx the day I asked Leah to marry me, I thought.

To those who recognized me, I seemed to be a source of considerable embarrassment, the ex-husband who had the effrontery to
make an appearance at the beatification of the saint he had never
deserved.

"Hello, Harriet."

"Hi." Harriet Hecht was wearing Reeboks. A Nike sweatband
absorbed the perspiration from her forehead. As always her nipples were at attention, although scaled lower against the damp
T-shirt that said CAMP BEVERLY HILLS. Harriet did not seem disposed to carry the conversation any further and as I turned away
I heard her companion say, "Who's that?"

"Her asshole ex-husband."

"He came here?"

"Exactly."

"Anyway this person on the cable car tries to put his hand under my skirt . . ."

"The Missoni?" Harriet Hecht said.

"The red suede."

"I thought the red suede was a culotte . . ."

I made my way to the stairs. Leah's office was on the second floor. The Shadow blocked my way. "You can't go up there, man."

"As it happens, I own this building and I can go any fucking place I want."

In a tight spot, talk tough and talk dirty, Leah had always advised. Perhaps good advice for a five-foot-two-inch woman, but I questioned the value of a six-foot man trying to intimidate The Shadow with tough talk. He did, however, hesitate. "I know you, motherfucker?"

"You know me, Shadow."

"You was married to that bitch, right?"

"Right."

The Shadow stood aside and let me pass. I did not look back as I walked up the stairs in case he changed his mind. Leah's office door was locked. I heard someone inside and knocked. I was not surprised when Bobby Gabel cracked the door an inch. I had lost my capacity for surprise.

"I was wondering when you were going to show up, man," Bobby Gabel said. As he locked and bolted the door behind me, I saw Bitty Crane sitting at Leah's desk. Jimmy Dana's sixteen-year-old last love. Whose mother Bev was Jimmy's penultimate love. Both gifts to Jimmy from Bobby Gabel if I remembered the scenario correctly. It seemed an aeon since Jimmy's funeral. Bitty Crane had a Baggie of grass and was sifting seeds.

"Bobby, what are you doing here?"

"We came up for the Jefferson Starship concert tonight," Bitty Crane said.

Bobby Gabel shrugged. "What're you going to do?"

"And what is that gorilla doing at the bottom of the stairs?"

"What gorilla?"

"The black guy. He's about the size of Kentucky. You can't miss him."

"The Shadow . . ."

"The midget wanted him," Bitty Crane said.

"Ramona?"

"She's afraid of the Merc for some reason, man," Bobby Gabel said.

"With good fucking reason." I was beginning to shout. "He made her blow him . . ."

"The midget?" Bitty Crane said, suddenly interested.

"Not proven," Bobby Gabel said. "Her story. You haven't heard the Merc's side of it . . ."

"The Shadow's his bodyguard, for Christ's sake."

"Used to be," Bobby Gabel said. "They had a falling out. Creative differences. Over that series idea. The Shadow didn't want to get iced in the fourth episode. So the Merc unloaded him. He's cool. I dropped some bread on him. He's on our side. Not to worry."

I suddenly felt exhausted. I had heard the rap before. It was like Musak. We were all getting too old.

"There's something I want to talk to you about, Jack."

"I'm not sure I'm up to it, Bobby."

"Listen, I can get behind that. There's been too much dying, man."

"I like the Dead," Bitty Crane said, as I knew she would. Bobby's girls never changed.

"What is it, Bobby?"

"Leah, man."

"What about her?"

"Her story. It has all the elements. There are people who'll back a picture like that. People I don't want to name, if you know what I mean."

At that moment, I think my brain waves went almost as flat as my father's. Because I could not think of anything else, I said, "I suppose you'll want Lottie to play her."

"Lottie won't touch it. She's gone straight. She won an Academy Award, man. She even thanked Frank Sinatra."

I looked at Bitty Crane. She had taken a Walkman from her bag and was inserting a tape. She adjusted the earphones and then began to hum, bobbing her head, sucking in her lower lip, snapping her fingers to the rhythm of the tape I could not hear. "I can't talk about this now, Bobby."

"I'm hip," Bobby Gabel said. "Back burner. Low simmer." He lifted one of Bitty's earphones. "We have to split." Then he took a ski mask from his pocket and rolled it on until his face was covered except for the slits around his eyes. "I don't believe in giving the feds pictures, man." He grabbed my thumb in a brothers' handshake. "We'll go out the back way."

They were gone.

I do not know how long I sat there alone. I had not cried, I could not cry. It was as if my spiritual drought had dried up my tear ducts. I had made a virtue of noninvolvement and my neutrality had hardened into a theology. I thought of Leah. Unlike me, she had spent a lifetime staying awake. I wondered why she had stayed with me through marriage and divorce, in sickness and in health, until death did us part. And suddenly I knew why. From the day we met, she knew that I would always love her, whatever the provocation. I would always be there, her safe haven, her home port.

Dearest Leah.

Never brainwashed by moral exhaustion.

Then I heard a key in the lock and the door opened.

"Jack." It was Bea. Hair fluffed and rinsed with blue. She was carrying a large flat box with grease stains on the bottom. Bea, who was always current, Bea, who had sent me brownies when I was in Vietnam, laced with hashish, Bea, a woman in her sixties. "Those people downstairs must be absolutely famished. I made up some hors d'oeuvres with Ramona. She has a real knack. Cheese Dreams. Rumaki. Angels on Horseback . . ."

I went over and put my hands on her shoulders. I had talked to her on the telephone, but this was the first time I had seen her since my arrival. Her face was so shiny it might have been buffed. "Those flautas you and Leah used to love so much . . ."

"It's all right, Bea." As if I could convince her and me that it was.

"Ramona and Aurelio will pass. I think I forgot the serving plates . . ."

"It's all right, Bea . . ."

"Make do, that's my motto . . ." She looked up at me, eyes blinking too fast, her bright smile collapsing, a mother with too few years left. Her voice broke, a sound I think I shall never forget. "Oh, Jack . . ."

And finally the tears came.

I left The Justice Department an hour later. Out the front door unnoticed and unmissed by the people drinking jug wine and trying to remember the lyrics of "Nosotros Venceremos." Aurelio Lira and Ramona Leon were passing Bea's hors d'oeuvres. Ramona said she and Aurelio were going to get married and that she was going to help Bea in her catering business. Leah was so happy for us, Jack, Ramona said. Aurelio had a small paunch and was minus most of his hair. He was playing in a mariachi band in East Los Angeles, weddings and *quinces* his specialties. You should see him in his serape and sombrero, Jack, Ramona had said.

Dejalo triste y apasionado.

It was drizzling outside. There were a number of police cars on the street. Interior lights lit, red and blue roof lights spinning. I paused and looked up at the roofs of the adjoining buildings. Atop the H & R Block office, I could see a zoom lens pointed at me. Slowly and deliberately I gave the finger to the photographer on the rooftop who was taking my picture for the files of God knows what agency. A policeman made a grab for my arm. I yanked it away. He made another lunge. Fuck off, I said. Then I saw the policeman's hard plastic nameplate. Shannon. And pinned to Shannon's shirt above the nameplate a small round campaign button that said, RICH IS BETTER. I was suddenly overcome by rage. Shannon came at me and with all the force I could muster I swung my foot squarely into his balls. He doubled over, frozen in pain and surprise, and I hit him once in the face before I was engulfed by a wave of blue uniforms.

Fritz Finn arranged my release from custody. I attended Bro's funeral at Old Saint Mary's the next morning with my arm in a sling, my nose broken and both eyes blackened. My father sat in his wheelchair directly in front of my aisle seat in the first pew. Fritz mounted the pulpit and talked about the fevers of violence.

When the Mass was finished and the cardinal's blessing of Bro's casket completed, I managed to maneuver my father down the center aisle of Old Saint Mary's with my one good arm. The weather had broken and we stopped in the sunlight at the top of the church steps on California Street, my father and I, the last of the Brodericks.

IV

And so when the trial began, we left the country. I did not care what happened to Richie Kane. His fate was in the impersonal hands of the state of California and I was happy to leave it there, whatever the outcome. I only wanted to stay away from his magnetic field. Once I had wandered into it and the end result was that the only two people I ever really cared about wound up dead. I stopped watching television when I saw a clip of Megan Kane leaving San Francisco city jail. She said that Richie was fine and had eaten grapefruit and toast for breakfast and creamed chipped beef for lunch and that Monsignor Lomasney at Holy Sep had taken him holy communion and before she cracked she said that he missed Rick and Kerry and little Eileen. That night I systematically destroyed every single tape and every single transcript I had made for *Grunts* because I knew that sooner or later the Richie Kane material would be subpoenaed by both the district attorney and defense counsel, each for his own ends. One morning there was a flurry of messages on my answering machine from Skip Kenna, who I knew was going to be an expert witness for the prosecution, and that afternoon, anticipating the subpoena I knew would ultimately arrive for me, I bought the tickets for Lizzie and myself.

We were gone for three months. Hong Kong first, with no layover in Honolulu beyond a few hours in the transient lounge. Singapore. Jakarta. Kuala Lumpur. Bangkok. Calcutta. Cities where news of a murder trial in San Francisco did not make the local English-language newspapers. Three months and no news of discovery motions or suppression hearings or jury demographics or the cross-examination of expert witnesses in San Francisco.

We left Rawalpindi two days before the earthquake and, under Liberian flag, steamed across the Indian Ocean to Diego Garcia where we learned that our hotel in Rawalpindi had collapsed in the quake. Up the east coast of Africa to Port Said and then through the Levant. In Istanbul we were highjacked for twenty-five minutes. The highjacker was a demented Albanian who was shot and killed by an Iraqi businessman in the first-class cabin who was wearing a flak jacket under his three-piece Giorgio Armani suit. How did the Iraqi get the Galil-10 with folding stock past the metal detectors in his Vuitton attaché case, I asked the Turkish airport authorities. There were smiles and apologies and no answers and we were on the next plane to Paris. But the aborted highjacking had put my name on the wires and when we arrived at Charles de Gaulle the press and the TV cameras were there. There had been a verdict in San Francisco.

Not guilty by reason of insanity.

Incarceration at the state mental facility in Napa.

I look at the photographs of that moment and see not myself but a tall man in his later forties with a slightly bogus Hollywood look, from the Burberry raincoat draped too casually over the shoulders, to the old tweed jacket custom-tailored at Tartaglia in Beverly Hills, to the navy turtleneck sweater and the faded jeans and the Gucci loafers and the white tennis socks. The tall man with the slightly bogus Hollywood look is bending toward the reporters as he receives the news of the verdict in San Francisco, his brows knit and his face grave, as if he cared about the verdict in San Francisco, cared how the verdict in San Francisco reflected the quality of justice in America.

Did I have any comment on the verdict in San Francisco?

I passed through customs and continued to say no, I had no comment, no, no comment. Then Lizzie and I were in a cab and I

told the driver to take us to the Plaza-Athénée, certain that the reporters would overhear. With the help of a hundred-franc tip, the
driver shook the pursuing press and I redirected him to that small
hotel near the Place des Vosges where I have stayed for years, no
elevator, no credit cards, not the place the wire services would
consider checking immediately. It has only a dozen or so rooms
and nestles so closely to the fifteenth-century Gothic church next
door that a flying buttress from the church flows through the wall
into the room I always book, forming an imposing stone canopy
over the bed. We unpacked and then Lizzie lay on top of me
under that flying buttress and she whispered that she was still
enough residual Italian Catholic to wonder if what we were doing
in that church annex was sacrilegious, an affront to the sacrament
housed in the altar tabernacle just a wall away.

When Lizzie slept, I tried to think about the verdict in San
Francisco, and my own part in it. If I had not been fascinated by
the Dixon Ticonderoga number three soft, if I had not gone to
Department 34, if I had not decided to teach Rem. Eng. Comp. II,
if I had not had lunch with my father, if I had not seen Richie's
sound truck—the ifs multiplied, metastasized—then what happened might not have happened. I was, it turned out, the trigger
of my misfortune.

The telephone began ringing two hours later.

"Connie King, Mr. Broderick. UPI. I was wondering if you had
any comment on the verdict in San Francisco today?"

Yes.

Oh, yes.

Yes, yes, yes, yes.

"No."